Mountain Folk

Book One of the Folklore Cycle

JOHN HOOD

DEFIANCE PRESS
& PUBLISHING

Mountain Folk

ISBN-13: 978-1-948035-85-9 (Paperback)
ISBN-13: 978-1-948035-87-3 (ebook)

Edited by Janet Musick
Cover designed by Spomenka Bojanic
Interior designed by Debbi Stocco

Published by Defiance Press and Publishing, LLC

Bulk orders of this book may be obtained by contacting Defiance Press and Publishing, LLC.
www.defiancepress.com.

Public Relations Dept. – Defiance Press & Publishing, LLC
281-581-9300
pr@defiancepress.com

Defiance Press & Publishing, LLC
281-581-9300
info@defiancepress.com

To Traci fair — companion, mate,
To love no thousand tales could sate,
From her such inspiration sprang,
Of her the lowly bard once sang:
"Come sing of waves and sand and shell.
Come, Water Maiden, cast your spell."

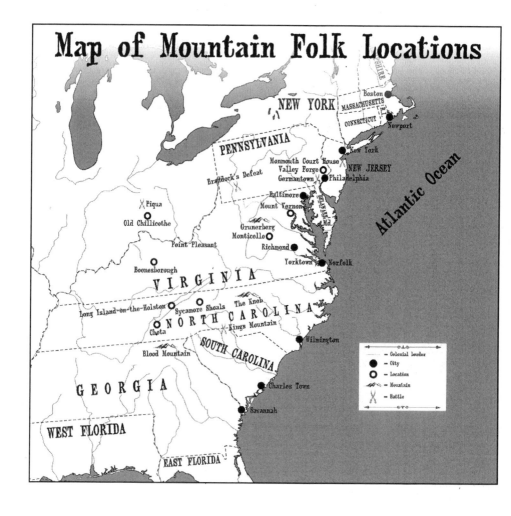

Chapter 1 — The Hunters

September 1751

DANIEL THOUGHT HE SPOTTED WINGS in the trees, but he couldn't be sure. He'd been hunting on the rugged mountain since morning. Now it was nearly dusk. He was tired and more than a little hungry. To make matters worse, the fog rising above the little creek he'd been following was getting thicker, swirling around the oaks and pines on the hillside. But Daniel never let fog or waning sunlight keep him from bagging game back home in Pennsylvania on Neversink Mountain. He wouldn't leave this mountain empty-handed, either.

He knew his mother Sarah would already be at the campfire, boiling beans and preparing spits for roasting whatever he brought back. They had some venison left from previous hunts, so no one would go to bed hungry. But quail, partridge, or even pigeon would be a welcome respite from chewing on stringy venison.

Truly, though, it was now a matter of pride: Daniel, the best hunter in the family, rarely returned without a prize. He usually returned with several.

Sure, hunting was easier in familiar surroundings. Back home, he'd known intimately the hills, valleys, and forests that lay between their farm in Oley and the bustling city of Philadelphia. Now these familiar places were far behind them. Over many months, Daniel and his family had traveled hundreds of miles, following the path of other settlers through Virginia into the backcountry of North Carolina. Some days earlier, his father had spotted rocky cliffs thrust improbably high against the otherwise flat horizon. The family had headed for them. Now their camp lay in the shade of the tallest mountain. Daniel had traipsed up and over it, following the sound of rushing water to a striking waterfall and the little creek beyond.

The place was unfamiliar, yes — but hunting was hunting. Even at sixteen, Daniel was a master. Everybody said so. Back in Pennsylvania, he'd earned more selling furs and hides in Philadelphia than he had working his father's fields and forge. He knew from experience that where there was fresh water, there was bound to be game.

He wasn't about to be defeated this night, on this mountainside, by a few wisps of fog.

What was that?

Daniel saw movement in the thicket. He stopped short, placing one moccasin silently next to the other in the soft leaves as he hefted his well-worn hunting rifle and peered into the tangle of low trees and vines. He stayed frozen in place for what seemed like an eternity. Although confident in his ability as a marksman, Daniel didn't want to risk his game taking flight. With a rifle, it was a whole lot easier to hit a treed bird than one on the wing. Folks usually needed a fowling gun for the latter.

Daniel listened intently. Presently, his keen ears picked up some rustling in the thicket, along with the sound of tree branches scraping together behind him and what seemed like footfalls in the fallen leaves much farther down the creek. Were there three birds in earshot? Or something else? Slowly, carefully, he cocked his rifle.

Then several things happened at once. The thicket suddenly exploded into a mass of shaggy fur, bared teeth, and beastly rage. Behind him, he heard a rustle of branches. And he heard a faint, eerie scream — like nothing he'd ever heard in years of hunting and tracking.

Perhaps that's why he jerked. Perhaps that's why his finger yanked the trigger prematurely rather than squeezing it. Perhaps that's why Daniel Boone missed.

▲▲▲

The huge black bear — for, of course, that's what was charging the young hunter at ferocious speed — wasn't at all startled by the report of the rifle. Daniel swore, drew his hunting knife, and turned to run. He'd tangled with bears before. There was no chance for him to reload. There was little chance of playing dead and placating the bear. And there was little chance of outrunning it, particularly since Daniel had been following the creek downhill and would now have to run up a slope. There was, in fact, little chance of surviving the encounter at all. But Daniel Boone was no coward. He'd run as fast as he could and then put up a determined, probably doomed, fight.

As he turned on a heel to begin his flight, he saw wings. He'd have paid them little heed had the wings been attached to what he expected to see: the back of a gamebird. But what Daniel Boone beheld was just about the furthest thing he'd ever expected to see along that creek, in those woods, or anywhere on God's green earth.

He saw a small, lithe, human-like body flying through the air.

Daniel saw the wings beat and then straighten as the little creature banked toward the rampaging bear. He saw one slender arm holding a bow and another slender arm pulling an arrow back to a faintly whiskered chin. He heard the minuscule bowstring twang.

Fast as lightning, Daniel whirled to see the bear stiffen, an arrow sticking out from its neck. He saw the bowman reloading his weapon and lifting his left wing to bank around the head of the bear, whose jaws were thrown open in pain and rage. And Daniel saw, even before the archer did, a furry paw swinging up with blinding speed. It struck the winged creature with tremendous force, knocking the little man against a pine trunk. From there, the bowman fell to the ground, hard.

Even as he witnessed the savage swipe, Daniel was hurtling toward the wounded bear, holding his knife in the reverse grip of his right hand and wielding his rifle as a club in his left. He'd never heard of a man beating a bear in a hand-to-paw fight, but he didn't hesitate. The wonder he felt upon seeing a real-life fairy — for that was, surely, what lay senseless or worse before him — did not keep Daniel Boone from acting. The deepest instinct of self-preservation, to kill or be killed, combined with the highest instinct of honor, gave speed and strength to his limbs. With his left arm, Daniel dealt the bear a terrific blow with the butt of his gun. Then, with his right, he plunged his knife deep into the breast of the bear, through the shaggy hide into the savage heart.

How he got close enough to deliver these attacks, Daniel didn't know. He'd killed bears before, but with a bullet from his rifle. He knew the look of death. The bear fell forward on its face, wrenching Daniel's blade from his grasp, and moved no more.

A moment later, Daniel was crouching below the pine tree, gazing in astonishment at the crumpled form of the fairy. The little creature was lying on his stomach, his apparently undamaged wings of yellow-tinged feathers, glistening in the twilight as if dusted in gold, retracted onto his back. He wore a cloak of forest green over what appeared to be a leather jerkin and woolen stockings. From a rough belt hung a couple of leather pouches and a blade that bore no small resemblance to Daniel's own hunting knife, except in its tiny size. Another strap, bearing a quiver of arrows, crossed the fairy's torso from right shoulder to left hip. The bow lay a few inches away. The fairy was about the height of a large raccoon, Daniel judged.

Unsure what to do, he reached out a hand and carefully turned the fairy onto his back. The creature's face was youthful and handsome, but his delicate features were contorted in an expression of anguish. Fearful the fairy had sustained a mortal blow, Daniel was both surprised and delighted when the little eyelids fluttered open, revealing light-brown eyes. Daniel was even more surprised, if not exactly delighted, to see the fairy's lips move and to hear a soft voice uttering words he understood.

"You…you blundering human," the fairy said haltingly, between winces. "Your recklessness almost got us both killed by that fearsome beast."

Daniel's concern gave way to annoyance. "I just killed that beast and saved your life, sir," he pointed out. "You should be more grateful."

"Grateful?" The fairy coughed and tried to sit up, grimacing. "You did not save me. And because of you, my quarry may have escaped. Thanks to you, my first solo ranging may end in failure. I may not get another chance to become a journeyman for a long time."

Daniel would have responded in anger, with little of the Christian charity his parents Squire and Sarah Boone had tried to teach him. But his feelings of sympathy and wonder took over. This was a fairy lying before him — a real flying, talking fairy! It was one of Mother's bedtime stories come to life. It was impossible and ridiculous, but it was happening.

Daniel stroked his chin, smiling quizzically.

"Maybe I ought to be the one upset, friend," he said. "I wasn't hunting bear. I was hunting fowl for supper. Even so, I reckon I would have hit the beast square on the nose and finished him if you hadn't distracted me with that weird little shout."

"What shout?" the fairy demanded, his eyes showing sudden enthusiasm. "What did you hear? I was too busy rescuing you to notice. Perhaps your gigantic ears can hear far-off sounds that my normal ears cannot."

Bemused, Daniel looked at the little man. Normal ears? The fairy's small ears were elongated and ended in points.

"I heard what sounded like wings fluttering behind me, and then a strange cry," Daniel said. "I figured you did it. I've heard Indian friends do battle cries before. Wasn't you?"

"No, of course not," the fairy responded, shakily getting to his feet.

"Now that I figure it," Daniel continued, "seems like the sound came from downhill a ways. I thought I heard something down there. At the time, I thought it was a bird."

The fairy shook his head. Whether it was to indicate disagreement or to regain his senses, Daniel couldn't tell.

"What you heard was the cry of the beast I have been tracking for a while — for days in your time," the fairy explained. "I was so close. I almost had it. But then I chose to help you. I may have saved one life at the cost of many more."

Daniel watched as the fairy moved his hands down to one of the leather pouches hanging from his belt. He rummaged inside it, let out a cry of alarm, and withdrew two small cylinders. Daniel drew closer to examine them.

"It is destroyed!" the fairy wailed. "Now I will never be able to find the beast again."

Daniel saw that the object was a silver-colored musical instrument broken cleanly in two.

"How can that little pipe help you track game?" Daniel asked.

The fairy glared at him for a moment, then his expression softened. "I suppose there is no harm in telling you," he said, still rubbing his forehead where his hard fall had raised a welt. "I will not need it to produce simple spellsong, which is all I will need for you. And, now that I have lost my quarry, I might as well tell my troubles to someone. I have been alone on the trail so long that even a conversation with the likes of you would be welcome."

"Well, that's mighty generous of you," Daniel said, a playful smile curling his lips. "I've only been hunting since breakfast but I wouldn't mind a little company, either, even from the likes of *you*."

For an instant, irritation mingled with frustration on the fairy's face. Then he caught Daniel's twinkling eye and let out a snort of merry laughter. "Well said, sir, well said! And well met — my name is Goran. Whom have I the pleasure to meet?"

"I'm Daniel Boone," said the young hunter, shaking the fairy's proffered hand. "My family's camped a little ways from here. We've only just arrived in these parts, looking for a good piece of land to settle on. We're originally from Pennsylvania."

"Pennsylvania, you say," said Goran. "I know it well. My Folk stayed there for many of your years, within the shade of a low mountain in a place the humans call Bucks County."

"Why, that's not far from where I grew up, in Berks County!" Daniel replied eagerly. "You're a long way from home, just like I am."

Goran looked searchingly at Daniel for a moment, then smiled. "You have no idea. Yet, in a way, the histories of your people and mine are intertwined. Where humans live, we live. Where you go, we are unlikely to be far behind."

Now it was Daniel's turn to gaze meaningfully at the fairy, who still seemed dazed as he rose fully to his feet and returned the broken flute to his pouch. "What do you mean by that? And why do you keep saying 'my years' instead of just years? Do you reckon the days differently?"

Goran sighed and looked longingly into the fog. "It is a long story, and more trouble than it is worth for me to tell you. You will never remember it, anyway."

Daniel pursed his lips. "I may not be as skilled at reading and doing figures as some, but nobody's ever doubted my memory. That's one reason I'm pretty good at hunting. It doesn't take me long to draw a map in my head of where I've been. I can recall just about every bird call I've ever heard. I can tell one footprint from another. Trust me, friend, my mind's like a bear trap."

"Trust me, *friend*," Goran repeated the phrase with a chuckle. "After you and I part, that memory trap of yours is going to be empty, at least when it comes to me. I am not such a novice that I need my flute for that."

The fairy held up a hand as Daniel began to reply. "Hold on, listen to me," Goran objected. "I said I would explain about the flute. I will tell you what you need to know. If you are such a skilled tracker, perhaps I can still catch up to the beast. Perhaps my ranging will not be in vain."

Daniel Boone had countless questions. He didn't like to be told no, but the idea of tracking unfamiliar prey intrigued him, while Goran's implied test of Daniel's abilities excited him. Holding his tongue, he nodded to the little man.

"Back in my village, I am an apprentice in the Rangers Guild," the fairy began. "We train for many tasks. We scout. We track game to fill our larders and dining tables. We convey messages across long distances. And, when it becomes necessary to deal with humans, we are trained for that, too. That is why I know your language."

"I was wondering about that," Daniel said. "Does that mean you also know…"

"Please do not interrupt," Goran interjected. "If there is still a chance to find the beast, it will not last long. Let us proceed while I talk."

Daniel stooped over the bear, withdrew his knife, and cleaned the blade on the tail of his buckskin shirt. Returning the knife to its sheath, he picked up his rifle and began walking briskly along the creek. Goran fluttered his wings, gingerly at first, then with deliberate strokes.

"Another job of the ranger, perhaps the most important of all, is to find and track the monsters that prowl beyond our borders — beyond our walls of magecraft and spellsong that protect us from the Blur."

"The what?" Daniel asked.

"The Blur. It is a word we use to describe your human world," Goran said. "You see, we Folk are not from this realm, not originally. We experience time differently from the way you do. In our villages, behind our Shimmer walls, time passes at a rate that is normal for us but would seem extremely slow to you. A day in our time is like a score of days in yours. If we stand at the very edge of our domains and look through the magical barriers that protect us, the grass, trees, waters, and creatures of your world look like they are in constant motion. To us, it is a blur."

"I don't understand what you're saying," Daniel said, his brows knitted in a questioning frown.

"To be honest, Daniel, I do not understand it very well myself," the fairy admitted. "The details are really a topic for mages, not rangers. I do not know how magecraft works, or even how the spellsong used by rangers works. I just know that it does. We spends years — that is *our* years — learning how to wield the magic of music. We sing spells to cloud the senses and conceal ourselves. We use it to find other magical creatures and exchange messages over short distances. And we use it to alter emotions. With the right verse or melody, I can make you feel proud or fearful, joyful or wistful, even bring you to laughter or tears."

Daniel chuckled softly. "That doesn't sound so different from what I've seen a good fiddle-player or hymn singer do back home. Were they fairy bards, too?"

"That is an interesting question," Goran replied with a knowing smile. "Perhaps they were. As I said, we can use spellsong to influence the moods and perceptions of humans and other weak-minded creatures. You may well have met some of my kind before, but you do not recall them, at least not the way you are seeing me now. Our spellsong alters memory, too."

Daniel found this explanation hard to grasp. He wasn't sure he wanted to grasp it.

"But back to what you need to know," the fairy said. "For more complicated feats of song magic — for those involving highly resistant targets, for example — our unaided voices can prove inadequate. We use instruments enchanted by our craftsmen to focus and amplify spellsong."

"Like your broken flute," Daniel cut in. "Now I'm beginning to see your trouble. Without it, you can't use your power to track that magical beast from far off because it doesn't want to be tracked. It'll resist you."

Goran swooped in front of Daniel's face and hovered. "I can see fortune has been most generous. You are not just brave but rather perceptive — for a human. So, you will help me complete my mission?"

Daniel stooped and set down his rifle by the creek, plunging both hands into the cool mountain water and cupping them to bring drink to his lips. He stood up, ran a damp hand through his dark, unruly hair, and turned back to the fairy still suspended in midair, his wings beating a graceful, steady rhythm.

"From what you've been telling me, I'm not sure how a mere human could be of much service," Daniel said drily. "I can't conjure up spells. All I can do is hunt fowl and rabbit and deer and, occasionally, bear. I even killed a cougar once, though I wasn't rightly hunting it at the time."

"Fortune truly favors us!" exclaimed the fairy. "That is exactly what I am after — a giant cat!"

"Well, cougars *are* way bigger than ordinary cats and mighty powerful," Daniel replied, picking up his gun and resuming his rapid pace. "I wouldn't want to tangle with one if I didn't have to. But I'd hardly call them giants."

"What I have been tracking is no ordinary wildcat, Daniel," Goran said, his expression suddenly grave as he flew alongside Daniel. "It is something far more dangerous. You could not pronounce the name in our tongue, I suspect, but humans sometimes call it a Wampus Cat. It is a bit longer than you are tall, powerfully muscled, incredibly fast, with long, sharp teeth. As you may have guessed, it draws on magical forces to enhance its strength and speed. And — this is a bit gruesome — the Wampus Cat does not feed on its kills in a normal way. It bites the neck and…well…it drains the lifeblood from its victims while their hearts still beat."

Daniel cast a revolted look the fairy's way but didn't interrupt his stride. "I've heard campfire stories about big cats, but never anything like that."

"You heard only shadows of the truth," Goran said. "Back in what you call the British Isles, where my Folk resided before we journeyed to America, local humans also told stories of monstrous cats with magical abilities. The Scots called them the Cait Sith. In Cornwall, where I was born, I often heard human bards sing of a legendary beast, Cath Paluc, that slew one hundred eighty people before a hero named King Arthur managed to overcome him. It did not really happen like that, of course."

"I'm beginning to think that lots of things I thought I knew, or perhaps lots of things that lots of us thought we knew, have not been quite so," Daniel said with another chuckle. "But if the giant cat we're talking about is really that fearsome, how do you expect to defeat it? I mean no offense, Goran, but if we're talking about some kind of giant cougar, it would dwarf the likes of you. Even my trusty rifle and I may be no match for it."

The fairy shrugged his shoulders in what struck Daniel as a very human expression. "I never had any intention of facing it on my own. Capturing or, if necessary, killing a monster of this size is a job for hunters or even warriors, not of rangers. Our task is to establish a clear location of the quarry and then use spellsong to send the location back. Teams of Folk stand ready to respond to such calls. They arrive and take care of the beast."

"What do you need me to do, then?" asked Daniel.

"We Folk have many talents and skills but, as you pointed out, we are comparatively small in your Brobdingnagian world," the fairy said.

"Hey, I know that word — you've read *Gulliver's Travels*? That's one of my favorite books!"

"Please stop interrupting — of course I am familiar with the adventures of Gulliver, more personally familiar than you would ever guess," Goran said, clearly relishing Daniel's astonishment. "But we were talking about the realm of men. You are fitted to it. Your senses are attuned to it. I never heard the footfalls. That piercing cry? I did not hear that, either. I am hoping that, with my spellsong and your sharp ears, working together, we can corner the prey."

Trying desperately to suppress his curiosity, Daniel stopped short and reached for his powder horn. "All right, Goran," he said as he began loading his gun. "Let's try whatever you had in mind. While the beast may well be ahead of us, it's also possible it's changed direction. Better be sure we're headed the right way."

The fairy grunted his assent. He banked, turned, and landed lightly on Daniel's left shoulder. The young hunter was taken aback for a second, then relaxed. He had made friends with Goran and agreed to help him, after all. Time to follow his lead.

Clearing his throat and turning his face upward, Goran sang. To Daniel, whose ear was very close to the fairy's mouth, it seemed as if the song wasn't coming from just that one place but from every direction at once. It sang of misty mornings, of cool evenings, of damp hiding places, of hunger, of longing. It was a song Daniel had never heard before, yet it felt like a familiar dream of countless nights. He recognized not a single word of the language Goran sang. But, by searching his feelings, Daniel found he could understand its meaning a little. Perhaps a great deal more than that.

And then the young human heard himself answering the fairy's song with a plaintive cry of his own.

No, wait, that's not my voice at all, Daniel realized.

It was a shrill, high-pitched sound. It was like the cry he'd heard just before the bear came crashing out of the thicket — only this time, Daniel could sense some of its meaning, a hint of loneliness, an eagerness to find comfort, but also the suggestion of wariness, of barely restrained ferocity.

Feeling a thrill of excitement, Daniel gave a nod. "I can hear it, Goran. Keep singing and follow me."

▲▲▲

For the better part of an hour, the two searchers followed the cries. Sometimes Goran flew high, extending the range of his spellsong. Other times he alighted on the human's shoulder and let Daniel propel the two, as the effort required to amplify his spellsong without his enchanted flute fatigued the fairy ranger. Slowly but surely they gained on their quarry.

Daniel longed to ask Goran why the cat wasn't running toward them since the fairy's song sounded more enticing than menacing. That was only one of many questions Daniel had. How would the other fairies find them? How could the fairies be so close that they'd arrive in time? And, given the tiny size of their bodies and weapons, how could even a squadron of fairies manage to subdue the monster Goran described?

But there was no time for questions. The fairy needed to sing. Daniel needed to listen, track, climb, and run. And he also needed to think about what he would do when they caught up with the beast.

The moment came without warning. It had been a few minutes since Daniel last heard the cat's responsive cry. As the young hunter weaved his way through a line of trees, he heard it again — so loud it was almost deafening. Then the searchers broke into a small clearing, formed by a handful of downed trees and rotten logs, and Daniel glimpsed for the first time what they'd been chasing through the cool Carolina evening.

The monster was a cat, yes, and more. Its face was feline but elongated, its jaws jutting forward with an almost lupine suggestion. It was improbably massive, frightfully imposing, and covered with stripes. Its legs, short and stubby, were out of proportion to its long body. Its paws were out of proportion, too, wider and with claws that made Daniel's hunting knife look like a dainty piece of silverware fit only for a Philadelphia dinner table.

Most terrifying of all were the cat's huge tawny eyes. They weren't just filled with enormous yellow-orange pupils. The eyes *glowed* yellow-orange. To Daniel, they looked like a blazing fire — no, on second thought, like yellow-orange thunderclouds about to erupt with yellow-orange bolts of lightning. And those eyes, those fiery eyes of that fiery cat, were looking directly into Daniel's eyes of cold blue.

Without hesitation, in a move honed to perfection from years on the frontier, with a calm assurance that had failed him earlier in his confrontation with the bear, Daniel Boone lifted his rifle to a solid shoulder, trained a steady eye down its barrel, took careful aim at a target of yellow-orange, and smoothly squeezed the trigger.

The rifle shot rang out and, from high above Daniel's head, something else rang out — a new song from Goran, a very different one, short, focused, commanding.

Daniel couldn't tell if he'd scored a hit. Then what happened next captured his attention. The air around him began to shimmer with light and crackle with sparks. He felt a great force against his body, like a wind first pushing relentlessly against him and then, as if this were possible, passing rapidly *through* him.

An instant later, Daniel found that he, the fairy, and the Wampus Cat were no longer alone. The clearing was filled with many other figures. They were Goran's size but dressed and outfitted differently. Some of the fairies, aloft, held bows with arrows fitted. Others had their bows strapped across their backs and instead held thin spears, their points directed squarely at the cat, their ends connected to ropes coiled in the fairies' other hands. Still others stood stoutly on the ground in what looked like a military formation, holding thicker spears and round shields. Both the bronze bosses on their shields and the scale armor worn by these grounded fairies glowed metallic red.

Strangest looking of all, in the opinion of their human beholder, were the fairies who stood along the perimeter of what Daniel could now see was a bubble of shimmering light encompassing the entire hunting party and its prey. These new arrivals wore not short cloaks like Goran's but, instead, flowing robes extending to their feet. The robes were variously colored and decorated with a bewildering array of signs, runes, and other figures Daniel didn't recognize, as were the pointed hats on their heads. They were the only ones not looking at the Wampus Cat. Instead, their gazes were fixed on the shimmering walls of the encircling bubble, and on their own hands — from which glistening beams of moonlight, or something like it — kept emerging.

As Daniel took it all in, this weird and wondrous tableau, the stuff of bedtime stories and childhood daydreams, its elements moved swiftly. Daniel saw the flying archers release their arrows and reload. He saw the flying javelinmen hurl their darts and grab onto their ropes with both hands. He saw the armored spearmen march forward and around their quarry. And he saw the cat, that lightning-eyed cat not out of a dream but of a nightmare, its mouth snarling and biting the air, lose its footing, stumble, and sink to the ground. Twice it struggled to rise and fend off its attackers, knocking some roughly to the ground with powerful swipes of its paws. Twice it failed. Then the Wampus Cat rose no more.

▲▲▲

"You hit it, Daniel, you hit it right in the head!" exclaimed Goran some time later, after Daniel had sunk to the forest floor himself in a state of shock. "You did not deal it a mortal wound, thankfully, but you definitely stunned the beast and made it easier to capture without loss of life."

The fairy ranger swooped down to sit on a fallen log. "You were very brave, my friend, and I couldn't have tracked it without you. My first solo ranging has ended in success. I am sure to get my Guild invitation."

Daniel nodded, rubbing his eyes in fatigue, just to make sure he hadn't been seeing things all along.

"Those arrows of yours — they aren't just pointed sticks, are they?" he asked the fairy.

"No, Daniel, they are not. Our craftsmen forge the arrowheads with enchanted metal. The ones we used tonight are designed to bring on sleep. So are the tips of the spears we used. As I told you, we prefer to subdue the monsters, to confine them. We only kill as a last resort."

"I hunt for food, or to make pelts to sell," Daniel said. "I guess that's not what your people have in mind."

Goran's disgusted expression was all the answer Daniel needed.

"That means, then, that even that bear back there, the one I thought I saved you from, was already going to keel over before I ever charged it," Daniel said. "You really saved me from him, like you said."

"Not necessarily," Goran assured him. "That was an enormous animal. A single piercing by my sleep arrow may not have brought it down for some time, if at all. As you can see, it took numerous shots to bring down the Wampus Cat, and your bear was actually a bit larger."

"Larger? Yep. But a bear is just a bear. This thing is something more. It's magical, just like you and your friends. Spellsong? Magecraft? Shimmer spells? I can't begin to take it all in."

Goran stood up and leveled a gaze at Daniel. "You will not need to, Daniel," he said reassuringly, but also with a tinge of sadness. "You have had quite an adventure this day. Please know that I will always appreciate the service you rendered to me, my profession, my Folk, and indeed your own people — because monsters are as great a threat to you as they are to us."

The fairy looked the young hunter up and down. "Are you injured? I can call one of the mages over. You will find that magecraft is superior to any healing arts your people possess."

"I'm fine, Goran, just fine and dandy," Daniel said. He sighed and got to his feet. "You were talking about our adventure tonight. I think you were about to tell me that I won't remember any of it tomorrow."

"That is right, Daniel — you are most perceptive. When our work brings us in contact with humankind, our Ranger Code requires us to sing songs of forgetfulness afterward."

Daniel picked up his rifle and began to reload it. Goran looked startled.

"You never know — I might still be able to get a pheasant on the way home," Daniel explained. "Don't like the idea of showing up without what I went hunting for."

"Oh, I see," the fairy said, visibly relieved. "I thought for a moment that you had some wild idea about trying to resist. Believe me, I wish there were some other way. I have made a new friend today."

Daniel looked back at Goran, a new light in his eyes. "A while ago, you said something about how where humans live, you live, and where humans go, you are unlikely to be far behind. What did you mean? If I'm to lose my memory, what's the harm in satisfying my curiosity for the moment?"

The fairy laughed. "Why not, indeed? You speak plainly. You cut right to the heart of the matter. So I will speak plainly, too."

He waved his hand at the fairies finishing their work, trussing the Wampus Cat in strands of what looked like ordinary rope — but probably wasn't.

"We are not from your world, Daniel, but we must live alongside it," Goran said. "We only want to survive, as you do. We act to protect our homes and families. But we also act to protect you humans. When we find that we must intervene in your affairs, sometimes it is to save ourselves. Other times, it is to save you from yourselves, from your human follies. It is nothing you need to worry about, though. We only do it for your own good."

Daniel didn't much like the sound of that. But he chose to keep his own counsel on the matter.

Instead, he asked, "If your spells are so good at scouring memories, Goran, then how come I knew what you were when I saw you? How come we humans know about fairies and magic and monsters at all?"

The fairy shook his head in amazement. "Again, Daniel, very astute of you. Our spellsong is far from perfect. Nothing in your realm, or any other, can be perfect. As a rule, our songs eliminate any memory of us from a human mind. There are, however, exceptions to every rule. Some human memories survive spellsong. But they are hazy, jumbled, incomplete. Such memories pose little danger — half-recalled daydreams suffused with fantasy and longing that fuel your imaginations and inspire your storytellers."

Goran turned and nodded at the other fairies who circled the bound, unconscious monster. Daniel gaped as the robed ones made signs with their arms and appeared to *draw in* the shimmering light previously emanating from their fingertips. Daniel again felt a mysterious wind and saw a flicker like the flame of a candle. In an instant, the fairies vanished.

All except Goran. He fluttered his wings and lifted off the fallen log. "I know you will not understand this either, Daniel, but I am an exception myself. You see, for most of my Folk, existing in your world beyond our protective Shimmer is possible for only brief passages of time before we go mad or perish. A few of us are born different, though. We possess certain qualities that allow us to live long stretches of time in your world. We become rangers."

Goran looked into the distance with a melancholy expression, as if seeing not what the fairy's eyes beheld in Daniel's world but instead what lay in the fairy's own memories.

"We do not have all the answers ourselves, make no mistake," Goran continued. "No one knows for sure how long even highly resistant, well-trained rangers can survive in the Blur. But tasks must be performed there. We need resources, supplies, protection. And the monster peril must be contained."

The fairy was right — Daniel hadn't understood what Goran said, not fully. But he could read the signs that were as plain as the nose on his new friend's face. He knew their conversation was nearing its end.

"One final time, Daniel, I offer you my deepest appreciation for all you have done. And I extend to you my heartfelt goodbye."

"Farewell, friend," the human hunter responded. "Best of luck until we meet again."

"Alas," the fairy said, "we will never meet again." And then he began to sing.

▲▲▲

It was a tired Daniel Boone who trudged along the banks of the mountain creek. On top of that, he was mighty hungry. He was looking forward to beans and venison when he got back to camp.

Should I try one more time to shoot up some game?

Daniel had great confidence in his skill with his rifle, but even the greatest marksmen who ever lived would struggle to hit a bird, treed or otherwise, in the pitch black of night. Besides, he'd already fired his rifle twice that day. Shot and powder weren't easy to come by, not back home in Pennsylvania and certainly not in the more remote Carolina backcountry.

Daniel supposed this would just have to be one of those rare times he went on a hunt and came back with nothing but a tall tale. Actually, in this case he'd have to come back with even less — and besides, there wouldn't be anyone awake to hear a tale. The Boones would all have been asleep for hours when he got back to camp. Or would it be daybreak by then?

Daniel got to thinking again about the cold beans and dried venison. "I wonder what fairies eat for supper," he asked out loud, to no one in particular. "I never got a chance to ask, and Goran never volunteered anything about it."

Oh, well, the fairy was free to keep whatever secrets he wished.

Daniel was good at keeping secrets, too.

Chapter 2 — The Knob

DURING HIS WEEKS AWAY FROM home on his first solo ranging, Goran had taken every opportunity he could to soar above the tree line, above the world of humankind. Aloft, he felt safe and free. Aground, he felt small and alone. Now, having finally completed his mission, Goran was flying west as fast as his tired wings could manage, through the stillness of a moonlit night, to the Knob. He was flying toward a warm welcome, a sumptuous feast, a father's pride, a sister's embrace. He was flying home.

The journey would be brief. While Goran had tracked the Catawampyrie back and forth for weeks, zigging and zagging through forests and hills, his hunt had ended on a mountainside only about twenty miles east of his home. Almost immediately he could see the Knob's distinctive gray cliffs shining in the moonlight, which also danced across the leaves of its green-topped dome. The sight thrilled Goran and spurred to him to beat his wings still harder.

Rangers born to the task and rigorously trained could spend long stretches in the Blur. It was their responsibility. Many even found meaning, diversion, and pleasure in their work beyond the Shimmer. But the human world would never be theirs. It would never be home.

As he approached the Knob, Goran banked left and turned to approach the south entrance to the Sylph village. Landing first on the branch of a chestnut oak, he glided to the rocky ground next to a rhododendron bush, its palette of pink-purple blossoms conjuring up cherished memories of wandering through his mother Wenna's elaborate garden.

Of course, there had been no flowers native to America in that garden. Goran's childhood had been spent far over the sea, in Cornwall. The Sylphs had lived there for generations atop a hill the humans called Brown Willy.

Wenna's garden there had boasted daisy, buttercup, spring squill, broom, and gorse, along with ferns, heath, a range of medicinal herbs, and a small apple tree. But the garden was on the far edge of the Sylph settlement, distantly removed from the village proper.

The garden was, therefore, still back on Cornwall's Brown Willy. It hadn't made the Crossing.

Goran remembered the Crossing as if it were yesterday — indeed, it hadn't been all that long ago, although his lengthy trips in the Blur meant that the Crossing was further in his past than it was to his friends and family. The Sylphs had, in truth, only just arrived in the Carolina backcountry a few months earlier. Before that, their village had been secreted for some years on a low ridge in Pennsylvania called Haycock Mountain. Before that, before the Crossing, the Sylphs had lived on Brown Willy for generations.

So it wasn't really the sight of the Knob itself that filled Goran with longing. The sight of Haycock Mountain wouldn't have, either. What thrilled him was the mental image of the Sylph village within, of its cherished halls and walls and faces. That, not the distinctive outline of the Knob, was what truly drew him home.

Looking past the rhododendron bush and up the cliffside, Goran saw a tell-tale glow. It was the Shimmer, the wall of magecraft and spellsong that surrounded the village, contained its time and energies, and protected it from incursion. Most earthly creatures couldn't see it at all. Magical creatures had no trouble spotting the wall but couldn't traverse it without voicing or playing the proper musical phrase. Goran approached the Shimmer and began humming. He felt the familiar tingle of magic from head to foot. He felt the wall give way as he pushed through.

As Goran headed toward the settlement, his eyes scanned instinctively for flora in the orange light of dawn. Perhaps his meandering thoughts about his mother's Cornish garden had suggested the idea. But, of course, there were no lush gardens here. Not yet. The Sylphs hadn't been on the Knob long enough. Sylph greenweavers were still experimenting with the local vegetation, learning how to infuse the plants with magic so they could sprout and flourish in surroundings quite different from their native soil — in a place where time could not be reckoned by the rising and setting of a sun that streaked through the heavens twenty times a day.

It was one of the oddest things to get used to in the Blur, that sun.

Behind the Shimmer, in a Folk realm, the sun was barely discernible in a sky shrouded by mist and refracted by magic. As a child, Goran had spent hours lying in the cool grass, gazing up at that misty sky. It lightened and darkened on a nearly hourly basis, cycling through a spectrum of hazy, diffused colors.

In the Blur, however, the colors became sharper, lusher, and slower. The daytime sun burned so fiercely that direct observation was impossible. During his first ranging into the Blur, what had really captured Goran's attention — and his imagination — was the moon, that lustrous nighttime visitor. As rangers traveled most safely by night, anyway, the moon had become his constant companion during his hunt.

Goran bore to his left to give a wide berth to the monster pens on the outskirts of the village. If there had been a lush green garden, he'd have been heading into it. In fact, he glided over a small enclosure and a plowed field beyond, but they contained only a few spouts here and there — greenweaver experiments that might one day blossom into beds and groves. That "one day" remained far off.

Indeed, the village greenweavers would have been further along in their enchantments had they retained the services of their most talented gardener. But she hadn't made the Crossing, either. Wenna's grave marker lay back in Cornwall, in her Brown Willy garden beneath the spreading branches of her prized gillyflower apple tree.

Goran mused for a moment about the Knob. The Sylphs had been fortunate to find the place — a mountaintop so well-crafted for magical conceal-ment that it must have been the site of a village long since abandoned by some other Folk. At best, the sharpest-eyed human could have seen nothing more than an occasional, mysterious glimmer in the foliage above the cliffs. Even when some human eyes saw through the Shimmer, they couldn't make sense of what lay beyond — an expanse of grass, trees, buildings, and streets far more extensive within the Shimmer than could be seen from without. With scarcely a hundred strides, humans could trace the perimeter of the village and never guess that an entire community of Sylphs lived within its seemingly tight confines.

But, of course, humans lived non-magical lives. Goran felt sorry for them.

As he landed and walked into the settlement, the orange sky began its transformation to light blue. Halls and homes bustled with activity.

Tradesmen and craftsmen clad in tunics and stockings of brightly colored wools and linens were pushing carts along streets or carrying bags and baskets as they flew overhead. Mages, greenweavers, and other scholars wearing luxurious robes and fur-lined cloaks either scurried on their way to appointments or wandered aimlessly, seemingly lost in thought. Armored soldiers leaned against walls and posts, polishing the bosses on their shields or telling ribald jokes or doing not much of anything at all. Two hooded hunters stood in front of a butcher shop, holding aloft the opposite ends of a pole from which two skinned rabbits hung — the result of a recent larder hunt, no doubt. Mothers and fathers minded playful children or hustled them homeward. Some Sylphs were talking. Some were laughing. Some were arguing. It was all delightful.

"Goran! You have returned!"

The young ranger felt slender arms wrap tenderly around him and draw him into a tight hug. Turning, he found his sister Ailee looking up with joyful eyes. Her long chestnut hair stretched halfway down the back of her dark green gown, which was cinched at the waist with a buff-colored belt. "We have only just heard the news from the hunting party, Goran. You did it! You found the monster! I am so proud of you."

Goran gave Ailee an affectionate kiss on one flushed cheek and freed himself gently from her embrace. "I missed you all, Little Curlew," he said, using the affectionate nickname he'd given her when they were children. "I would love to tell you of my adventures, but first I have to report to the guild."

"You're quite right, young man. Get a move on!" The dark eyes of his father Brae glowered beneath shaggy white brows as the thick-set man strode toward him on squat, muscular legs. But the stern expression on that weather-beaten face soon gave way to a broad, toothy smile.

"I always knew you had it in you," Brae stated proudly, too loudly to be meant for Goran and Ailee's ears alone.

"A strong branch off the old family tree, there is no doubting that," his father added as a crowd of onlookers gathered. "You were the most talented apprentice the guild had seen in many an age; that is what they all said. You will be a grandmaster one day!"

Goran felt his face reddening with embarrassment. "As you say, Father. I best be off to the guildhall," he said, shaking Brae's proffered hand and then several more as he resumed his course down the street. "I will come home as soon as I can."

"Please do, Goran," Ailee called after him. "We will be sitting down to dinner shortly. The spread we have prepared will astound you. And yes, you need not even ask, that includes your favorite: roast grouse with gravy."

Goran's mouth watered. Then the mention of grouse reminded him of the human hunter he'd just met. Daniel Boone had proved to be a skilled tracker and brave hunter. He was also intelligent and curious. The other humans Goran had met in his travels seemed small by comparison. Most never noticed Goran at all, due to a mixture of inattentiveness and Goran's spellsong. Of those humans who did catch a glimpse, or to whom he chose to reveal himself, some fainted at the sight. Others, convinced Goran was a demon or ghost, tried to attack him or to flee. None escaped his memory charms.

Daniel hadn't either, Goran thought sadly. It was, he supposed, a shame that such a refreshing curiosity would have to remain unsatisfied. But that was the way of things.

The guildhall of the rangers was just north of the village square, its stone walls adorned with brightly hued banners and ringed at the top with sculptures depicting a wide variety of magical creatures. The menagerie included many that Goran recognized readily from his studies or from the fabulous stories that his father Brae and other retired rangers had told around the dinner table. A few shapes he now knew from personal experience. Some statues exhibited outsized or oddly misshapen forms of animals that would have been familiar to any human: felines, canines, ursines, bovines, equines, cervines, porcines, rodentia, avians. Others, Goran, thought, would appear fantastical, even to imaginative humans such as Daniel. Fish-like creatures of sea, lake, river, and bog. Spheres of light and spirits of shadow. Serpents with two legs or four, serpents with three heads or nine, serpents with wings, with fins, with the beaks of birds or the jaws of lions. Some forms were stranger still.

Goran ascended the steps and knocked on the massive doors of ash and bronze. Soon, as a journeyman, he'd be able to push his way right in; he wouldn't need to knock. But not just yet.

The doors creaked open. "Well, Apprentice Goran, it took you long enough," said the owl-faced Sylph who beckoned him inward. "We expected you to transport with the hunters, not take the scenic route. But perhaps you have grown so fond of the Blur that you decided to linger a bit among the English. It has been known to happen…"

Goran wasn't fooled. He knew when he was being teased. "I could not have been more than a few minutes behind the hunting party, Ceredan," he said, pretending offense. "It only took me about half an hour of Blur time to reach the Knob. And, yes, while I 'lingered among the English,' it is only because I had to sing a memory spell."

Ceredan and Goran had been walking along the hallway toward the council chamber. Now the older ranger halted and faced the young man. "Yes, I heard about that," he said, a little hesitantly. "There is always a chance of encountering humans on larder or monster hunts. Each of us has had the experience, but rarely do we enlist a human's aid. Did you really deem that wise?"

Goran looked back at his long-time teacher, now less sure he was being teased instead of scolded. "I had no choice. My flute was broken by accident. Without the keen ears of the human, I would have lost the quarry."

Ceredan cocked his head sideways and considered. "There are worse things than a failed ranging. You could have returned home and gotten a new instrument. Perhaps the Catawampyrie would still have been in the area. Or perhaps you would have had to embark on a new journeyman trial. Involving humans in hunts invites danger."

Goran offered a deferential nod of his head. "I understand your words, Ceredan, but there was something about Daniel that inspired confidence. Besides, I knew that even with a broken flute I could still cast a memory spell."

"Such a spell can treat the memory, Goran, but it cannot treat a broken limb or, worse, a broken neck," Ceredan responded. "Still, all rangers must make judgment calls. I suppose you did what you thought best. You can explain it to the other guildmasters. They have assembled to receive your report and evaluate your trial."

Ceredan preceded Goran into the council chamber, where a dozen rangers ranging from middle-aged to elderly sat behind a semi-circular table. Goblets of wine sat before each, as did plates filled with pastries and sweetmeats. The sight reminded Goran of his own hunger and thirst. He resisted the impulse to seek refreshment. Now was the time to report. And he knew his family had a celebratory feast waiting.

The most ancient of the rangers, Grandmaster Cono, clapped his hands to silence the others. "We welcome you home, Apprentice Goran, and congratulate you on the successful capture of your quarry," the elder said with a quivering voice that nevertheless commanded the guildmasters' rapt attention. "We are eager to hear the details of your ranging and the lessons you have taken from it."

Goran complied. He told the masters about receiving his assignment from Ceredan, who'd relayed stories of mysterious attacks in the Carolina backcountry. He told them how the details of the attacks had convinced him some kind of monstrous feline, likely a Catawampyrie, was responsible. Goran described the painstaking process of surveying the countryside, flying by night and moving stealthily through forests by day, singing and playing summoning spells to entice the cat. On two earlier occasions, he explained, the beast had responded to the call but was so far away that even Goran's most skillful spells had failed to pinpoint its location. For weeks he had tracked the beast, stopping only to eat, rest, and avoid the occasional human hunter, trapper, or party of settlers.

Finally, in what was nearly two days ago in the Blur but only a couple of hours to the Sylphs of the Knob, he'd picked up the trail. After sending a preparatory signal, he'd headed after the beast. Goran related his encounter with Daniel, his decision to enlist the human's aid, and the final confrontation with the monster. Then he fell silent.

The guildmasters looked at each other, some conversing, some speaking more with their eyes than their tongues. Presently, Cono spoke again.

"Apprentice Goran, the Catawampyrie is one of the most elusive of magical creatures in the wilds of the New World. The only event of your report that strikes us as noteworthy is your decision to attack the bear to save the human hunter. While we wish no harm on any human, you could have been injured or killed during your rescue, leaving the Catawampyrie to continue ravaging the countryside. Explain yourself."

Goran looked at the floor for a moment, then lifted his gaze and squared his shoulders. "It was an impulsive thing to do," he admitted, responding first to Cono and then looking each guildmaster in the eye in turn. "I do not have a clear explanation. It just seemed wrong to let the human die before my eyes, not when I had a chance to save him."

Another guildmaster, a small man with graying temples and a long, thin nose, cleared his throat. "Goran, to say that something is noteworthy is not necessarily to say it is wrong," said Bren, a long-time friend of his father's. "I, for one, think your actions were admirable."

"We are all quite well aware of your thoughts on the matter, Bren," said yet another master, a burly Sylph with a shiny bald pate and a massive grey beard extending halfway down his nut-brown tunic. "Your voice at council is ever for greater engagement with humans. Where the rest of us see peril, you see opportunity."

"Yes, I do, Borva — and why not?" Bren answered, the volume and pitch of his voice rising in his excitement. "For generations, we have seen our humans merely as providers of sustenance. We send our rangers to human homes to obtain food, cloth, building materials, precious metals. They make offerings. They give us what we seek in exchange for a few magic tricks. We profit from their superstitions. And what, really, do we offer in return?"

"What, indeed?" snorted Borva. "We risk our lives to track and capture the monsters that would otherwise overrun and slaughter them. What we get for this service is scant payment, to my mind."

"Borva only scratches the surface of the truth," Grandmaster Cono broke in, and the others fell silent. "What our humans receive from us goes beyond just protection from beastly attack. There is much more to it, as we all know."

Almost all of the seated rangers nodded in assent, some vigorously, some more hesitantly.

Bren was the exception. "I agree that our actions sometimes benefit our charges," he told his fellow guildmasters. "But it is not by design. We protect our humans much as they protect their own herds of cattle and flocks of sheep — and for the same reason, because the safety of the herd is in our interest. The difference is that humans are not cattle or sheep. They are reasoning beings."

Borva again snorted derisively. "In my experience, human behavior rarely meets that test," he insisted. "I have found them to be ignorant, simple-minded, and violent. Even the best of them suffer from impatience, arrogance, and perpetual dissatisfaction. They have no facility for spellsong, magecraft, or any of the higher arts. Their appetites are insatiable. They enslave their fellow humans and treat them like beasts. And they are constantly at war."

"I will remind you that warfare is hardly confined to the human realms," Bren said icily. "We have warred with other Folk from time to time. With the Pixies of the Cornish coast. With the Gwyllion and Coblynau of the Welsh highlands. And have you so soon forgotten the border conflicts that prompted us to leave the human colony of Pennsylvania for another new home?"

"Our memories are quite intact, Bren," replied Grandmaster Cono with a sharpness that startled Goran. "We need no reminders. And, as you also know, we undertook our southward journey from Pennsylvania for many reasons, not just because of border conflicts. Besides, the Council of Elders has already discussed your ideas at great length, and found some of them persuasive. Even the latest orders brought over the sea from our own King Briafael bear some similarities to your argument for more engagement with humans. So why are we debating here? This is an examination judgment, not a council meeting."

Both Bren and Borva bowed their heads in acknowledgement of the ancient one's authority.

"Goran," said Cono, returning his attention to the young ranger standing before them. "Thank you for your service. You will be judged fairly by the masters of your guild. If you are invited to become a journeyman, you will be assigned your first long ranging. That is all for now. You are excused."

▲▲▲

The table was set for six but there was food enough for thrice that many. Salads of tossed greens and crisp vegetables. Platters of sliced fruits and cheeses. Trays of roasted grouse, turkey, and pork. A huge bowl of steaming rabbit stew. Sausages of venison, cured and delicately spiced. Trout pan-seared in butter. Loaves of freshly baked bread. Cakes, cobblers, and pies.

Goran sat to his father's right, the place of honor, longing to grab at the roast grouse. Weeks in the Blur eating field rations, wild onions, and an occasional charred haunch of rodent had left Goran famished. Just how ravenous had not become evident until he neared the house and smelled the aromas of Ailee's handiwork. His pace quickened, his pleasantries little more than perfunctory when he reached the doorway. Almost immediately, Goran was sitting at the table awaiting his father's blessing and the beginning of the feast.

Both came quickly. "For the bounty before us, we give thanks to the Maker of All Things," Brae intoned, "as we do for the victory we commemorate today."

Then the clanking and chewing began.

"Welcome back, brother," said a broad-shouldered Sylph sitting across from Goran as both began lifting generous portions onto their plates with their hunting knives. Kaden, his elder brother, had joined the Warriors Guild two years before the standard age of admission. Demonstrating impressive skills of body and mind, Kaden soon commanded his own squad and was studying advanced warcraft with his guild's grandmaster, General Eyrn. "I was drilling spearmen today and could not join the hunting party. I trust the battle was a glorious one."

Goran had just stuffed his mouth with a hunk of bread dipped in stew. He waved helplessly to Kaden, swallowed so quickly he nearly choked himself, and then took a drink of ale.

"As it turned out," he said momentarily, "the battle was fairly short. You might have been a bit disappointed, Kaden."

Now it was his brother's turn to finish chewing before replying. "I have never battled a Catawampyrie before, but the tales say it is massive and dangerously quick. Did your fearsome prey turn out to be nothing more than a little kitten? Or an old grandmother cat on her last legs?"

Kaden's friend Jodoc exploded in guffaws, nearly spraying Ailee with half-chewed trout. She glared at the young soldier, who immediately began profuse apologies as she turned up her nose. It was a pattern Goran had witnessed many times before. Jodoc was very interested in Ailee. She was very uninterested in him.

Although Kaden initially flashed a mocking smile, his expression quickly turned apologetic. "I meant no disrespect, brother. Just making a little jest."

Goran believed him. As children, the two had quarreled, as siblings do. But they also had great affection for each other. Goran was immensely proud of Kaden's prowess as a soldier. He could tell Kaden felt the same way about his little brother's ranging.

"Of course, Kaden," Goran reassured him. "To answer your original question, the reason we took down the monster so rapidly is that it sustained a wound from an instrument of human design — a hunting weapon called a rifled musket."

His brother perked up at the mention of weapons. "The Warriors Guild has been studying gunpowder, cannons, and muskets for many years, ever since rangers brought samples from the Blur," Kaden said. "We have even heard lately of cannons with grooves cut into their barrels to spin the metal shot and make it more accurate. The humans call that rifling. Are you saying they rifle their shoulder weapons, too?"

"Some do, it seems, although I do not know how widespread the practice is," Goran said. "The weapon has a very long barrel and takes quite a while to reload. It is a useful tool for hunting. But I am not sure how practical it would be in a pitched battle."

Kaden looked intensely interested. "I will ask my captain about this tomorrow. Most human guns are too large and heavy for us to wield, even if we could get enough of them to outfit more than a handful of warriors. As for making our own shoulder weapons, I understand the Craftsmen Guild has tried. So far, they have failed with bronze and brass. The humans often use iron, but of course iron and magic do not mix well."

Goran cut off another hunk of bread and put it on his plate. "I will ask if there is an updated ranging report on human musketry I can pass along," he said. "At the very least, if our Folk could produce a few rifles and learn to use them as Daniel did, it would make both our larder and monster hunts easier."

"Making things easier does not necessarily mean making them better," Brae cut in, sounding annoyed. "Do not be so quick to throw out the tried and the true. The old ways have served us well. They have filled our tables and defended our borders for generations. I will take tradition over comfort any day."

"I have no taste for ease, Father," Kaden said. "Our soldiers train hard, and well. The Warriors Guild is as strong as ever. And I would still rather have a good bow or a stout spear in my hands than some human contraption belching smoke and fire. But what if some other Folk figure out the secret of firearms? We owe it to our Folk to be prepared for anything — even if that means borrowing an idea from humans."

"It is not as if we shy away from 'borrowing' other things from them," Jodoc said, laughing at his own joke and glancing not-so-discreetly at Ailee for a sign of approval.

It never came.

"Always be prepared — that is what I always say," said Brae. He looked back at Kaden. "I am sure your guildmasters know best, just as the masters of our guild know what is best for ranging. Speaking of: Goran, when will you receive their judgment of your application?"

Goran smiled. "I am not sure, Father. But, after a meal like this one, the prospect of some rest and relaxation with my family is sounding better and better. Perhaps it will take the masters a week to make up their minds, or a month."

▲▲▲

It took only a single day.

Goran was at the back of the house the following afternoon, fixing a door latch, when he heard a knock on the door and Brae's deep, loud voice conversing with someone. When he came around to the front, he saw his teacher Ceredan.

"It is time, Goran," he said simply. "Pack up your kit and come with me to the guildhall. I shall wait."

Goran went to his room to get ready. He pulled out two clean tunics, an extra pair of stockings, a bedroll, and his hooded travel cloak. He stuffed them in his knapsack, then filled his pocket pouches with writing paper and his spare spellsong flute, feeling its familiar contours and finger holes as he stowed it away. He strapped on his hunting knife and picked up his unstrung bow and quiver of bronze-tipped arrows. Compared to that of hunters and soldiers, ranger equipment was sparse and light. Yet he still felt the weight of responsibility as he turned to make his goodbyes. He supposed he ought to have been more excited — Ceredan wouldn't have asked him to pack if the news were bad — but he had hoped for more of a respite.

"I did not think your first journeyman mission would come so soon," Ailee said, wiping a tear from her eye with one hand and pulling him forward for a kiss with the other. "This time, you may be gone for more than just a few days. Here, put these in your pouch." She handed him several thick squares of cornbread and a roll of venison jerky.

"You are headed back out so soon because you impressed them so much," a beaming Brae assured Goran. He clapped his son on the back and turned to Ceredan. "Is he not a branch off the old tree, my friend? Did I not tell you?"

Brae clearly had, many times. Ceredan nodded his head good-naturedly and motioned for Goran to follow.

When they reached the guildhall, Ceredan paused for a moment at the door. "You have done well, Goran. You are about to take a new and fateful step in a long journey, in a lifetime of service. The masters think you are ready. I think you are ready. But you must *know* you are."

Goran took the old ranger's hand. He understood, even if he wasn't as sure of himself as the moment required. *Will I ever truly be sure?* he thought. Ranging was an unpredictable and varied profession. You had to be part scout, part hunter, part scrounger, part diplomat, and wholly committed to the safety and wellbeing of your Folk.

Goran had studied. He had trained. He should be up for what lay ahead. Was he? Time to find out.

They walked into the council chamber. A much smaller cast of characters greeted him this time: the aged Cono, the pensive Bren, and the irritable Borva.

"Welcome back, Ranger Goran," said the latter, his long beard trembling as he spoke his words forcefully. "You have been awarded the rank of journeyman. May you range long, range wide, your song your guide."

"Range long, range wide, our song our guide!" echoed the other Sylphs, repeating the familiar chorus of their guild spellsong.

Borva pointed to an empty chair. Goran sat.

"Ranger Goran," began Cono, "what I tell you is meant for your ears and ours alone. You are bound by the Code to secrecy, and to the successful completion of your mission."

"Understood, Grandmaster," Goran replied.

"While you were in the Blur, the Council of Elders received a ranger sent all the way to the Knob from Cornwall, from King Briafael himself," Cono began. "His message generated significant debate among the guild grandmasters. We understand its import and are obligated to carry out the king's directives. Still, there are mysteries and uncertainties here."

Borva, his arms crossed over his barrel chest, grunted his assent. Bren stroked his chin and looked searchingly at Goran.

"In brief, Briafael expressed concern about the current state of human affairs," Cono continued. "Their realms have been unstable for as long as Folk have recorded their history, since the bygone days of the Arrival. Of late, however, the events of the Blur have become even more turbulent, more unpredictable."

Cono paused, seemingly shaken. Bren cleared his throat and picked up where the grandmaster left off.

"Goran, King Briafael observes that the kingdoms of Europe continue to be at constant war. For the most part, we Folk seek to stay out of such conflicts. But, as long-time residents of Britain, and now of the British colonies in America, we do have an interest in making sure the balance of power is maintained — that the Crown maintains its authority over all the lands we inhabit. We also have, I might add, a moral obligation to lift up those humans among whom we have lived for generations."

"You may keep your personal opinions to yourself, Bren," snapped Borva. "This is not about the welfare of humans. It is about our own protection. With any domination of the humans by a foreign power would inevitably come domination by a foreign Folk. This is *our* domain. We will not surrender it to the Goblins of Paris, the Duendes of the Spanish plains, or the Kabouters of the Dutch marshes."

"Be that as it may," began Cono, his voice once again calm and authoritative, "we have been ordered by King Briafael to find out more about potential threats to Britain's North American colonies. You, Goran, will act on our behalf in these matters."

The young ranger looked in stunned disbelief at the three masters across the table. "Why me?" he heard himself ask. "This sounds like a complex matter of intelligence and diplomacy. I am only now a journeyman. Surely a more experienced ranger would…"

"Silence, Goran," said the grandmaster, not unkindly. "It is not your place to challenge your guildmasters. Your duty is to carry out your assigned mission."

"Or, if you wish, you could refuse the assignment," Borva suggested with a mocking leer. "We do not conscript into the Rangers Guild. Perhaps this pursuit is not for you. Perhaps you would be better suited to your late mother's occupation of greenweaver. Or to your father's current occupation of village…"

Borva stopped short, seeming to realize he'd gone too far but disinclined to make apology. The other two masters glared at him, then turned their attention back to Goran, whose face had reddened.

"I meant no disrespect," said the young ranger, "nor did I mean to suggest hesitation. I accept the assignment, of course. I will do my best to live up to your expectations."

Cono gave a brief nod and leaned back wearily in his chair, eyes closed. Bren smiled and inclined his head in approval. Borva merely gave Goran a sideways, sneering look, as if to say that living up the level of his expectations would require no great effort on Goran's part.

Chapter 3 — The Wagoners

July 1755

DANIEL WAS SICK TO DEATH of stumps. He was sick to death of mud.

He was sick to death of bouncing up and down on a rough wooden seat as he drove his wagon slowly over the stump-filled trail, and sick to death of having to climb down to help work his wheels out of mud-filled ruts. He was sick to death of the sheer boredom of his months-long trek — first from the Yadkin River Valley into Virginia with the Carolina militia, then to Alexandria, then along the Potomac to western Maryland, and now deep into Pennsylvania.

Daniel was sick to death of living on musty bread and rancid meat. He was sick to death of weary days and restless nights. He was sick to death of arrogant British officers and contemptuous British soldiers. He was sick to death of the whole affair.

The one thing Daniel Boone wasn't — for which he was most grateful — was quite literally sick to death. The same couldn't be said for some of the other men who had marched, rode, or chopped their way into Pennsylvania with him. The afflicted looked deathly ill. Doubled over in pain, incapable of keeping down food and water, some had stumbled along with the column. Others had given up. At least Daniel hadn't seen a man die from the bloody flux or one of the other diseases afflicting the expedition, although he'd seen many a poor horse succumb to excessive exertion and inadequate fodder.

That is, he corrected himself, he hadn't seen a man die *yet*. Perhaps that was about to change, given the miserable condition of the young officer lying in the back of Daniel's wagon.

While their pace seemed pitifully slow, his lightened wagon was moving fast enough to pass the other supply wagons and marching men following the newly cut road. A couple of days earlier, the young officer had, in between groans and grunts, ordered Daniel to unload all his cargo and race to the front of the column, where General Edward Braddock was preparing to lead his British regulars and colonial militia in an assault on the French stronghold of Fort Duquesne.

That his passenger, an officer in the Virginia militia, was so desperate to reach Braddock and join the attack struck Daniel as ridiculous. The man was in no shape to attack anyone. In fairness, he looked every bit the soldier — big, six feet tall or more, with strong features chiseled into a broad, intelligent face. Healthy, the young Virginian might have been an imposing sight. But sprawled in the back of Daniel's wagon, his head lolling from side to side, his limbs alternating between sickeningly limp and contorted in pain, the colonial officer just looked sick. Perhaps even sick to the point of death.

Daniel had come to like the young man, who he judged to be about the same age as his own twenty years. He prayed that Colonel George Washington wouldn't die, especially not in the back of his wagon.

▲▲▲

At first, Daniel's service as a wagoner and blacksmith for the Carolina militia had felt more like an adventure than an ordeal. And he'd believed their cause was a just one.

Daniel had known many Indians growing up. He agreed with his father that whites and Indians ought to be able to live together and learn from each other. But, in response to widespread Indian raids encouraged by the French, Daniel was willing to defend his former neighbors in Pennsylvania as well as his new ones in North Carolina.

During the grueling march, though, Daniel's enthusiasm had faded. Still, there was a bright spot. The expedition had given him a chance to make new friends among his fellow wagoners. One of them, John Finley, told him tantalizing stories about a wondrous country beyond the high mountains where the land was lush and the game was plentiful. Daniel was also delighted to discover that another wagoner was his own eighteen-year-old cousin, Dan Morgan.

Seeing a throng blocking the road ahead, Daniel slowed his team and glanced back at his passenger. Colonel Washington was sitting up, his eyes glassy but nevertheless taking in the scene around him. The rough "road," such that it was, had only just been cleared. On either side, the trees stood tall and thick. As his eyes followed Washington's searching gaze into the forest, Daniel caught occasional glimpses of the blue coats of colonials and the brown shirts and skins of the handful of Indian scouts who had remained with the column. They were in the woods screening the advance of the British regulars who were marching along the road in bright red uniforms.

Daniel was glad he didn't have to wear a red coat. If the French and their Indian allies attacked, he thought, those in red would be the easiest targets.

"Driver, can you keep us moving?" Colonel Washington asked. "We must be getting close to the fort. I must reach General Braddock before he orders the assault."

"I can try, sir," Daniel replied. "But, if I may say so, you're in no condition to go into battle."

"I will manage," the young officer said, sitting up straighter and buttoning up his waistcoat. "My duty is clear. And I have a score to settle."

Daniel understood. He'd heard the story from John Finley. Two years earlier, George Washington had made his first trip to western Pennsylvania as a newly minted lieutenant colonel in the militia. His mission was to deliver a letter declaring the Ohio Country a British domain and demanding that the French stay in Canada. The French rejected the demand. On the way back to Virginia, Colonel Washington had identified the spot where the Alleghany and Monongahela Rivers met to form the Ohio as an ideal location for a fort. But it was the French who got there first. They'd built Fort Duquesne.

Sent out again with militia to challenge the French, Washington had built his own stockade, Fort Necessity, and recruited allies among the local Mingo Indians. When the Mingos found a small French force encamped between the two forts, Washington agreed to attack. Among the slain was a French officer. The man hadn't just been killed. He'd been scalped. The French were outraged and came to Fort Necessity to get their revenge. Vastly outnumbered, Colonel Washington had given up the fort. The formal surrender was written in French, though, so Washington hadn't realized he was admitting to a role in "assassinating" the French officer.

Now it was the British who were outraged. That was why General Braddock had come to America. That was why the British redcoats and American militia were marching toward Fort Duquesne. That was why Daniel was there, driving the wagon carrying George Washington to the front of the column. The young Virginian officer clearly had something to prove. And it looked like Washington wasn't going to let a bout of the bloody flux keep him from doing so.

As the wagon approached the crowd blocking the road, Daniel saw that the cause wasn't a fallen tree or a wheel stuck in the mud. Some British officers were standing in a circle, along with a short, thick-set man dressed in buckskins. They were having a spirited discussion. Groups of soldiers stood a fewer paces away, leaning on muskets and taking the opportunity to rest their feet or drink from wooden canteens.

"That's General Braddock!" Washington exclaimed. "We have arrived in time!" The young officer began staggering to his feet. "Driver, what is your name?"

Daniel looked dubiously at the still-weakened man. "Daniel Boone, sir."

"Mr. Boone, you have done me a great service," Washington said. "Now I wonder if I may ask another favor. I must walk to General Braddock on my own power to show I am ready to rejoin the column. But I fear that, if I try to carry my equipment, I will stumble. Will you carry it for me, and offer a shoulder if I need it?"

Daniel looked down at Washington's "equipment," which consisted merely of a sword in its scabbard, and a bedroll. Then he cast a questioning glance at the officer. "I'll be happy to oblige, but I don't know if it will do you much good."

Washington lowered himself gingerly from the wagon and began smoothing the wrinkles from his uniform. "I have not come this far only to prove wanting when battle is joined. I am Braddock's aide-de-camp. I will not shirk my responsibility. Once on my feet and walking around, I will recover my strength."

Daniel suspected Washington may have been reassuring himself as much as his wagoner, but said nothing. Instead, he picked up the officer's equipment and followed a step behind as Washington approached the group.

"Welcome, Mr. Washington," said a distinguished officer in a resplendent uniform. "I am surprised but pleased to see you up and about."

"Thank you, General Braddock," Washington replied, standing ramrod straight. "Providence has been kind. My health is restored and I am pleased to return to your service."

"That is good news," Braddock said. He turned to the other British officers. "Perhaps our beardless young American friend can help inform our conversation. He has been here before."

Some of the officers snickered at Braddock's "beardless" jibe. Daniel took an instant disliking to them.

Braddock looked at one of the officers who didn't laugh. "Colonel Halkett, state again for the benefit of Mr. Washington your suggested course of action." Sir Peter Halkett, Daniel recalled, commanded one of the two regiments of British regulars in the expedition.

"Sir, we have only some fourteen hundred troops available," Colonel Halkett said warily. "Colonel Dunbar's regiment remains far to our rear, guarding our baggage train. We know Fort Duquesne is strong and well-defended. We don't really know how many Indian allies the French have recruited. I still advise we wait for Dunbar's regiment to reach us so we can attack at full strength."

"Thomas Dunbar is a cowardly old woman," General Braddock snapped. "If we wait too long, we may lose the initiative — and that, gentlemen, is precisely what I mean to keep."

The commander turned to another officer, one who *had* snickered at Washington. "And what is your view, Colonel Gage? If we proceed with the attack, you will command the advance guard."

That was another name Daniel had heard before, Thomas Gage. The officer seemed disinclined to answer. "We will do our duty as always, sir," he said tentatively.

Standing next to Gage was a young officer. Daniel recognized the slovenly looking man in a lieutenant's uniform as the one who'd laughed the longest at Washington's expense. The lieutenant cleared his throat and thrust out his chest, reminding Daniel of a strutting turkey. "General, the regiment will more than simply do its duty. We will write a new chapter in the history of our glorious empire. Like the phalanxes of Alexander, we will conquer all who…"

"That will be quite enough," Braddock snapped. "If we have need of a history lesson, gentlemen, we have only to call on our schoolmaster, Charles Lee, to do the honors."

Now it was Lee's turn to be the target of the others' chuckles. He stepped back, scowling.

Braddock turned back to Washington. "It was at your suggestion, as I recall, that we left our slower units and supplies behind so we could move quickly. Should we now hold so Dunbar can catch up?"

Washington considered the matter. "I would judge the additional troops to be most welcome, sir. But I would not advise waiting for Dunbar. His horses are exhausted. It would take many days for him to catch up. I was only able to do so because of the assistance of a skilled wagoner who shed all his cargo."

General Braddock looked past Washington to the figure of Daniel Boone standing behind him, dressed simply in his hunting shirt and leggings. "We are most appreciative of your services," he said, giving a curt nod. Not knowing what else to do, Daniel attempted a clumsy salute. It triggered another round of laughter from the officers. Daniel felt ridiculous.

"I am inclined to agree with you," Braddock told Washington. "But there is something else to consider. This scout here — what is your name again?"

The buckskin-clad colonial stepped forward. "I'm Evan Shelby, sir," he replied in a thick Welsh accent, nodding pleasantly to Colonel Washington but pointedly ignoring the British officers.

"Yes, well, our man Shelby here has learned that France's Indian allies may not be firmly attached to their cause," Braddock continued. "Perhaps they are finally hearing our message, that we are here as much in their interest as in ours."

"This is yet another compelling reason to wait," Colonel Halkett chimed in, immediately regretting it in the face of Braddock's icy glare.

Washington cleared his throat. Daniel thought he looked hesitant to say what he was thinking. But, finally, the Virginian spoke again.

"That prospect may change matters. If the Indians can truly be persuaded to abandon the defense of Fort Duquesne, we could accomplish our objective with little risk. If there is even a chance…"

"I will remind you the British domains in America were not won without risk, Mr. Washington," Braddock interrupted, "and I hardly think they can be defended without it. We will talk again in a few hours."

With that, the general walked briskly away. The circle of officers began to break up. The scout, Evan Shelby, nodded amiably to Washington once again and strode off toward the front of the column. Then Daniel saw Washington sag slightly and hurried over to provide a shoulder. But the officer quickly regained his composure.

"Thank you again, Mr. Boone, for rendering me a great service," he said, taking his sword from Daniel's hand and strapping the scabbard to his belt. "And now, I believe I shall go find a suitable mount."

▲▲▲

Daniel spent the next few hours at his wagon, tending to tired horses and checking his wheels as soldiers marched past. He wasn't certain what he was supposed to do. No one had given him any orders.

His militia company was at the back of the column. So were John Finley, Dan Morgan, and his other wagoner friends. Should Daniel turn back and rejoin them? Should he wait for them to catch up? Or should he move forward with the troops if General Braddock ordered an attack? Daniel guessed he wouldn't be much use in the latter case. Of course, he was a good shot with his hunting rifle, which he kept stowed in his wagon. But Daniel had only fired at fixed targets or wild game. He'd never fired at a man. He'd never been charged by someone with bayonet or tomahawk.

What would I do? Daniel shuddered at the possibility that he might find out.

He wished he could be in the forest instead of the road. Daniel looked longingly into the trees, hoping to catch another glimpse of a friendly Indian or an American ranger like the Welshman he just met, Evan Shelby. Then he gasped, his eyes widening in shock. Daniel *did* see a ranger lurking among the trees — or, to be more precise, he saw a ranger lurking *in* a tree.

Daniel beheld a form he had seen only once, four years earlier, and thought he'd never see again. It was Goran, the winged fairy, perched on a branch and peering up the trail at a British sergeant, who was loudly ordering dawdling redcoats to their feet.

As if feeling the force of Daniel's eyes trained on him, the fairy began looking around uncomfortably. Then he pulled something out of a pouch and raised it to his lips. Out came a darkly beautiful melody. After a minute or so, the song ended and the fairy repocketed his flute. Seemingly relieved, Goran glanced around again. His eyes met Daniel's. The fairy blinked. Then he started in alarm.

Daniel tried a reassuring grin. The smile wasn't just for Goran's benefit. Many times since he first met the fairy on top of that Carolina mountain,

Daniel had questioned his memory. Had he fallen asleep and dreamed it up? Had his active imagination concocted a fairy story out of some birdwings, glimpsed through the fog of a darkening sky, and a scary encounter with a wildcat?

Now Daniel was relieved. He hadn't dreamed it. He hadn't imagined it. There was the proof, right there in that tree — Goran, his green cap askew, his wings folded, his bow slung over one shoulder, looking back at him.

After several moments of strained silence, Daniel left the road and walked to the tree. Goran made no effort to challenge him or fly away. He just sat on the branch and watched Daniel approach, his initial expressions of surprise and dismay fading from his face. Daniel was glad to see Goran. And, unless Daniel was very much mistaken, Goran was glad to see him.

"Do you...do you remember my name?" the fairy asked haltingly.

"Of course, Goran. I remember it all — the bear, the Wampus Cat, the other fairies, everything."

"Amazing, simply amazing," Goran said. "Your resistance to spellsong is far beyond anything I have ever experienced. My teacher Ceredan told me that only one human in a multitude could retain even a hazy image of a Folk encounter."

Daniel lifted his broad-brimmed beaver hat to scratch an itchy scalp and looked more closely at Goran. "You don't seem to have changed a bit, friend, except this time your magic flute appears to be in one piece."

Goran pulled out the instrument and looked thoughtfully at it. "That is another surprise. You should not be able to see me, much less converse with me. My spellsong of concealment does not seem to work on you, either."

"I got no answer for you, Goran," said the wagoner. "I heard your flute. I heard your song. But I still see you just fine."

The Sylph stepped off the branch, hovered for a few seconds as he looked around, then landed. "Daniel, I never expected us to meet again. I am not here to see you. I am here to learn more about your war. My mission is of vital importance."

Daniel was puzzled. "I thought you fairies tried to stay out of our affairs. What's this mission of yours?"

Goran glanced down for a moment, seeming to gather his thoughts, and then looked up at Daniel, who was leaning against the tree and trying to mask his curiosity.

"I have a strong feeling I can trust you, Daniel," he began. "After all, King Briafael's policy is intended to benefit your people, not harm them. I will tell you what I know."

Goran and Daniel walked and talked for hours, hardly noticing the passing time as they headed deeper into the forest. Goran talked of becoming an apprentice and then being sent out immediately on his intelligence mission. Each ranging had taken him farther and farther away from home. He had visited market towns, ports, and provincial capitals. Goran had even traveled to Philadelphia, where he learned a great deal by reading newspapers, listening to conversations, and watching public meetings from magical seclusion.

"As best I can determine, during the four of your years since I saw you last, I have spent almost two years here in the Blur," Goran said. "To you, that might not sound like much time. But, for most rangers, their trips into the Blur are short and sporadic. Mine have not been."

Daniel saw a shadow darken the fairy's face. It aroused his sympathy. "Been hard on you, Goran? I sometimes dream of spending months away from home hunting and exploring. I take it you get too homesick to enjoy it."

"It is not exactly that, Daniel," Goran said. "Remember that, for my people, time passes at a different rate than it does here. Every day for us is like twenty days in the Blur. I can spend the better part of a month here and then, when I return home, it seems to family and friends that I have been gone just a day. I have an elder brother named Kaden. I have always looked up to him despite the fact that he was born just eighteen months before I was. But now that I have spent more time than that in the Blur, Kaden and I are essentially the same age. Soon I will look and feel much older."

Daniel stopped, knelt, and placed a hand on Goran's shoulder. "I'm still trying to understand this fairy time of yours. But I know what it's like to have older brothers to look up to. I reckon Kaden will always be that for you, no matter how old you look."

"Thank you, Daniel," the fairy said. "Ranging can be a lonely calling. I knew that when I began the training, but the mission I received was not what I expected."

"Help me understand that," Daniel said, seizing the opportunity to change the subject. "Why'd you get sent on this mission?"

"We Folk crave security and stability," Goran explained. "For the most part, we have enjoyed both during many centuries living alongside humans in Britain and now in America. But, in recent times, Britain has fought many wars against multiple, exceedingly dangerous foes. Occasionally, at critical moments, the British have had help — from us or other Folk with an interest in defending them."

"And no one's been the wiser, I take it," Daniel said, shaking his head in amazement.

"That is correct, my friend," Goran said. "However, we grow increasingly concerned. So far, Britain has managed to find allies and use its naval power to balance the scales. Our King Briafael and his council worry Britain's luck may run out."

"I wouldn't pretend to understand politics or empires," Daniel said. "What I do know is that, here on the frontier, the French are making it harder and harder for folks to settle new lands. They urge Indians to attack us and supply them with guns to make those attacks more dangerous. That's why we're here. It's not about some dispute back in Europe. It's about security, like you said — *our* security, the people of America."

Goran shot his companion a reproachful look. "I know that is how you see it, Daniel. But what of the Indians? What of their security?"

"We could live peaceably with them if the French weren't constantly stirring up trouble," Daniel protested.

"I am not so sure," Goran replied. "That is precisely why I am here. I followed General Braddock's expedition to learn more about the Indian communities over the mountains, both those allied to the British and those allied to the French. I am trying to determine if…"

Suddenly, from far off in the distance, they heard a gunshot. Then two more. Then so many that they rumbled like thunder.

"The army!" Daniel exclaimed. "General Braddock must have ordered the attack! And here I am talking to you!"

He turned and started running as fast as he could through the thick forest. Goran flew behind his human friend, banking right and left to avoid trees. As they worked their way laboriously toward the battle, it became easier to hear the barked orders of officers, the whoops of Indians, the whinnies of anxious horses, and the anguished cries of wounded men.

Daniel wished he could say the sounds aroused some heroic feeling within him. The truth was far different. What he was feeling, deep in the pit of his stomach, was fear. Still, he didn't know what to do other than get back to the road, find his wagon, and at least arm himself with the rifle stowed inside it.

After what seemed like an eternity, Daniel and Goran reached the road and found themselves surrounded by clouds of smoke. The chorus of musketry continued, punctuated occasionally by the deeper shouts of cannons. Then, as the thickest smoke blew past, Daniel glimpsed familiar coats of red. They belonged to the scores of British regulars he could see running rapidly through the smoke.

Running toward him.

Some weren't so much running as hobbling along, limping on wounded legs or holding up wounded comrades. Others were backing up more deliberately, stopping periodically to load their muskets or fire a shot into the impenetrable smoke. Daniel also saw splashes of red on the ground. Some were the coats covering the backs of fallen soldiers. Others were red blood-stains on white waistcoats of those lying face up.

"Form up, men, rally and form up!" cried a British officer, his terrified horse rearing up on its hind legs. Daniel recognized the determined face of General Braddock trying to make himself heard over the din of battle. Some of the redcoats heard him and stepped into ragged ranks. Others didn't hear, or at least pretended not to.

"General, the militia…let me order the militia into the trees!" boomed the voice of another mounted officer. It was Colonel Washington, his face streaked with soot and sweat. Daniel could see at least two places where musket balls had ripped large holes in the Virginian's clothing, one through his coat and another through his hat.

"Certainly not! They must form up as well!" General Braddock shouted in reply. "We must hold the line!"

"There will soon be no line left to hold," Washington argued. "There will be only death here in the road. Let my men fight behind cover. Perhaps they can hold off the Indians long enough for us to retreat in good order."

Braddock shook his head resolutely — and was then thrown unceremoniously to the ground as a shot struck the flank of his horse. Scrambling to his feet, the general looked up at Washington and then to the redcoats continuing to run or hobble away.

"It has come to that, has it?" Braddock roared. "Well, if retreat we must, we will execute a fighting retreat to protect our wounded and supply train."

He waved to a passing British horseman. "Dismount and bring your mount to me! They may have shot four horses out from under me, but I still command this column!"

The officer complied. Braddock sheathed his sword and put one foot in the stirrup. As he swung over the saddle, Daniel saw something seem to grab the British general and hurl him back to the ground with great force. The general groaned, then coughed up blood.

"General Braddock!" shouted Washington. He spurred his horse to the fallen general's side. Then he spied Daniel, transfixed by the scene. "Mr. Boone, do you still have your team at the ready?"

"I don't know, Colonel," Daniel replied, "but I'll find out soon enough."

Daniel tried to regain his bearings and locate his wagon. But it was nearly impossible to see through the smoke and the bedlam of desperate men.

"Follow me!" said a high voice from overhead. Then Daniel remembered Goran. The fairy must have flown above the fray and spotted the team. Daniel raced after him. There was the wagon! Somehow, the team remained hitched up and unhurt.

Daniel leapt to the seat and drove back to where Washington was stooped over Braddock, helping two other men lift the general. It was hard to believe the rangy young Virginian was the same sickly man Daniel had transported. The soldiers carried the general to the back of Daniel's wagon and placed him gently inside.

Washington sprinted back to his horse and mounted. "Let's go, Mr. Boone!"

They headed down the road toward the rear of the rapidly disintegrating British column. As the wagon rolled along, the wounded Braddock continued to issue orders to Washington and the other officers congregated around him. Presently the party came to a small stream and forded it. On the other side, exhausted soldiers were catching their breath while the wounded sat or lay on the ground. At Braddock's insistence, several men removed him from Daniel's wagon and propped him up against a tree.

"You have your orders, Mr. Washington!" Braddock cried. "Rally as many troops as have not yet entirely lost their nerve, and hurry forward to screen our retreat!"

The American officer, a determined expression on his grimy face, rode off to comply.

Daniel gazed with growing horror at the bodies strewn around him. He saw arms and legs crushed by musket balls and mangled by tomahawks. He saw chests torn open by bayonets. Lying among the dead was someone Daniel recognized: Colonel Peter Halkett, the very commander who had spoken against sending his regiment into the attack. Now Halkett would never speak again.

Before long, Washington returned with a couple of hundred soldiers walking behind him. "Let someone else take them from here," Braddock said in between gasps of pain. "I have another task for you, Mr. Washington. Ride to Colonel Dunbar and deliver a message. Tell him to rush forward with haste and reinforce our position. The entire campaign depends on it!"

"Yes, sir," Washington said, and turned to comply. Then he caught a glimpse of Daniel, still seated on his wagon seat in stunned silence.

"Again, Mr. Boone, you and your wagon have done us a great service," Washington said. "But now its usefulness is complete. Leave it there and ride to the rear with me."

Daniel responded instantly, welcoming the chance to leave the wounded and stay with Washington. He unharnessed one of the horses and jumped on its back, his rifle tucked under one arm. Off galloped Washington with Daniel close on his heels and Goran flying overhead. Every few seconds Daniel heard the report of a musket. Often he heard a ball whiz by. Miraculously, none hit home.

As they reached a bend in the road, Daniel suddenly felt his crippling fear return. From the forest emerged a fearsome-looking Indian with red hawk feathers in his hair and a musket in his hands. The warrior's face lit up in triumph when he saw Colonel Washington. He ran forward and lifted his gun to fire. The motion drew Washington's attention, but the American officer had no time to evade the attack.

Then, from above, Daniel heard an eerie sound emanating from Goran's magic flute. The muzzle of the Indian's musket, previously aimed at the breast of his target, now moved slightly to the right. He fired — and the ball tore yet another ragged hole in the tail of Washington's coat.

The Indian groaned in frustration and reached for his tomahawk, but then thought better of it when the two Americans galloped past. As the warrior began reloading his musket, Daniel breathed a sigh of relief at the realization they'd be out of range before the Indian could get off another shot.

For several more miles, the two Americans rode along the road. The sounds of battle grew ever fainter. Ahead, Daniel caught sight of fresh troops marching forward and, behind them, the supply train. They had reached their destination.

"Providence has again favored us, Mr. Boone," Washington said. "But now I think you should take your leave. What is needed now are soldiers, not wagoners."

Daniel stared back at the colonel, a mixture of relief and embarrassment washing over him. It was true — he was no soldier. He knew nothing about forming ranks and fixing bayonets. But, somehow, when it was Washington stating that simple truth instead of himself, it stung him like a hornet.

"Off with you now," the Virginian said. "And, Mr. Boone, make sure to take your fairy friend with you. This is no place for him, either!"

The American officer galloped off. Daniel turned his own horse in the direction of the other wagoners, many of whom were doing exactly the same thing he'd done earlier — abandoning their vehicles and leaping on unharnessed horses to make their escape. As Daniel rode into the mass of other wagoners, he looked up to see Goran still flying above him, clearly exhausted but seeming to share his relief as they headed away from the battle.

Two familiar figures rode up next to Daniel — his friend John Finley and his cousin Dan Morgan. Daniel whispered a prayer of thanks that neither was lying back on the roadbed in a pool of blood. They waved and smiled. Neither turned their gaze upward to look at the Sylph flying above their heads.

Daniel had no doubt Goran's concealment spell was working on them. But the militia colonel was another story. He must have seen Goran plainly! And, based on the officer's lack of surprise and matter-of-fact comments, Daniel reasoned that Goran was not the first fairy George Washington had encountered. The conclusion filled him with wonder.

Chapter 4 — The Long Island

November 1761

NO MATTER HOW MANY TIMES Goran saw Daniel Boone in action, he never stopped being amazed at his human friend's uncanny ability to find his way, noiselessly and unerringly, through a forest.

Over the years, Goran had encountered other frontiersmen. Many were skilled trackers and stealthy hunters. But Daniel stood shoulders and head above the rest. As Goran watched those shoulders and head leaving the bank of the Holston River and entering the nearby woods, he felt grateful once again to have Daniel's company on yet another journey. He flapped his wings and followed.

In the years since the two had renewed their friendship, during the disastrous Braddock expedition of 1755, Goran hadn't been able to spend as much time with Daniel as he wanted. The Sylph's responsibilities as explorer and diplomat frequently took him far away from Daniel's home on the Yadkin River. When he wasn't gathering information about colonial affairs or Britain's war with the French and Indians, Goran returned home to the Knob. His guild instructor had told him many times about the perils of staying too long in the Blur. It took a heavy toll on the body and mind. A ranger needed time behind the Shimmer to rest. Goran had followed Ceredan's teachings faithfully, taking lengthy breaks. But he did so because he was supposed to, not because he felt he needed it.

Even if Goran *had* set aside more time for long visits with Daniel, his friend's new responsibilities would have made them challenging. Daniel was a husband now, and a father. Rebecca Boone had borne Daniel two sons, James and Israel, and a daughter named Susannah. Goran had seen Rebecca once and found her most striking for a human. Long, raven-black hair. Dark, intelligent eyes. As fond of a good song and a good laugh as her husband was.

Goran was happy for Daniel. Yet the thought of Daniel's family also made Goran uncomfortably envious. Both spent much time away from home. When Daniel wasn't serving in the militia, he often went on long treks to hunt and trap. As for Goran, he went on ranger missions and the occasional hunt. The difference was that, no matter how far Daniel traveled and how long he was away, there would always be a wife and children waiting for him when he got back home. Goran had neither.

The longer he spent in the Blur, the more he grew apart from his family and friends. From their perspective on the Knob, it had been only six months since Goran had been admitted to the Rangers Guild. But during that time, he made multiple, lengthy rangings. From Goran's perspective, then, his admission to the guild had occurred years ago. His father Brae, being a former ranger, had at least some inkling of what Goran was experiencing. But even Brae had spent comparatively little time in the Blur before a leg injury had compelled his retirement.

Goran observed and learned a great deal. In addition to observing Braddock's defeat firsthand, Goran documented other battles in the war and submitted detailed reports of colonial officials, prominent citizens, and military commanders. Goran had also established diplomatic relations with other Folk communities residing within British America, such as a Brownie village hidden underneath the new College of Philadelphia and an extensive settlement of Gnomes on New York's Staten Island.

As Goran's intelligence reports indicated, British fortunes in the war had made a turn for the better beginning in 1758. A new expedition that year to expel the French from Fort Duquesne proved successful. Subsequent British campaigns in Canada resulted in the capture of Fort Ticonderoga and Quebec. To the south, however, a new threat arose when a combination of misunderstandings, border disputes, and successful French diplomacy prodded the powerful Cherokee nation to attack frontier settlements in Virginia and the Carolinas.

After more than two years of tough fighting, the Cherokees had been defeated. Colonial militiamen, including Daniel Boone, had laboriously cut a road across North Carolina's highest mountains and reached the South Fork of the Holston River that flowed through the "land of the Tanasee," as some called it. The militia occupied a four-mile-long island and built a new stronghold, Fort Robinson, on the riverbank across from it. For generations,

Cherokees had come to "Peace Island" to settle disputes. Now, hundreds of homeless Cherokees had come to Long Island-on-the-Holston, as it was also known, to negotiate a treaty with the British colonies.

Goran was on hand to observe. But, with the talks not to begin for another day, Daniel had convinced Goran to accompany him on a hike up a heavily forested mountain overlooking Long Island-on-the-Holston. The human's thirst for exploration seemed unquenchable.

Daniel threaded his way silently up the wooded slope, Goran fluttering closely behind. About halfway up, the pair heard voices. There were two of them, male and female. They seemed to be quarreling, but in a language Goran didn't know.

Daniel stopped and raised a hand to signal caution. Mouthing the word "Cherokee" to Goran, the hunter carefully placed one moccasin-clad foot on the ground, then the other, his hands gripping his loaded rifle with enough force to turn his knuckles red. Goran swooped forward and landed on Daniel's shoulder, removing his flute to play spellsong. But, even as the Sylph lifted the instrument to his lips, he heard a sound that made him stop short.

Someone was singing. It was a high voice, singing in round tones a melody very similar to his own spellsong of concealment. Accompanying the voice in rhythmic cadence was a rattling sound — soft when the melody dipped low and louder when the notes were high. The effect was lush and mesmerizing. Most remarkable of all, perhaps, was that the words of the song were in clearly articulated Folktongue, his own language. Goran had expected the unfamiliarity of Cherokee.

His human companion heard the spellsong, too. Daniel looked at Goran in amazement and then scanned the trees to find the source. Taking another few tentative steps, Daniel stopped short again and, using his eyes and a slight shake of his head, drew Goran's attention to the upper reaches of a white oak. After a few moments, the Sylph found he could discern a small form standing on a limb.

Well, not exactly standing. The form was dancing, the legs and body twisting back and forth in perfect rhythm with the rattling sound.

As the two hunters continued to watch, the music ceased and the form grew still. Only then did Goran realize they were on the edge of a small clearing in which two humans stood, talking quickly and gesturing to each other. The Cherokee man was tall and muscular, dressed in deerskin leggings and a mantle of brightly painted leather. On one side of a thin belt hung a long knife. On the other side hung a tomahawk that had the appearance of frequent use. Clean shaven except for a clump of black on the top of his head, the man sported yellow feathers tinged with blue in his topknot of hair and brass wires circling his ears from top to lobe. Another piece of polished brass, a gorget, hung around his neck. The man's close-set eyes blazed. The nostrils of his long nose flared. His face — marked on both cheeks with signs of having survived a bout with smallpox — was contorted in rage.

The Cherokee woman looked just as angry, but there the resemblance ended. She was shorter, more rounded. Her leggings were made of wool, as was her ribbon-trimmed skirt and a light-blue blouse intricately embroidered with floral patterns and gathered at the waist by a dark-brown sash. Into the sash was thrust, incongruously to Goran's eyes, a tomahawk covered in painted designs and decorated with feathers. Her long hair draped over bare shoulders. Around her neck hung multiple loops of white, green, and brown beadwork. The woman's almond-shaped eyes were widely spaced, her nose small, her lips full. While both she and the man were debating contentiously, she repeatedly punctuated her points with an ironic smirk or grin, her eyes dancing. The man never smiled.

As Goran took all this in and pondered what to do, the decision was taken out of his hands. Turning away from the woman in frustration, the Cherokee man caught sight of Daniel standing not ten paces away. In one fluid movement, the warrior slid his tomahawk from his belt with his left hand and drew the knife with his right. Wordlessly, he bounded toward Daniel, fury written darkly on his face as if by printer's ink.

Goran gasped and flapped his wings, lifting off as Daniel instinctively put the rifle to his shoulder, cocked, and aimed squarely at the breast of the charging warrior.

In the instant before Daniel could pull the trigger, however, Goran again heard spellsong. It was the same high-pitched voice, now sounding urgent instead of calming. The rattles were constant instead of measured. As if yanked by an invisible string, the warrior veered off, his momentum directed not at Daniel but at a nearby thicket of mountain laurels. For his part, Daniel dropped his rifle to his side and watched the Cherokee's deflected charge with a mixture of astonishment and amusement. As the warrior crashed into the vegetation, he slowed to a halt, dropping his arms and looking around in confusion.

"Tsiyu Gansini!" cried the Cherokee woman. She ran toward him, her arms outstretched in a plaintive gesture.

The warrior stared at her coldly, then at Daniel. He seemed not to notice Goran fluttering above. He shot the woman a final, murderous look, sheathed his knife, and stormed into the forest.

The Cherokee woman sighed and shifted her gaze to Daniel — and then, unmistakably, to the Sylph hovering in the air. "You might as well come down here and join us, Tana Song Snake," she said loudly in more-than-passable English. "I have a feeling you and I have more in common with these strangers than might first meet the eye."

Goran saw motion in the oak tree on the far side of the clearing. A figure leapt deftly from branch to branch, then alighted on the ground. As the figure came closer, Goran could make out a female clad in a deerskin shirt and skirt, her copper-colored legs bare except for two large anklets, her wavy dark hair encircled by a cloth headband of dark green. Fine jewelry of copper and precious stones glistened on her fingers, arms, neck, and earlobes. She was about his height, Goran guessed, and carried a long pole that he supposed was some kind of walking stick. Her slender form reminded Goran of an Elf ranger he'd met a couple of years earlier in Georgia. He doubted the approaching figure was an Elf, however.

Then the figure spoke in Folktongue. "You are a Sylph," she stated matter of factly. "I have never met one of your people before, although the chief of our clan lodge once told me a scurrilous tale about a Sylph village and a flock of lovesick buzzards."

Goran didn't quite know what to say to that. Instead, and quite spontaneously, he guffawed. After a moment, the other fairy joined him in gales of laughter.

"Uh, Goran?" Daniel inquired, the corners of his own mouth twitching. "Would you mind letting me in on the joke? I figure I'm about to giggle, and I'd like to know how come."

"We are called Nunnehi, the 'immortal travelers,' in the Cherokee tongue," the female fairy said, also in more-than-passable English, as she, Goran, Daniel, and the human woman left the clearing and headed back up the wooded slope. "I am Tana, of the Azalea Clan. We forage and scout. But on this journey, I act in neither capacity. I am here for her."

Tana nodded to the human woman, who smiled uncomfortably and returned the nod.

"My name is Nanyehi," she said, "although most whites started calling me Nancy Ward after I married my second husband, the trader Bryant Ward."

Tana turned to Daniel. "Are you a Virginian or a Carolinian?"

"I'm Daniel Boone," he replied in a shaky voice, his face reflecting an expression close to awe as he stared at the tiny woman. "My home is in North Carolina, but during the worst of the war, I moved my family to Virginia to keep them safe."

Tana appeared amused at Daniel's fascination with her, and chuckled. "I take it I am the first of my Folk you have ever seen. You are hardly the first white man I've seen. Quite a few have entered our hunting grounds, and during my visits with Nanyehi I saw Bryant Ward many times. But, as far as I know, you are the first white person who has ever seen *me*."

Nanyehi, having recovered her composure, looked up at Goran, still hovering above Daniel's shoulder.

"And *you* are the first of your kind *I* have ever seen," she said. "I thought the time I glimpsed a Tlanuwa soaring over a far-off mountain would be the most thrilling moment of my life — more thrilling even than my visit to the cave of Tana's people. But, in a way, seeing you up close fills me with still greater wonder."

"You mean," Goran speculated, "that my wings impress you even though I am so small. May I assume that a Tlanuwa, as you call it, is of great stature?"

"The Tlanuwa is one of the fiercest monsters that roams our domains," said Tana as the group continued up the slope. "It is a bird of prey, shaped and colored much like an ordinary red hawk, but of gigantic size. Its feathers are hard as metal and nearly impossible to pierce without enchanted weapons. Tlanuwa live in caves, much as we do, and hunt in pairs or groups."

"Among their prey are we Cherokee," added Nanyehi. "As a girl I heard many stories about ferocious Tlanuwa swooping into a town and carrying off children to their nests to feed their young. I used to think them just scary tales told by mischievous grandmothers. Now I know better."

Tana was looking more closely at Goran, taking in his gold-flecked wings, his clothes of brown and green cloth, and the bow and quiver of arrows strapped across his torso.

"You travel the Land of Shadow without a magical shield," she observed. "You must be a scout like me."

"We are called rangers among our Folk," Goran replied, "but yes, I am a journeyman in our guild. I accompanied my friend Daniel here on a commission from my guildmasters — although the orders originated with the king of all Sylphs, Briafael, back in England."

"So you are ruled by a king, then, like the humans?" Tana asked, sounding doubtful.

The question made Goran feel defensive. "Our king guides our policy, if that is what you mean, although most village affairs are governed by our Council of Elders. It would be impractical for King Briafael, separated from us by long stretches of land and sea, to attempt to make all our decisions."

At the vanguard of the little party as it continued languidly up the mountain, Daniel had been dividing his attention between following the conversation and scanning the trees. A force of habit, no doubt. At the mention of kings and councils, however, Daniel turned his head.

"That's not so different from how our colonies are set up," he said. "We're all subjects of the crown, yes. And King George appoints our royal governors. But we Americans elect provincial legislatures to make laws and levy taxes."

"And did your provincial legislatures also decide to make war upon my people?" asked Nanyehi pointedly. "Or was war forced upon you by your king-over-the-water?"

Daniel stopped short, seeming to struggle with conflicting impulses about how to respond. Goran glanced first at Nanyehi, who had also halted with her hands on her hips, waiting for an answer, and then at Tana, whose face reflected the same apprehension he felt.

"Ma'am," Daniel began carefully, "I don't claim to know everything that led up to the war or why the Cherokee joined up with the French. What I do know is that your warriors attacked our farms and settlements along the frontier. My neighbors and I had to flee our homes. Some people I know got killed and scalped. Had we no right to defend ourselves?"

Nanyehi stood motionless for some time, looking squarely into Daniel's face. He spoke no more himself, and merely stared right back at her. She bowed her head briefly, hands leaving her hips to hang by her sides, and then looked back up at Daniel.

"There has been too much fear and too many deaths on both sides," she began. "I spoke against going to war, as did my uncle Attakullakulla and a number of other chiefs, despite the many provocations and the justice of our cause. But other chiefs demanded revenge and compensation. When our most peace-loving elders went to South Carolina to try to negotiate a truce, they were insulted and captured. I turn your question back on you: Had we no right to defend ourselves?"

Nanyehi's reply seem to leave Daniel both disarmed and puzzled. "What provocations do you mean?" he asked.

The Cherokee woman sighed. "The entire tale would be a whipping snake — long, twisted, and best suited to strike, not to conciliate. To shorten it: our warriors had fought alongside yours, helping to force the French from Fort Duquesne. But instead of receiving their just rewards, the Cherokees were ill-treated, their horses and provisions seized, then they were ordered to make a long, difficult march home. By the time they got to Virginia, they were compelled to resupply themselves with new mounts and supplies. The local settlers saw themselves as victims of the Cherokees and attacked. Our people retaliated. All too soon, reason gave way to war."

"I've heard of Chief Attakullakulla," Daniel said. "So you're his niece, then? You supported him when he spoke for peace to the other chiefs?"

"Nanyehi speaks for herself at council, not simply as a kinswoman," Tana interrupted. "She is Ghigau, 'Beloved Woman.' She is a warrior and leader of her people."

Daniel inclined his head to Nanyehi. "I meant no disrespect," he said. "Ever since I was a boy, I've had Indian friends. We've explored together, hunted together. We haven't always agreed. But I always learn new things from them. Today is no different."

Nanyehi returned his nod. "Neither of us is here to refight the war."

The group had nearly reached the top of the ridge. Through the trees, they could see Long Island stretching several miles within the South Fork of the Holston River. Nanyehi gestured at the Cherokee and militia camps visible along its length. "Your people and mine have come here to reestablish a peace between us. Well, at least *most* of my people came here to do so."

Goran had a sudden flash of insight. "Might one of the exceptions be the man you were arguing with when we met?"

"Yes," Nanyehi admitted. "He is Attakullakulla's son, my cousin Tsiyu Gansini. The name means 'he who is dragging his canoe.' While most feel we have no choice but to end the conflict and learn to live together in peace, Dragging Canoe and others do not agree. They lack trust. They do not think the British authorities or the white settlers will abide by any treaty for long. I cannot say their doubts are baseless, but I still think peace is the right path."

Goran cast a glance at Tana, who was looking sympathetically at Nanyehi. The fairy caught his eye and shrugged her shoulders in resignation.

"My Folk have faced much the same choice in the past," Tana said. "We have warred with Pukwudgies to the north, with the Yunwi Amayine Hi and Este Lopocke to the west and south, and sometimes with the Yunwi Tsunsdi, whose mound is not far from our home on Blood Mountain. We war over hunting grounds for the most part, although it has not always been clear whether the rewards were worth the lives spent."

"That reminds me of a question I wanted to ask earlier," said Daniel. "You've mentioned hunting a couple of times now, and that giant bird with the metal wings. Do you hunt monsters the same way Goran's people do?"

Goran marveled again at his friend's natural talent for diplomacy. Daniel had a knack for knowing when to divert conversations from painful or awkward subjects.

"I do not know if we hunt the same way," Tana began, "but, yes, the most common task of a scout is to locate game and then signal hunters from the Fox Clan to secure it. For magical game, we often summon warriors from the Rattlesnake Clan, as well."

"Your spellsong was stunningly beautiful," Goran said, alighting on the ground next to Tana. "Do you channel the magic with an instrument? I play the flute." He pulled it out of his pocket pouch and showed it to her.

"If you heard me singing, you must have heard my shackles, too," she said, pointing to her bulky anklets. Goran saw that they were fashioned out of shards of turtle shells. It occurred to him that they must have been mage-crafted so the pebbles inside them rattled or swished only when Tana wanted them to. "These are why I am called Song Snake."

"I thought perhaps that cane you carry was some kind of musical instrument," Goran said.

Tana hefted the long pole in her left hand and tossed it deftly into her right. "No, this serves a very different purpose," she said, and Goran felt a tingle in his feathers at the unmistakable hint of menace in her voice.

Then Goran felt the earth tremble beneath his feet. Had Tana's words really stirred so much fear in him?

There, he felt it tremble again! He wasn't quivering out of fear. He wasn't imagining it. Something was causing the mountain to shake. And this time, Goran also heard a sound — a loud, scraping noise, as if two great rocks were rubbing against each other.

The others clearly sensed the same things. Daniel lifted his rifle reflexively and looked around. Nanyehi's hand slipped down to her sash and touched the hilt of her tomahawk. Tana's free hand was moving, too — it disappeared inside her skirts and reappeared with a very short arrow tipped with copper and fletched with eagle feathers.

"Nanyehi, we have traveled much too far to call for aid," Tana said hurriedly. "The Rattlesnake Clan hunts Tlanuwa in the southern hills. We are on our own."

"Is it what I think it is?" Nanyehi asked. Her voice sounded panicked.

"Yes," Tana confirmed. "It is a Stoneclad — and a big one, I suspect."

Goran wondered if he should be panicked, too. "What kind of creature is a Stoneclad?" he asked as he lifted his bow over his shoulders and filled his right hand with an arrow.

"It is a stone giant of the mountains," Tana explained, "twice as tall as a human and powerfully muscled. Its skin is hard as stone. That makes it highly resistant to all methods of attack, magical or otherwise. One finger on each massive hand is elongated and ends in a point like a spear. It uses that to pierce its prey. And Stoneclads have a particular fondness for human flesh."

Daniel looked at Nanyehi in disgust and alarm, then threw a protective arm around her shoulder. "Don't worry, ma'am. Goran and I have been in tough scrapes before. We'll get you out of this somehow."

Nanyehi surprised Goran by smiling broadly. "Your concern does you credit, but I am no child or old one to be protected. I am a War Woman." Then Nanyehi drew her tomahawk and looked down its sharpened edge with a practiced eye.

Whether Daniel would have protested the Cherokee woman's bravado would never be known, for at that moment the ground shook yet again, longer and more violently. The scraping sound of stone on stone was coming closer to their position near the top of the ridge. Unfortunately, it was below them, not above them. Escaping meant running farther uphill. All three of the foot-bound appeared to conclude independently it was not their best option. And Goran was certainly not going to fly away and leave the others behind to their fates.

Then he saw two tall pine trees bend impossibly low, in opposite directions, as the Stoneclad pushed its way into view. Tana's description had scarcely done it justice. The creature looked something like a giant boulder with two squat legs, two oversized arms and, jutting up from its rocky surface, a bullet head split from one side to the other by an enormous mouth out of all proportion to the rest of its savage face.

Daniel took no time studying the monster. He fired. The report of his rifle seemed to startle the Stoneclad for a moment. But the ball either missed or ricocheted off its stony hide. Daniel grabbed his powder horn and began reloading.

"Its joints are the only vulnerable spots!" Tana shouted. "Aim for armpits, elbows, knees, or neck!"

Even as she spoke, Goran nocked an arrow, aimed at the monster's neck, and shot. The arrow bounced harmlessly off the creature's chest as it opened its ragged maw and screamed a low, gravely challenge. As Goran drew another shaft, he saw Tana scampering off to the right of the beast, holding her cane with one hand and slipping her short arrow point-first into its top. Then the fairy knelt, brought the end of the cane to her lips, and aimed at the Stoneclad's left knee.

Tana's blowgun found its target. The monster roared in pain as the missile sank deeply into the exposed flesh. "That won't hold it for long," she called to the others. "My sleep darts are expertly enchanted but our quarry is massive. It will take some time for the magic to work."

"More mass just requires more magic!" Goran yelled as he shot again at the Stoneclad, then grunted in frustration as the arrow broke against a rocky forearm.

As Daniel lifted his rifle to fire again, Nanyehi touched his arm. "Without enchantment, our weapons may only serve to enrage the beast without doing it much harm," she said in a calm, authoritative voice. "There is another way for us to help. The Stoneclad has used the slope of the mountain against us. We need to use the mountain against it."

Goran could tell that Daniel didn't understand what Nanyehi meant. Nevertheless, the young hunter lowered his gun and ran after the Cherokee woman, who had begun sprinting around the left side of the Stoneclad.

Meanwhile, Tana shot two more darts at the beast with her blowgun. One missed and the other just grazed an elbow. Goran fired two more arrows and was relieved to see one embed itself in the Stoneclad's left armpit. As puny as their weapons looked when compared to the size of the giant, Goran felt hopeful that the magic might begin to slow the beast down, at least.

His hopes were dashed when the Stoneclad roared again and, quicker than Goran would have expected, swung his right arm toward the crouching Tana, who was slipping another dart into her blowgun. Just in time, the fairy sensed the pointed finger swinging at her head and danced off to the side. The finger buried itself in the ground far enough that it took the Stoneclad several tries to pull it out.

Tana lifted her blowgun to her lips for another shot — which almost proved to be her undoing as the Stoneclad's other arm swung around to impale her. Tana saw that blow coming, too, and managed to swing her blowgun up to parry. Her weapon broke in two as the spear-tipped finger struck it. The blow knocked Tana to the ground, and forced the air from her lungs.

Goran gasped and hurled himself into the air directly at the head of the Stoneclad, hoping at least to distract it from delivering a killing blow. Then he heard unexpected sound from an unexpected direction — from behind the monster.

It was, as best he could tell, the gobble of a turkey. It gobbled several more times.

The Stoneclad whipped its head around.

Then another set of sounds came from behind the monster. This time, Goran thought he heard the howl of a wolf. A few seconds later came another howl, then a gobble.

Leaving Tana senseless on the ground, the Stoneclad wheeled, shook his head for a moment, and started lumbering downhill toward the sounds. Goran flew along after him, trying without success to get a clear shot at the small slits of exposed flesh moving within its rocky mass. The giant crashed through the trees, knocking some aside with its massive bulk and flattening others with a stomp of its feet. With its every step, the ground trembled — and the monster's pace quickened.

The howl came again, this time to the left of the Stoneclad's current track. The monster shifted accordingly, lifting its flat head slightly in a manner that reminded Goran of his father straining to catch a whiff of Ailee's blackberry pie. It was an odd thought to pop into the ranger's head at such a moment. But, as he had felt something close to uselessness during the fight so far, Goran's mind began to wander. He thought of the Knob — of his Folk going about their day, largely oblivious to the momentous events he had been witnessing in the ever-changing human world. For all he had learned so far, Goran still wasn't sure he was the Sylph for the mission he'd been given. Did he truly understand its purpose? Couldn't he be doing more good by planning larder hunts and tracking monsters?

Snap out of it, Goran told himself. *No need to track this monster. It is right in front of you.* There were no hunters or soldiers to call. His spellsong wouldn't work quickly enough on such a creature. The only tools available were his bow, his knife, and his courage. Tana was down. Daniel and Nanyehi had run off. Now it was up to Goran.

Once again the monster shifted its momentum to the left, responding to a gobble. And then, abruptly, forest canopy gave way to open sky. Goran followed the giant onto a long, broad ledge dotted with clumps of grass, a few rocks, and some fallen trees. Directly in the path of the rampaging monster, behind a fallen oak, the two humans crouched low. Fearing he was about to see them crushed or speared, Goran swooped forward and called out a warning.

Daniel gobbled. Nanyehi howled. Then they spun out from behind the log, one in each direction, each rolling up on one knee.

The Stoneclad saw its prey move to either side but was by this time barreling along so quickly it couldn't arrest its momentum. One wide, stone-soled foot struck the heavy oaken log, then the other. The monster tripped. As it fell, it twisted sidewise and reached for Daniel with its elongated arm while using the other arm to try to regain its balance.

"Now!" Nanyehi commanded. "It is not all the way there yet!"

Daniel brought his rifle to his shoulder and fired. Goran, now seeing the object of the plan, loosed an arrow. A dart whistled past his left ear. And Nanyehi flung her tomahawk.

The bullet smashed into the Stoneclad's head. The arrow struck it in the chest. The dart caught it in the shoulder. And Nanyehi's tomahawk, thrown expertly end over end, found its mark in soft flesh between rock-hard chin and rock-hard breast.

The impact of the four missiles, striking nearly instantaneously, was enough to help propel the Stoneclad to the edge of the ledge — and beyond. The handle of the tomahawk protruding from its neck, the roaring creature plunged over the side.

Goran rushed to the edge, followed closely by a shaken but conscious Tana, clutching the shard of her broken but still usable blowpipe. Both began to sing, the Song Snake accompanying their harmonics with the rhythmic rattle of her ankle shackles. No matter where the Stoneclad fell, and in what condition, any whites or Cherokees in the vicinity would never see a thing.

▲▲▲

For some time, the four stood in a rough circle on the ledge, panting from their exertions. No one spoke at first, but they exchanged glances that communicated much. Relief. Respect. Satisfaction. Triumph. Finally, Goran could contain his curiosity no longer.

"I *thought* it might be you two making those animal sounds," he told Daniel and Nanyehi. "But I do not for the life of me understand how this crazy scheme of yours actually worked."

The two humans merely shrugged and looked at each other conspiratorially.

"For one thing," Goran continued, "how did you know there was a ledge down here with fallen trees placed just where they might trip the giant?"

"I can explain that," Nanyehi replied. "Many times have I journeyed from my home in Chota north to Long Island-on-the-Holston. I know these mountains like I know my daughter Betsy's face. There was nothing random about the path we baited the Stoneclad to take."

"But that is the other factor I fail to understand — the bait," Goran insisted. "Why did the Stoneclad abandon an easy kill in Tana and instead go chasing down the hill after a gobbling turkey and a howling wolf?"

Tana began to laugh playfully and didn't bother to use her magic to muffle her shackles. So, for every guffaw, there was a loud, joyous rattle.

"I think I can answer that one for you, Goran," she said presently, trying to stifle another chuckle. "It was not the animal calls that accomplished the task."

Daniel looked surprised. He tried, without success, to look offended. "I've won prizes for my turkey call. I'm very proud of it."

"I, too, have earned much praise over the years for my ability to mimic the cry of the gray wolf," said Nanyehi good-naturedly. "Are you saying the Stoneclad wasn't fooled?"

"Not for a second," Tana replied. "Remember what I told you. It does not crave dry turkey breast or stringy wolf meat. Nor are we Folk much to its liking. The Stoneclad has a particular taste for human flesh.

"And an excellent sense of smell."

Chapter 5 — The Dragoon

September 1763

PETER MUHLENBERG HAD GONE FISHING. That's what had started all the trouble in the first place — going fishing. But he couldn't imagine starting a beautiful day like this one without it. Slipping a worm onto his hook, Peter tossed his line into the fast-moving water of the Saale River and thought about home.

As a boy back in Pennsylvania, some of Peter's happiest days had been spent lounging alongside Perquaminck Creek, watching the sun rise and hooking the occasional perch, shad, or catfish. Sometimes his younger brothers, Frederick and Henry, slipped away with Peter, carrying their own poles. Other times, Peter fished alone. Either way, he always enjoyed himself.

There had been one added benefit to fishing alone, however. It meant only Peter, not his brothers, got in trouble with their father.

The Reverend Heinrich Melchior Muhlenberg was an important man. For generations, Germans had being immigrating to the Pennsylvania colony. They built homes, farms, and new towns such as Skippack, Conestoga, and Oley. They also founded churches, though they had no formally trained ministers. Eventually they had asked church leaders back in Germany to send missionaries. The first to arrive, in 1742, had been Heinrich Melchior Muhlenberg. Peter had been born in the largely German-speaking town of Trappe four years later.

What was that?

Peter's thoughts of home were interrupted by a noise from upstream. He glanced that way but trees blocked his view. Thrusting the end of his fishing pole into the soft mud, Peter wiped his hands on his leather breeches and looked over at his coat, crumpled up on the ground next to his hat, sword, scabbard, and boots. He decided against recovering them. Instead, he strode over to the trees and peered down the riverbank. He saw and heard nothing. Shrugging, he returned to his fishing — and his reminiscing.

It hadn't been easy growing up as the son of a famous father. Reverend Muhlenberg was frequently away from home, founding congregations in German communities across New York, New Jersey, Pennsylvania, and Maryland. Peter once heard a minister call Reverend Muhlenberg the founder of the Lutheran Church in America. Peter just called him Father.

Peter loved and respected his father, but he came to dread what happened every time Reverend Muhlenberg got home. He'd ask to see Peter's lessons. He'd ask how many books Peter had read. And, when he deemed Peter's answers unsatisfactory, which was usually, he scolded Peter for wasting time at field and stream.

Reverend Muhlenberg was determined that his sons follow him into the ministry. Peter had been just as determined to find his own way. Still, when his father announced in early 1763 that Peter, Frederick, and Henry were to attend school in Germany, Peter had initially looked forward to a grand adventure across the sea. But when they arrived at their final destination, the university town of Halle in Saxony, Peter had quickly discovered that, unlike his brothers, he wasn't cut out to be a student. It hadn't helped matters that the faculty and students considered the Muhlenbergs to be unlettered rubes. They laughed at how Peter and his brothers dressed, how they wrote, how they talked.

His brothers could sluff off such talk. Peter couldn't. Within days of arrival, he'd gotten into a fist fight. While the other boy was on the floor, nursing a bruised jaw, Peter had rushed to his room, packed his meager possessions, and fled the school.

There it was again! Peter was sure this time he heard a voice.

Straining to hear more, he almost toppled over and lost hold of his fishing pole. After he recovered his balance, Peter looked over again at his pile of clothes. If his regiment had broken camp and was coming this way, he should expect a dressing down — or worse — from Sergeant Ehring for leaving camp without permission. But if Sergeant Ehring found Peter out of uniform, fishing in the river, the "or worse" was guaranteed. Discipline was harsh in the Light Dragoons.

That clinched it. Peter yanked his pole out of the river, dropped it, and sprinted to his equipment. He wriggled his feet into his high black boots and slipped his uniform coat, bright red trimmed in black, over his straw-colored waistcoat. Attaching his sword and scabbard to his white belt and donning his black cocked hat, Peter turned and looked upstream again. He could still hear the voice. But it was so faint he couldn't make out any words. It also hadn't gotten any louder, so whoever it was must not have been heading in Peter's direction.

He looked longingly at the pole on the ground. Had he let panic cheat him out of another good hour of fishing? Peter concluded he wasn't to blame. It was whoever was talking loudly upstream.

Peter strode along the riverbank, his annoyance growing with every step. He even considered drawing his sword and giving the intruder a good scare. When he reached the trees and glimpsed a bend in the river ahead of him, however, prudence reasserted itself. The sword stayed in its scabbard. His steps became more cautious. Perhaps Peter would find fellow dragoons wading in the Saale. Perhaps he'd encounter villagers drawing water.

No amount of speculation could have prepared Peter Muhlenberg for what he actually saw as he came around the bend. It was a tiny man sitting on the riverbank, holding a fishing pole of his own and humming a song.

Peter halted in mid-step and looked more closely. The fishing man looked to be about four feet in height, but stout and powerfully built. He was wearing a dark-red cloak over a light gray tunic and trousers and a jerkin of boiled leather. A long cap of the same color as his cloak drooped down to cover one ear. His face was unlined and youthful, with a yellow beard hanging down to the top of his jerkin. Lying next to him was a bulging pack with some kind of stringed instrument alongside.

The little man was grinning broadly as he hummed. The whole scene reminded Peter of a bedtime story about an endangered princess fleeing into the woods and taking refuge with a group of merry Dwarfs. Even before hunting and fishing had captivated Peter's attention, his fixation with fantastic tales had been another source of friction with his father. Peter and his brothers had spent hours making up their own stories and acting out their favorite scenes — hours they were supposed to have devoted to their studies or chores.

Peter returned his attention to the little man. He was taller than Peter would have expected of a Dwarf. Other than that, he might as well have walked right out of Peter's own childhood imagination.

Or perhaps I am still just imagining it, Peter wondered. He decided to find out, and stepped out of the woods.

At the crunch of the young dragoon's heavy boots on the fallen leaves and twigs, the Dwarf started, stopped humming, and dropped his pole in the river. Sweeping his cloak aside with one hand, the Dwarf yanked something from his belt with the other. Peter saw to his alarm a wicked-looking handaxe.

"Hold on!" Peter shouted, drawing his sword defensively but holding up the other hand in a gesture he hoped wouldn't be as threatening. "I just want to talk!"

The Dwarf responded, but neither in Peter's native language of English nor the German that Peter spoke so fluently. Instead, the Dwarf began to sing, his words unrecognizable but his face showing just as much panic as Peter felt.

The two stood facing each other awkwardly, weapons in hand. As the moments passed, panic gave way to puzzlement on the Dwarf's face. Presently he stopped singing altogether, gripped his axe tightly, and began looking furtively around him. Was he seeking an escape route, Peter wondered, or expecting company?

As if on cue, Peter began to hear footsteps — far off at first but coming rapidly closer. He couldn't tell how many were approaching, or even whether it was the sound of feet or hooves. He prayed for the latter. Indeed, it was the first time since Peter joined the Saxon Light Dragoons a few weeks ago that he found himself hoping to see the distinctive red coats and saddlecloths of his fellow mounted soldiers.

Peter had never thought of a military career. But when, during his flight from school, Peter almost literally ran into the Light Dragoons loitering in Halle, joining the regiment had seemed like a handy way to make good his escape. His regrets hadn't been long in coming. The school rules he found so constricting were nothing compared to the rigors of soldiering. At this moment, though, as he faced a mysterious, axe-armed stranger with what was now a grimly determined look on his face, Peter welcomed reinforcements.

It quickly became clear he would get them. The sounds had become distinct hoof beats, punctuated by an occasional whinny.

The Dwarf heard them, too.

"So that is the way of it!" he snapped in perfect German to a surprised

Peter Muhlenberg. "I have no wish to hurt you, but I cannot let you and your fellows capture me!" And with that, the Dwarf did something else that surprised Peter — he lifted his axe behind his right ear and hurled it in the direction of the young dragoon's head.

Peter instinctively ducked. He felt his hat lift off his head as the spinning axe struck one of its three corners and slammed into the trunk of the tree behind him. Momentarily fascinated by the still-quivering handle of the weapon, Peter failed at first to see the Dwarf scrambling away. By the time he noticed him, the Dwarf had reached his pack. Pulling another handaxe out of his pack with one hand and picking up the musical instrument with the other, the Dwarf whirled and headed toward Peter.

The young dragoon was no coward, but he had also never wielded a weapon in battle. Peter lifted his sword in a half-hearted attempt to block whatever the Dwarf might throw at him. But the running Dwarf paid him little heed. Striking aside Peter's sword blade with a sweep of his axe, the Dwarf rushed past the soldier and ran up a slight hill to the road beyond.

Unsure whether he should accept his good fortune or test it by chasing the Dwarf, Peter simply stood and watched as the little man reached the road. Just then, two troopers of Peter's regiment came into view, their horses trotting at a leisurely pace. As soon as they spotted the Dwarf, the dragoons spurred their mounts into a canter and drew their swords. Peter recognized one of them as Dietrich, a solder in his own troop.

"Halt, boy!" Dietrich ordered the Dwarf, mistaking him for a burly child. "You dare to wave a weapon at us? We'll soon teach you some manners!" The soldiers prodded their horses into a gallop and pointed their swords at him.

The Dwarf seemed unperturbed. As the first rider came near, he swung his axe again and neatly deflected the first dragoon's point, then dove and somersaulted under the blade of the second, coming back up to his feet with both hands still full.

The dragoons swore and reined in their mounts to turn and charge again. At the same time, three other red-coated dragoons rode into view, took in the scene at a glance, and spurred their own horses. Peter regained his fortitude and sprinted forward, preparing to yell something at his fellows, at the Dwarf, or perhaps at all of them — although not yet sure what that something ought to be.

Then the Dwarf did one more surprising thing: he dropped his axe and sat right down in the middle of the road.

Was he surrendering? Before Peter could call out to the others to halt their charge, the Dwarf placed the instrument on his lap — Peter suddenly remembered seeing one like it in his father's church and someone calling it a "scheitholt" — and began to pluck the strings with one hand while holding a wooden stick against the strings with the other. The Dwarf also began to sing, his voice clear, though the words again sounded like gibberish.

Was the little fellow some kind of madman? Or a wandering minstrel hoping to placate the enraged dragoons with a song? Either way, Peter feared that the Dwarf would get trampled underfoot in spite of himself.

Two sword-wielding dragoons galloped directly at the Dwarf from one direction, three dragoons from the other, while all along the Dwarf sang and played his song — a gentle, leisurely tune that struck Peter as ludicrously out of place. He felt a strong impulse to look away, but macabre curiosity got the better of him. Peter watched, utterly fascinated, as the two groups of horsemen converged. He continued to watch, utterly bewildered, as they galloped past each other, looked around in confusion, and stopped.

"What do you think you're doing?" Dietrich asked the three dragoons that formed the other group of riders. "Why did you charge us with naked blades? It's too early in the morning for that kind of game."

One of the other troopers sneered contemptuously. "It was you who came at us. I thought perhaps you were chasing a rabbit or something."

The dragoons continued to argue and trade insults. All the while, the Dwarf still sat in the road, singing and playing his scheitholt. Presently, the little man nodded to himself in apparent satisfaction, rose, and walked amiably back toward his pack by the river. He didn't seem to notice Peter following him with his eyes.

Stowing the scheitholt and axe away, the Dwarf heaved the pack onto his back, walked over to the stand of trees where Peter had spied on him, and yanked the other axe out of the tree trunk, threading it through a loop in his belt. Then, without another sound or backward glance, the Dwarf headed off along the river.

Peter let him go while he stood there, trying to make sense of it all, Dietrich saw him and exclaimed, "There you are, new recruit! Sergeant Ehring sent us to look for you. He's madder than I've ever seen him."

Peter wasn't thinking about angry sergeants at the moment.

"How did you miss him?" he asked the dragoons. "He was just sitting there in the road. You charged right past him, and then you let him go."

"Sergeant Ehring?" Dietrich asked. "Why would we be charging Sergeant Ehring? He's back at camp. And besides, even if he *was* here, I'd rather him stay mad at you than draw any attention to me."

"No, of course I'm not talking about him!" Peter insisted. "I'm talking about the Dwarf. He bewitched you all somehow with his magic…"

"A magic Dwarf!" snorted another trooper, provoking another round of laughter at Peter's expense. "You saw a magic Dwarf? Was there an Elf, too, or a Devil?"

"Was the Devil riding a Unicorn?" Dietrich asked derisively.

As the ridicule continued, a sinking feeling came over Peter like a wave. Just as the students of Halle had done, his fellow dragoons had already been making fun of their new recruit for being a half-civilized American. Now they had found even more grounds to ridicule him.

"Devil Pete! Devil Pete!" the troopers chanted as they rode away from the miserable young man.

Chapter 6 — The Moot

HAR HAD NEVER WANTED TO be a ranger in the first place. His experiences in the Blur over the past few weeks had done nothing to change his mind.

The day after Har left his village on the Brocken for his first diplomatic mission — a journey far to the east, to the Lusatian Highlands — someone stole all the food from his pack while he slept. The theft forced Har to stop repeatedly during the journey to forage, hunt, and fish. On the way back home, he'd been chased through the hills near Bautzen by a demented Woodwose, stalked outside of Dresden by a particularly bloodthirsty Roggenwolf, and even attacked near Halle by a troop of mounted human bullies wearing long red coats and waving swords at him.

Now, as he followed a familiar trail up the eastern slope of the Brocken, the mountain he called home, Har's relief warred with frustration. His diplomatic mission had failed, after all. His task was to convince Lord Boleslaw to attend the upcoming Dwarfmoot at the Brocken. But Lord Boleslaw wouldn't even agree to *see* Har. In fact, the belligerent Lutki guards had quite nastily rejected every request Har made, even for a decent meal and a good night's sleep. After demanding that Har bow repeatedly and hand over many gifts, demands that he steadfastly refused, the Lutki ordered Har to leave. He hadn't needed to be told twice.

It was not my fault the mission failed, Har reasoned.

Everyone knew that Lutki were a greedy and obnoxious Folk. They weren't proper Dwarfs, anyway. At best, they were distant cousins. Even if Lord Boleslaw had agreed to join his fellow lords at the Dwarfmoot, he probably wouldn't have contributed anything useful to the deliberations. He wouldn't have understood the great challenges the Dwarfkind of Germany were there to confront. Boleslaw wouldn't have cared.

Or so Har assured himself.

He looked over the tree line at the snow-covered top of the Brocken, the highest peak of Saxony's Harz Mountains. The Dwarf village buried deep inside it would be bustling with activity. There hadn't been a Dwarfmoot in a generation. There'd *never* been a Dwarfmoot at the Brocken. Har would have been more excited if the circumstances were different, if his sole role in the affair wasn't going to be reporting his own failure to the assembled lords. The Lutki would be the only one of the six invited realms of Dwarfkind to decline the offer.

Their loss, Har thought, but also his. Again he cursed the day he'd been made a ranger.

▲▲▲

Har had always been large for his age. As a baby, he'd been a curiosity. As a youth, he'd towered over the other children of the village. "Har the Tower," they had called him. The name stuck. Even his mother Frauke had taken to ordering him to do "the Tower's" household chores and to wash "the Tower's" hands for supper. When one of the neighbors needed a heavy door hung or a massive stone moved, it was always: "Call the Tower!"

Har never minded. The nickname suited him. He *did* tower over everyone he knew. Indeed, he had grown nearly a human foot taller than his father Daric by the time Har was eleven.

Har enjoyed putting his size and strength to good use. That's why he'd always expected to join the Craftsmen Guild and work a forge, like his father did. He'd even resigned himself to the possibility that old King Hibich might insist Har apply his imposing stature and bulging muscles to soldiering in the Warriors Guild.

But the trials had changed all that.

When Dwarflings reached the age of majority, they were sent to the Mages Guild for testing. The morning of Har's trials, his mother served up an enormous amount of breakfast — "a Tower must have strong foundations," Frauke insisted — and then served up an equally enormous amount of advice.

"Always volunteer to do more than the mages ask," she said, "and let no chance pass to impress them. Thank them profusely for the opportunity, and for all they do to keep our Folk safe. It never hurts to flatter those in high places."

"Frauke, do not fill the boy's head with such prattle," Daric growled as he chewed on a mouthful of eggs. "Har, just do what you are told and ask no impertinent questions. Magecraft will dictate the outcome of your trials, not statecraft."

Har arrived at the guildhall of the mages later that morning with no idea what to expect, only to discover that his trials were more tedium than terror. Har spent hours completing written examinations and answering verbal questions. The mages made him run, jump, skirmish, shoot at targets, roll on the ground, and perform other exercises upon command. All the while, they waved their hands and spoke incantations.

The trials gauged the strengths, weaknesses, and magical capacities of the Dwarflings. The candidates, their parents, and guildmasters weren't required to accept the recommendations, but they almost always did. Still, the results left room for interpretation. A Dwarfling could get high ratings on multiple attributes, suggesting the potential for success in more than one occupation. Someone equally skilled at melee weapons such as hammers and at missile weapons such as bows might choose to be either a warrior or a hunter. Or someone with great manual dexterity might make for a fine craftsman, producing intricate and subtly enchanted jewelry, or prove to be a talented greenweaver, transplanting delicate sprouts from a hillside or cavern floor into a box of carefully enchanted soil to produce pungent spices, medicinal herbs, or ingredients for magical elixirs.

There were, however, two improbable outcomes that, for all practical purposes, eliminated choice from the equation. If Dwarflings exhibited the highest capacity to store elemental magic in their bodies, they were admitted immediately as apprentices into the Mages Guild. If Dwarflings exhibited no capacity to store elemental magic at all, that meant their bodies were highly resistant to the adverse effects of the Blur. They were admitted immediately as apprentices into the Rangers Guild.

Har couldn't have been more shocked on the day after his trials, when the spindly old mage emerged from the guild, approached the waiting Har and his parents with a rapid gait, and then snapped, quite simply, "Ranger."

It had been the last thing they expected to hear. Truthfully, it had been the last thing anyone in the village had expected to hear about Har the Tower.

Rangers were usually the leanest, nimblest Dwarfs. They were scholarly. Har was none of those things. But his trials had indicated high resistance to the Blur. Few members of any Folk, and especially few Dwarfs, exhibited that rare trait. It had been Har's duty to become a ranger, whether he wanted to or not.

▲▲▲

As he hiked up the slope, dreading the report he'd have to give when he reached the village, Har consoled himself by looking at the marvelous shapes and colors of the wildflowers surrounding the trail. There were white ones the humans called Brocken flowers, yellow ones they called Brocken hawkweeds, and green ones with black berries they called Brocken myrtles.

Har's appreciation of the scenery ended abruptly when a stiff breeze passed over his shoulder, flipping up the dangling end of his cap. It hadn't been a windy day. Har also caught a fleeting sound of voices and the telltale sparks of a transport spell.

One of the Dwarf lords must have just arrived for the Dwarfmoot. Was it the first party to arrive or the last one? Har decided that, if it were the latter, he'd better not make the five Dwarf lords wait long for the news that the sixth wouldn't be coming.

Scrambling up the trail as fast as he could, Har soon reached a layered clump of lady's mantle and dashed around it to the mouth of a tunnel cut into the vegetation. The tunnel's entrance had the luster of Shimmer. The ranger hummed the necessary song, pushed his way through, and resumed his brisk gait. After only a few paces, the leafy canopy overhead gave way to a rocky ceiling.

As he walked through the narrow, torch-lit passageway, Har thought back to his Dwarf-lore lessons as an apprentice. Unlike his cherished memories of childhood, it gave him no pleasure to recall the many stultifying hours he spent listening to lectures and reading books on history, geography, and politics. It was for times like these, however, that Har and his fellow apprentices had studied so laboriously.

He could still picture the map in the front of his textbook, the map showing the nations of Dwarfkind. While small communities of Dwarfish Folk could be found across northern Europe, most were subject to one of six major realms. There were the Dwarfs of the Harz, Har's own people, ruled by aged King Hibich from the Brocken. To the west dwelt the Dwarfs of the Ruhr, ruled by the intellectually inclined King Goldemar from the catacombs underneath Hardenstein Castle. To the southwest were the Dwarfs of the Rhineland, led by the impetuous Lord Alberich, a former ranger himself. In the northeast corner of the German-speaking lands, out in the Baltic Sea, the stern Count Nickel ruled over the Dwarfs of Rügen Isle. To the southeast lived Lord Boleslaw's Lutki host in the Lusatian Highlands. And finally, far to the south, could be found the Dwarfs of the Tyrol, in the high Alps that marked the edge of the German lands. Their ruler was Queen Virginal, about whom Har had learned the least.

The moment one of the perimeter guards caught sight of the returning ranger, he bellowed: "Har the Tower! King Hibich has been looking for you. Come." The guard, clad in scale armor of polished bronze, turned and headed down another narrow tunnel.

Har stowed his equipment in the guardhouse and sprinted to catch up. The tunnel soon widened into a massive cavern, lit brilliantly by magecraft luminaries floating near its high ceiling. Dwarfs of all ages were packed along the sides of the cavern, one of the village squares of the Brocken. No Folk stood in the square itself, however. It had been completely cleared of the merchant stalls, huts, and carts that normally filled it.

Few noticed as Har and the guard entered. The crowd's attentions were fixed on a group of finely dressed Dwarfs attempting to walk majestically through the throng. Har guessed it must have been one of the Dwarf lords just arrived by magical transport. As he got closer, he realized why the Folk of the Brocken were so fascinated. The newcomers were Dwarfs of the Tyrol, their distinctive cloaks of royal blue and their hooked alpine swords setting them off from their ruder cousins of the Brocken.

At their head walked a woman. Har quickly decided he had never seen such beauty. Queen Virginal's long, braided auburn hair draped down over sloping shoulders and framed a round face dotted with freckles. She was short and stout, even for a Dwarf, but carried her frame regally in a long, glowing gown of blue and white. Despite the significant distance between them, Har thought he glimpsed perfectly shaped eyes of green — not a placid green of meadow grass but a lively green of alpine spruce swaying in a cool mountain breeze.

Virginal and her entourage exited the cavern through the same corridor the guard was leading Har to. But the common Folk were so crowded along the walls that Har and his companion found it impossible to make any headway. Then Har saw the familiar sparks and felt the familiar prickles on his skin that signaled magical transport.

He turned and watched another delegation arrive. The first to materialize were four mages, evenly spaced to form a square. Within the square, three more figures came into view: a distinguished-looking lord richly adorned in striped cloak and doublet of black and gold, accompanied by two Dwarfs carrying sacks of books and scrolls.

"That is Goldemar of Hardenstein Castle, I would wager," the guard said to Har. "They say he studied arcane lore and wrote textbooks on magecraft before he became king of the Dwarfs of the Ruhr."

As soon as Goldemar and his party left the square, it began to sparkle again. Har realized someone must have been using spellsong to coordinate the arrival of the delegations.

This time, six incoming mages materialized in the village square, encircling a single form. Where Virginal had a regal bearing and Goldemar a scholarly one, the newly arrived Dwarf lord, clad in simple clothes of dull gray, didn't so much walk as stalk through the crowd.

"Count Nickel," breathed the guard softly. Har nodded his agreement. The fearsome reputation of the lord of far Rügen Isle aptly fit the figure of the lord now exiting the chamber with his attendants, also wearing gray and scrambling to keep up with Nickel's brisk pace.

A gap appeared in the crowd. The guard motioned Har to follow him into it. "Lord Alberich of the Rhineland is already in the audience chamber, so we best get you to King Hibich. He wants to meet with you before the Dwarfmoot begins."

▲▲▲

That proved to be impossible. When the guards hustled Har into the audience chamber, it was evident the moot had already started.

"The Troop of the Black Forest have gone too far this time!" bellowed a wiry, ruddy-faced lord with a short black beard, whom Har recognized from his teacher's descriptions as Lord Alberich of the Rhineland. "Treaties mean nothing to Elves. They hunt where they wish and take what they want."

"They lack wisdom — that much is certainly true," said gray-haired King Goldemar, leaning back in his chair even as Alberich leaned forward with excitement. "Elves harvest so much from their towns that even the lowly humans realize something is amiss and lock up their doors and windows."

"That is just it, Goldemar," Alberich insisted. "Elves do not limit themselves to their own humans. Lately they have been sending their rangers into the Rhineland. Our humanware harvests are down by a third!"

Har saw his own King Hibich, a frail-looking man clad in the traditional dark-red raiment of the Brocken, raise an unsteady hand for silence.

"We all know why we are here," Hibich said, his faltering voice undermining his attempt at sounding authoritative. "We know the threat goes far beyond the supply of humanwares."

"Chairing the Dwarfmoot is the traditional prerogative of the host, Hibich," said Count Nickel, a languid expression on his ghostly face. "But do not presume to order us around, even in your own hall."

Har looked more closely at the pallid lord of Rügen Isle. All Dwarfs were independent-minded. Many were quarrelsome. But the Dwarfs of the Baltic Sea islands were especially prickly. They went out of their way to fill their local humans with fear instead of wonder.

Hibich moved his hand back and forth as if patting an invisible shoulder. "Now, now, Nickel. I presume no supremacy. I merely urge us to address the most serious matters. They are matters of magic, not matters of the Blur."

Goldemar nodded gravely. Alberich threw up his hands and leaned back. Nickel stared at Hibich with expressionless, ice-blue eyes. Har took all this in, wondering if a journeyman like himself should really be in the audience chamber hearing such talk.

Then a new voice cut the awkward silence in the room — a thoughtful, melodic voice. A voice accented by a tremble that suggested neither shyness nor anxiety but, rather, that at any moment the voice might dissolve into a laugh.

"I think, gentlemen, that before we go on, we might want to discover if our Dwarfmoot is fully assembled," said Queen Virginal of the Tyrol. The other lords, councilors, and grandmasters turned their attention to Virginal, sitting on the far right of the circle.

The queen turned and beckoned Har forward. "Am I to understand that you are just an improbably tall dwarf?" she asked with a chuckle as Har strode into the circle formed by the seated Dwarf lords and their retainers. "Or are you in fact an improbably short human?"

Har arrived at the center of the chamber and blinked. All were looking at him, some curiously, some dismissively. But Har only had eyes for Queen Virginal. Her green eyes were staring right back at him — piercing right through him, Har felt, like a spear to his heart. As he stood transfixed, he fancied that her face could never produce any expression for him other than an inviting smile.

"Well?" Virginal prompted. "Are we to suspend our Dwarfmoot so you will have time enough to find your tongue?"

Har blinked again and cleared his throat. "Illustrious King Hibich," he began grandly, "Great King Goldemar of the Ruhr, the inestimable Lord Alberich of the…"

"My dear young man," interrupted the queen with an impish smirk, "we already know who *we* are, more or less. Pray tell us who *you* are and what news you possess."

Feeling his face blush bright red, Har squeaked out a reply. "I am Har the Tower, and I have just returned from…"

"The *Tower*?" Virginal interrupted again, this time with glee. "Did your mother really name you Har *the Tower*? How delightful."

If it were possible, Har's face would have turned an even darker shade of red. He had blurted the name out without considering how ridiculous it sounded. "No, Your Majesty. Har is my given name. The Tower is my nickname."

"Well, it is the most accurate nickname I have ever heard," Virginal said, her eyes still dancing.

"Let us dispense with this silliness and get on with it!" snorted an impatient Alberich. "You went to see King Boleslaw, I take it? Is he or is he not coming to represent the Lutki host?"

"He is not, my lord," Har said. "The Lutki refused even to grant me an audience."

"Then our deliberations will be more thoughtful and productive," said Count Nickel of Rügen Isle, his thin lips forming a sneer. "Boleslaw is a knave and a fool."

"The Lutki face the same challenges we do," Queen Virginal said evenly.

"They have also warred over harvests and game with the Elves of the forests, the Kobolds of the towns, and the Nixies of the rivers. Like us, the Lutki have seen constant wars and disease ravage the humans. They have also watched as many human families and sometimes entire human communities leave our lands, sailing to new homes in America."

"Taking our source of humanwares with them," complained Lord Alberich.

"That is not all they take with them," said King Goldemar, looking at Alberich with barely disguised scorn. "You have seen the numbers. The declining game counts alone surely remove all doubt."

"I have heard your *theory*," Alberich said, "but my doubt remains. You think the monsters of our lands are somehow migrating to America with our humans. How is that possible?"

Goldemar made to respond but Alberich clearly considered his question rhetorical.

"The simpler explanation for the decline in game, both monster and animal," he continued, "is constant poaching by Elves. They fear us too little!"

"My rangers report the other Folk are also finding monster game to be scarcer," Goldemar said, keeping his voice level and refusing to take Alberich's bait.

Hibich, the aged king of the Brocken, looked nervously over at Nickel, then raised his hand. "Come, gentlemen, there is no need for this. Whether the cause is human emigration to America or encroachment by other Folk, the effect is the same."

Nickel had leaned so far back in his chair, his eyes so nearly shut, that it seemed to Har the pale Dwarf lord might have fallen asleep. But, at the king's words, Nickel suddenly perked up.

"That *is* the crux of the matter, Hibich, you are quite correct," Nickel said, to Hibich's visible relief. "Perhaps its origin is disputable. But the problem is here. It stares us in the face. It dares us to respond. We must take decisive action."

"If I am right," Alberich insisted belligerently, "then the right course of action is to join all our forces together and strike back at the poachers, starting with the Black Forest Elves."

"That is no solution at all," said Queen Virginal. "Our resources are already stretched thin. Our mages are exhausted from the frequent transport and Shimmer spells our hunting parties require. Waging war again will cost us dearly — and, if Goldemar's theory is right, there is little to gain from another war with the Elves."

Alberich looked at first like he was about to contest her argument. But then he sighed in frustration and sat back in his chair. "What would you have us do instead?" he asked, his tone defensive. "We *must* produce far more from our hunts and harvests to meet our people's needs."

"There is another solution," Virginal replied. "We can *reduce* our people's needs so that they more closely match our declining hunts and harvests."

The assembled lords and advisors stared at the queen of the Tyrol — some in surprise, some in confusion, some in horror. After a moment, Goldemar cleared his throat. "What precisely do you mean?"

"I mean," Virginal stated with equanimity, "that we have more Folk in our domains than we can support. Some should leave. They should follow the humans to America."

Her proposition provoked gasps of astonishment and spirited conversations throughout the chamber.

"This is hardly a novel idea," the queen continued over the din. "We have heard reliable reports of other Folk sailing west to settle in the New World — Sylphs and Brownies from England, Goblins and Lutins from France, Kabouters from Flanders. For all we know, some isolated Dwarfish tribes may have already stowed away on ships and found new homes among the Germans of America."

King Goldemar was listening intently to her, one hand tugging at his beard, but his eyes looked like they were seeing something far away.

"Your proposal has another argument in its favor," he said presently. "If magical monsters from our lands have somehow followed our humans to America, who would be better able to subdue them than those who have hunted those same monsters for generations? One might say we Folk have a clear duty to perform there."

Alberich's eyes had their own faraway look, but where Goldemar's seemed to foresee both honor and peril, Alberich's blazed with excitement.

"What wonders might our rangers and hunters discover there?" he said. "What glory might our warriors earn? It stirs the blood. If I were only twenty years younger…"

"There is nothing preventing you from joining the expedition, Alberich," said Goldemar with a wry smile. "Even if we agree to Virginal's proposal, there remains the weighty subject of which Dwarfs should make the journey, and who should lead them."

"You would like nothing better than for me and my Folk to leave the Rhineland," Alberich retorted, his suspicion instantly overwhelming his sense of adventure. "You of the Ruhr would move in and double the size of your domains."

This time, Goldemar did take the bait. Leaping to his feet, he touched the warhammer hanging by his side. "I did not come to the Dwarfmoot to suffer insults from ruffians like you," he said, his normally bookish manner replaced by unmistakable menace.

Alberich stood and faced Goldemar, a mocking grin on his face and a hand on the hilt of his sword. "I seek no answers in books, old man. I find my own answers. And I carve those answers with my own blade. So choose your questions carefully."

"Gentlemen, please," pleaded King Hibich, "this is neither the time nor the place for…"

"Sit down, both of you!" snapped Count Nickel, who had also risen to his feet, glaring icily. The sudden burst of volume and energy from the seemingly phlegmatic lord was startling. Among the startled were Goldemar and Alberich. Nickel raised a hand to stifle their protests.

"It is pointless to argue about which of our realms should relocate to America," Nickel stated matter of factly, "because the answer is clearly that none should do so."

Now it was Queen Virginal's turn to protest. "Do you really mean to offer your support to Lord Alberich's proposal of war?"

"Not at all," Nickel responded, taking his seat deliberately in a manner that had the effect of releasing the tension in the room. Virginal, Goldemar, and Alberich followed suit.

"You have jumped to the wrong conclusion," Nickel continued. "I see no alternative but immigration. We of Rügen Isle have long believed that, without the firm hand of Folk guidance, humans become restless, rootless, and potentially dangerous. A Dwarfish dominion in America is long overdue."

Virginal hid her surprise behind a graceful smile.

"However," Nickel continued, "the project requires careful planning. I suggest that each of us contribute mages, rangers, and other settlers to our

American colony in proportion to our numbers. That way, the balance of power, both there and here, will be preserved."

Har began to wonder if he had misjudged the man. Nickel might be arrogant, and perhaps even cruel to humans. But his suggestions about the colony sounded wise.

The other Dwarf lords and councilors in the room were clearly feeling the same mixture of emotions. Goldemar and Alberich, their harsh words seemingly forgotten, had turned to talk energetically with their advisors. Virginal sat quietly, still looking intently at Nickel — who also sat quietly, seeming to look at no one in particular.

"What do you think of that, young Har?"

The soft voice of King Hibich, now sounding more kindly than frail, brought Har's attention back to the fact that he had been standing quite literally at the center of history in the making.

"I do not...I do not know," Har managed to spit out before self-awareness kicked in. "That is, I mean to say, Your Majesty, it is not my place to..."

"Oh, tut-tut," the elderly king said, smiling indulgently at the ranger's nervous attempts at courtly talk. "I just want to know what you are thinking. This will be an endeavor of youth, not one for wizened sages or dried-up kings who have outlived their usefulness."

"Sire, that is not true!" Har insisted. His parents had always loved King Hibich, who had ruled the Dwarfs of the Harz for an astounding sixty-seven years — the equivalent of more than thirteen hundred years in the Blur. When Hibich was crowned king, the Roman empire had still ruled Western Europe. In his youth, Hibich had been a talented administrator, a skilled negotiator, a charismatic leader. He had guided the Dwarfs of the Brocken through many decades of conflicts with other Folk and through more than a millennium of complicated, strife-filled human history. Even now, with his health failing him, Hibich was a venerated figure.

"Come now, Har," Hibich said encouragingly. "I am not so doddering an old fool that I fail to see myself clearly in the mirror. But, pray, tell me true: does America call to you? Would you join the expedition if you had the chance?"

Although Har understood the logic behind the proposed immigration, he'd never once thought of making the journey himself. Har had only grudgingly accepted his fate as a ranger. Har had no interest in becoming a settler.

I owe it to my king to be forthright.

"Any such request would honor me, sire," Har began, "but as only a journeyman ranger — and not a particularly talented one, I would be the first to admit — I suspect someone else among your subjects would serve far better."

"That would be quite a shame."

At the sound of Queen Virginal's melodic voice from behind him, Har froze in place, his face again blushing crimson.

"I hear the American frontier is a rough country," Virginal continued, her mocking smile both pleasing and terrifying the young ranger as she walked up next to Hibich. "For our new American settlement to survive and thrive, I will have need of those who can take their size and strength into the Blur at least as much as I will have need of those more experienced or fleet of foot."

King Hibich and Har seemed to have realized the import of her words at the same time, looking at each other in slack-jawed astonishment and then back at her.

"Well, of course, the American expedition was my idea — so *I* should be the one to lead it," Virginal said, answering their unspoken question. "I will leave the governance of my alpine realm to the capable hands of my council. I will send no Dwarf to face perils I am unwilling to face myself."

With that, the queen whirled, her royal-blue cloak swirling dramatically as she strode confidently toward the door, her attendants falling in behind her.

"It would, indeed, be a shame," Virginal cried over her shoulder as she walked, "if Dwarfkind's new fortress in the New World did not include our tallest Tower."

As Har watched the beautiful queen exit the chamber, it occurred to him that she had made an excellent point.

Chapter 7 — The Warning

March 1771

THE SPELLSONG CAME EASILY TO his lips. That it could save a life, he knew well.

Will it save mine today?

When performed skillfully, the concealment song started out low and soothing, like crickets in summer. Later, its magic worked like a massive tree dropping thick piles of leaves over anything and everything the singer wanted to obscure. The listener might catch the tiniest hint of color here or movement there, but then tumbling wisps of autumnal reds, yellows, and browns would blot out the senses and cloud the mind.

He lay stretched out on a deerskin under the fading blue sky of a late spring afternoon, continuing to hum. But he also slid his hand slowly down to the hunting knife at his hip. He ought to be prepared in case the spellsong didn't work. Sure, he could recall the tune and hum it. But he didn't know any of the words. After all, Daniel Boone was no fairy.

▲▲▲

After nearly two years of exploring, hunting, and trapping, Daniel had gained a new appreciation for the rewards of caution — largely by being incautious and suffering as a result.

His friend John Finley had shown up at Daniel's home one fall afternoon in 1768 and asked him in no uncertain terms: "Isn't it about time we went to Kentucky?" It had taken months to recruit others and gather supplies they needed for the expedition. But, by the following May, they were ready.

Daniel, John Finley, and several others had set out from the Carolina backcountry, following the Elk and Watauga Rivers up and over the Blue

Ridge Mountains. They then continued north and west, through gaps, over ridges, until they finally reached the rolling hills of the Kentucky plateau. They made their camp along the Red River, near a rocky knob that reminded Daniel of the place so many years earlier where he first met Goran. The hunting party had spent the next several months bagging the most bountiful game any of them had ever seen. Indeed, they'd begun to worry about how they could haul all the skins and furs home.

A Shawnee hunting party relieved Daniel and his companions of that worry — by relieving them of their entire stock.

"You are trespassers here," the angry leader told them. "If we raided one of your farms and made off with your cattle, would you not hunt us down as thieves?"

Daniel tried to protest. "The way we reckon it, these 'cattle' don't belong to the Shawnees," he said. "Our governments signed a treaty last year with the Six Nations to buy this territory for hunting and settling."

"The Iroquois swindled you," the Shawnee responded testily. "These hunting grounds belong to us, not to our northern enemies."

Daniel held his hands up in supplication, made his friendliest face, and tried again. "The treaty was negotiated in good faith..."

"There can be no good faith from the Iroquois," his captor stated with finality. "We Shawnee did *not* surrender our lands. We would be within our rights to take your lives. But we will be merciful. Now, be grateful — and be gone."

Losing the fruits of their labors had been a severe blow. The others had abandoned Kentucky altogether. Daniel wouldn't be defeated, however. He started over, accumulating a second stock of skins and furs. Daniel's brother Squire Boone had arrived with fresh supplies, and later led a line of heavily laden pack animals back across the mountains to North Carolina. During the course of 1770, Squire Boone would make a second roundtrip. But Daniel had remained in Kentucky, alone.

While he always enjoyed company on long hunts — especially the occasions his fairy friend Goran came along — Daniel made the most of his solitude in Kentucky. He explored, hunted, trapped, read his well-worn copy of *Gulliver's Travels*, and dodged both wild beast and Shawnee alike. His months alone proved more than bearable.

Now Daniel's keen senses told him his solitude was over. Stretching out to rest on a deerskin after laboriously dragging another kill to camp, Daniel heard approaching footsteps. Lying still, he glanced over at his rifle, leaning on a tree and far out of reach. Then he looked around for some means of escape.

If only Goran were here, Daniel thought.

Which had trigged his wild idea. Daniel had heard Goran's spellsong of concealment so many times he knew the tune by heart. Why not try it? If it failed, there was always the recourse of drawing his knife and putting up a fight.

So Daniel continued to hum.

"Of all the wonders I thought I'd see in Kentucky, I never thought it'd be Daniel Boone singing me a lullaby," said a friendly voice.

Daniel withdrew his knife from its sheath, leapt to his feet, and whirled to meet the newcomer. It turned out to be not a Shawnee warrior but a hunter Daniel had met years ago, Casper Mansker.

"Well, you're a much pleasanter sight than I was expecting," said Daniel, relieved his failed magic trick had not doomed him. "Are you hunting alone or with a party?"

"Our camp is just a short ways from here," Casper replied. "Care for a little company?"

As the two frontiersmen walked through the forest together, Daniel narrated some of his adventures. In return, Casper related the latest news from home. Daniel wasn't surprised to learn of worsening tensions between Britain and the colonies. Parliament had tried several times to levy taxes in America to help pay off the debts incurred from fighting the French and Indian War. Every time, Americans protested the injustice of being taxed without the consent of their own provincial legislatures.

Daniel *was* shocked to learn, however, that British troops had opened fire on some Boston protesters, killing five.

"There's a new prime minister over there now, Lord North, and things have calmed down a bit," Casper said. "Parliament got rid of most of the taxes. But folks here are still plenty angry."

"What about the Regulator business in North Carolina?" Daniel asked.

"Backcountry folks are plenty angry about that, too, I hear," Casper replied. "They don't trust the judges and tax collectors. I guess you didn't hear what Governor Tryon did?"

Daniel winced at the name and shook his head.

"Well, he moved into a new Government House in New Bern a few months back, and it turned out to be quite the palace. Now folks are even *more* up in arms."

Daniel thought of Rebecca and the rest of his family. They were probably up in arms about Tryon's palace, too. Not for the first time, he felt a twinge of guilt about staying away for so long. But he had to think that his long hunt would be worth it.

Daniel decided to change the subject. "How's the hunting been, Casper?" he asked as they bore to the right to bypass a muddy stretch of ground.

"Good for the most part, ever since we left Long Island-on-the-Holston."

Daniel perked up. That was the place Daniel and Goran had first met Nanyehi and her fairy friend Tana.

"How are things with the Cherokees?" Daniel asked eagerly.

Casper shrugged his shoulders. "It's hard to say. I guess you know about the treaty they signed with Virginia a couple of years ago?"

Daniel nodded.

"Well, we all figured that treaty and the other one signed with the Iroquois up in New York had cleared things up. A Welshman named Evan Shelby founded a new settlement called Sapling Grove north of the Holston."

"Evan Shelby?" Daniel exclaimed. "The frontier scout? I met him back during the war."

"That's the one. Evan's got a store there now, and a stockade. I even heard the Shelbys are distilling whiskey on the premises."

Daniel let out a low, amazed whistle. The wild frontier didn't seem so wild any more.

"But marks on a map are one thing," Casper continued. "Moccasins on the ground are another. We've been raided more than once by Indians saying they aren't bound by the treaties."

"You're not the only ones, friend," Daniel said. "When we first got to Kentucky…"

They abruptly emerged from the woods onto a wide, grassy meadow that had clearly been trampled repeatedly by buffalo. Daniel halted Casper with a gesture.

"I've learned around these parts to be especially cautious out on open ground," he explained. "We'd best stay under cover and give the meadow a wide berth."

The two circled the clearing and then continued walking for another hour, reaching Casper's camp just before dusk. Daniel saw a couple of other hunters he knew, and got to tell his stories again over a rude supper of venison stew. Somehow, his second telling got more dramatic.

Early the next morning, Daniel reluctantly bade the hunters farewell and started back toward his own camp. As he approached the high meadow he and Casper had skirted the evening before, Daniel slowed his pace a bit and listened intently for any signs of man or beast.

His caution was well-advised. If Daniel had continued walking briskly, he might not have detected the low, rumbling noise now commanding his attention. It was exceedingly strange — not like any animal call he'd ever heard, and not like the grinding, rock-on-rock noise that had announced the approach of the Stoneclad that day on the mountain overlooking Long Island.

Then the low rumble gave way to a booming, trumpet-like call. As Daniel reached for his powder horn and began loading his rifle, a completely different sound reached his ears: human voices. His rifle at the ready, Daniel started forward again. Another human shout rang out from the direction of the meadow, followed by a response, and this time Daniel recognized the language as Shawnee, a tongue he knew passably well.

"Turn to the right!" the first said.

"My spear is broken — toss me another!" said the second.

If a party of warriors awaited Daniel, that was all the more reason to head in a different direction. Daniel turned left and stalked deeper into the forest, which sloped upward toward a low ridge. Another trumpeting call from the unknown animal prompted another round of answering cries from the Shawnees.

Daniel's discretion battled for supremacy with his curiosity. As the minutes passed, his resolve began to weaken. Surely, while he circled the meadow, it wouldn't hurt to take a closer look, he reasoned, as long as he stayed behind cover.

Through the thinning forest, he caught fleeting glimpses of human bodies speeding past the gaps. He crept forward and knelt behind a hickory stump. At first, Daniel saw nothing but grass across the broad meadow. Then a warrior came into view from the left, backing away from something that lay just out of Daniel's line of sight.

The warrior was dressed like most Shawnees Daniel had met: buckskin leggings and moccasins like Daniel's, a white cotton shirt acquired in trade, beaded belt and headband, and a topknot of hair through which dyed porcupine quills were thrust. The Indian was carrying a long spear tipped with a rounded flint, which Daniel instantly recognized as their weapon of choice for taking down buffalo. Shawnee hunters preferred rounded spearheads to pointed ones, because the latter were more likely to shatter against bone. No doubt some would be carrying guns as well, but Shawnees always took pride in their great skill at hunting elk and buffalo with traditional weapons.

The Indian stopped not fifteen paces from where Daniel crouched behind the stump. Cupping his hands around his mouth, the Shawnee screamed a challenge. Once more, Daniel heard the low rumbling followed by the trumpeting sound. Then he felt the ground shake, as if a herd of buffalo was approaching. The Shawnee man turned and sprinted out of sight.

Following the hunter, however, was no buffalo. It was far taller and lacked the buffalo's shaggy hide. Instead, Daniel saw leathery skin, light gray and creased with deep wrinkles. He marveled as he watched the wall of leathery skin keep moving across his field of vision. Could this really be a single beast?

When Daniel looked up and saw its head, he knew it was more than just a wild animal. The first image that came to mind was a woodcut he'd seen of an elephant from the East Indies. But the head of this beast was, if anything, stranger. Its head was flat and elongated, with two enormous tusks jutting out and forming a near-circle. Its trunk was elephantine, certainly, but also wider and longer than the one depicted in the woodcut.

The most telling signs of its magical nature were its eyes, set far apart and glaring out from underneath leathery brows. The eyes were glowing — not the tawny color Daniel had seen in the eyes of that Wampus Cat so many years ago, but instead a deep blue. And while the Wampus Cat's eyes had flashed with something close to barely contained lightning bolts, this creature's eyes reminded Daniel of embers left over from a dying campfire.

From the bottom of its stiff legs to the top of its elongated head, the monster stood at least fifteen feet tall. Yet, as it charged past and he saw four more warriors running swiftly behind, Daniel noticed that their gaze was directed *not* upward, at the monster's swinging head or switching tail, but instead at the level of its knees. Odder still, only one Indian was following closely behind the monster itself. The others were spaced out across the meadow as if chasing other beasts parallel to the monster, although Daniel saw and heard only that single beast.

"Turn the herd more to the right!" commanded one of the trailing Shawnees, who Daniel guessed was the leader of the hunting party. The man was tall and slender, dressed head to toe in buckskins and sporting a magnificent assemblage of colorful feathers thrust into his black hair. His large eyes flashed with excitement as he watched the hunters respond to his orders.

"We must be getting close to the mud pit!" cried a warrior.

"Yes, but keep your spears up," the leader replied. "Once their hooves get stuck, be ready to strike immediately."

As the Shawnees moved out of his sight, Daniel found the drama of the hunt too compelling to resist. He ran into the meadow to see where the Indians were herding their quarry. The Shawnees on the far side of the behemoth appeared to have stopped, aiming their long spears at a point somewhat below the monster's body. The trailing Indians were still yelping and prodding, driving their prey.

Then the creature's head appeared to take a dip and jerk. As Daniel got closer, the tableau came into sharper relief. The elephantine beast had stumbled into a broad section of soft ground above a natural sinkhole. Mud splashed all around as it struggled to free itself while swinging its head back and forth to defend itself from thrusting spears.

Once again, Daniel found the behavior of the Shawnees puzzling. While a couple of the hunters were aiming in the direction of the monster, most were standing to the left of it, on either side of the sinkhole, jabbing their spears at nothing but empty air.

Then, from the trees on the other side of the meadow, came the unmistakable sound of a wet drum beating out a regular rhythm.

Daniel had seen the Shawnees' distinctive wet drum years before at a trading camp. It was made from a "cypress knee" — a foot-and-a-half of hollow stump filled to its halfway point with a mixture of water and charcoal, then covered by a tightly stretched buckskin. Back then, Daniel had watched a dozen Shawnees dance gleefully, beating their bearclaw-clad feet on the ground, as two companions played wet drums three feet high. On this day, however, Daniel heard only a single drum. And from its high pitch, he figured it was smaller.

Even before an ethereal voice began singing a haunting melody over the steady pounding of the drum, Daniel had guessed that fairy magic was behind what he was witnessing. The song reminded him of Goran's illusion spell. Daniel had first heard it during the Braddock expedition, when Goran used it to misdirect the shot of the hawk-feathered Indian trying to kill George Washington. He had heard a similar song years later at the Holston River, when Tana had protected Daniel by deflecting Dragging Canoe's charge.

This time, the illusion song didn't so much deflect an attack as end one. The Shawnees standing on either side of the muddy sinkhole stopped stabbing their spears. Instead, they looked around in confusion.

An imposing broad-shouldered Shawnee, his hair swept back with a headband crowned with pitch-black feathers, turned to the leader. "What happened to the buffalo, Cornstalk?" the puzzled warrior asked.

The tall leader looked back at his companion with equal puzzlement. "I see no way the bulls could have escaped the mud, Blackfish, and yet escape they must have."

Blackfish put a hand above his eyes and scanned the horizon in all directions. Daniel noticed that the singing and drumming from the far woods had stopped.

"You, there," Blackfish called to the warriors on the other side of the sinkhole. "Which way did the buffaloes go?"

The other Shawnee shrugged.

"Fan out," Blackfish continued, "and see if you can pick up their trail."

At that, Daniel suddenly realized how exposed he was. It was too late. As one of the warriors turned to follow Blackfish's instructions, he spied Daniel. Letting out a cry of alarm, the warrior lowered his spear and started running. Another dropped his spear and unslung his rifle. Daniel heard whoops and curses from the others, too, but by that time he was running, as fast as his legs could carry him in the opposite direction.

In the race that followed, Daniel had two advantages. First, a head start of three dozen paces. And second, resistance to spellsong. Cornstalk, Blackfish, and the other Shawnees were strong runners, but the illusion spell must not have worn off completely. Daniel reached the trees before his pursuers had truly found their footing.

As Daniel hurtled through the forest, his mind raced. He knew he shouldn't head back to camp, given the risk that the Shawnees would track him. Daniel was as loath to give up his stock of skins and furs as he was to give up his life in a fight against superior numbers. So he bore west instead of south, hoping to shake pursuit by heading through dense bramble and then along the heavily wooded banks of the nearby river.

An hour later, dog-tired and bleeding from cuts and scrapes he picked up during his mad rush, Daniel was approaching his camp when it occurred to him he ought not to take any chances. Slowly, methodically, he inched his way forward, stopping after every step to listen. He heard nothing. Congratulating himself on his good fortune, he strode into camp, set his rifle down, and began gathering wood to light a fire.

"I take it you have heard spellsong before, human," said a voice.

Daniel jerked and dropped his armful of sticks. "Show yourself!" he warned, picking up his rifle and turning slowly around in a circle, his sharp eyes scanning for movement.

"Come now," the voice continued. "You and I should have nothing but plain talk between us. You are clearly one of those rare humans who possess the Sight. Why should I abandon my hiding place? It would appear to be my only advantage."

Daniel considered for a moment, then planted his rifle butt-first on the ground. "There's no need to talk of advantage, friend," he said in his most conciliatory tone. "I have made fairy friends before. I am happy to do so again."

"Talk of peace might meet with more success if you lay down your weapon of war," answered the voice.

Reluctantly, Daniel complied. He couldn't know if he was facing one fairy or many. Talking seemed wiser than shooting.

"Thank you, human. Fair is fair."

There was a sudden commotion. Ducking instinctively, Daniel heard a thud as something struck the ground a few paces from his feet. It was neither an arrow nor a spear but something in between, with a point of copper at one head and fletching of yellow and black feathers at the other. A second later, something else landed nearby. It was a smoothly crafted piece of wood with a groove running down its length, two side-by-side copper holes attached to one end, and a symbol on the other end shaped like a bee.

While Daniel speculated as to the purpose of the finely decorated stick, a small figure emerged. Daniel immediately thought of Tana. The trim, lithe-looking little man was outfitted much like a Shawnee warrior, although his hair was cut in Mohawk fashion — not unheard of among the Shawnees, but atypical nonetheless.

The fairy's most interesting piece of equipment was a cylindrical object strapped to his back with two leather straps. Daniel saw the familiar outlines of a wet drum. Here was the source of the illusion charm that had so flummoxed the Shawnee hunters.

"As I said, I see no reason not to speak plainly," said the fairy. "You have met a Pukwudgie before?"

"If you mean, have I met fairies before, the answer is certainly yes," Daniel said. "But I don't recognize the word Pukwudgie."

"The humans know us by many names. I am Atta the scout. Some call me Atta Yellow Jacket."

Daniel looked down at the bee device on the stick and the fletching on the short spear. He smiled. "I can see why. May I offer you food and a place at my campfire?"

"Thank you, no," Atta said, glancing up slyly at Daniel. "Speaking plainly, I will not have time for that. Neither will you."

Daniel stiffened. "What do you mean by that, friend?" he asked as he looked over longingly at his rifle.

"We may treat with each other honorably," Atta responded, and Daniel could tell that his averted eyes had given away his scheme. "We may even come to a mutual understanding. But you must know, human, that you and I can never be friends."

Opting to continue a diplomatic approach, Daniel shook his head in what he hoped the Pukwudgie would interpret as a good-natured gesture. "That's where you're wrong, Atta Yellow Jacket. As I told you, I already have friends among the fairies."

Atta arched his eyebrows. "You only think you do. Either the others you met were pretending — or else they are outcasts, not truly Folk."

Daniel knew he ought not take the bait, but he couldn't help himself. "What's so impossible about humans and fairies getting along? Are they such enemies where you come from?"

"Not, strictly speaking, enemies," Atta answered. "One does not think of one's livestock as enemies. They are simply resources."

Daniel felt his temper flaring. "I am no one's cow to be milked. I am a man."

"You are, indeed, just a man," Atta agreed. "Other than possessing the Sight, you are no different from the Shawnees I tricked into helping me catch the Yakwawi. They proved to be strong, fleet, and brave, though they thought all along they were just hunting buffalo. I have nothing but respect for the abilities of humans. When the task calls for feats of brute force, we Pukwudgies gladly make use of them. The massive, fearsome Yakwawi would be difficult for my Folk to subdue on our own. But we do not mistake the usefulness of humans for the highest qualities that belong only to Folk."

It occurred to Daniel that Atta, who had initially spoken in short, clipped sentences, had become more talkative and animated. Was Daniel's talent for making friends winning him over?

"That is not to say," Atta went on, "that all Folk possess those qualities to the same degree. Pukwudgies have overseen these domains for many centuries of your years. We know every riverbed, every plateau and high meadow, every hill and mountain. They are ours. We allow the Shawnees and other native tribes to hunt, fish, and gather in our lands, and take a portion of their harvests for the protection we afford them."

"Protection from what?" Daniel asked. "From magical monsters?"

"From that threat, yes, and from many others. We have warred against encroachers from the other, lesser Folk — against the Nunnehi and others who herd the Southern humans, against the Jogah of the Iroquois country, and now against the Folk from your white lands over the sea who seek to invade our territory."

Daniel had heard this kind of talk before, from the Indians. "I agree that newcomers should respect the customs of new places, and make fair treaties. But I don't agree that any one people can claim compete mastery over the wide-open spaces."

"Your agreement is not required," said Atta, who had turned around, stooped over, and let his drum slip to the ground. "Only your obedience — or, if necessary, your silence."

Then Atta began to drum. His hands struck a ponderous beat on the taut buckskin. The water sloshed around inside the drum, creating complex rhythms. Atta began to sing a frenetic, high-pitched melody.

"I thought you understood," Daniel said as he walked confidently to his discarded rifle and picked it up. "Your magic songs won't work on me."

Atta stopped singing and looked up. "My song is not meant for you. I do not need to recover my spear-thrower to solve the problem you present."

Then Daniel understood. From the forest came the sound of running feet.

"If you are remain until the Shawnees arrive, you will be buried here," Atta said matter of factly. "And if, somehow, you manage to escape, remember this. I am Atta Yellow Jacket. And the Shawnee camps are like wasp nests. If you are foolish enough to venture here again, the wasps and yellow jackets will swarm up and over you. You will not survive our stings."

▲▲▲

Once again Daniel found himself racing through the trees, clutching his rifle desperately and angrily cursing the loss of yet another stock of skins and furs. Even if he couldn't hear the sound of his pursuers, Daniel could *feel* their presence. It felt like a weight pressing down on his shoulders and chest, making it hard to breathe. Daniel had no idea which direction was best. He had no idea how to escape his seemingly inevitable fate. Yet, still, he ran.

Daniel abruptly reached the end of the forest and found himself on a rocky cliff. More than a hundred feet below lay the rapids of the river. Leaping into that shallow body of water was out of the question. But the Shawnees were almost upon him.

Then he spied the spreading branches of a sugar maple growing next to the river. He saw no alternative. Placing his rifle against the cliff and letting it slide down, then whispering a fervent prayer, Daniel leapt feet-first, his arms waving wildly.

As he crashed through the upper reaches of the tree, his descent slowed ever so slightly. Reaching out with both hands, Daniel felt several branches slip past his burning palms. Then his grip held. Somehow, he managed the sudden jolt without breaking any limbs. Looking up at the cliff, he saw Cornstalk, Blackfish, and the other Shawnees peering down at him with a mixture of righteous fury and grudging admiration.

▲▲▲

The store at Shelby Station was a rude affair — a cabin stocked with a few articles of clothing, spare flints and powder, knives, dry beans, and other goods a frontiersman might need. Located on the Shelby family farm called Sapling Grove, it was only infrequently manned by one of the Shelby boys, and even more infrequently visited.

But it just so happened that on this day in late March of 1771, twenty-year-old Isaac Shelby had finished digging a post hole on the upper field and headed to the store to refill his powder horn. As he approached the cabin, he saw a lean-looking man in a ragged shirt, leggings, and moccasins leaning against a stump, a battered-looking rifle propped against his knee.

"Welcome to Shelby Station," said Isaac, eyeing the stranger dubiously. He doubted the ragged man could afford to buy anything.

"Thank you kindly, friend," the man replied. "I'm Daniel Boone, and I'm wondering if I might get a flint and some supplies."

Isaac Shelby's jaw dropped. *Daniel Boone? The famous long hunter? Here at Shelby Station?*

"Why, uh, sure, Mr. Boone," Isaac managed to sputter. "Headed out or coming back?"

"Coming back, friend, and call me Daniel," came the reply. "And you?"

"I'm Isaac Shelby."

"Pleased to meet you, Isaac," Daniel said with a broad smile. "I met your father during the war. I see you take after him."

Isaac felt a bit more at ease. *Something tells me this Daniel Boone has a talent for making people feel at ease.*

"I've been away from home for two years hunting in the Kentucky country," Daniel continued, "and now I'm mighty eager to get back to my Rebecca and the children."

Isaac opened the door and led Daniel into the cabin. "The Kentucky country, eh? Is it as beautiful as they say?"

"Much more than anyone could say, and full of more game than anyone could imagine."

Isaac looked skeptically at Daniel's tattered clothes and then blushed when he realized the hunter had read his expression.

"Oh, I know it doesn't look it," Daniel said with a laugh, "but I had great success hunting. The Indians who took all my skins and furs got plenty of goods in trade for the fruits of my labors, I'll wager."

Isaac meant to apologize but Daniel stayed him with a raised hand. "I know I look a sight, Isaac. Now, where do you keep your flints?"

The two fell silent as Isaac showed his visitor the shelves.

"Daniel, if I may ask," began Isaac after a while, "where does your family live?"

"Our place is back east, on the banks of the Yadkin River," Daniel replied.

"I suppose after what happened in Kentucky, after losing everything you worked so hard for, you plan to stay home for a good long time."

"Why, no," said Daniel, his lined face forming another wide grin. "I'm going back to Kentucky — and this time I'm going to figure out how to take lots of other people with me. There's a certain yellow-jacket nest there that needs stomping. The more feet, the better."

Chapter 8 — The Newcomers

September 1772

PETER MUHLENBERG STOOD AT A great, sweeping bend of the Shenandoah River, looked out over the sparkling water, and wished he'd brought his fishing pole.

His regret reminded Peter of the many times fishing had gotten him into trouble. The memory made Peter smile. What would the famous Reverend Henry Muhlenberg have to say if he were here to witness his son gazing wistfully at this perfect fishing spot? Peter guessed he would quote Matthew 4:19: *Follow me, and I will make you fishers of men.*

That's precisely what Peter had become.

His journey had taken many twists and turns. After being unceremoniously expelled from the Saxon dragoons after just weeks, Peter had slunk back to Halle, penniless and desperate. University leaders had arranged an apprenticeship for him with an apothecary in Lubeck. It had proved to be the most miserable experience of all of Peter's miserable experiences in Germany. By 1766, desperate to return home, Peter had met a British army recruiter and enlisted in the Sixtieth Regiment of Foot, soon to embark for garrison duty in America.

Again released almost immediately from military service after his arrival in Philadelphia, Peter went home. While not exactly the "prodigal son" of scripture, Peter had indeed been welcomed with open arms by his family, very much including Dr. Henry Muhlenberg. Chastened by his experiences in Germany, and deeply touched by his father's forgiveness, Peter had resolved to enter the ministry.

After years of study, Peter had been ordained a minister of the Evangelical Lutheran Church. His responsibilities took him to multiple congregations in Pennsylvania and New Jersey. At one of them, he met a young woman,

Hannah Meyer, who became his wife in 1770.

The following year, his father had come to Peter with a problem. German settlers from Pennsylvania, streaming south into Virginia and the Carolinas, were founding churches on the frontier. Ordained ministers were needed to lead them. The most pressing invitation had come from Muellerstadt, a settlement on the Shenandoah River in western Virginia. Called Woodstock by English speakers, the town had been founded by the legislature in 1761 thanks to the efforts of Colonel George Washington, a planter and veteran of the French and Indian War.

Peter answered the call to Woodstock. But the laws of Virginia required churches to be headed by ministers from the Church of England. Although Peter's time in Germany had made him greatly appreciate the freer life of British-ruled America, he still chafed at such restrictions. Seeing no alternative, however, he'd sailed to London in 1772 and received a second ordination from an English bishop. Finally, after arriving back in Philadelphia, Peter and Hannah set out immediately for their new home in Virginia.

Woodstock lay next to the North Fork of the Shenandoah, which wound its way like a giant snake along the west side of a ridge of mountains. The South Fork of the river followed a similarly serpentine path along the other side of the ridge. During his first weeks in Woodstock, Peter spent most of his time helping Hannah with the new house and meeting members of his congregation. Now, he was taking his first day off to explore.

The tree-covered ridge just across the Shenandoah was a luscious shade of green. It struck him as an excellent place to start.

As he headed up the slope, Peter marveled at the mountain's natural beauty. The thick stands of chestnut and red oak reminded him of Pennsylvania. He passed shrubs covered with colorful blossoms and bushes covered with luscious blackberries and huckleberries. Within the space of an hour, Peter spotted two turkeys and a white-tailed buck. At the riverbank, he'd regretted leaving his fishing pole behind. Now his regrets turned to the long Pennsylvania rifle hanging over the door of his new house.

Peter paused to rest at a rocky outcropping. First he looked down at the river — there were now seven distinct bends visible near the Woodstock settlement. Then he directed his eyes up the ridge. As Peter observed the forest-covered peak, some of the trees seemed to bend down suddenly to one side, as if buffeted by a strong wind. But the day was sunny with only the hint of a breeze. Deciding he must have imagined it, Peter began to turn away — but then, out of the corner of his eye, he saw the same thing happen again. This time, the trees swayed low in a different direction, as if being pushed down by some giant hand.

Am I about to get caught in a storm?

Prudence counseled that he seek shelter. But within the distinguished new minister of Woodstock, there still lived young Peter Muhlenberg, the frequently truant boy with perpetually muddy feet, as well as "Devil Pete," the frequently absent dragoon with perpetually muddy boots. What was a little rainstorm to them?

So Peter kept climbing. To his surprise, he felt no wind, no drizzle. He heard no thunder. He saw no more trees bending low.

A passage from Isaiah came to mind: *And there shall be a tabernacle for a shadow in the daytime from the heat, and for a place of refuge, and for a covert from storm and from rain.*

The Shenandoah Valley was the new home Peter and Hannah had faithfully chosen. Serving the settlers here was the commission Peter had faithfully accepted. He expected challenges. There would be mountains to climb, in a sense. Perhaps today's climb was a symbol of that. Peter resolved to make this place — this river, this valley, this mountain — a refuge.

Feeling exhilarated by the thought, and by the beautiful vistas, Peter began to hum a merry tune. While far from a skilled singer, Peter loved music of all kinds, from stately church hymns and the chamber pieces he'd heard in London to the folk songs and marches he'd learned in Germany. He couldn't quite remember where he'd first heard this particular tune. But it must have made quite an impression on him, since Peter was finding no trouble humming along as it continued for verse after verse…

"What is happening here?" Peter asked aloud.

He *had* been humming along, but to a song that, he now realized, was actually being played nearby on some kind of stringed instrument. Now that Peter considered the matter plainly, he couldn't remember hearing the melody before. The sound he had found so familiar wasn't the song itself. It was the plucking of the strings. Peter racked his brain. During his time in Germany, he'd visited many taverns and market squares where musicians plied their trade. Was he remembering one of those times? No, that didn't seem quite right.

Then Peter remembered. The Dwarf!

He was hearing the scheitholt the Dwarf had played when Peter's fellow dragoons had tried but failed to attack the little man. Many times over the subsequent eight years, Peter had wondered if his imagination had gotten the better of him that day near Halle. Truth be told, he'd attempted several times to convince himself of that. But the attempts always failed.

Now, somehow, Peter knew that, if he just kept climbing, he'd see the Dwarf again.

Confirmation wasn't long in coming. Peter reached another clearing with a clear view of the mountaintop. What he saw there was that same red-cloaked little man he'd seen back in Germany. This time, the man sat underneath a chestnut tree, the scheitholt on his lap. The Dwarf was plucking the strings with one hand and pressing the neck of the instrument with the other. He was also singing in a deep, rich baritone.

Perhaps it was seeing as well as hearing the Dwarf, but for whatever reason Peter felt the song begin to fill his senses and stir his emotions. He didn't recognize a single word. Nevertheless, it was as if the song had become a long, invisible quill, dipped in ink, reaching across the expanse and writing directly onto his mind. What it wrote was a single, simple, powerful word: *home.*

As Peter stood spellbound, a flicker of light appeared in the air just above the Dwarf's head. Then came another, higher and a few feet to the right, then another even higher and leftward. The air itself seemed to ripple, as if it were a pond into which someone was rapidly throwing a series of stones. Small, fleeting flickers of light became streaks, then entire walls of multi-colored illumination. The trees he'd previously seen bent low were now bucking and swirling as if in a gale. The only exception was the chestnut at the very top, the one beneath which the Dwarf sat. It stayed perfectly still.

Next came the wind. At first, Peter felt a light breeze against his face. Then it was a constant pressure against his entire body, and finally a shove. But instead of lifting him off his feet, the mysterious wind appeared to push *through* him and disappear. Reflexively, Peter looked down at his chest, as if expecting to see that something had punched a hole in him. All he saw were his shirt and waistcoat, untouched.

When he returned his attention to the peak, Peter saw that the Dwarf had ceased playing his song. The little man stood up and began walking around the chestnut tree, stopping after every few steps to examine the ground as if looking for something. It didn't take long for him to find it. Peter watched the dark-red cap of the Dwarf dip toward the ground, then out of sight.

Concluding that the Dwarf had stumbled upon some kind of cave or tunnel, Peter resolved to follow. He had many questions. Some were eight years in the making. Other questions were prompted by the amazing events of the past few minutes. They all needed answering. And, as Peter recalled, the Dwarf spoke excellent German.

The young minister sprinted as fast as he could toward the chestnut. He'd given up any attempt at stealth, so his boots made quite a racket. Above the noise of his own making, however, he managed to hear a sliding sound, like a heavy object being dragged along the ground, seconds before something smashed into him, knocking him against a nearby tree. He sank to the ground, gasping for breath and clutching his chest.

A moment later, he looked up and saw rapid movement toward the peak. It was too fast, and the distance too great, for Peter to tell who or what had sideswiped him. Although every step made his ribs ache, Peter rose to follow — while again regretting his choice to leave home that morning with no more equipment than a canteen and a hunting knife.

Peter's hand shot to the hilt of the knife as he reached the tree and caught sight of the object pointing at him. It was a tail — charcoal gray, scaly, and twitching. Peter recalled the settlers telling him that timber rattlesnakes were native to these mountains. They were quick as lightning. Their bites could sicken or even kill. But this tail was far, far too large to be attached to a rattlesnake. Peter judged it nearly a foot in diameter. And there was no rattle on the end.

A few steps more and Peter could see that the tail broadened into a thick serpentine body plunged into a hole. He guessed a giant snake had tried to follow the Dwarf but couldn't force itself all the way in. It shook repeatedly as if thudding against some unseen barrier.

Peter considered his options. Pitifully armed, his safest course of action was to head back down the mountain, leaving the snake and Dwarf to their respective fates. But he still had all those questions. And Peter Muhlenberg never lacked for courage. So he grasped the wriggling tail and pulled hard. The beast didn't budge. He heaved again, still harder.

That second time produced three unexpected results. First, Peter heard not a snake's hiss but the enraged roar of some colossal cat. Second, the tail jerked easily toward him as the entire body of the beast — nearly fourteen feet long, scaled in ominous gray and glistening gold — slithered back from the tunnel, coiled, and turned around.

And third, the face now regarding him with menace was not that of a snake. It was that of a cat — a broad, maned leonine face with massive jaws and dark, glowing eyes. Even though Peter had been chasing a Dwarf — an *actual Dwarf* out of a fairy story — encountering such a bizarre-looking monster came as a complete shock.

His shock was almost his undoing because, even as Peter stood there, mouth wide open, the monster was moving rapidly toward him, propelled both by its undulating body and by two cat-like front paws. At the last minute, with the beast's jaws heading directly for his throat, Peter realized his danger and dodged, spinning around to stand before a tall bank of cardinal flowers and holding his knife in front of his face. The puny weapon wouldn't pose much of a threat to the snarling monster. But it was all Peter had. Wielding it made him feel better.

As the cat-snake poised for another attack, Peter saw two more unexpected sights beyond it. One was a shimmering wall of light within the tunnel the monster had tried to enter. The second was a figure emerging from the shimmering wall. It was the Dwarf.

"Tatzelwurm!" he shouted in German as he hefted a doubled-bladed battleaxe and charged the monster from the rear. Instantly an image came unbidden to Peter's mind. He was a small child, sitting on his mother's knee and listening to a story about a venomous snake monster the terrorized the Alps.

"Don't let it breathe on you!" said the Dwarf, lifting his axe over his head to strike. It was a well-timed warning, for the Tatzelwurm had lunged directly at the human's face. Peter dropped to the ground and rolled. Looking up from the ground, he saw a dense mist spread out over the cardinal flowers.

Then the Tatzelwurm roared in pain as the sharp axe found its mark, producing a shower of red sparks and leaving a foot of writhing tail on the ground.

"Help is coming!" cried the Dwarf. "We need only keep it busy."

If that "help" consisted of more little men, Peter wasn't sure it would do much good. Losing the tip of its tail only served to enrage the massive

Tatzelwurm. Its head whipped around, spying the Dwarf and emitting another roar. Perhaps a large party of men with rifles could take down such an enormous monster, but a few Dwarfs with axes, and one man with a hunting knife, struck Peter as hopelessly outmatched.

He couldn't just watch while his would-be rescuer bore the brunt of the beast's fury, however. So Peter rushed forward, wrapping his left arm with great difficulty around its twisting body and stabbing with his right.

He might has well have been stabbing a boulder with a bent twig. His knife bounced harmlessly off the dark scales. On Peter's third try, he kept the knife exactly perpendicular to the Tatzelwurm's body and shoved with all his might. Like a twig would have done, the knife simply broke into pieces. Then, for good measure, Peter lost his grip on the monster with his left arm, fell face-first into the dirt, and again felt sharp pains in his ribs.

He didn't see the battle between the Tatzelwurm and the Dwarf. He did, however, hear it — the feckless scrape of the axe against the monster's thick scales, the roar as it lunged at its attacker, the thud of the Dwarf hitting the ground.

Peter stumbled to his feet. Just a few paces away, the incongruously feline face of the monster was dipping toward the dazed Dwarf. Peter watched in horror, weaponless, helpless.

Then the wind returned. This time, Peter felt the cold gust only briefly as it passed over and through him.

It was as if the wind had blown a mask from his eyes. Where before Peter saw nothing but the grotesque Tatzelwurm and the prostrate Dwarf, Peter now saw a squadron of little people surrounding the monster. Some were dressed like the first Dwarf, in dark-red cloaks and caps, their hands filled with warhammers, double-bladed axes, or smaller hatchets. Other Dwarfs, dressed in cloaks of black and gold, wielded long, two-handed spears topped with axe-heads. There were green-clad archers with arrows pulled back to their chins. And there were a few javelinmen, noticeably smaller and slighter than the others and dressed in shabby clothes of black and tan.

Only for an instant did the newcomers seem frozen in place. Then they sprang into action. Arrows and javelins flew. So did the little hatchets, spinning through the air end over end. The Dwarfs in black and gold swung their long halberds while the others leapt in close with their hand weapons.

The scales of the Tatzelwurm's body and the tough hide of its forearms turned many weapons aside. A few penetrated the beast's natural defenses, however, and dealt scrapes, gashes, bruises, or punctures. Whether hits or misses, the weapons always produced showers of red sparks and screams of rage from the monster.

Its eyes burned dark with anger — and with some mysterious power. Peter saw two Dwarfs go down under its paws, one howling as a razor-sharp claw sliced into his chest and the other falling completely silent as his head hit the ground hard. At the other end of the monster, the stub of its severed tail had smashed one of its attackers into the trunk of the chestnut tree, breaking both of the Dwarf's legs with a sickening crack. Then the tail knocked another Dwarf off his feet and down the side of the mountain, where he landed with an agonized grunt.

Most horrible of all, as one of the javelinmen scurried forward to retrieve his weapon, the Tatzelwurm turned and breathed a dense mist right into the face of the little man. He shrieked and fell back, clutching both cheeks. Peter could see blood dripping from the victim's hands.

It was the next moment that Peter realized the newcomers weren't all men. He heard a woman's voice snap a command in a language he didn't understand. Instantly the Dwarfs who were still on their feet reassembled in a circle around the Tatzelwurm, nocking fresh arrows or otherwise preparing themselves for another assault. Through a gap in the circle marched a female Dwarf, followed by three males. All were dressed in resplendent clothes of snow white and royal blue. Each carried long bronze blades with hooked ends.

At a second command from the woman, the archers, javelinmen, and axe-throwers fired another volley. The Tatzelwurm sustained a few more wounds but, more important, was distracted by the flying missiles. The four Dwarfs in blue sprang forward in concert. All swung their hooked swords at the same spot on the monster's serpentine body, just behind its feline head. Sparks flew as each hook found its mark along a seam between two tough scales. Two of the male Dwarfs jumped on top of the beast and twisted over to their stomachs, still clinging to their swords. The other male and the female dove to the ground.

Peter quickly recognized the brilliance of the tactic, even before three archers sank three bronze-tipped arrows deep into the flesh of the Tatzelwurm through the opening in the scales created by the hooked swords. The lion's head uttered an anguished cry as the beast bucked and rolled. Whether it was trying to get to the embedded arrows or just writhing in pain, Peter couldn't tell. A few moments later, the motions of the cat-snake slowed appreciably. Then they ceased entirely.

Peter released the breath he'd been holding. He watched as several warriors rushed in with thick ropes and began binding the Tatzelwurm. Winded and slightly wounded Dwarfs regained their feet and looked each other over. The seriously wounded sat or lay on the ground, calling out for aid. A few lay unconscious.

For the first time, Peter noticed there were other Dwarfs on the mountain besides the ones that had taken part in the battle. Dressed more as scholars than warriors, they stood in a rough circle, waving their raised hands and speaking in low tones. Beyond them, Peter saw a strange wall of light. It surrounded the mountaintop and extended several feet into the sky, where it curved into a dome. It was as if everyone there — Dwarf, Tatzelwurm, and human — were enclosed in a shimmering bubble.

As he tried to make sense of it all, two of the scholarly Dwarfs left the circle and hurried to the sides of the most seriously wounded Dwarfs. One waved his hands as he'd done before. The other removed a flask from a pocket and began pouring luminous liquid into the mouths of the wounded.

His attentions focused elsewhere, Peter was startled to discover the Dwarf he'd first met in Saxony now standing before him. The little man sported a big bruise on his face. His light-gray trousers were ripped at one bloody knee. In one hand was his battleaxe, one blade missing half its edge.

Before Peter could speak, the Dwarf held up a hand and began to sing. Behind the singer, the finely dressed woman strode forward, slipping her hooked sword into her belt. Her much-shorter stature prompted Peter to notice that the "little" man singing in front of him was by far the tallest Dwarf of the group.

Nonplussed and aching from his wounds, Peter simply stood there as the singer sang. The faces of the three exhibited their increasing confusion. After a couple of minutes, the Dwarf stopped singing. The woman spoke to the singer and waved a dismissive hand at Peter. The singer responded at length. The woman seemed lost in thought for a moment, then nodded. She cast a searching look at Peter, who immediately felt the weight of her appraisal.

"I suppose you must have questions," said the male Dwarf in German. "I have one or two of my own. You may call me Har. And you may call the queen 'Your Majesty.'"

▲▲▲

The three sat together for a long while. Most of the Dwarfs had departed in another burst of wind with the unconscious Tatzelwurm. But two on the perimeter remained, each holding his arms aloft and emitting light from them.

Har told Peter about the Shimmer and the Blur, about Folk and monsters, about rangers and other guilds, about magecraft and spellsong. Peter told Har about his schooling and military service in Germany, his family in America, and his new ministry in the Shenandoah. Queen Virginal mostly listened, adding a few details here and there and asking pointed questions.

Peter learned of the Dwarfmoot and the expedition to America. Each of six Dwarfish nations had contributed settlers and resources for the new colony, including javelinmen, greenweavers, and mages from the Lutki of the Lusatian Hills, who hadn't attended the Dwarfmoot but later decided they would lose face if they didn't participate. The Dwarf lords had readily agreed to Queen Virginal's proposal to lead the expedition, though Har and Virginal suspected the motivation was more to weaken her position in Germany than to strengthen the colony in America.

After assembling at King Goldemar's keep on the Ruhr River, the colonists had used magical transport to jump to Amsterdam, then to London, and eventually to a ship bound for Philadelphia. Magecraft and spellsong had kept hundreds of Dwarfs and their supplies, livestock, and personal possessions secreted in a tiny corner of the ship's hold. Upon arrival, Har and the other rangers had fanned out to look for suitable locations. The Dwarfs were used to living either on mountains or under rivers, so finding places with both features had been one consideration. Another had been proximity to German-speaking humans.

It was Har who had scouted the Shenandoah and found it ideal. Through a series of jumps, the colonists had just transported into a spacious cavern within the mountain when the Tatzelwurm attacked.

"Among the creatures we hunt, it has one of the strongest attractions to magecraft," Har explained. "It consumes magical energy, which strengthens its armor and venom. It could not breach our Shimmer wall by brute force alone, to be sure, but as it continued to draw magic from the door, it may eventually have broken through."

"It was a brave thing you did, Peter, attacking the Tatzelwurm with nothing but a knife and your bare hands," Virginal stated. "Even Folk of great power would not be so bold."

Peter shook his head sheepishly. "I think my Hannah would use a less complimentary word. I didn't know what I was getting myself into."

"True enough," said Har, getting up and motioning Peter to follow. "Look over here where you dodged the Tatzelwurm's venom."

Peter saw the cardinal flowers that had been behind him during the monster's attack. The previously green leaves were now brown and shriveled. The previously red blossoms were dried and blackened, as if dropped into a roaring fire. Peter shuddered at the thought of what would have happened if the beast's venomous breath had struck him in the face.

Virginal came up beside them.

"I have heard stories of rare humans who possess such rich imaginations and keen insight that they are immune to spellsong," she said. "You, Peter Muhlenberg, appear to be one of them."

"I suppose so," he replied, "although I never thought of myself as special. To be honest, I've usually distinguished myself from other people by getting into trouble."

"You may have succeeded at that again," Virginal said with a laugh. "What are we to do with you?"

Har looked first at the Dwarf queen, then at Peter, and spoke up.

"Your Majesty, I think we can trust him," Har said. "He proved his courage against the Tatzelwurm. He has earned the chance to prove himself."

Virginal considered the matter. "The stories do tell us that, in some cases, humans gifted with the Sight became trusted friends to the Folk. But I have never met one before. Are you such a human?"

Peter turned, looked out over the Shenandoah, and thought of his father, the most learned man Peter had ever known. Doctor Muhlenberg was a scholar, a leader, an innovator. He had sacrificed to come to America and build the Lutheran Church here. Father had hoped and prayed that his sons would become part of his great mission. Peter had answered that call.

Now he faced a different challenge, a different call to action that would require faith and perseverance. The Dwarfs had immigrated to this valley, too. They would build a new life here. They would hunt for food, and remove monstrous threats to both communities. They would, inevitably, come into contact with the human settlers. It was up to Peter to keep that contact as friendly, and as limited, as it could be.

He turned back to the Dwarfs.

"I am a minister of the Faith," he began, "and I look to Scripture to grant me comfort and wisdom. One of those verses is from the Book of Colossians: *For by Him were all things created, that are in heaven, and that are in earth, visible and invisible, whether they be thrones, or dominions, or principalities, or powers: all things were created by Him, and for Him.*"

Virginal and Har exchanged meaningful glances. Then the Dwarf queen directed a brief nod to Peter, wheeled, and started issuing orders to the two mages sustaining the Shimmer wall.

"Until we meet again, Reverend Muhlenberg," said Har, shaking Peter's hand.

A moment later, the four Dwarfs vanished.

Peter stood for a moment, staring at the empty space they'd vacated. *This mountain had, indeed, become a refuge.*

Chapter 9 — The Courage Song

March 1774

AS HIS CATTLE GRAZED ON tall grasses and took leisurely drinks, Isaac Shelby looked at a small, forested island in the middle of the river and imagined he was taking a leisurely drink of his own — a drink of black coffee.

On this brisk day, he'd have welcomed hot coffee. But such comforts would have to wait. Isaac had driven his cattle eight miles from Shelby Station that morning to feed and drink along the South Holston River. It took longer than he expected. He'd be lucky to get home by nightfall.

Coffee beans had been a recent addition to the Shelby store, and something Isaac had enjoyed learning how to brew. It proved to be a profitable new skill. Many of those who frequented the store had grown up drinking tea. But that was before all the trouble.

First, the British Parliament had imposed a host of taxes. To quell the resulting uproar, Parliament had repealed all the hated taxes — except the tax on tea, left in place to make a point. Then Britain had aggravated the situation by passing the Tea Act. American colonists saw it as another interference in their affairs. So, a few months ago, a group of protestors in Boston had stormed cargo ships and thrown chests of tea into the harbor.

When Americans heard what happened, they expressed their solidarity with the Bostonians by boycotting tea. Some started drinking coffee instead. Among them were the Shelbys of Shelby Station. Thinking about the Boston protest prompted Isaac to recall the chorus to "The Liberty Song," one of his favorites:

In Freedom we're born and in Freedom we'll live.
Our purses are ready. Steady, friends, steady;
Not as slaves, but as Freemen our money we'll give.

Isaac had first read those words in the *Maryland Gazette* in 1769, back when the Shelbys lived in Maryland. Even as a boy, Isaac had read every newspaper he could get his hands on. He loved to learn — about commerce, farming, politics. After the family relocated to its frontier settlement on the Holston River, however, reading material got a lot scarcer.

Occasionally, a visitor would share an old copy of the *Pennsylvania Journal*, the *Virginia Gazette*, or the *Cape Fear Mercury*. But, for the most part, Isaac had to make do with two books his grandparents, the elder Evan Shelby and wife Kate, had brought over from Wales. One was *Robinson Crusoe* by Daniel Dafoe. The other was *The History of Tom Thumb* by Richard Johnson.

Isaac had read them so many times he could quote them extensively by heart. Living on the frontier, Isaac had strongly identified with Robinson Crusoe. But, to his surprise, he had also thoroughly enjoyed the tales of Tom Thumb. They were utterly ridiculous, of course. Nothing practical in them. Yet, somehow, the adventures of the diminutive man in the courts of King Arthur, the Fairy Queen, and the King of the Pygmies had always delighted Isaac. *Perhaps it's the Welsh in me*, he thought, recalling the strange legends his Nana Kate used to tell him in her thick Welsh accent.

A loud noise jolted Isaac out of his reminiscences. Then he heard several more.

The sounds were coming from the cattle. As Isaac looked their way, two cows began to edge from the water while a third, standing on the riverbank, continued to snort and grunt. Fearing the cows might have run across a venomous copperhead or water moccasin, Isaac grabbed his father's old fowling gun and ran to the water's edge.

Something had, indeed, spooked the cattle. Isaac could see a form lying on the soft mud. But it wasn't a snake. Isaac stopped and stared. It didn't look like anything he'd ever seen before.

It was blue. It was small. And it was a woman.

At first, Isaac thought it might be a child's doll. But when he stooped over to get a clearer look, he saw that it was too finely detailed. The face was beautifully molded, the tiny hands and feet perfectly shaped. The pale blue skin shone in the afternoon sun. The figure was clothed in a short gown of darker blue, fringed with shapes that looked like the fronds of riverweeds. Its mass of long, wavy hair matched the color of its gown and covered one of its curiously pointed ears. Around the neck hung a string of dark, tightly fitted shells.

The only explanation Isaac could think of was that he was looking at a decorative figure of porcelain — something that belonged on a fine table in Philadelphia or Baltimore. How it got all the way over the mountains and into this remote stream was a complete mystery. But no matter. Isaac decided he'd take it home to see if his mother or sisters could find some use for it.

Then it coughed.

Isaac Shelby was a sober, sensible man of twenty-four. He was no fool.

This is a prank, he thought.

Perhaps a concealed trickster was pulling a string to make the doll jerk. Isaac turned all the way around, searching in vain for a hiding place big enough for one of his brothers, or for his friend John Sevier. Then he turned back to the doll. It was motionless.

Was it my eyes that played the trick on me?

No. The tiny woman coughed again and spit up, her motions making her shell necklace rattle.

Isaac was forced to accept the fact that he was looking at a living being. He was also looking at someone in great distress. Kneeling in the mud, he reached carefully beneath the little creature and turned her on her side facing away from him, using two fingers to thump and rub her back. She coughed once more, spitting up water in shuddering heaves.

Only after she was on her side did Isaac see a knob on the back of her right thigh. Closer examination revealed the wooden nock and fletching of an arrow. The point must have passed all the way through her leg and broken off. Isaac realized the arrow fragment had to come out if the creature was to survive. But, if he yanked it out now, lacking any way to staunch the bleeding and cleanse the wound, she would also die.

There was but a single choice. Isaac removed the handkerchief from his neck and wrapped the blue creature in it. He'd take her to Shelby Station.

▲▲▲

Her shiny, strangely hued skin marked quite a contrast to the palette of dry yellow straw as the blue woman slept in the Shelby stable. Isaac was no surgeon, but he'd had years of experience tending to injured cattle and horses. The strip of cloth binding her leg wound was clean and tight. When

Isaac arrived home, late in the evening, he managed to hide his wrapped bundle under a coat until he could get her into the stable. Then he rushed to the store for supplies. Now Isaac was standing guard to make sure the strange creature wasn't discovered. He was lucky most of his family was away visiting Jacob Brown's farm on the Nolichucky River.

As he stood over her, Isaac tried not to stare. He failed. So when the blue woman abruptly turned over to face him, Isaac was unprepared and embarrassed. Her big blue-green eyes, which turned up at the corners, stared back at his big brown ones, which drooped down at the corners.

After what seemed like a long while, she blinked, smiled, and spoke softly in what Isaac immediately recognized as Welsh, although he knew too little of it to get her meaning.

"I don't understand," Isaac said, shaking his head.

She smiled again and nodded. Then her eyes and mouth suddenly widened in alarm.

"The village!" she exclaimed.

"Calm yourself," Isaac said, trying not to show that her fluency in English surprised him. "There's no village here. You're at Shelby Station. I'm Isaac Shelby."

"No," she insisted, "*my* village! How far are we from the island? I must find them!"

She tried to sit up but then winced, arching her back in pain and clutching her thigh.

"If you don't lie still, you'll reopen the wound," Isaac said, trying to be stern even as his curiosity grew by leaps and bounds. She relaxed and lay back on the straw, nodding her assent.

Isaac managed a reassuring grin. "I'll try to answer your questions if you promise not to do that again."

She opened her mouth as if to argue the point, then closed her eyes and gave another nod.

"Dela," she said quietly.

"I don't recognize that word," Isaac admitted. "Is Dela the name of your village? The name of your people?"

"It is the name of *me*," she said, her eyes softening in amusement. "In Wales, my people are called the Gwragedd Annwn. The English call us Water Maidens."

Now it was Isaac's turn to be amused. "That's as good a name as any. If my daddy came home and asked what I had in the stable, I'd probably say something like 'a water maiden.'"

"We are not all maidens, naturally," Dela said wryly. "But among my Folk, most with the talent for ranging happen to be female. So, when humans remember us at all, they remember us as maidens."

"A 'talent for ranging,'" Isaac repeated. "What do you mean by that?"

Dela sighed. "It would take a long time to tell you, Isaac of Shelby Station, and I am not at all sure you would understand even after the telling."

Isaac looked down at her sternly. "You're not going anywhere. And neither am I, not for a long stretch of time. We might as well make practical use of it."

▲▲▲▲

The Shelbys returned home the following afternoon to find Isaac loading a small shoulder sack with provisions. "Where are you off to, son?" asked Captain Shelby, setting his rifle against the door and wiping his hands on the tail of his hunting shirt. "Mam and the girls will be cooking bacon and beans before long."

"Can't stay," said Isaac. "When I took the herd south a couple of days ago to graze, I got distracted and left something behind at the river. I better go back and get it."

"Left something behind, eh?" his father said with a puzzled look. "That's not like you, Isaac. What's so important it can't wait until tomorrow?"

Isaac averted his eyes for a moment, then met Captain Shelby's gaze. "I left the fowling gun. One of the cows saw a copperhead and I got to chasing it down the river…"

"Well, then," the older man said matter of factly, "I guess we'll just see you later."

It wasn't until about a mile from home that Isaac felt it safe to open the sack and let Dela peek out. Although still weak, the Water Maiden was nevertheless more alert and able than Isaac would have thought possible. Much as the practically minded Isaac Shelby found it hard to believe Dela's talk of fairies and magic, he couldn't argue with the simple truth that her rapid recovery should have been impossible.

Not to mention the fact that she had blue skin, blue hair, and — as he had discovered to his shock — blue blood.

"So, *that* was Evan Shelby," said Dela as they continued on the path. "I heard some of the other settlers talking about your father while I was scouting locations for our village. The talk made him seem like a very big man. It was hard to see through the sack but, next to you, he didn't look that big."

"Daddy *is* a big man around these parts," Isaac replied, "big in what makes a man important. He was a hero during the war. He's the bravest man I've ever known."

Dela looked at her new friend with kind eyes. "No doubt he *is* brave, Isaac. I just meant that you are taller. Perhaps you will prove to be braver, too."

Without realizing it, Dela had touched a sore subject.

Would I be brave? Isaac wasn't convinced. He was certainly no weakling. Isaac was heavy-set, as were all the Shelby men, and had spent much of his life outdoors. He'd even been a teenaged deputy sheriff back in Maryland. But he'd never had to do what Captain Shelby did during the war. He'd never been in battle. He'd never had to kill another man.

Isaac felt Dela's eyes on him — those big, blue-green eyes turned up at the corners and set between two pointed blue ears. He blushed and tried to think of a way to change the subject. No way occurred to him in time.

"I always thought I could be brave when I had to be," Dela said, startling Isaac with the notion that perhaps she had read his thoughts. "But I failed the test. I ran."

"Is that how you were shot in the leg?" Isaac asked — then instantly regretted it.

"Yes," Dela replied, her face showing no sign of offense. "Remember when I told you how my Folk came to be ambushed at the island? My mission was to find our new home. I spent weeks exploring up and down the river you call the South Holston. I was sure the place you found me was the right spot to build our village. I was sure it was safe. I was wrong."

"You did the best you could…" Isaac began.

"My best fell short," Dela interjected. "The Pukwudgie ranger must have tracked me for a long time. I never realized it. He let me think the island was safe. He let me call my Folk."

"And all the while, he was planning an ambush," Isaac said gravely.

"How many Pukwudgie warriors were there?"

"More than I had time to count. My Folk were not outnumbered, and we are excellent fighters with trident and net. But we expected no army to be waiting for us in the caverns under the island. We were unready. We paid a great price."

Isaac saw Dela shudder uncontrollably. "How…how many?" he asked hesitantly.

"More of *them* than I had time to count, too. I saw one of my best friends fall with a spear through her heart. I saw my brother go down under the weight of three Pukwudgie warriors. I saw — and then I ran."

"So you didn't fight?" Isaac asked, trying to imagine himself in the same situation.

"No, I managed to stab one of the warriors," Dela responded. "But when he fell, I lost hold of my trident. That is when I ran."

"You were unarmed! What were you supposed to do?"

"Fight on with my bare hands, if necessary," she said. "Fight on alongside my family and friends."

Isaac shook his head. "From what you've told me, you are a scout, not a soldier. It was your responsibility to survive and find a safe place for your people. Most of them can't survive in the human world, right? By saving yourself, you were doing your duty."

"And getting myself shot by one of those Pukwudgie spear-throwers, anyway," Dela said bitterly. "Folk time may pass much more slowly than human time, Isaac. But by my getting wounded and having you carry me off, I may have lost my chance to save my people."

Isaac said nothing, but he quickened his pace.

"That Pukwudgie scout knew it all along," Dela went on. "After he shot me, he taunted me. 'You could not escape my sting, just as your Folk cannot escape the fate they earned when they invaded our river.'"

"What did you say his name was, again?"

"He called himself Atta," Dela recalled with another shudder. "Atta Yellow Jacket."

After racing through the forest in silence for more than an hour, Isaac was forced to stop for a rest. As he sat underneath a red oak tree, he heard Dela's voice again. But what came from the sack was not another explanation, or story, or question, or regret.

It was a song.

Isaac didn't have much experience with music other than a few Presbyterian hymns. Even that "Liberty Song" Isaac liked so much had been only words on a page. He'd never heard anyone sing it.

Isaac had, in truth, never heard anyone make any sound so hauntingly beautiful as the one Dela was making. The song was in a language he didn't know. But without knowing why, and soon enough without caring, Isaac found that the song spoke to him.

It spoke of long journeys. It spoke of toil, and privation, and danger. It spoke of tridents bristling from tight formations of warriors, of armor hot and heavy under a summer sun, of arrows filling the sky and the fallen filling the ground. It spoke of enemies in ranks of bronze. But it spoke of other enemies, too: of giants and dragons and other monsters. It spoke of pain. It spoke of terror. It spoke of hopelessness, of loneliness.

But then that song, that hauntingly beautiful song of the Water Maiden, spoke something different to Isaac. It spoke of love, of friendship, of loyalty. It spoke of underground caverns and underwater channels. It spoke of hours drilling with trident, net, and sword, of hours sewing scale mail and fletching arrows, of heated rods of metal pounded on anvils and supple rods of yew bent back to form longbows. It spoke of barked commands, meant to be obeyed, and sage counsel, meant to be trusted. It spoke of honor, of perseverance, of victory.

Most of all, the song spoke of courage. It spoke its words of courage to Isaac. And, he fancied, it also spoke its words of courage to its singer, to Dela.

After what seemed like an eternity, Isaac realized Dela had stopped singing. He found he had no words to offer in response. They would have felt wholly inadequate. And so Isaac and Dela continued their dash to the Holston.

A couple of hours later, they reached the very spot where he'd rescued Dela. He lay the sack on the ground. Dela crawled out, rose unsteadily to her feet, and stretched.

"I must go there," she pointed to the forested island. "I must find out if the battle still rages. If not, I must find where my people have gone."

"How can I help?" Isaac asked. "What would you have me do?"

"You have done more than enough, Isaac Shelby," Dela said, walking forward and putting a small blue hand against his leg. "Where I go, you cannot follow."

"I can wait here until you return," Isaac insisted.

"Have you forgotten so soon what I told you about the Shimmer and the Blur? Once I enter the cavern, I could be in there for days or weeks of your time and, if the battle still rages, I may never return at all."

Isaac gazed down at her and nodded grudgingly. "I suppose you're right. I'll go back home. But, if you need me, now you know where to find me."

"I do, Isaac," said Dela deliberately, "and now I must know something else."

Then she sang. Once again, Isaac didn't recognize the words. But images, jumbled and indistinct, flashed across his mind. He saw Shelby Station. He saw himself driving the herd to the river, cows bellowing, a snake at the water's edge, aiming his gun at it. He saw a leisurely walk home. He felt himself enjoy a comfortable, untroubled sleep.

Confused, Isaac focused his eyes back on Dela and asked, "What's happening to me? Why am I daydreaming?"

The Water Maiden returned his gaze, stopped singing, and smiled.

"I suspected as much," she stated. "You have the Sight. Memory and concealment spells have little power over you. We learn about the Sight during our training, but only in a theoretical sense. I have never met a human with it, nor has anyone since the time my grandmother ranged."

"Your grandmother?"

"Her name is Nimue," Dela said, "but that is a story for another day. I must go. Thank you, Isaac, for all your assistance. Someday, I hope to repay your kindness."

Isaac felt tongue-tied and decided it might be best simply to bow. When he raised his head, the Water Maiden was gone.

▲▲▲

When Isaac got home that evening, a stranger was waiting at the store. The newcomer brought a recent edition of the *Maryland Gazette*. That was how Isaac learned the latest about the Indian troubles. That was how he learned the latest about Daniel Boone.

When Isaac first met Daniel at Shelby Station years earlier, the bold hunter had vowed to return to Kentucky in force. That's exactly what Daniel had done. The Boones and other families had set off to found the first permanent settlement in Kentucky under the terms of treaties signed with the Iroquois and Cherokees. But the Shawnees didn't consider themselves bound by treaties they didn't sign. They'd decided to make an example of the Boone expedition.

In October, Daniel's sixteen-year-old son James and several other settlers were moving supplies when they were ambushed by a war party. The Shawnees had tortured and killed James Boone.

The outrage was clearly meant to scare the whites away. But the instant Isaac read that awful story in the *Maryland Gazette*, he knew the Boone murder would bring war — and that he, Isaac Shelby, would be among those called to wage it.

▲▲▲

Almost exactly seven months later, in October 1774, Lieutenant Isaac Shelby sat with his father, Captain Evan Shelby, and several of their Holston River neighbors. Surrounding them were hundreds of other militiamen, their campfires dotting a high, triangular meadow at the convergence of the Ohio and Kanawha Rivers on the far western frontier of Virginia. The plan was to meet up with another militia column led by Lord Dunmore, the royal governor, so they could smash Shawnee Chief Cornstalk and his warriors once and for all.

But Lord Dunmore wasn't there when the Shelbys and the other militia arrived at the bluffs. And some of the most experienced Indian fighters, including Isaac's father, doubted the wisdom of Dunmore's plan. "Cornstalk is no young sapling we can fell with a single stroke," Captain Shelby told the others. "He'll be on the move. He'll already know about Lord Dunmore."

"*Lord* Dunmore," snorted Isaac's friend John Sevier. "I'd wager there's more going on here than meets the eye."

"What do you mean?" Isaac asked.

"I mean the royal governor is more interested in keeping us in line than he is in protecting us from the Indians," Sevier said.

"I have no love for Dunmore," Captain Shelby began, "but I can't believe..."

Before he got a chance to finish his sentence, a gunshot rang out, followed by shouts of alarm and the sound of running feet. The Shelbys leapt up just as a militiaman hurtled into the light of their campfire. Isaac recognized Valentine Sevier, John's brother.

"The Indians are upon us!" the newcomer cried. "To arms, to arms!"

Isaac snatched up his rifle and hat. Others grabbed their own equipment, checked the flints on their guns, slipped on coats, or took final swigs from their canteens.

"Get up, you young dogs, and follow me!" Captain Shelby yelled as he took off running. The rest of the company hurried after him, some hooting and hollering with abandon.

Isaac couldn't see anything through the early morning fog that hugged the high meadow between the two rivers. Then, all at once, the fog turned orange and Isaac heard the roar of musket fire. At the front of the Virginia line, he saw a red-coated officer jerk, double over, and fall. Other militiamen fell, too. Isaac saw a man kneel down to fire — and then scream as his rifle, and the hand holding it, exploded in a burst of shot and splinters. The blast of guns, the shouts of fighters, and the groans of wounded men formed a continuous din so loud and horrifying that Isaac imagined it would cause even the stoutest heart to shudder. He found he could scarcely hear anything else.

The exception — the glorious, welcome exception — was the sound of his father barking commands. "Keep it at, fellows!" Captain Shelby would say, or "Close the gap!" or "That's it — answer with fire!" Even as Isaac fired and reloaded his own gun, he saw two more officers get hit. One stumbled past Isaac toward the rear, bleeding from the chest and holding his mangled left arm with his right. The other officer took a musket blast to the head and never moved again.

That left Captain Shelby as the last officer standing. Isaac's heart leapt as his father ran from side to side, shouting words of encouragement and urging fresh troops forward. "Cover the flanks!" he ordered, and the men expanded their battle line so that it stretched all the way from the Ohio to the Kanawha. Through the fog, Isaac was able to glimpse Indians rushing forward along each of the rivers, clubs and tomahawks in hand, clearly intending to surround and attack the company. Captain Shelby's order to cover the flanks had come just in time.

Isaac felt pride swell in him. "Daddy *is* a big man — a very big man!" he said out loud, then thought of Dela.

Hours passed as the battle intensified. The fog lifted a bit but was replaced by massive clouds of obscuring smoke. As the afternoon wore on, the gunfire turned sporadic. Virginian and Indian alike resorted to hand-to-hand fighting. Isaac saw militiamen use gun butts, tomahawks, hunting knives, and bare fists against Indians doing the same. Wave after wave of warriors attacked the militia line, only to be rebuffed.

As the sun dipped low on the horizon, the enemy tried another frontal assault. Isaac was now closer to the action and could see into the mass of Indians for the first time. Among them was a tall, lean-faced man with colorful feathers thrusting high above his head. The man was shouting orders and directing warriors to fill gaps in the attack line as the occasional Indian fell to American gunfire. Isaac guessed it must be the Shawnee leader Cornstalk, and he marveled at how much the chief reminded him of Captain Shelby — not in stature, dress, or color, of course, but in bearing.

Firing his rifle into the approaching Indians, Isaac turned it around and brandished it like a club, looking over at his father and hoping he could draw enough bravery from the sight to propel him into the melee.

Then Captain Shelby turned and saw Isaac looking back at him. "Isaac! Hurry to me!"

Isaac reversed his grip on the rifle and cleared the space between them with a few large bounds.

"We're in a tight spot, and most of the officers are done for," his father said quickly. "Consider yourself promoted to captain."

Isaac gulped.

"Here's what we need you to do. Take those men" — he indicated three militia companies standing at the bluff overlooking the Kanawha — "and find a way to get around the Indians. They tried to outflank us. Now let's outflank them."

Isaac dashed to comply. When he reached the militia, Isaac cupped his hand over his eyes and looked down the steep bank into the river. "It's not too deep down there," he told the other soldiers and captains. "Let's stay in the water as long as we can."

The men worked their way down the slope and stepped waist-deep into the Kanawha. They crouched low, using the high riverbank as cover while they waded slowly forward. Isaac felt himself shiver, and not just because of the cold water. For the first time that day, his father was entirely out of his sight. Even surrounded by dozens of other men, Isaac felt alone.

Can I really lead these men into battle, perhaps to their deaths?

Isaac again thought of Dela. He thought of the courage song. Slowly, haltingly, he tried to hum the melody. He recalled the first part, then his memory failed him. He started over. And stopped again, frustrated and anxious as he and the other men continued sloshing up the cold river.

Then, in a sudden flash of insight, it came to him. He began to hum, seeking the song's power, caressing each note. It surrounded him. It filled his senses. He imagined he could *see* the song, *feel* it, even *taste* it. His breaths seemed to rise and fall with the rhythm, each beat punctuated by something that sounded like a rattle.

As before, the song painted a series of mental images — only this time, he saw not rows of bronze-tipped tridents but of iron guns. He saw the laughing face of his friend John Sevier, long and angular rather than round and broad like Isaac's. He saw his father's face, also round and broad, smiling with pride.

Isaac cast sideways glances at the other men. He'd imagined he was singing so loudly that everyone, even the faraway Shawnees, could hear him. But no one looked his way. All seemed fixated on the task ahead. And all seemed willing to trust their young captain to see them through.

Presently they reached a little creek branching up and to the left. They followed it. Once they had passed entirely behind the mass of attacking Indians, Isaac stopped humming. Motioning his men to follow, Isaac stepped cautiously out of the creek and up a small ridge.

He needn't have tried to be stealthy. The fog was so much thicker here, and the din of battle still so loud, that the Shawnees didn't notice the militiamen until most had emerged and formed ranks.

"Fire!" Isaac Shelby commanded. The men obeyed.

"Puckeshinwau!" shouted several Indians in horror as a broad-shoul-dered, brightly painted man in the front rank toppled to the ground with multiple wounds. The Virginians' first volley had torn a ragged hole through the warriors. Those who escaped unscathed were reeling from shock. Behind them, however, Isaac could see hundreds of other brightly painted bodies — fierce, experienced men armed with muskets capable of spraying multiple colonists with devastating blasts of ball and shot. Isaac knew his men were exposed and outnumbered, but he also knew their task was important. He was determined to exact a price for every man he lost.

Isaac Shelby found his courage that day on the Kanawha. He would never lose it.

As he considered how to deploy his men for the expected Shawnee charge, Isaac was astonished to see their foes begin to back away, stoop-ing to pick up dead or wounded comrades as they withdrew, including the groaning Puckeshinwau. The Shawnees showed no panic. They retreated in good order. Some continued to fire their guns or to fend off attacks by small groups of pursuing Americans. Fearing a trap, Isaac ordered the company to form up and march deliberately forward rather than scampering after their apparently defeated foes.

As the last Indians swam or floated across the Ohio River in the fading light, Isaac ordered an end to the pursuit. His men were spent. Many were aching or bleeding with wounds. The rest of the column advanced to meet them. Isaac was relieved to see his friend John Sevier and other unwounded friends running forward. Isaac saw his father striding behind them, pride evident on his smoke-smeared face.

Out of the corner of his eye, Isaac thought he saw a small figure, lithe and blue, land with a splash on the surface of the Kanawha and begin swim-ming rapidly and gracefully upriver. But it was nearly dark, and Isaac was exhausted. He couldn't say for sure it wasn't his imagination.

Chapter 10 — The Shoals

March 1775

NANYEHI HAD SEEN DANIEL BOONE'S face many times before. She'd seen it first on that day, nearly fourteen years ago, when they first met on the mountain overlooking Long Island-on-the-Holston and faced the perils of the giant Stoneclad together. Since then, she and Daniel had repeatedly encountered each other as he hunted or visited friends and she traveled the frontier with her Nunnehi friend, Tana.

On the previous occasions Nanyehi had seen Daniel's face, it had made her smile. In fact, she'd watched him have that effect on nearly everyone he met. Daniel had spent his life doing what he loved. It was a message his joyful face had been able to communicate across gaps of distance, language, and culture. It had been an infectious joy.

It was absent from Daniel's face this day. As Nanyehi, her daughter Betsy, and other companions from Chota walked through the cane field toward Daniel, who was standing beneath a massive sycamore tree, she could see clearly what lay behind his brave smile. She could see sorrow in his eyes. She could see weariness in his hollow cheeks. She could see grim determination in his clinched jaw.

Nanyehi turned her head slightly and looked down at Tana Song Snake, walking with the Chota party but unnoticed because of her magical conceal-ment. Tana returned her gaze and nodded gravely. She had read the same signs on Daniel's face. Nanyehi pulled her shawl of white swan feathers tighter over her shoulders, though it wasn't only the late winter wind that made her shudder.

Daniel was standing not far from the cabin where the whites were displaying their trade goods for inspection. As the rest of the Chota party headed for the cabin, Nanyehi turned to her daughter. "You go on with the others. I'm going to talk to my friend."

"That is Daniel Boone, right?" Betsy asked. "I would like to meet him."

"You will, Little Doe," Nanyehi replied. "But not now. I will catch up in a little bit."

As Betsy moved reluctantly away, Nanyehi resumed her walk, Tana at her side, and discovered that Daniel had been joined by another white man. While Daniel was lean and wiry, the other, younger man was round and heavy-set. While Daniel was dressed in his familiar buckskins and stiff beaver hat, the other wore a long hunting shirt, cloth breeches, hard leather shoes, and a floppy hat. While the pain Nanyehi could see in Daniel's expressive eyes made her wince in sympathy, the other man's large eyes, turned downward at each corner, gave him an analytical look.

"Daniel, it pleases me to see you again," Nanyehi said, letting go of the shawl to offer him greeting.

"You're a sight for sore eyes," Daniel replied, brightening noticeably as he took her hand and then directed a subtle nod down at Tana. "Beloved Woman Nanyehi, meet my friend Isaac Shelby."

"It's a pleasure, ma'am," Isaac said. His manner was courteous but she saw his appraising eyes flick from her to Daniel and then all around the ground beneath the sycamore tree. It made her feel uneasy. But she had a higher priority.

"I was so sorry to hear about your son James," said Nanyehi, still holding Daniel's hand.

"Thank you kindly," he answered. "It's been more than a year, but it still feels like a fresh wound."

As she and Daniel stood together in quiet reverence for a moment, Isaac continued to glance around in a way that heightened her unease. Presently, the young man broke the silence.

"Is that some kind of title, 'Beloved Woman'?" Isaac asked.

"Yes, Mr. Shelby, it is," said Nanyehi, opting for friendliness over wariness, "but feel free to call me Nancy Ward. Most whites do. Daniel is an old friend and honors me by pronouncing my given name."

She smiled conspiratorially at Daniel, who seemed genuinely delighted.

"Among the Cherokee, our names help tell the stories of our lives," she explained. "As our stories change, so do our names. For example, you have probably heard of my uncle Attakullakulla."

Isaac, who had just then been looking searchingly at Daniel, answered with a quick nod.

"His name is widely understood to mean 'Little Carpenter,'" she continued, "which the whites consider a fitting description, both because he is a short man and because he is skilled at building. At building trust. But, among the Cherokee, his name is pronounced Adagalkala, which means 'Leaning Stick.' And, as a boy, he was Okoonaka, or 'White Owl.' Sometimes I still call him that, and it makes him chuckle."

Isaac had now turned his full attention back to her. "I must have made my Mam chuckle right from the start," he said, again mixing pleasant-sounding words with a calculating expression. "My name comes from the Bible. It means 'one who laughs.'"

Nanyehi willed herself to smile along with Daniel, although she continued to wonder what this crafty Isaac Shelby might be up to. *What is this man looking for? Why do I feel like I am being judged?*

"Nan-ye-hi," Isaac said slowly, pronouncing her name well for a first time. "You haven't yet explained what your name means."

She glanced at Daniel, who gave a subtle shrug.

"It is a name I earned in childhood. There is a Cherokee story about a spirit people we call the Nunnehi. They are 'those who travel anywhere.' When I was a child, I liked to go alone among the trees and imagine I was walking and talking with the Nunnehi. My mother found my tales endearing and decided I must be a 'traveler,' as well."

Isaac's face suddenly beamed with a triumphant expression.

"As a boy," he said excitedly, "I pretended I could talk to little people, too, although my inspiration came from an old story book about Tom Thumb. But I take it you didn't need to use your imagination at all. You had something better. You had someone like her."

Isaac was pointing directly at Tana, who started suddenly as Daniel and Nanyehi looked on, mouths wide open in surprise.

▲▲▲

The three humans and the fairy sat underneath the sycamore tree for the better part of an hour, swapping stories. Daniel spoke of Goran, the Sylphs, and his conflict with the Pukwudgie scout Atta in Kentucky. Nanyehi and

Tana spoke of the Nunnehi of Blood Mountain, the Yunwi Tsunsdi, and the other Folk of the Cherokee lands. And Isaac told them about his encounter with the Water Maiden.

"I have never seen the blue-skins before," Tana said, running her fingers up and down her blowpipe absent-mindedly. "But another scout reported that he caught a glimpse of one at Long Island-on-the-Holston. I wonder if it was your Dela."

"I'd like to think so," Isaac said. "She told me that the Gwragedd Annwn prefer to create their underground villages on islands. Perhaps enough survived that they were able to build a new home there."

"The part about the Pukwudgies concerns me," Tana said. "They haven't ventured so far south in many years. The Holston Valley lies within the territory of the Cherokee, not the Shawnee or Lenape."

Isaac looked first at her and then at Nanyehi. "There are white settlers living on these lands south of the Holston, along the Nolichucky and the Watauga. Many are friends of mine: John Sevier, John Carter, the Browns, the Robertsons. When they settled, they thought they were building on lands opened by treaty. When they found out they were wrong, they came to the Cherokees and paid generously to lease the land."

"It was my uncle Attakullakulla who struck that agreement," Nanyehi said. "He said it was 'but a little spot of ground' and that he pitied the plight your friends had gotten themselves into. But not all of our leaders agreed. And not all have come here today, to Sycamore Shoals, to help Attakullakulla make yet another peace with the Long Knives. His son Dragging Canoe, my cousin, is one who believes we should drive all the white settlers out."

"And what do you think, Nanyehi?" said Daniel, a determined look returning to his face. "The words of a War Woman and Beloved Woman carry great weight."

Nanyehi sighed. "I feel like a river flowing between two steep banks. I share Dragging Canoe's frustration with selling territory to the settlers. How are we to preserve our people without preserving our lands? But I also share the desire for peace that drives my uncle. Every year brings more settlers. Every year brings more Long Knives to the frontier. We are a powerful nation with powerful allies" — Nanyehi and Tana shared a meaningful look — "but I fear another war would win us only devastation."

Isaac had followed Nanyehi's gaze to Tana and appeared to guess something of its import. "You told me earlier that Beloved Woman was a title. Now Daniel has used another title, War Woman. What do your titles mean?"

"I can tell you how Nanyehi became a War Woman — because I was there, and her modesty would leave you guessing," Tana said, shrugging off Nanyehi's attempted protest.

"It was the year 1755 on your calendar," the fairy related. "For many years, the Cherokee had been warring with the Creeks. War Chief Oconostota led some five hundred Cherokee warriors into battle against a much larger force of Creeks at Taliwa, on the Etowah River."

"My first husband Kingfisher was one of those warriors," Nanyehi broke in. "He was my first love."

And Bryan Ward my second, although we both knew he would not stay long among the Cherokee. As her thoughts wandered a different path, one of joy and of heartbreak, the others waited impatiently for her story to continue.

"So Kingfisher went off to war…" Tana prompted.

"…And I resolved to go with him," Nanyehi continued, flashing her friend an appreciative smile. "I loaded rifles and brought water to the wounded. When Kingfisher made me take safety behind a log, I took out a pouch of his musket balls and chewed on them to make their edges rough and dangerous to the Creek invaders."

Isaac looked both fascinated and horrified.

"Then I saw Kingfisher's breast explode as a Creek musket ball hit him," Nanyehi said. "I saw him die." The memory of her loss made her shudder, and she couldn't help but look over sympathetically at Daniel.

"And so," Tana continued the story, "Nanyehi picked up Kingfisher's rifle and fired back at the enemy. 'Rise, warriors, and avenge Kingfisher!' she cried. 'Rise and find victory!' That was when the tide of the battle turned. The defeated Creeks withdrew south of the Chattahoochee River. In gratitude, her people named her War Woman, for bravery in battle, and Beloved Woman, for her sage counsel."

Daniel had heard the story from Nanyehi before, but now gave Tana a questioning look. "You say you were there at Taliwa," he said. "I never knew that. Is that how you two met?"

Tana shook her head.

"Nanyehi and I have been friends for most of her life. It was I she met and talked with in the woods when she was a little girl. I had never encountered a human being who could resist my songs of concealment and memory. I was fascinated. She could resist me but, I found, I could *not* resist her." The memory brought smiles to the faces of both women.

"And so you went off to war with Nanyehi and her husband?" Isaac asked.

"No, we Nunnehi try to stay out of the wars of human beings. I was at Taliwa for a completely different reason — as a prisoner."

By this time, Daniel and Isaac had both become mesmerized by the tale.

"My captors were two scouts from Folk living in the forest near Augusta," Tana explained. "I believe you call them Elves. I ran into them while hunting a Stoneclad. I tried to escape but the Elves overpowered me. They were taking me back to their village when we happened on the battle at Taliwa. They had never seen Indians fight before and decided to observe. They had not counted on one of the humans seeing them."

"Nanyehi," breathed Daniel.

"I was exhausted from the battle, and almost out of ammunition," Nanyehi said. "But, as I walked back to camp, I saw Tana struggling with the Elves on the limb of an oak tree. She managed to break free for a moment, so I took aim and fired my last shot. I missed but the Elves fell from the limb, anyway. When I reached the tree, they were gone. Only Tana remained."

"And now you know why, Daniel, when Nanyehi travels from Chota, I seek always to be by her side," said Tana, once again gripping her blowpipe with clenched knuckles. "I owe her a debt I can never repay."

"You owe me nothing but your friendship, Song Snake," Nanyehi assured her. "But I am always grateful for the company."

Out of the corner of her eye, Nanyehi saw her daughter Betsy emerge from one of the cabins. "And now I think, Tana, that you and I best be going. There are many ears that must not hear talk such as ours."

"It was a distinct pleasure to meet you," Isaac said as they all rose, "to meet *both* of you."

"As it was to meet you, Isaac of Shelby Station," Nanyehi replied.

"Let's hope this conference brings peace to the frontier at last," Daniel said.

"I always cling to hope," Nanyehi answered as she turned to leave, "even when the slope is steep and the ledge is narrow."

▲▲▲

That night, after her daughter and most of the other Cherokees were asleep, Nanyehi slipped away from camp, crossed the cane field, and entered a dark forest. Tana, as always, fell in beside her. As the two women crossed a small creek, they heard wings flutter and a voice behind them. Both sounds were expected.

"Ho, there," said Goran the Sylph, circling the two women and alighting on a stump. "Thank you for meeting me."

"I think Daniel would be put out with me if he knew," Nanyehi scolded. "I honored your request for a private meeting, although I do not understand the reason."

Goran looked crestfallen. "I wish I could tell him, but duty requires it. My mission is sensitive, and involving Daniel in it could imperil both it and him."

"But you do not mind imperiling me, I take it?" Nanyehi asked, again with a scolding tone.

"Oh, it is not that," Goran insisted, sounding wounded by the accusation. "My task is to gather information about both the Cherokee and the Folk who live among them. I do not want Daniel to get mixed up in matters that might hurt his relations with both."

Tana eyed Goran dubiously.

"I consider us to be friends, Goran, and our Folk have never had reason for conflict," the fairy woman said. "But all this talk of secrecy and spying makes me suspicious. What would you have of us?"

Goran wiped his hands nervously on his forest-green cloak. "I value your friendship highly, Tana — and yours, too, Nanyehi. What I have been instructed to say is not intended to harm anyone, least of all you. In fact, I was sent to seek your help in keeping the peace."

Mystified, Nanyehi looked over at Tana and held up her hands questioningly. Tana signaled her own confusion with a shrug.

"As I told you when we first met," Goran began, "I am acting on the orders of King Briafael. He believes it is in the interest of peace to preserve British authority here. Britain has fought many wars with France and its allies. He believes another war would be even more costly."

"I agree," Nanyehi said. "But I seek to prevent another outbreak of war between my people and the settlers. Is your Sylph king truly concerned about that?"

"In a way, yes," Goran replied. "But his concerns extend further. The relationship between Britain and its colonies has deteriorated. Parliament thinks Americans have unreasonably refused to help pay the debts from the last war. The colonists think both Parliament and royal governors have abused their power. In North Carolina, where my Folk live, the conflict even erupted into armed rebellion."

"I know about the War of the Regulation, Goran," Nanyehi said. "Some Regulators who rose up in arms and were defeated chose to move over the mountains and settle here, along the Watauga and Nolichucky Rivers. Their presence is one of the reasons for this peace conference."

"Yes," Goran agreed, "I was here at Sycamore Shoals three years ago when John Carter, Jacob Brown, and the others created their Watauga Association. Later, I saw a letter from Lord Dunmore calling the association 'dangerous' because it was 'distinct from and independent of his majesty's authority.' My guildmasters said it was just the kind of event King Briafael had warned about — a break from tradition that might lead to large-scale war."

Tana still looked unconvinced. "I do not see what any of this has to do with the Cherokees or my Folk."

"My guild sent me here to find out what the Cherokees might do if there is a rebellion against British rule," Goran explained. "Would they side with King George or the colonists?"

Nanyehi crossed her arms in thought as both Goran and Tana watched expectantly. "That would depend on a great many things," said Nanyehi after a time. "Our people have long been divided. When it comes to relations with the settlers, there is a peace faction and a war faction. There are also some chiefs, such as my uncle Attakullakulla, who have long had friendly relations with the British while other chiefs still remember fondly the ties our people once had with the French in the north and the Spanish in the south."

"If you had to hazard a guess, though, what will the chiefs decide?" Goran pressed.

"I think most would try to remain neutral," Nanyehi answered. "But some might strike out on their own." *And Dragging Canoe would almost certainly be one of them.*

"What about your Folk, Tana?" Goran asked, turning to the Nunnehi scout. "Sylphs usually stay out of human conflicts unless we perceive great danger. Given the orders from King Briafael, he clearly thinks an uprising in the colonies could meet that test."

"Whether the lands to the east of the great mountains are ruled by local humans or faraway humans does not greatly interest my Folk," Tana said. "If the British government had enforced its own laws and kept settlers from crossing the mountains, things might be different. But they have not, nor do I think they could if they tried. I believe Nanyehi is right in seeking a peaceful solution. And I do not believe the Nunnehi would be inclined to join someone else's war."

Goran nodded and sat on the stump, visibly relieved. "Neither of your answers surprises me. I still hope each side will see reason. And, if I may stop being a ranger and just talk to friends, I have never experienced a harder time than now in the Blur. It exhausts me."

Tana walked over and sat next to Goran, taking his hand. "I should have greeted you with understanding, not suspicion. I, too, know the burden of the trail, the loneliness. It helps me to confide in Nanyehi. Can you not confide in Daniel?"

"I would like nothing better," Goran said. "But I know Daniel's feelings on the subject. Even if King Briafael is right, that preserving British authority would be best for everyone, I doubt Daniel would agree. He resents being told what to do."

"Daniel needs a friend now more than ever," Nanyehi said.

"Oh, I came to him as soon as I heard about the gruesome murder of his son," Goran said. "I tried my best to offer consolation. I think he appreciated the gesture, but the tragedy has only made Daniel more dead-set on settling Kentucky. He sees it as a vindication, as a way of bringing meaning to his son's death."

"Daniel may also seek revenge," Nanyehi added. "His face has a hardness that I never used to see."

She turned to Tana. "It is time we were getting back to camp. Goran, will we see you at the treaty conference?"

"Yes, I will be there," Goran agreed, rising to his feet. "I will be sure to pay my respects to Daniel. Perhaps we can watch it together, Tana."

"I would like that," Tana said, falling in behind as Nanyehi started to leave. "And give my regards to Daniel when he introduces you to Isaac Shelby."

Goran's expression of surprise made both women grin.

▲▲▲

There were nearly two thousand people camped at or near Sycamore Shoals. Only a few were present in any official capacity. Some made the journey to deliver, inspect, or barter trade goods. Others were on hand to provide protection and support to their respective peoples. Daniel Boone had assembled axemen and other frontiersmen for an impending expedition to the Kentucky country. Still others were at the shoals simply to satisfy their curiosity, to witness history.

It seemed to Nanyehi that all two thousand had tried to crowd into the place where the negotiations were underway. Too many succeeded. The small clearing was so packed it was hard to see and hear the speakers. Richard Henderson, the leader of the Transylvania Company, had just detailed his offer to buy the Cherokee claim on Kentucky. As Chief Attakullakulla stood to address the gathering, Nanyehi edged closer.

"I am an old man who has presided as chief in council, and as president of the nation for more than half a century," Attakullakulla began. War Chief Oconostota and other elders grunted in respect, as did some of the younger, dissident chiefs.

Attakullakulla detailed his long service as a peacemaker and diplomat, including a trip to England to meet the king. "From long standing in the highest dignities of our nation," he concluded, "I claim the confidence and good faith of all in defending and supporting the rightful claims of my people to the Kentucky country, now in treaty to be sold to the white people."

Ostenaco, another aged chief who'd traveled to England with Attakullakulla, stood to offer his support for the treaty. "The guns, clothes, and other supplies will make our people strong and contented. The way of peace with the Long Knives is the way of wisdom."

Nanyehi saw her cousin Dragging Canoe stand and face the other chiefs. She could tell he was seething with rage.

"Whole Indian nations have melted away like snowballs in the sun before the white man's advance," said Dragging Canoe, sweeping his hand to illustrate the point. "They leave scarcely a name of our people except those wrongly recorded by their destroyers."

Nods came from many of the younger chiefs, while many older ones listened intently. Nanyehi looked over at Richard Henderson standing in the corner. His face betrayed no emotion but she could see his hands become tight fists.

"We had hoped that the white men would not be willing to travel beyond the mountains," Dragging Canoe went on. "Now that hope is gone. They have passed the mountains, and have settled upon Cherokee land. They wish to have that action sanctioned by treaty. When that is gained, the same encroaching spirit will lead them upon other land of the Cherokees. New cessions will be asked. Finally the whole country, which the Cherokees and their fathers have so long occupied, will be demanded, and the remnant of our people, once so great and formidable, will be compelled to seek refuge in some distant wilderness."

There was another round of nods, grunts, and groans. And, when Nanyehi glanced again at Richard Henderson, his mask of indifference was gone. There was fear in his eyes.

"Should we not therefore run all risks, and incur all consequences, rather than submit to further loss of our country?" Dragging Canoe demanded, raising his arm in defiance. "Such treaties may be all right for men who are too old to hunt or fight. As for me, I have my young warriors about me. We will have our lands. I have spoken."

With that, Dragging Canoe dropped his arm, threw his blanket over his shoulder, and strode confidently from the clearing, followed by other young chiefs. Nanyehi understood exactly how they felt. Dragging Canoe's words had moved her, too. But she couldn't help but think they followed her cousin, not to victory, but to death.

▲▲▲

Dragging Canoe's exit brought a dramatic close to the first day — but the peace conference was far from over. The next day, Richard Henderson and his partners put on a great feast. There was enough venison, fowl, vegetables, and rum for all. In the latter case, Nanyehi observed with dismay, some of the chiefs consumed far more than enough.

Attakullakulla spoke again, urging his people to take what they could get in trade for the land rather than fight an unwinnable war. He even agreed to another proposal from Henderson to confirm the land purchases of the white settlers on the Watauga and Nolichucky.

As soon as it became clear that the treaty would eventually be signed, Nanyehi resolved to return immediately to her home in Chota. First, though, she and Tana sought out Daniel Boone and Isaac Shelby to say their good-byes. They found the two talking to Richard Henderson.

"So, you'll be off, then?" Henderson asked Daniel as Nanyehi approached.

"Now is as good a time as any," Daniel replied. "My men and I will make first for Long Island-on-the-Holston. Then we'll blaze your trail north along the old hunting path."

"I wish I could go with you, Daniel," said Isaac wistfully. "I have some business of my own at Long Island. But my militia service isn't up yet. I have to go back to the fort."

Henderson turned to the younger man. "Captain Shelby, isn't it?"

Isaac nodded.

"I've heard the tale of your bravery at the battle with the Shawnees," Henderson said. "Did Chief Cornstalk really come shake your hand after he signed the peace treaty?"

"He did. I wasn't expecting anything like that, I assure you."

"How would you like to come work for the Transylvania Company after your service is up?" Henderson asked.

"I'd welcome the chance," Isaac replied enthusiastically. Daniel gave him a wink.

Nanyehi saw her chance. "Gentlemen, I must take my leave," she said. "It is a long…"

She broke off when she saw Dragging Canoe stalking toward them. The others saw him, too. Isaac planted his two feet firmly and squared his shoulders. Henderson visibly tensed. Daniel didn't move a muscle.

The chief came straight at Henderson and pointed a trembling finger.

"We gave you our Kentucky claim, and still you ask for more?" Dragging Canoe said accusingly.

Henderson stammered. "If you mean the land leases for Jacob Brown and the others, surely you must see that…"

Dragging Canoe cut him off. "When you have this, you have all," he said. "But there is a cloud hanging over it. You will find its settlement dark and bloody."

Nanyehi feared that her cousin had never spoken truer words.

Chapter 11 — The Crown's Man

AS GORAN SOARED OVER THE forests and fields of North Carolina, he couldn't help but marvel at the changing landscape. During his first journeys into the Blur, much of this country had been wild. Now, flying northward from Charlotte Town, Goran could see many new settlements. To his family and friends on the Knob, it had been little more than a year since Goran joined the Rangers Guild. In human terms, though, more than twenty years had passed. The Carolina backcountry was rapidly becoming settled. The true frontier was shifting westward, up to and then beyond the high mountains.

Goran alighted to rest on a tree branch. Before him lay one of those new frontier settlements, at Town Fork Creek in Surry County. Goran had once spent several weeks there, obtaining supplies and studying it closely because of its proximity to the Sylph village on the Knob. Goran had been particularly struck by a man named Joseph Winston, a young farmer and hero of the French and Indian War.

If the rupture between Britain and its colonies led to armed conflict in the Carolinas, Goran mused, Joseph Winston would likely play a role in it.

As he resumed his northward flight, Goran considered the disturbing events he'd just witnessed in Charlotte Town. While the leaders of Mecklenburg County were meeting to discuss ongoing tensions with Britain, a rider arrived with the news that British regulars had fired on militiamen in Massachusetts. War was no longer just a possibility. It had come.

The Mecklenburg Committee of Safety had responded by declaring that "all laws and commissions confirmed by, or derived from the authority of the King or Parliament, are annulled and vacated, and the former civil constitution of these colonies for the present wholly suspended." They had also begun stockpiling weapons and ammunition. Other communities would likely follow Mecklenburg's lead, Goran knew.

Anxious to deliver his latest report, and hopeful that King Briafael or the Council might still have come up with some way to head off calamity, Goran beat his wings as fast as he could. Soon he spied the Knob looming above the morning mist. As always, he felt his heart leap at the promise of what lay beyond it.

▲▲▲

When Goran entered the guildhall, he knew something out of the ordinary was afoot. The corridors were empty. He guessed all the rangers must be in the council chamber, listening to news so compelling that none was willing to hear it secondhand. And Goran could guess what that news was. The Knob had received its own messenger from Lexington and Concord.

"By the time the British column got back to Boston, at least two hundred soldiers were dead, wounded, or missing," said Guildmaster Bren as Goran hurried in. Bren, wearing a traveling cloak similar to Goran's, was winded and red-faced.

"When I left Boston, I counted about some fifteen thousand rebels surrounding the city," Bren said. "The British have many advantages. Professional soldiers, supplies, and control of the sea. But it would be a mistake to underestimate the rebels. They control the countryside."

As the assembled rangers buzzed about Bren's report, Goran saw he'd guessed correctly. Virtually the entire guild membership was crowded into the council chamber. He saw Borva, the burly guildmaster, talking animatedly to Grandmaster Cono. Then Goran caught the eye of his father, who was standing with a small group. Brae beamed and loudly called out, "Goran, my boy, back so soon?"

The other rangers stopped their conversations and turned toward Goran. "Journeyman, come forward and report," Cono ordered.

"My report will likely add only more details to Bren's report without changing its import," Goran said. "War has come. And it is not just a rebellion against King George by a few colonists in a few cities. There are rebel committees across Virginia, Georgia, and the Carolinas. Each area also contains many supporters of the Crown. I just came from Mecklenburg. Most of its leaders are for independence. But they do not speak for everyone."

"What of the Indians?" Bren asked. "In the North, the Iroquois and most of the other tribes intend to stay neutral, while the Shawnees and Mingos will support the Crown."

"Something similar will happen in the South," Goran said. "There are conflicting factions among the Cherokees, although I am told most will seek neutrality. The Creek lean toward the British, while the Catawba nation will probably help the rebels."

"Folk affairs concern me far more than idle speculations about human tribes," said Borva gruffly. "Are there Folk foolish enough to involve themselves in this civil war?"

Bren and Cono both looked disdainfully at Borva. He met their gaze with defiance.

Goran tried to think of a quick way to sum up the many conversations he'd had over the past several months. "In general, most of the rangers from Indian country say their Folk are inclined to neutrality," he said. "As for other Folk, the Pixies of Norfolk, the Redcaps of Cross Creek, and the Merfolk of Cape Fear are already firmly convinced that British authority must be maintained in America. The Lutins of Charles Town and Elves of Georgia said they were willing to follow our lead. I've also heard reports of Dwarfs, Gwragedd Annwn, and a few other Folk colonies on the frontier. But I was unable to locate them."

"No doubt you will next time, Goran," said Brae proudly. "What you have already done is most impressive. I dare say no ranger has ever accomplished so much in such a short…"

"Thank you, journeyman," Grandmaster Cono said to Goran, gracefully interrupting Brae without seeming to insult him. "Bren, what about the Folk of the North?"

"Most are also inclined to follow our lead, Grandmaster," said Bren as he scratched the tightly cropped whiskers on his chin. "The Brownies of Philadelphia, the Ellyllon of inland Pennsylvania, the Gnomes of New York, and the Sprites of Boston already favor the Crown, as do the Pukwudgies to the west. Other frontier Folk have yet to commit themselves."

"We have yet to commit ourselves, as well," Borva insisted. "Sending rangers out to gather intelligence was wise, but you speak as though the decision has already been made."

"It *has* already been made," Bren stated firmly.

Borva swore. Other guildmasters flapped their wings or shook their arms in an attempt to be recognized. Around the room, apprentices and journeymen began talking. Goran had eyes only for Bren, who continued to stand calmly in place and stroke his chin.

"Silence," commanded Grandmaster Cono. Everyone obeyed.

"Guildmaster Bren is quite correct," Cono continued. "While he and Goran were ranging, we received another courier from England. King Briafael has made his decision. He commands us to render whatever aid we can to help the royal governors maintain control over the colonies."

No one spoke. Goran suspected they were doing the same thing he was: considering what the king's order meant for them.

It was Goran's father who broke the silence. "Well," Brae said with as much pomposity as he could muster, "if King Briafael thinks this is the wisest course…"

"The king is over the sea," Borva interrupted belligerently, his beard shaking. "We are here and must live with the consequences."

"Indeed, we must," Bren agreed. "And that is precisely why the king's reasoning is sound. As I have long said, we cannot treat human affairs as distant from our own. Our fates are intertwined. Their well-being is our responsibility."

"It is as it was in my younger days, during the time of the human King Alfred and his line," said Cono, his voice seeming to grow stronger as he recalled his youthful exploits. "Constant wars among the Britons, Saxons, and Danes had disturbed the peace and comfort of the Sylphs and other Folk of Britannia. Human warriors foraging for food interfered with our larder hunts. And, when foreign Folk followed the invaders to our shores, our monster hunts grew less productive as well. We decided enough was enough. So we helped the kings of Wessex conquer the others. We helped make them kings of England."

Borva snorted. "That hardly brought an end to war!"

"No, it did not but, without a king ruling over the English, both Folk and human would have been worse off," Bren said, maintaining his composure despite Borva's provocations. "The English needed us then. These Americans need us now. When humans make a mistake, they need us to correct it for them."

"But *are* they making a mistake?"

Goran was just as startled as everyone else to discover that he had asked aloud the question that had been on his mind for months. Cono coughed and glared. Bren narrowed his small eyes into slits. Borva looked at Goran with surprise written on his wide face.

Goran's father was again the one to break the silence.

"How clever of you, Goran," he said, affecting a toothy smile. "You ask a rhetorical question so we can better grasp the humans' point of view. That way, we are better able to carry out King Briafael's commands and bring the rebels back in line."

A few rangers seemed satisfied with Brae's explanation. Most still looked at Goran dubiously. But Bren, a crafty expression on his thin face, pounced at the opportunity.

"You are quite right, friend Brae, and well done, *Journeyman* Goran," he said, with an unmistakable emphasis on the young ranger's rank. "Just as a teacher must understand how his student thinks if he is to instruct the student well, we must strive always to understand how our humans think."

Borva scowled but then seemed to master his frustration as he posed his own question. "Do you intend our soldiers to go into direct battle with the rebel humans?"

"It is not for me to dictate strategy," Bren answered cagily. "That's a matter for the Council to decide. Still, I suspect they will choose a different course. Our warriors are well-trained and courageous, but we must be prudent. Our magical and material resources are limited. The magecraft needs alone would be daunting."

"In other words," Borva said, "the burden will fall on those who can enter the Blur without magecraft. It will fall on the Rangers Guild. On us."

"A better way to say it is that we rangers will have the *opportunity* to serve," Bren corrected him, "and to earn glory for that service. We will protect our village, our king, and our Folk. Once again, we will range long, range wide, our song our guide."

"Range long, range wide, our song our guide!" repeated the assembled rangers, many clearly tantalized by the opportunity for glory Bren described.

Folk may be immune to the mood alterations of spellsong, Goran thought, *but magic is hardly the only means of manipulating people.*

After Goran's first successful ranging, his sister Ailee had prepared a sumptuous feast to welcome him home. After every subsequent mission, she seemed intent on outdoing herself. As troubled as Goran had been by the meeting at the guildhall, he couldn't help but enjoy his first Folk-cooked meal in weeks. And he couldn't help but enjoy Ailee's company. She was more than just a sister to him. She was affection. She was familiarity and comfort. She was home.

His father and brother were another story. Brae came back from the guildhall no less troubled than Goran was — but what clearly troubled him was Goran's impertinent question.

"You should know better than to challenge the wisdom of your king and your guildmasters," Brae scolded him. "Who do you think makes promotion decisions?"

"I hardly think my guild career is the most important consideration, Father," Goran replied. "These human 'rebels,' as we call them, have legitimate grievances with Britain. Some of them are friends of mine."

"Are they?" sneered his brother Kaden, draining his mug and wiping his mouth on his sleeve. "That was your first mistake. You should choose your friends more carefully."

"I *have* chosen carefully," Goran insisted. "Daniel Boone and the others are thoughtful and brave. I enjoy their company. And I would trust them over some Sylphs I have come to know."

Kaden looked at his friend Jodoc, also at table, with incredulity. Brae was shocked into an uncharacteristic silence. Even Ailee seemed bothered by Goran's statement. "I know that all that time in the Blur can take its toll, my brother, but surely you have not forgotten where your loyalties lie."

Ailee could not possibly know what it is like, he thought. From her perspective, Goran left for a few days at a time and then came home. It was no different from a greenweaver or monster tender who might spend a few nights in their gardens or barns and then come home. Goran had a job to do, as did they.

But for the ranger, it wasn't like that at all. Goran had stopped keeping close count of the weeks and months that passed during his rangings. But he had spent something like nine years in the Blur. He was now, truly, Kaden's much-older brother, and felt the difference keenly. Indeed, he had already spent more time in the Blur than his father had during Brae's entire ranging career.

"My loyalties will always lie with my family and Folk," Goran said wearily. "It is not disloyalty to question whether the decision King Briafael has made is truly in the interest of the humans and of ourselves."

Brae dropped his spoon into his stew with a loud clank. "The Sylphs are a great and noble Folk. We have always prized wisdom, and I am sure King Briafael has benefited greatly from the advice of the elders. But the time for such deliberation is passed."

"Now is the time to do our duty," Kaden added. "We of the Warriors Guild are ready to do ours. And I am sure, little brother, that you will not fail to do yours."

Little brother. Kaden's unintended joke made Goran smile.

"This is hardly a laughing matter," Brae protested. "What will you…"

"I was not making light of Kaden's call to duty," Goran interrupted, opting for conciliation when he saw the pained expression on his sister's face. "I was thinking only of the many years I have spent exploring the human world. Perhaps I understand these Americans in a way other Folk do not."

"I think you are mistaking knowledge for wisdom," Kaden said. "You have learned many facts. But, in doing so, you lost your perspective. Ever since the Arrival, we have had to live alongside these humans and supply ourselves from their world. That does not mean we should ever consider ourselves a *part* of their world. We can never be. But it does mean we should have a hand in the *affairs* of their world. The humans need stability. They need order. They need protection from their own worst instincts."

Goran looked at his brother in a new light. Kaden had never been one to make speeches. He'd always been drawn to more physical pursuits. This wasn't like him.

Goran decided to try levity. "Has the Warriors Guild become a debating society in my absence?" he asked, lifting the platter of roast grouse and using his knife to refill his plate.

Kaden answered with a smile, and Goran could feel the tension leaving the others, as well.

"Not likely," his brother said. "Drill fills our days, as always. And we are still working with the Craftsmen Guild to cast firearms."

"Any progress?" Goran asked.

"We have two good working models of cannon, one with a rifled barrel. If some hostile Folk ever try to take the Knob, they will be in for a rude surprise."

"So, I guess you have not been reading books on Blur lore in your plentiful spare time, either," Goran joked, trying to keep the dinner conversation light.

"No," Kaden said, reaching for another skewer of rabbit. "But I have been attending Bren's lectures."

Goran stopped short. "Bren's lectures?"

"For the past few months, Bren has been giving lectures on humanity for anyone who wants to come," Kaden explained. "They are a revelation. I tried to get our sister to come with me, but she always seems to be working late at the greenweaver nursery."

Ailee shrugged her shoulders and got up to fetch the dessert platter.

"That sounds interesting," Goran said carefully, trying to keep the alarm he felt from creeping into his voice. "Perhaps I will have some time to go hear the lectures for myself."

"Now, that sounds like a capital idea!" Brae said enthusiastically. "Impressing my old friend Bren can only speed your rise to guildmaster. All the young up-and-comers go see him for the same reason. They know what it takes to get ahead. You do not want to be left out, do you?"

"No, Father, I suppose not," Goran said.

"I *knew* you were still the Crown's man," Brae continued. "You just need to make sure Bren and the other guildmasters know that, too."

As much as Goran thought he'd learned about humanity during his years in the Blur, it occurred to him that he still had a lot to learn about his own people and how *they* felt about humanity. It was a knowledge gap he resolved to fill as quickly as possible.

Chapter 12 – The Sermon

January 1776

"YOU'RE UP EARLY THIS MORNING, Reverend Muhlenberg."

Peter nodded politely to Henry Long as he passed the old man. A few minutes later, Peter did the same to another group he passed, the widow Catherine Pence and her family. It *was* early, the crack of dawn. Peter had hoped to slip away to his favorite fishing spot without meeting any of his congregation heading to town for Sunday services. But he should have known better. For folks such as the Longs and the Pences, coming into Woodstock for services was the high point of the week. They took great pride in the simple log church they'd built. They often arrived early and stayed late on Sunday to pray, to sing hymns, and to visit with friends.

They were a happy, faithful people. They'd welcomed Peter and Hannah with open arms more than three years earlier and helped make the couple's life in the valley joyful and fulfilling. Now Peter Muhlenberg would have to leave them. He already felt the pain of it, the loss. Would they feel abandoned? Would they feel betrayed? Perhaps his early morning meeting would test that proposition.

▲▲▲

Har the Tower was already sitting by the river, his fishing pole dangling loosely in his hands. The Dwarf wore his usual dark-red cap and cloak over a light gray tunic and trousers. Despite the bitter cold of a January morning, Har was dressed as he always was. Peter grimaced. Shivering underneath multiple layers — a thick greatcoat over suitcoat, waistcoat, breeches, shirt, cravat and undershirt — Peter found himself envying the Dwarf's resistance to the extremes of weather.

"Biting today?" Peter asked.

"Not a nibble," Har replied, shrugging his shoulders. "But I hardly noticed. I've got a lot on my mind."

Peter's heart sank. If Har was already worried about something, was now really the time to tell him Peter's news? Still, the Dwarf would hear about it sooner rather than later, anyway. "What troubles you? Perhaps I can help."

"Oh, I doubt it," said Har. "You have your own worries. Are you not leaving soon?"

Peter looked at his friend's earnest face and chuckled. "And here I thought I was about to spoil our fishing with ill news. How did you find out?"

Har shot Peter an exasperated look. "I *am* a ranger, Peter. When you journeyed to Williamsburg for the Fourth Convention, I already knew its purpose: to respond to Lord Dunmore's declaration of martial law. I knew that response would be to organize the defense of Virginia. And when you got back a few days ago, I already knew your return would be brief. I take it the legislature gave you a commission?"

Peter nodded his head. "I'm to serve as colonel of the Eighth Virginia Regiment. Actually, I'll be *forming* the regiment from among the men of the Shenandoah and nearby settlements. Then we'll go wherever they want us to go."

"Perhaps they will send you to join your friend George Washington in Massachusetts," Har suggested. "I hear his army surrounds Boston but lacks enough men to take the city."

During his time in Virginia, Peter had made many friends. But Har and George Washington had become his two closest companions, even though Washington made only occasional visits from his Mount Vernon home. Both men shared a love of hunting and fishing. Washington proved to be an excellent shot with his rifle, although Peter usually outshot him.

As for Har, he was highly skilled with his throwing axes at close range but only passable with a bow at faraway game. Where Har surpassed the other two was at fishing. His catches always seemed to be more frequent and more impressive. Peter suspected Har was somehow using spellsong to bait the fish. The Dwarf laughed off the suggestion — albeit with so much delight that it only heightened Peter's suspicions.

Of course, Peter had never gone hunting or fishing with both friends at the same time. He was duty-bound not to disclose the existence of the Dwarf colony to anyone. Perhaps Har could cloud the memory of anyone who found out. And perhaps George Washington could be trusted with the secret. But it wasn't Peter's secret to share.

"I'd like nothing better than to serve in General Washington's army," Peter confirmed. "But I heard talk in Williamsburg of Britain conducting a Southern campaign. They might reinforce Dunmore at Norfolk or invade the Carolinas. Once I recruit enough men for the regiment, we may be ordered any number of directions."

Peter sat down next to Har, who had returned a distracted gaze to the fishing line in the icy river. After the two shared the stillness of the Shenandoah for a time, Har spoke again.

"It is really your fault that I find myself in such a mess. Well, not your *fault* exactly, but it is your rebellion against your monarch that has set me against mine."

"*Against* Queen Virginal?" Peter asked incredulously. "You've always spoken highly of her. You've never talked of dissention or rebellion before."

"Oh, I mean nothing like that," Har assured him. "Our colony of Grünerberg has gotten off to a praiseworthy start, and Virginal deserves a great deal of credit. We settlers came from all over the Dwarfish lands. Our lords have rarely seen eye to eye. Our communities have even warred from time to time. But here in America, Virginal has kept the peace by keeping us busy. She has made good decisions so far. I just do not agree with her decision about you."

"Why would your queen concern herself with a human pastor?" Peter asked.

"Again, not you personally. I mean her decision about the American rebellion. She thinks the Folk of Grünerberg should just keep to ourselves."

Peter found himself shocked by the turn in their conversation, but resolved not to let it show. *Do fairies actually get involved in the wars of mankind?* He'd never considered the possibility. "I take it you don't agree with her policy," he said carefully.

Har sighed. "No, I do not. Some Folk have chosen to aid the English king against the rebels. I was pleased when Virginal rejected that idea outright. But the more I think about it, the more I think her neutrality policy will not work, either."

Peter was aghast. "Are you saying the other fairies will attack our armies?"

"Not likely, Peter," Har assured him. "We Folk have intervened in human affairs from time to time, but rarely so crudely. When our armies take the field in battle, it requires great feats of magecraft to sustain the Shimmer walls. Also, after you humans developed iron, our Folk soldiers lost some of their advantage. Our enchantments do not work well on that metal."

"Well, then," Peter began, "how do…"

Har cut him off with a wave of his hand. "You are thinking too much like a human. Great moments in your history can turn on the smallest of details. Imagine what an army can do if a precise map of enemy deployments drops mysteriously into its lap. Imagine an important general never showing up because he falls asleep. Imagine soldiers suddenly growing fearful, or confused, or attacking what they think is an enemy unit that is in reality their own? With spellsong, we can conceal, surveil, misdirect, manipulate. We can win battles without lifting an axe."

Peter began to see the picture Har was painting. It terrified him.

"Of course, we Folk are few compared to humans," Har continued, "and it can take us months of your time for our leaders to reach decisions. That is why those who can survive in the Blur, the rangers, are often given discretion. Still, Folk interventions do not always work as intended. To our leaders, the Blur really *is* a blur. Human affairs are constantly in flux and hard to follow. When rangers do get orders, they are sometimes out of date. They can even lead us to favoring the wrong side."

"Which is why, I'm guessing, your queen doesn't want you Dwarfs to intervene."

"That is part of it, yes," Har agreed. "But she also sees no need for Grünerberg to take sides in the first place."

The Dwarf's answer gave Peter the opportunity he'd been waiting for. "Har, help me understand why fairy folk would *ever* see the need to take sides in a human war."

Har stood up, planted the end of his pole in the mud, and rubbed his eyes with one stubby hand. "A good question, Peter, for which I have too many answers. To many Folk, your people are just a source for humanwares. To others, humans represent unwelcome competitors for game and perhaps even potential threats to us, much like the monsters we hunt."

Peter was about to protest but Har again cut him off with a gesture.

"These matters are complicated, Peter, and my explanations will fail to do them justice. All I can say is that, in your case, I do not think we can or should remain neutral. If other Folk intervene to crush your rebellion, they will gain at our expense. In the long run, your grievances with Britain will continue to fester. You can no more be ruled from over the sea than our colony could be ruled by the Dwarf lords back in Germany. The next war could disrupt our hunting and foraging to an even greater degree."

Har's argument sounded reasonable. But it didn't sound like the whole story.

The Dwarf seemed to guess what his friend was thinking. "If I am being honest, Peter, there is another reason Grünerberg should aid the rebels. Your cause is just. I have read the declaration written by your John Dickinson and Thomas Jefferson, the one that pledges you will fight for the preservation of your liberties. That is something worth fighting for."

"I know Mr. Jefferson well," Peter said. "We have served in the legislature together."

Har turned to face Peter. "That acquaintance points to another consideration. The conflict has become personal for me. You are my friend, Peter, and you are about to march off to war. I do not want you to go alone. I would like to help you, if I can. But the queen forbids it."

Har's words touched Peter deeply. *Greater love hath no man than this, that a man lay down his life for his friends.*

"Nothing would please me more than to have you with me," Peter said. "And, as you say, our cause is a just one, although I struggled at first to reconcile it with the vow I took as a minister to affirm that 'the king's majesty, under God, is the only supreme governor of this realm.' It was the Parliament who first trampled our rights. Now that King George has declared America in open rebellion, I believe my duty is clear. Still, leaving my family and friends is proving to be far harder than I thought."

"They will understand, Peter, surely."

"It's not just about me, though," Peter said. "I'll be recruiting their husbands, their sons, their brothers, and their friends to go with me. It's one thing to *speak* of liberty, of a choice between submitting to tyranny or resisting by force. It's another thing to march into danger, or to watch your loved ones do so."

Har reached up and touched Peter's upper arm. Although tall for a Dwarf, he couldn't quite reach Peter's shoulder. "I have always envied your way with words," Har told his friend. "I know you will find the right ones."

Peter placed his hand over Har's and looked out over the Shenandoah. He'd miss these early mornings most of all — the colors of the dawn, the songs of the birds, the sounds of lapping water, the faint mist hugging the river and then dissipating under the rising sun.

"There's a verse in the Book of Proverbs about finding the right words," Peter said. "It reads: *The words of a man's mouth are as deep waters, and the wellspring of wisdom as a flowing brook.*"

Har smiled and nodded.

"Perhaps you can find the right words as well, the ones to convince Queen Virginal," Peter suggested.

Har shot him a questioning look. "It is not my place to argue with the queen's commands. I am just a journeyman."

"You said our cause was just," Peter said. "Well, one of the liberties we defend is the liberty to speak our minds. Surely the principle applies as well to your people as to mine."

Now it was Har's turn to look out over the river, lost in thought. "I will think on it, Peter," he said presently. "I do not wish to be disrespectful, or make Virginal angry with me."

"What she thinks of you matters greatly, doesn't it?" Peter asked, his mouth broadening into a knowing smile.

Har reddened at Peter's implication. "My concern is reasonable. Does not everyone want to stay in the good graces of his sovereign?"

Peter exploded. "Did you really just ask me that?" he said between gales of laughter.

Har quickly caught his meaning and laughed even harder than Peter. Then the Dwarf pulled his fishing pole out of the mud, wound the line around it, and lifted it to his shoulder.

"As I said, I will think on it, Peter," said Har the Tower. "Do you really think there can come a time when even a queen might welcome the...uh... the counsel of a lowly ranger?"

"I do," said Peter — and now he had yet another reason to be grateful to his Dwarf friend. Har's words had given Peter an inspiration. Peter now knew what he should do, and say.

▲▲▲

When Reverend Peter Muhlenberg rose to deliver his sermon, he looked out over a crowded church. He saw the familiar faces of regular churchgoers. The widow Catherine Pence and her family sat smiling at him from the front row. Old Henry Long and his people sat just behind. But other faces were less familiar. And beyond the door — thrown wide open, despite the biting January cold, so those standing outside could see in — there were faces Peter barely recognized at all.

Of course the news of his officer's commission had already spread throughout the valley. Peter shouldn't have been so naïve. They'd guessed, without Peter having to say anything, that the sermon he would deliver would be his last for a long while. So they'd dressed in their Sunday best and flocked in record numbers to the little log church, filled it to capacity, and then spilled outside it, the onlookers hoping to catch at least snippets of his farewell sermon.

As Peter stood in his long clerical robes, he felt all eyes on him. He felt what those eyes conveyed — anticipation, respect, affection.

When the Committee of Safety had formed two years earlier to discuss how to respond to escalating tensions with Britain, it was Peter the locals had called upon to moderate the meeting. Then he'd chaired their Committee on Resolutions. "We will pay due submission to such acts of government as his Majesty has a right by law to exercise over his subjects, and to such only," Peter's committee had declared. "Every act of the British Parliament respecting the internal policy of America is a dangerous and unconstitutional invasion of our rights and privileges." The Shenandoah people had sent Peter to Williamsburg to represent them in legislatures and conventions. They'd made him a politician, ignoring his objections. They'd followed his lead and embraced the case for rebellion. But would they now follow the lead of their minister-politician into battle?

Peter began the sermon by reading Psalm 89, one of his father's favorites. When he finished, he paused for a moment to sweep his eyes across the sea of expectant faces.

"David sings here of the strength of God, his righteousness, his faithfulness," Peter said. "In times of peril, the language of holy writ pledges that the Lord of Hosts shall indeed arm the righteous. Justice and judgment shall indeed inhabit the Lord's throne. Truth shall indeed go before the Lord's face. We face such a time of peril today. And the Lord of Hosts shall be with us."

Peter looked over at Hannah. Their eyes met, and he lingered longingly in memory of intimate moments that could not come again for months, perhaps years. She smiled bravely and nodded. Peter felt a power swelling within him.

"We are told in the Book of Ecclesiastes that to every thing there is a season, and a time to every purpose under the heaven," Peter said. "We learn there is a time to be born and a time to die, a time to kill and a time to heal, a time to rend and a time to sew, a time of war and a time of peace. As for me, there is a time to preach, but that time has passed away."

With that, Peter threw off his black clerical robes. As they swirled to the floor, the congregation saw him standing there in full uniform. Blue coat faced in buff, with gold lace epaulets at each shoulder. White waistcoat, cravat, shirt, and breeches. High boots of black leather. A red sash tied at his right hip, his brass-hilted sword hanging at his left.

"The time to fight has now come!" Peter shouted.

Gasps dissolved first into applause, then into cheers. As Peter strode down the aisle and out the church door, some cried "For Liberty!" and "Liberty or Death!" and "Huzza for Colonel Muhlenberg!" Other sang "A Mighty Fortress Is Our God."

Before the end of the day, scores of young men, mostly German-speaking settlers of the Shenandoah country, had volunteered to serve in the new Eighth Virginia Regiment. Before the end of the week, it was hundreds.

Chapter 13 — The Drum

April 1776

THE BASKET WAS ALMOST DONE. Woven of honeysuckle and dyed orange with broom sedge, it needed only the black accent stripes Nanyehi would add with butternut dye. As she pounded the squash seeds into a fine powder, she heard hoof beats on the south trail. Nanyehi set aside her dye bowl, rose to her feet, and sighed. She could guess what the sound meant. She could guess what might come next.

As Nanyehi emerged from her clay-walled cabin onto the primary street of Chota, she glanced first across the square at the large, seven-sided Council House and then toward Chota's south entrance. Other Cherokees were also emerging from their homes or coming in from fields and orchards, looking in the same direction. The first thing they all saw was a pack mule. Protruding from the bundles on its back were exactly what Nanyehi expected and feared she would see: gun barrels. Behind the first mule walked a long line of mules and horses, most similarly burdened with guns, ammunition, and other supplies.

Two horses bore human cargo, however. One was Nanyehi's cousin Dragging Canoe, who'd left weeks earlier to meet the supply expedition from Florida and guide it to Chota. The other rider was a white man, whom Nanyehi supposed must be the British agent who had supplied the arms.

At the sight of what the pack animals carried, cheers arose from many of the young men of Chota. Nanyehi felt only foreboding. As she watched Principal Chief Attakullakulla and War Chief Oconostota emerge from the Council House and saw the grim expressions they directed at the arriving party, Nanyehi welcomed the small comfort that at least she was not alone in her misgivings.

▲▲▲

"Are we never to reclaim our lands from the invaders?" Dragging Canoe asked in exasperation.

The meeting in the Council House the following day had gone better than Nanyehi expected. The assembled chiefs watched from their respective corners, each corner filled with a delegation from one of the seven clans, as Dragging Canoe had advocated an immediate attack on the white settlers of the Holston, Nolichucky, and Watauga River Valleys. Attakullakulla and Oconostota had advocated patience and another try at diplomacy — as Nanyehi herself had argued, in her role as Beloved Woman and head of the Council of Women.

What had really made the difference, though, were the words of Henry Stuart, the British agent who'd arrived with Dragging Canoe.

"Now is not the right time to attack," Stuart said, "and the Overmountain settlers are not the right target. There are many loyal supporters of the Crown among them. We implore our Cherokee brothers to heed our counsel in this matter."

That's what prompted Dragging Canoe's angry outburst. Frustrated, he turned and sat down next to his brothers. Their father, Attakullakulla, regarded Stuart with skepticism. "Why do the British supply my son with arms if they do not wish him to attack the Americans?"

"I do not speak against attacking the Americans," Stuart said. "I speak only of the right time and the right place. His majesty's generals and admirals have a plan to bring this rebellion to a swift and decisive end. With a coordinated strike against the Southern colonies, we will rob the rebels of half their strength and prompt them finally to see reason."

Dragging Canoe shook his head dismissively.

"You would have us strike over the mountains into the Carolinas," he said. "We have already discussed your plan. You want your allies to do only *your* bidding, to advance only *your* interests. When will you act in ours?"

"When the rebellion is at an end, we will be in a position to deal with the squatters in the north," Stuart explained. "The Loyalists among them can have the pick of other lands to settle, from Florida or from lands confiscated from the rebels. We can finally enforce the king's laws against encroaching on your territory. We can finally reestablish the king's peace."

Chief Attakullakulla sighed. "*Reestablish* the king's peace," he repeated with weary sarcasm. "I have wanted nothing more than to establish a firm peace with our white brothers for most of my life. But it has proved more fleeting than the fleetest buck. And your idea of peace, it seems, is for my people to start another war."

Dragging Canoe jumped to his feet, his pockmarked face towering over his elderly father. "The war is already upon us. We can either fight or succumb to a dismal fate. There is no other choice."

War Chief Oconostota stood up next to Attakullakulla and gave Dragging Canoe an icy stare. "I was leading men into war before you were as much as a beat in your mother's heart," he said, spitting out the words in a voice suited more to battlefield command than council debate. "It is not cowardice to deny your enemy a battle on *his* terms. It is not surrender to refuse to fight today, against impossible odds, so you may live to fight for your people on another, better day. To fight in another, better way."

Dragging Canoe stared back at Oconostota for a long while.

"Your words sound like wisdom," he finally admitted, "and yet we have heard such words many times before. Have they preserved our lands from the invaders? Have they preserved our hunting grounds? We who still have strength to fight will not be satisfied with words, whether they be from our own people or from our British 'brothers.'"

Then Dragging Canoe exited the Council House, followed by other young chiefs. Nanyehi, sitting with her Wolf Clan, watched them go and felt a resurgence of optimism. Perhaps there was still a chance to avoid calamity.

▲▲▲

Nanyehi's optimism outlasted the day. Indeed, it lasted for many weeks. Grudgingly, Dragging Canoe agreed to a final attempt at a peaceful resolution of the conflict with the settlers. Henry Stuart wrote a letter demanding they relocate back over the mountains to Virginia and the Carolinas, or even to British-occupied lands in Florida.

Nanyehi didn't really expect all the settlers to leave, although some would likely flee in fear. The rest, though, could at least relocate from outlying farms to the security of fortified settlements. That would mean fewer scalps for Dragging Canoe's raiders. And, because his raiding parties wouldn't be much use against forts, pitched battles would be less likely, reducing casualties on both sides.

She knew her goals were not Henry Stuart's. He wanted to protect Loyalists and redirect Dragging Canoe eastward, against the American rebels in Georgia and the Carolinas, rather than northward against the Overmountain settlers.

Nanyehi longed to know more of what those settlers were thinking. If only Tana were available to scout for her! But her Nunnehi friend was on a diplomatic mission to another fairy people, the Yunwi Amayine Hi, whose village lay far to the southwest of Chota, underneath a bend of the Great River. The two nations had long warred. Tana's task was to negotiate a lasting peace. She had left weeks ago nursing a cautious hope, much like Nanyehi's.

It was on the day a delegation of fourteen Indian chiefs arrived at Chota, their unfamiliar faces painted in black, that Nanyehi's newfound optimism began to waver. She watched as a tall, imposing-looking man with a clutch of colorful feathers in his hair approached Attakullakulla, who had just emerged from his cabin. As Nanyehi hurried forward to stand with her uncle, she saw the tall man offer the traditional sign of greeting and open his mouth to speak.

"I am Cornstalk," he said, immediately bringing to Nanyehi's mind the stories she'd heard about the Shawnee chief from Daniel Boone and Isaac Shelby.

"I have come with other chiefs of the Northern tribes," Cornstalk stated gravely, "to speak of betrayal, alliance, and war."

▲▲▲

The Grand Talks, as they came to be called, commenced ten days later at the Council House. Cornstalk had requested delegations from every Cherokee town to attend. He was not to be disappointed. Nanyehi had never seen so many chiefs assembled at one time and place. Also present were the British agent, Henry Stuart, and several Tory whites who remained loyal to Britain. Nanyehi recognized two of them: Alexander Cameron, a close friend of Dragging Canoe, and a South Carolinian named David Fanning.

The talks began with a great feast. The delegations enjoyed stews of venison, elk, and rabbit meat cooked with wild onions, beans, squash, and mushrooms and accompanied by many cakes of cornbread. Then the Cherokees crowded into the Council House to hear the visitors' proposal.

First to speak was the chief of the Mohawk. He was a broad, muscular man with the scars of battle on his face and breast and a single stripe of graying hair running along the top of his head. The Mohawk described a long series of trespasses and betrayals by the colonists of New York and other Northern provinces.

Nanyehi tried to listen closely to his tale but found herself distracted. Someone outside the Council House had begun to drum. It was a steady, ponderous beat. There was nothing unusual about a beating drum in Chota. Still, there was something distinctive about this drum, something hypnotic. She made a concerted effort to concentrate on the words being spoken.

"The British will soon strike their rebellious colonies with full force," the Mohawk chief was saying. "Will you not seize this opportunity with your brothers to strike our common foe?" With that, he removed a war belt from his waist and offered it first to Principal Chief Attakullakulla and then to War Chief Oconostota. Both elderly chiefs refused it.

Again, Nanyehi's attention was drawn back to the drumbeat. Its tempo had quickened Now, instead of throbbing ponderously, it pounded an insistent call to arms. She saw Dragging Canoe rise to his feet, face the Mohawk chief, and take the war belt.

Next came a representative of the Ottawa nation. Again, a chief painted in black related the crimes of the Americans and asked for alliance. Again he offered a war belt to Attakullakulla and Oconostota. Again they refused it, and Dragging Canoe accepted it.

By then, Nanyehi could hear a voice singing along with the drum, which was beating ever faster, as if ordering an attack. Although she couldn't understand the words, the language sounded vaguely familiar. No doubt it was the tongue of one of the visiting Northerners. The song conjured up memories of the war song Oconostota and his warriors had sung two decades earlier at Taliwa, before their battle with the Creeks — the battle that had taken the life of her first husband, Kingfisher.

Nanyehi could see the long-ago moment as clearly as if it were yesterday. The twenty-year-old memory thrilled her. She felt a sudden urge to leap up and perform the war dance that she'd watched Kingfisher do before

Taliwa. Perhaps she could persuade Oconostota into joining her…

No! she thought. *What is happening to me? Why do I feel so exhilarated and yet so angry?*

Then it came to her. The reason the music filling the Council House sounded so familiar. She hadn't heard its melody before. But she knew it was spellsong.

The realization shocked her out of her daydream and back into the reality of what was unfolding before her. Nanyehi saw the Raven of Chota, who had only a year earlier signed the Sycamore Shoals treaty, stand up and proudly accept a war belt from a Lenape chief. Other Cherokees were shouting words of encouragement to Dragging Canoe and the Raven.

Nanyehi felt both panicked and paralyzed. She could see the magically enhanced war fever spreading around the room. Only the whites, Attakullakulla, and Oconostota seemed unaffected. She guessed that the song's magic wasn't aimed at whites. And she guessed, or perhaps just hoped, that decades of experience had left her uncle and the war chief resistant to the spell, although of course they gave no sign of even hearing it.

She knew she should try to do something, but the magic's effects had not yet entirely left her. And when she fully freed herself, what options did she have? No one would believe her story of magical beings and enchanted songs.

Then Cornstalk, the most commanding presence in a room of commanders, rose to speak. The beat of the drum quickened again, as if to accompany a frenzied dance. The Shawnee leader held up a massive war belt of his own, woven and beaded in brilliant shades of purple.

"In a few years, the Shawnee has been reduced from a great nation to a handful," Cornstalk said in a deep voice. "They once possessed land almost to the seashore, but now have hardly enough ground to stand on."

As Dragging Canoe and the others watched intently, Nanyehi could see their heads nodding and feet tapping to the frenetic rhythm of a song they could not hear.

"It is plain that the white people intend to wholly destroy the Indians," Cornstalk said. "It is better for the red men to die like warriors than to diminish away by inches. Our cause is just, and I hope the Great Spirit who governs everything will favor us."

Then he held his war belt with one hand, removed a small vessel from his mantle, and poured its contents over the belt. The red paint covered its surface and dripped to the floor of the Council House like the blood of a slain enemy.

"Now is the time to begin," Cornstalk declared.

The chief offered the red-stained war belt to Henry Stuart. The British agent paused, glancing around the room at the swaying Cherokees. Then he clinched his jaw.

"I agree that the cause of my Indian brothers is just," Stuart said. "But your grievance is with the settlers who trespass, and the rebel leaders who abet their trespasses. It is not with all Americans, many of whom remain loyal to his majesty's government. I am here to make war against our common foes, the rebels. I have no authority to embrace the broader war you seek."

Cornstalk turned dismissively from Stuart and strode across the room to Dragging Canoe, who was glaring at the British agent in contempt. "I accept your belt, your alliance, and your friendship on behalf of all true Cherokee," Dragging Canoe snarled.

Then he passed Cornstalk's belt to another chief, whom Nanyehi recognized as Osioota from the town of Chilhowie. Osioota held the purple belt high over his head and let the red paint drip from its surface to cover both cheeks of his excited face. Issuing a cry of war, the young chief lifted his tomahawk and struck the pole in the center of the Council House. The sharp sound was like a rope yanking dozens of chiefs to their feet. Osioota began to sing and dance, following the rapid tempo of the drum. Others followed his lead, forming a circle of dancing chiefs.

Finally finding herself in full control of her limbs, Nanyehi took advantage of the commotion to slip out unseen. Freeing her own tomahawk from her sash, she let her eyes adjust to the darkness and then began to scan the nearby paths and cabins of Chota. The spellsong seemed to come from everywhere, and from nowhere.

As Nanyehi crept stealthily from cabin to cabin, she could still hear the sound of singing and dancing coming from the Council House. Some of the chiefs had stumbled out and continued their war dance on the grassy town square. Finding no sign of the drummer anywhere in Chota, she decided to search the neighboring trees.

Once Nanyehi passed through the gate, the spellsong stopped being a pervasive presence. Now she could pinpoint the source: a large holly bush at the edge of the woods. Breaking into a trot, then a run, Nanyehi headed for it.

Suddenly, the drumming stopped, as did the voice accompanying it. Nanyehi wasn't surprised to see movement in the bush and was ready. She halted, took careful aim, and threw her carefully balanced tomahawk end over end with a practiced flick of her wrist. She heard a grunt, followed by a cry of pain mixed with rage. A sixth sense prompted her to treat the cry as a warning. She dove, flattening her body. She felt something fly just past her left ear and heard it strike the soft ground. Glancing quickly behind her, Nanyehi saw a short, thick spear imbedded in the dirt, its end still quivering from the impact.

In an instant, she was back on her feet and headed for the holly bush. When she got there, however, she saw only her tomahawk lying on the ground, its blood-stained edge testifying to the fact that it had at least wounded its target. The drummer was nowhere to be found.

With her attention directed into the forest, Nanyehi didn't notice the man approach from the clearing until he was almost upon her.

"Nancy Ward!"

She whirled, crouching in a fighting stance, only to see the face of Isaac Thomas, a white trader she had met many times before.

"Thank God it's you," Thomas said, removing his hat and wiping his sweaty forehead with a handkerchief. "I have a message from the Watauga settlement to Henry Stuart. Do you know where to find him?"

Nanyehi straightened and gave a frustrated sigh. She wanted to catch up with the fairy drummer, but she also recognized the potential importance of the message Isaac Thomas carried.

"Come with me," she said. "The British agent was in the Council House when I left town." Then she cast a last, longing look back at the holly bush and, only few paces away, the missile still protruding from the ground. She noted its distinctive fletching — alternating yellow and black feathers — and then headed back to town.

▲▲▲

When Nanyehi conducted Isaac Thomas into the Council House, she found the chiefs continuing their war dance. Henry Stuart, standing with the other whites, watched the dance with a wary expression. Attakullakulla and Oconostota sat on the far side in stony silence.

"Henry Stuart, you have a visitor," Nanyehi called out loudly, prompting Dragging Canoe and several others to stop dancing. Stuart rose as Thomas ran to his side. The two spoke for a few minutes in low tones.

"Allies have no secrets in our Council House," Dragging Canoe exclaimed. "Will our British brother share his news?"

Stuart paled. Then, once again, Nanyehi saw his cheek bulge as the British agent gritted his teeth in determination. "It is a response from the Watauga settlers. They insist they have legally purchased the land they inhabit from your people. They will not leave."

Dragging Canoe seemed unsurprised. "The treaty was the work of old men without teeth, too old to hunt or fight," he said, ignoring the glares of the two elderly chiefs in the corner. "I and my warriors are young, and we will have our ground."

Not only was Dragging Canoe unsurprised, but he also knew his man. There was more to tell. "And?"

Although clearly reluctant, Stuart complied. "They further state that the Cherokee should not fight with the British and those Americans loyal to King George. They claim that, if you do so, there is an army of six thousand Virginia militiamen who would march not east to fight his majesty's army but instead west and south to destroy your towns."

"They dare to threaten us!" Dragging Canoe cried. "It would have been better to have attacked the Wataugans at once, without writing that letter. It served only to put them on guard, and caused them to prepare to come against us. By this time they will have all their people removed."

Henry Stuart could see just as clearly as Nanyehi did where events were leading. "There are Loyalists among them, men like David Fanning here. The foes we must strike now lie to the east, in the Carolinas and..."

"You told us to assist the king," Dragging Canoe broke in. "Now, when there is a white army planning to come against our towns, your king will not assist us. We must do it ourselves. We must keep them back."

Cornstalk and the other Northerners cheered his words, as did most of the other chiefs. Sensing his strong support, Dragging Canoe began issuing commands. Isaac Thomas and the other American traders in Chota were to be seized and imprisoned. Cherokee delegations were to return to their towns and prepare for war — war against the American rebels in the Southern colonies, yes, but also war against the trespassers on the Holston, the Nolichucky, and the Watauga. War against them all.

Nanyehi felt physically ill. That her cousin was committing a grievous error, one that would hurt their own people more than anyone, she was firmly convinced. That he and the other chiefs were at least partly under the spell of some fairy power, she was convinced no less firmly. She wished her friend Tana were here. Even with her help, however, Nanyehi could think of no way to stop the coming war.

▲▲▲

Dragging Canoe and his closest friends immediately left Chota. As the days passed and they failed to return, Cornstalk and the Northern chiefs grew restless. Nanyehi grew no less apprehensive. During Dragging Canoe's absence, the warriors readied for war. They selected new guns, filled their pouches with ammunition, and sharpened their knifes and tomahawks. Their wives prepared rations and mixed war paint. Emulating the Northerners, the warriors would paint themselves mostly in black.

When Dragging Canoe returned, it was with four white scalps. Cornstalk accepted them as a conclusive token of alliance. Then he and his delegation took their leave. *They will not be here when vengeful Americans retaliate for what was about to happen*, Nanyehi thought bitterly.

A few days later, Nanyehi heard Dragging Canoe explain his attack plan to other chiefs. The Cherokees, with Shawnee and Creek allies, would form three war parties. One group, led by the Raven of Chota, would move northwest against John Carter's settlement. Another group would attack the Wataugans at Sycamore Shoals. Dragging Canoe would lead the main force against the settlements near Long Island-on-the-Holston. Meanwhile, the Cherokee of the Lower and Middle Towns, led by Alexander Cameron and other chiefs allied with Dragging Canoe, would attack the Carolina backcountry.

On the night before the warriors left Chota, it fell to Nanyehi as Beloved Woman to prepare the War Drink. Made by boiling the leaves and branches of the yaupon holly into a dark, thick brew, the War Drink bestowed courage and fortitude. She resolved to perform the ceremony. Nanyehi loved the men of Chota and hoped for their safe return. Perhaps the ceremony would help to accomplish that end. But the War Drink, and the ensuing celebrations, would also incapacitate the men for some time. She planned to use the distraction to good effect.

After the ceremony, as the warriors drank, danced, and purged, Nanyehi slipped away and found the cabin where Isaac Thomas and the other traders were being kept. She lifted the latch on the door and saw the surprised look of the prisoners.

"Quickly, before we are discovered, follow me," she ordered. They obeyed without question. Once they reached the outskirts of the town, she told him of Dragging Canoe's plans and urged them to warn the settlers to flee or take refuge in their forts.

If we are all fortunate, there will be only raids and not massacres, Nanyehi thought as they ran off into the woods.

▲▲▲

Dragging Canoe's attacks proved to be much more than raids but far less than massacres. Heeding Nanyehi's warnings, most of the settlers were in hiding or behind fortifications when the war parties arrived. John Sevier, John Carter, and other leaders were able to turn back Cherokee attacks on the Wataugan settlements with little loss of life. At Long Island-on-the-Holston, however, Dragging Canoe found himself in an open-field battle with hundreds of whites commanded by James Shelby, Isaac's brother.

"They must have had warning." Dragging Canoe spit out the words in between groans of pain as Nanyehi removed the crude bandage on her cousin's wounded thigh and began probing to see if the rifle ball had remained in his leg or passed cleanly through it.

"We lost a dozen warriors at the Island Flats," he continued, "but we avenged our loss with eighteen dead whites on the banks of the Clinch River."

"If you do not hold still so I can bind your wound properly, you may yet lose this leg," Nanyehi replied, trying to sound playfully stern while her insides twisted themselves into knots. In the dim light of her house, she looked around for a moment, locating her basket of healing herbs in the corner.

As Nanyehi tended to his wound, Dragging Canoe looked at her with a tenderness she had not seen in his eyes for many years. "I know what you would say," he said. "Yes, of course I know the Americans will attack. I know my war has only just begun. But I will move south and west, to the banks of the Chickamauga Creek and the Great River. I will stay one step ahead of them. I will fight alongside the British, the Tories, and the Northern tribes. And, if necessary, I will fight alone."

"The war you fight will never be yours alone," Nanyehi said sadly. "We will also suffer for it."

"We were already suffering," he said, and the brief softness she saw in his eyes turned once more into hard flint. "The difference between you and me is that I would rather suffer the physical wounds of battle than the spiritual wounds of surrender."

Chapter 14 – The Rescue

June 1776

WHEN GORAN FIRST MET HIM, Daniel Boone was all of sixteen years old. Now Goran's friend was forty-one, married with nine children, and living on the frontier of the Kentucky territory in a settlement named after himself: Boonesborough.

Goran had changed, too. He wasn't quite as old as Daniel. He was twenty-seven, including his time in the Blur, although Goran was still a teenager in the eyes of his family back on the Knob. But he had witnessed much. He had never felt more isolated, more alone. And now, as the Sylph spied the settlers' cabins in a distant clearing, he knew what he had come to say would make him feel even lonelier. But it had to be said. Daniel deserved to know the truth.

Although its name made it sound like a town, Boonesborough was really just a couple of rows of small cabins forming a rough rectangle in the clearing, with crude blockhouses at each corner and some newly planted fields beyond. Not far to the east was the Kentucky River, flowing north and then turning to the west of the settlement. As Goran landed on a post and started looking for Daniel, he could see several men hauling logs to a spot between two of the blockhouses where they had begun erecting a high wall. Once they completed the stockade between all four blockhouses, they'd have a proper fort. Daniel wasn't among the workmen. Nor could Goran see him anywhere else in Boonesborough.

Perhaps he is out hunting. That would be just like him.

Goran guessed that fortifying the settlement hadn't been the priority for the settlers when they arrived on the spot a year earlier. Since then, though, tensions with the Indians had gotten worse. Many Shawnees, Mingos, and Cherokees never accepted the legality of the treaties that paved the way

166

for the founding of Boonesborough and other Kentucky settlements. Now that the war had broken out, British agents had been arming Indians and encouraging them to attack.

Goran had come to Boonesborough to warn Daniel about that, although the partially completed stockade suggested the settlers already knew the danger. But the fairy ranger had also come to tell Daniel that Britain would have other allies in the war: Goran's own people.

After learning of King Briafael's decision, Goran had decided to stay on the Knob for a while to better understand the pro-British policy he was being asked to carry out. He attended Bren's lectures on humanlore, paying attention not only to the guildmaster's presentations but also to the response they got from audiences of young Sylphs. Apprentices and journeymen from every guild on the Knob, most responded enthusiastically to Bren's call for greater Folk guidance of human affairs.

"The humans are clever and resourceful, there is no doubt about that," Bren had admitted during one of the lectures. "Have Folk benefitted from their innovations? Of course. The humanwares they produce have made our lives more comfortable. In my grandfather's day, we wore coarse tunics and robes of simple design. Our tools and weapons were cruder. Now they are superior in every way. Material comfort, however, cannot be our primary concern."

There had been loud agreement from the audience, including Goran's brother Kaden.

"Not all human innovations have been praiseworthy," Bren had continued. "Some are destructive. Too many humans have lost their way. They have abandoned the places, crafts, and practices that gave meaning to their lives. They crowd into cities teeming with vice, or crowd onto ships bound for faraway shores. As their traditional ties fade away, the humans grow uneasy. They quarrel. They fight. They even rebel against their rightful rulers."

Bren had shaken his head in disbelief at that — more as a dramatic flourish than from genuine concern, Goran guessed.

"The resulting wars not only cost the humans dearly but also disrupt our hunts and our access to humanwares," the guildmaster had said. "Although they do not realize it, the humans' actions are a call for help — a call to all Folk from a benighted people bereft of magic and bereft of hope. Indeed, many Americans do not favor rebellion. They rightly fear the calamities that are inseparable from a state of war. Will we turn our faces away? Will we leave the humans to the dark fate this torrent of violence must bring both sides?"

Most of Bren's audience had erupted in support for intervention. It would be for the humans' own good, after all. Of course, few had ever met a human before — and none could match Goran's years of experience with them. Most humans he'd met seemed happy and hopeful, not miserable and restless. Goran was open to the possibility that his judgment was wrong, but at least it was based on real encounters with real humans.

▲▲▲

It was about an hour after Goran's arrival at Boonesborough that its namesake walked into view. Daniel hadn't been hunting, as Goran had supposed, because he wasn't carrying his rifle and freshly killed game. Instead, Daniel carried a tanned deerskin.

He's probably been smoking it over a fire pit, Goran thought.

Placing the skin on a pile next to one of the cabins, Daniel glanced up briefly and winked an acknowledgement before going inside. Goran flew off the post and landed on the roof. From there, he could hear the voices within.

"Think I'll head out to the smoker again before dark," he heard Daniel say.

"Are you sure that's safe?" said a female voice that Goran recognized as that of Rebecca, Daniel's wife.

"I'll be just fine, no need to worry," Daniel replied. "I won't go alone. I'll have my guardian angel with me."

"Your what?" Rebecca asked.

"My rifle, Mrs. Boone — my trusty guardian angel," Daniel said with a playful lilt.

There was no more talk. Goran fancied he heard Daniel kiss his wife reassuringly. Then Daniel emerged, picked up his gun, and began a leisurely walk out of the settlement. Goran followed, staying far above the human's head until they reached the forest.

"I was wondering how long it would take you to find us," said Daniel as he leaned against a tree and watched Goran flutter down beside him.

"It may seem like a year since we were together," the fairy replied, "but to me it has only been a few weeks. After Sycamore Shoals, my ranging took me to Charlotte Town and then home to consult with my guild."

"Did you get a chance to spend some time with your family, Goran? As hard as it's been to build up this place, I can't tell you how much of a relief it's been to have Rebecca and the children with me this time."

"I did, yes," Goran said, but the hesitation in his voice wasn't lost on his friend.

Daniel looked at him appraisingly. "Still having a hard time adjusting, I suppose. Sorry — as much as I've tried to make sense of fairy time, I reckon no human ever could."

Goran smiled. "I appreciate what you are trying to say, Daniel, although you are mistaken on one point. There *have* been humans who came to understand what it was like, as least for a time. Sometimes a ranger will bring an injured or diseased human through the Shimmer to be healed by magecraft. Other times, rangers bring humans to be interviewed by guildmasters. In a few cases, humans have found their own way in."

"How's that possible?" Daniel wondered.

"No one knows," Goran admitted, "but whatever the explanation for their entry, when the humans are returned to the Blur, they often find it has been months or even years since they left. Of course, for most, their distress is only temporary. Spellsong relieves them of the burden."

Daniel eyes widened. "You said in *most* cases."

Goran nodded. "Yes, Daniel, there are exceptions. After you and I met for the second time, and I realized my memory spell had not worked on you, I spent much time in the guild library studying obscure works of humanlore. For most humans resistant to spellsong, the memories they retain are jumbled and confused. We Folk have never been particularly concerned about them. If they try to explain what they recall, other humans just hear it as a funny child's tale or a fantastical campfire story."

"I grew up hearing such tales from my Ma," Daniel said.

"Most humans do. The effect even makes it easier for rangers to collect humanwares. When we appear and offer household chores or magical wishes in exchange for supplies, humans remember the tales and comply without much of a fuss. Of course, we still wipe their memories clean, just to be safe."

"Which doesn't always work."

"No, it does not, and we cannot always tell in the moment," the fairy said. "Shortly after I began my education, back in England, a human subject was brought to the Rangers Guild. He was a special case — a human who had somehow traversed Shimmer barriers on multiple occasions, in multiple locations. He also exhibited remarkable resistance to magic. So, as a test, our guildmasters had all the apprentices and journeymen form a chorus and subject the human to hours of intensive spellsong."

Daniel seemed fascinated by the story. "And that worked?"

"It did, after a fashion. After placement back in the Blur, the subject still recalled some of his experiences. But his memories were so contorted and exaggerated that they bore only a passing resemblance to the truth. We found out later that the man left England for Ireland and befriended a clergyman there, a writer who used the faulty memories as inspiration for a book."

Goran saw Daniel start as recognition set in. "Surely you don't mean…"

"Of course I do," Goran interrupted. "Our spellsong subject was a sea-faring surgeon named Lemuel Gulliver."

Daniel shook his head and laughed softly. "Every time I think I understand, you tell me something new, something I'd never guessed."

Even as his friend continued to chuckle, Goran felt a painful stab of regret. He did, indeed, have something new to tell Daniel, something Daniel would never have guessed. The levity of the past few minutes was about to vanish.

"Daniel, I tracked you down, all the way to Kentucky, because I have news."

"Oh, if you mean the Indian troubles, we know about them now," Daniel assured him, matching Goran's quick transition to seriousness. "There was an attack south of here by raiders led by our old friend Dragging Canoe. They killed and scalped four whites. Shawnees and Mingos have also been raiding across the Ohio. Some settlers fled back over the mountains. But we're building up our defenses. We'll be ready if they come in force."

Goran sighed, wishing he didn't have to say more but knowing he must.

"Your predicament goes far beyond just raids, Daniel," he said. "The Indians are being supplied by British agents — from Fort Detroit to the northwest and from Saint Augustine to the southeast. The British are using the frontier raids as a distraction so the Americans will be unable to concentrate their forces to the east against British and Loyalist forces."

Daniel cast him a puzzled look. "Many settlers moved here to get away from the war. They never much liked the Southern planters or the Northern politicians. They don't want anything to do with the rebellion. Some still feel loyal to Britain."

"And how do you feel, Daniel?"

"I feel crowded and pushed around," Daniel said. "I want to build something new here in Kentucky. I want us to be left alone to do as we see fit."

Goran heard the determination in his friend's voice. It saddened him.

"That will not be possible," Goran said. "The raids will get worse. The British will keep supplying and encouraging the Indians. The Americans will respond. The war will not remain in the East. It will spill over the mountains. In fact, it is already here."

Daniel shrugged his shoulders. "You may be right, and I appreciate you coming all the way here to warn us, but we're not giving up our homes without a fight."

"You will have to fight more foes than you realize," said Goran, weighing his words carefully. "Britain has powerful allies."

Daniel looked taken aback. "I always take Indian nations seriously, even when other whites foolishly dismiss them. And if you mean other powers will come to Britain's aid, I don't follow you. I figure the French and Spanish will be happy to see Britain stuck in a new war."

"Those are not the allies I mean," Goran said, not daring to look Daniel in the eyes. "The Sylphs of the Knob have decided to help Britain crush the rebellion. So have many other Folk."

Neither spoke for a time. Goran's curiosity overcame his discomfort and he cast a glance at Daniel's face. He had expected to see incredulity, confusion, even rage. Instead, the face he saw was rigid and expressionless. Daniel's eyes were cold.

"Have you come to deliver commands from your fairy king?" Daniel said, with no hint of either playfulness or resentment.

Goran would have preferred a passionate argument or an angry tirade. He found Daniel's cool detachment far more painful — and more chilling. For the first time in the hunter's presence, Goran didn't feel like a companion. He felt like prey.

"It was not my decision, Daniel," he protested, "and no one sent me here to deliver anything. I came of my own accord because you are my friend.

If the guildmasters knew I was here telling you this, they would be furious. They might remove me from the Rangers Guild."

"The threat we face isn't losing our place in some club," Daniel said icily. "We face death at the hands of Indians — and now, I take it, death at the hands of fairy folk like you."

It felt like Daniel had stabbed him with a knife. "I would *never* harm you or your family," Goran insisted, his own resentment building. "And the Sylphs are unlikely to enter the war directly. There are other ways, subtle ways that will nevertheless prove difficult for your people to overcome. The rebellion will surely fail, Daniel. You must see that now."

"The rebellion?" Daniel said. "What politicians and kings say doesn't interest me. We will *not* be chased off our land — not by foul weather, not by ferocious animals, not by Indian raids, not by red-coated or blue-coated armies with guns, and not even by fairies with spells. Take that message back to your Knob. Tell them to leave us alone."

With that, Daniel picked up his rifle and began trotting back to Boonesborough.

"Wait, Daniel, please," Goran said. "Let me try to explain. My duty is…"

"There's no duty higher than friendship," Daniel called over his shoulder, his bitterness now unmistakable. "And there's no duty that could've ever made me your enemy. I guess fairies see it differently."

Goran was horrified and deeply wounded. How could this man he'd known and trusted for years think so little of Goran's character? How could he be so unreasonable in the face of undeniable truths and overwhelming odds?

"I am not your enemy, Daniel. I could never be your enemy!" he cried.

But the human was already gone.

▲▲▲

Daniel wanted nothing to do with Goran. He'd made that very clear weeks ago. Still, the Sylph ranger couldn't bring himself to leave Boonesborough. He couldn't leave his closest friend in great danger, even if the man no longer thought of him as a friend.

Daniel knew. He was too skilled a woodsman to miss the signs, despite

Goran's attempts to stay out of eyesight and earshot. But the human made no effort either to talk to the Sylph or to chase him away.

From a distance, Goran watched the workmen finish the first wall of the stockade and start on the second. He saw the settlers work their fields, convert the local game into food and fiber, improve their rudely constructed and furnished cabins, and try to eke a living out of a remote wilderness. He watched as Daniel and the others went out on scouting parties. In fact, Goran scouted the woods around the settlement himself, hoping against hope that Indian raiders would choose a different target.

It was on a Sunday afternoon in mid-July that the situation changed.

Goran was ranging west of the settlement. Hearing voices, he flew rapidly to the northeast, crossed the river, then landed on the first of a line of sycamore trees, singing a concealment spell in low tones. He immediately caught sight of a canoe floating downstream. It carried three girls. Goran recognized Daniel's thirteen-year-old daughter Jemima Boone. From a snatch of conversation he'd overheard a week earlier, Goran figured the other two other girls were probably Jemima's friends Fanny and Betsy, the daughters of another Boonesborough founder, Richard Callaway.

Why are they so far away from the settlement without armed escort? Goran tried to think of a discreet way to sound a warning.

It would have come too late.

When the canoe floated close to the north bank of the river, Goran was horrified to see five Indian warriors scamper from behind bushes. One grasped the canoe and began pulling it to shore, holding up his arm to fend off Jemima's spirited whacks at him with a paddle. The girls screamed. Then a warrior grabbed the hair of one of the Callaways and traced his finger along her scalp. The message was unmistakable. The girls fell silent.

Whatever his duty to the Sylphs and their alliance with the British, Goran resolved not to let Daniel Boone's daughter and the other two girls come to harm. Lifting his bow over his head and pulling an arrow from his quiver, Goran began considering his options.

"Your assistance is not required, ranger."

The voice came from Goran's left. He turned his head to see a Pukwudgie standing on the limb of a neighboring sycamore. From his lithe physique to his hair cut in Mohawk fashion to the black-and-yellow fletching of the short missile fitted onto the spear-thrower pointed at Goran, he could be none other than Atta, the scout Daniel Boone and Isaac Shelby spoke of.

Goran thought quickly. "This is your doing, then?" he asked, lowering his bow and hoping the Pukwudgie would do the same with his weapon. Goran nodded toward the Indians who were leading their captives away into the woods. "Is this the entire raiding party or are these humans the vanguard of a larger attack?"

Atta regarded Goran with half-lidded eyes. Goran noticed for the first time a gash running along the scout's jaw line from ear to chin. Its color suggested the wound was recent, and that the Pukwudgie hadn't had a chance to get it healed properly with magecraft.

"I am told the Sylphs have joined the Great Alliance," Atta said. "That is wise. The American threat must be contained, swiftly and firmly." He still had his spear-thrower raised.

"But is there a broader assault to come?" Goran persisted. "No doubt you can oversee a simple abduction. If the Indians plan to attack Boonesborough, however, you may benefit from my help. Two voices sing stronger spells than one."

The Pukwudgie's nostrils flared. "*Boones*borough. How arrogant to name this squalid place after himself. I neither require nor desire help to deal with him. He was warned. Now I shall sting Boone where it will be most painful."

"So, it is a personal matter, then," Goran observed, trying to sound calm while his mind raced. "I try not to pay too much attention to individual humans myself. I find it a distraction."

"I am not distracted," Atta said, still watching Goran carefully. "Terror is an indispensable weapon of war. The raids by our humans have chased many cowardly settlers back over the mountains. Only a couple of hundred remain. The more they fear for the safety of their wives and children, the more they will flee. And, if soldiers come here in response, all the better. That will mean fewer soldiers to resist the British armies."

The raiding party had vanished into the forest. Goran faced an immediate decision. Should he pursue the girls or take the news to Daniel? Either way, he must first elude this Atta.

"You seem to have things well in hand. I will be on my way, then." Goran flapped his wings and lifted off the sycamore limb.

"I think not," said Atta. "You and I will remain here. I would like to hear of the mission that brings you to Pukwudgie territory."

"Just gathering information," Goran said, trying to sound cordial as he continued his flight and began to raise his bow.

The first indication his subterfuge had failed was a lancing pain as Atta's copper-tipped missile drew a bloody line across Goran's thigh. With a yelp, he sank to the ground, still clutching his bow with his left hand while his right moved reflexively to cover his wound.

Atta leapt from the limb and fitted another missile into the groove of his spear-thrower. Raising it over his head, he flung it at Goran, who managed to knock it aside with a sweep of his bow. Then the Pukwudgie cast aside his thrower, drew a finely crafted tomahawk from his waist, and came at Goran, his lips forming a contemptuous snarl.

Wincing in pain, Goran drew his hunting knife and assumed a fighting position. Atta chopped down with the tomahawk but struck only empty air as Goran managed to spin away, albeit with great difficulty, on his wounded leg. He tried a knife slash as he spun but Atta was no less nimble, dodging to his left and raising the tomahawk for another strike.

This time, Goran caught it on the upper limb of his bow. The copper blade sunk into the yew and stayed there. Thinking quickly, Goran cast the bow away, which had the effect of yanking the tomahawk from Atta's hand. Sensing a sudden advantage, Goran raised his knife to strike — but Atta was swift, and unwounded. He grasped the wrist of Goran's knife hand and punched the Sylph in the jaw.

Even as Goran sank to the ground, dazed, he heard for the first time shouts and running feet. The girls' initial screams must have attracted attention. Atta heard them, too, and broke his grip on Goran.

"Another time," snapped the Yellow Jacket as he turned and ran into the forest. "Your debt to me remains. You will pay it in blood."

His leg throbbing with pain from the bloody gash, Goran managed to get into the air and find a perch in a pine tree as a group of humans came into view, led by Daniel. They crossed the river and began examining the ground. It took Daniel only seconds to read the footprints.

"There were four or five Indians and they took the girls into the trees," he told the others. "Let's find their trail."

While Goran watched from the tree, he tore a strip of cloth from his traveling cloak and tied it around his thigh to stop the bleeding. He sheathed his knife and then realized he'd forgotten about his other weapon. At that precise moment, he saw Daniel stoop and pick up Goran's bow — with Atta's tomahawk still embedded in it.

"What's that you got there?" said one of the settlers.

"Oh, nothing of interest," Daniel replied, flinging his find into the river. Goran saw it land in the shallows. One limb of the bow must have planted itself in the riverbed, because a few inches of the other limb still protruded above the water line.

Then Daniel announced with satisfaction the discovery of the abductors' trail. "It's too late to follow it, though. We'll camp tonight and start out fresh in the morning."

Goran had great confidence in Daniel's abilities, but the Indians' head start troubled him. What might happen in the time it took for the rescue party to catch up with them? Still suffering from the leg wound and weakened by the loss of blood, Goran decided to act. He didn't have Daniel's tracking skills. It was too dark to track the Indians on the ground, anyway. But Goran had the advantage of mobility. He'd fly all night if he had to. He'd find the girls.

Realizing he'd have a better chance if he recovered his bow, the Sylph crept silently to the edge of the tree branch, leapt into the air, and soared gracefully to the shallows. Hovering over the spot where the bow was sticking up above the river, Goran managed to free it with a couple of pulls, dropping Atta's tomahawk back into the water. Then he took to the air.

▲▲▲

His first night and day of searching the Kentucky wilderness turned up nothing. The next day's search would have proved no more fruitful had Jemima Boone lacked resourcefulness. But she was her father's daughter.

At her long, agonizing shout of pain, Goran whirled in midair and swooped rapidly in her direction. When he reached a clearing, he found her lying on the ground, clutching her foot and writhing with pain. The two Callaway girls were on the ground with Jemima, comforting her, while the five Indians stood in a ring around them. Goran concluded from their dress and equipment that three were Cherokees and the other two Shawnees. He also noticed an old horse standing a few paces away, snorting and stamping its feet.

"Get up, little squaw," ordered one of the captors, a short, thickly built man with a bundle of hawk feathers thrust into his hair.

"She's injured herself falling off the horse, Hanging Maw," said another warrior.

The one called Hanging Maw laughed. "I suspect she is a better rider than she would have us believe." He stooped down, pulled Jemima to her feet with one powerful arm, and pointed to the Callaways with the other.

"Come, we still have a way to go before nightfall," he ordered as he led Jemima out of the clearing. The others followed behind. As Hanging Maw passed the old horse, now chewing on a tuft of grass, he slapped its flank.

"Go on now, Soquili, we have no more need of you," he said. The horse took off in the opposite direction.

Then Hanging Maw turned to Jemima. "I admire your courage, girl, but do not try my patience further. We've already caught you breaking twigs and dropping bits of cloth. We've removed your shoes so you can no longer press your heels into the dirt. If your people are tracking us, they will get no more help from you. I will not permit any further delay. I must return home quickly. My nephew Dragging Canoe is about to launch his attacks along the Holston, and I will not be left out."

"Pa won't rest until he finds us," Jemima snapped defiantly. "You don't scare me. You are the one who should be scared."

Hanging Maw laughed again. "You are indeed a fine little squaw. When we get to the Shawnee village, many a young man may wish to have you for a wife. But, if you continue to resist, you will never know such an honor."

Jemima and the Callaways looked at each other fearfully. The other Indians joined Hanging Maw in laughter. Goran had heard enough. It was time to act. Drawing an arrow, he fitted it to his bow and took careful aim.

Perhaps his arrow would have struck Hanging Maw had the long wooden stick not smashed into Goran's bow, spoiling his aim. He looked up just in time to see the triumphant face of Atta Yellow Jacket looking down from a higher branch, swinging the stick again — this time at Goran's head.

The Sylph dodged the blow and jumped out of the tree, hovering and reloading. Now he was the one with the advantage. Other than the stick, Atta was unarmed. Goran had nine more arrows. Surely one would find its mark.

What Goran failed to consider was that Atta might not be alone. "Wound him!" shouted the Pukwudgie, "but leave the killing stroke to me!"

Atta's command gave Goran a split-second warning. He banked left as three spears flew past him. Straining his wings to gain altitude, Goran looked down and scanned the tree line. Soon he spotted the three other Pukwudgie scouts. Each wielded enchanted spear-throwers similar to that of Atta, who'd dropped to the ground among them.

Goran could simply have eluded them by flying away. But that meant leaving the three girls behind. Instead, Goran fitted another arrow to his bow, said a prayer, and dove toward the Pukwudgies.

Not expecting him to charge into overwhelming odds, Goran's foes scrambled for cover rather than launching another round of spears. He fired as he swooped past. He saw his arrow strike a fallen log. One of the Pukwudgies leapt from behind cover and loosed a spear. It soared over Goran's head as the Sylph glided along the clearing and then banked right to climb once more into the air.

"We will soon pluck those feathers!" Atta cried, snatching the weapon from the other scout and demanding the remainder of the latter's stock of throwing spears.

Reloading, Goran decided to try a different approach. Rather than diving in low, he hovered above the clearing, hoping to stay safe while picking them off with his longer-range weapon. Unfortunately, his next three arrows also missed their targets.

"You waste your stock while we recover every spear we throw," Atta taunted. "Soon you will have to come down and face us, bird-man."

Goran's next shot, however, struck home. One of the Pukwudgies screamed as the arrow struck him full in the breast, sinking so deep that the fletching was barely visible on his bare chest. The scout fell lifeless. Atta glowered and lifted his weapon to the ready.

After loosing two more shafts to no effect, Goran paused. He had only two more shots. Even if each found its mark, he'd have to face the remaining warrior on the ground, where his wounded leg would present a significant disadvantage. More likely, he'd have to face two or three foes. The odds of survival were long.

He decided to fire words rather than arrows.

"You call the humans cowardly, Atta, yet you are the one making war on women and children," Goran accused. "You are the one willing to lie to these Indians, to claim to share their grievances, when all you really want are dispensable warriors to employ in someone else's war."

Atta's thin lips formed a sneer. "You speak meaningless words, bird-man. How little you know. *Of course* we use the Shawnees, the Cherokees, and the others for our own ends. But the British are no less tools in our hands. We care nothing about their king or his meaningless treaties. We care only about protecting our domains. We will let no others displace the humans we herd. And we will let no other Folk encroach on our territory."

"You are the one speaking nonsense," Goran said. "You might as well stand in the river and command it to stop flowing. All your efforts will come to naught. In the meantime, you will be merely the lackeys of other Folk and the abusers of young girls."

Red-faced and sputtering with rage, Atta shook his fist at Goran and opened his mouth to hurl another taunt. Then he abruptly shut his mouth. Gone was the angry scowl. In its place was Atta's previous composure, framed by half-lidded eyes and the faintest hint of a smirk.

"Your tactic has become obvious, ranger," the Pukwudgie said. "We will not snap at your bait. We will not lose track of our true mission."

With that, Atta Yellow Jacket nodded to the two surviving scouts. They ran into the woods. Goran found a branch and alighted to rest. He'd long since lost track of which way the Indians had taken the girls. He could only hope that Atta had, as well.

▲▲▲

The next morning, Goran resolved to find a waterway and then follow it until he saw a familiar landmark. Presently the Sylph saw a little creek, swooped down to take a drink from it, then flew back up to follow its path. Within minutes, he spotted a party of men walking along the creek. He rec-ognized the familiar beaver hat of Daniel Boone.

Are they lost, too?

Goran thought of the fearful girls he'd tried to rescue. He wondered if they'd already been delivered to captivity in some Indian village, or perhaps to a worse fate.

The search party halted. Daniel pointed out something on the bank of the creek. Then the men broke into a trot along what appeared to be an old buffalo trail. Heartened at the humans' sudden burst of speed, Goran flew above them, nocking an arrow.

When Daniel and the others reached a clearing, they dropped to their knees and began crawling stealthily through the canebrake. Goran looked beyond them and spotted the smoke of a cookfire. The raiding party! Either Hanging Maw had become reckless or he thought he was so far ahead of his pursuers that caution was no longer necessary.

In any event, it proved to be a misjudgment. Goran drew in a breath as Daniel knelt, aimed his rifle, and fired. One of the Indians cried out as the bullet struck home, throwing a splash of blood to the earth.

"That's Pa's gun!" cried Jemima exuberantly.

The other men fired, too. As Goran hurtled toward the raiding party, he saw one of the Shawnees raise his war club and hurl it at one of the Callaway girls. At the last moment, she ducked beneath it. Then the Indians fled into the canebrake, two of them carrying the man Daniel shot and Hanging Maw running alongside the remaining warrior, his arm around the man's shoulders. The fifth Indian must have been wounded, as well.

Goran pulled up from his dive and sang a concealment spell. As far as he could tell, none of the humans had seen him. He watched Daniel hug his daughter and the other men help the Callaways to their feet. After some conversation, the girls began walking with their rescuers back the way they came.

All except Daniel.

"I'd like to poke around the camp; maybe they left something behind," he explained. As soon as they were out of sight, Daniel looked up at the hovering fairy.

"Have you been following us the whole time?" he asked as Goran alighted next to him. "I'd have thought you'd at least offer to help, although I wouldn't have wanted it."

Hurt once again by an insult from his long-time friend, Goran struggled to find his words.

"You do not understand," he finally said. "I have been trying to..."

"Good thing this wasn't my first time tracking raiders," Daniel broke in, reaching for his powder horn and pouch to reload his rifle. "I knew we'd never catch up tracking them through the woods. So I guessed where they were headed, took a shortcut down the creek, and that was that."

Goran fell silent. Daniel truly *hadn't* needed his help to find the girls.

Goran's admiration for his friend soared to new heights. But what would have happened if Atta and the Pukwudgies had been with Hanging Maw during the final attack? Perhaps Goran's delaying tactic had proven useful after all.

Rather than risking an argument about it — or worse, another hurtful accusation from Daniel — Goran said nothing.

"I've got to see the girls safely home," said Daniel, who'd finished reloading and was now looking Goran in the eyes. "I'll leave you with this. I don't know how much of *Gulliver's Travels* were real and how much were dreams you put in his head. Still, remember when the king of Lilliput orders Gulliver to help him conquer Blefuscu? Gulliver refuses to employ his great power to aid an unworthy cause. He suffers for it, but he makes the right decision."

Goran recalled the tale.

"Gulliver makes the right decision," Daniel continued, "even though he's just an ordinary, non-magical human like me. What does that say about you and your Folk?"

Chapter 15 — The Palmettos

COLONEL PETER MUHLENBERG STOOD ON the side of the road watching the men of the Eighth Virginia Regiment, his regiment, march into the bustling seaport of Charles Town. Dressed in hunting shirts, waistcoats, and breeches dyed blue, as well as coats of varying colors and felt hats cocked on three sides, the men of the regiment looked tired but hopeful as they entered the town. They were hoping for rest and a good meal. They were hoping not to have to march again for a long time.

The Lowcountry of South Carolina was a long way from the Shenandoah Valley of Virginia. In March, after reaching its full strength of nearly seven hundred men, Peter's regiment had first been ordered to coastal Virginia to help defend the province against raiding by Lord Dunmore. Then they'd been sent to accompany the new commander of the Southern Department, General Charles Lee, to North Carolina to defend against a British invasion there.

The invasion never happened. The British commander, General Henry Clinton, had hoped to join forces at the mouth of the Cape Fear River with loyalists marching down from Cross Creek, but patriots had stopped the loyalists at Moore's Creek Bridge, about twenty-four miles inland.

Invading North Carolina no longer made sense. Where would General Clinton go next? Concluding Charles Town would be the target, General Lee ordered the units under his command, including Peter's regiment, to march south yet again.

It had been a lot to ask. The Virginians' supplies were limited, their equipment far from standard. Most were armed with hunting rifles, not military-style muskets. That meant few had bayonets, so Peter knew the regiment was ill-suited to stand against redcoats in a hand-to-hand fight.

On the other hand, the Shenandoah men were excellent shots, having hunted most of their lives to help feed their families. Some had also skirmished with Indian raiders or were veterans of the 1774 war against Chief Cornstalk. Over the past four months, Peter trained his men as much as circumstances and his own limited knowledge allowed.

Before the war, during Peter's hunting trips with George Washington, his friend had talked of meeting Charles Lee during the disastrous Braddock expedition. The meeting hadn't gone well. Washington disliked the man, Peter knew, calling him "fickle and violent in his temper." But Washington also recognized that, as a veteran British officer now willing to fight for the American cause, Charles Lee was a valuable asset.

During the long march from Virginia to Wilmington, North Carolina, and then to Charles Town, South Carolina, Peter found General Lee to be an able leader, if sometimes hard to get along with. In turn, Lee several times praised the deportment of Peter's regiment. Of course, his Virginians had yet to be tested under fire. If the British ships clearly visible on the horizon were any indication, that test could be administered soon enough.

▲▲▲

"Colonel William Moultrie of the Second South Carolina Regiment, I have the pleasure of introducing Colonel Peter Muhlenberg of the Eighth Virginia."

General Charles Lee sat astride his horse, motioning the South Carolinian forward to shake hands with Peter, also on horseback. Peter recalled that Lee and Moultrie were about the same age — in their mid-forties, while Peter was only twenty-nine — and yet he was struck by the stark contrast between the two. Charles Lee was an exceedingly thin man with a sickly complexion, a bony face that often bore a scowl, and a large nose overlooking a weak chin. His uniform was ill-fitted and poorly maintained. As for William Moultrie, he was stocky and unpretentious, with a ruddy complexion. He filled his uniform with ease and grace. The line of sweat across his brow made him look vigorous, not pallid.

"I am pleased to make your acquaintance, sir, and even more pleased to have your Virginians here with us," Moultrie said. "We believe the British will make an attempt to force Sullivan's Island any day now."

Peter looked to the structure from which the South Carolinian had walked. The square-shaped fort on the southwestern end of the island was unfinished. Only the seaward walls were complete, and Peter wasn't sure how they'd stand up to broadsides. If the British silenced the guns on Sullivan's Island, Charles Town itself would be their next target.

The fort's walls consisted of large mounds of sand pounded flat between two high rows of straight, light-colored logs. The flag waving above them bore a white crescent moon in the northwest corner of a dark-blue field. Peter had heard in town that Colonel Moultrie designed the flag himself to inspire his fellow Carolinians. It was too far away for Peter to make out the letters stitched into the crescent. But he'd been told they spelled "Liberty."

Peter took a closer look at the fort's bastions, one per corner, guns protruding from each. They were constructed of the same light-colored logs that made up the fort's walls. "What kind of timber is that, Colonel Moultrie? I don't think I've seen its like."

"Palmettos," Moultrie answered. "They are a common sight here. We have found them to be excellent material for our defenses — tough but flexible, just like our people."

Peter took an instant liking to the man.

"Well, sir, at the risk of sounding didactic or incurring an accusation of prolixity, I feel compelled to restate my concerns about the fortification," said General Lee, who had a reputation for wordiness. "Your walls of sand and palmetto reflect considerable exertions, of that I have no doubt. However, I fear they will prove less an impediment to British incursion than a slaughter pen for hundreds of Americans best deployed to defend the town."

Peter could see Moultrie bristling, but the South Carolinian said nothing.

"Still, I recognize the General Assembly has countermanded my recommendation to relocate you to the mainland," Lee continued. "Let us hope it will not be necessary to evacuate in the midst of enemy fire."

"We will beat them," Moultrie said simply.

General Lee pointed at the British vessels anchored off-shore. "I have heard some say that when those ships come to lay alongside your fort, they will knock it down in half an hour."

"Then we will lie behind the ruins and prevent their men from landing." said the South Carolina colonel, his determined face mirroring the stubbornness in his voice.

Peter and General Lee resumed their ride up the length of Sullivan's Island, passing dune after dune, until they reached its northeast tip. There, several hundred Continentals and militia were encamped with their commander, Colonel Thomson. Peter could see two cannons and a line of riflemen behind their own line of fortifications, also made of sand and palmetto.

General Lee called Peter's attention to another island across the narrow channel. "British regulars gained that position a few days ago. They have explored the possibility of an incursion over the inlet several times, so far without success. For now, your regiment will remain on the mainland, as General Clinton may opt to attack there. But if this advance guard appears hard-pressed, your men will reinforce Thomson. Colonel Moultrie's fort would be just as imperiled from a successful British landing here as it will be from bombardment from the sea."

"Yes, sir," Peter said. "The regiment is at your disposal."

▲▲▲

It turned out that the Virginians would enjoy only a few days of rest in Charles Town. Shortly after breakfast on June 28, Peter heard the report of a signal cannon. Hurrying to the dock, he saw nine British warships sailing toward Sullivan's Island. The first rank dropped anchor and began firing broadsides into the fort. Colonel Moultrie's defenders responded with their own artillery. The roar was deafening to Peter, even from his vantage point on the mainland. He'd tried to prepare himself for the potentially overwhelming sights of war. What he hadn't reckoned on was the overwhelming *sounds* of war.

He could also hear cannon and gunfire coming from the other end of island. Had British soldiers managed to establish a beachhead there? It was impossible to see what was happening because of distance and smoke. Peter couldn't tell how the palmetto fort was faring, either, although various rumors spread through the waiting troops. Some claimed Moultrie's batteries had blasted the British ships to pieces. Some claimed the ships had blasted the fort to pieces. Some claimed Moultrie's force was out of gunpowder and about to evacuate.

Peter knew better than to credit the rumors of anxious men far removed from the action. The claim that the fort had already fallen was highly improbable. Three British frigates had tried to move around the tip of the island, presumably to shoot into the fort's poorly protected rear. But they were stuck in the shoals. None of the warships had moved closer to Moultrie's position, and the American artillery continued to fire, albeit sporadically.

The rumor about a gunpowder shortage gained credence early in the afternoon, when one of the fort's defenders crossed the water to ask for resupply. The news soon spread among Peter's men. He walked among them, offering words of encouragement, some in English, some in the native German of many of his men.

Shortly before three o'clock in the afternoon, the guns in Moultrie's fort suddenly fell silent. At just that moment, Charles Lee rode into the ranks of the regiment. "Colonel Muhlenberg, a moment if you please," he said. Peter sprinted quickly to the general's side.

"There will be a supply run to the island," Lee told him. "I have a mind to journey over to the fort myself and take stock of the situation. I have need of another set of eyes. Have your lieutenant colonel prepare your regiment for imminent deployment, and then follow me."

Presently the two officers, accompanied by several soldiers, were in a boat headed toward the palmetto fort. The British ships continued to fire broadsides but now there was no answering fire. "Put your backs into it!" General Lee shouted to the rowers.

As Peter watched with dismay, a British cannonball smashed the fort's flagpole. The blue flag with the crescent moon tumbled from sight. Peter heard groans from the troops and townspeople watching from shore.

When the boat reached the island, the small party ran to the unfinished gate of the fort, which had been barricaded with several timbers. Defenders pulled them away to let the party inside. The scent of gunpowder and sweat, mixed with the usual smells of a sweltering midsummer day on a Carolina beach, washed over Peter, making him feel queasy and disoriented. He caught a glimpse of the fort's commander standing a few paces away. Then he saw a sergeant appear beside William Moultrie.

"Colonel, don't let us fight without our flag!" cried the sergeant.

"What can you do?" Moultrie asked. "The staff is broken."

"Then, sir," the sergeant replied, "I'll fix it to a halberd and place it on a merlon of the bastion, next to the enemy."

Peter looked on with amazement as the man sprang outside the fort, retrieved the flag, strapped it to one of the sponge staffs used to clean a cannon between shots, and planted it in the sand of the wall. The flag waved again for all to see. "God save liberty and my country forever!" the sergeant shouted. Peter had never seen anything more thrilling. The roars of approval from the fort's defenders signaled their agreement.

Peter returned his attention to Lee, who was in a spirited conversation with Moultrie. Spying Peter, the general motioned him over.

"The colonel ceased fire because several men reported seeing British regulars among the dunes beyond the fort," Lee said. "He deemed it prudent to conserve powder in case it proves necessary to fend off an infantry assault. See if you can determine the veracity of the account. Quickly now!"

Unsure how to proceed, Peter ran to the northward-facing wall and began asking the troops what they'd seen.

"I saw a boat land and a score of redcoats get out," said one soldier. Another said he spotted artillerymen wheeling a gun into position. A third man, a North Carolina militiaman named John Lemmond, said he saw British grenadiers running between two dunes.

Peter climbed onto one of the gun platforms and looked over the wall. He saw nothing but sandy desolation. It seemed improbable that the British had landed on the island but made no effort to fire on or assault the fort. Peter scanned the dunes carefully.

What was that?

A flash of red caught his eye. Something had darted behind a dune, but it was far too small to be a British redcoat.

There it is again!

This time, Peter got a clearer look before the figure disappeared into a hole. Before he met Har the Tower, the sight would have struck him as preposterous. Now he knew better. The fairy Peter saw diving into the sand was a bit shorter than a Dwarf, and slighter of build. His dress was similar to Har's. But the red cap on his head pointed straight upward, while Har's drooped down over one shoulder.

Peter felt prickles in his scalp. He was being watched. Looking at the spot of beach where the fairy had disappeared, Peter soon discerned two eyes peering over a lip of sand.

As he stared back at the eyes regarding him, they widened in shock. Slowly they rose, along with the rest of the fellow, until he was standing in stockinged feet on the sandy beach of Sullivan's Island, the fairy's mouth moving as if asking a silent question. At first Peter thought the creature was using spellsong, but he heard no sound. Apparently the fellow had already tried his spell on Peter, to no effect. That's what left him mystified and, it seemed, fearful.

Then, without a backward glance, the little man scampered to the edge of the beach, leapt into the water, and began swimming toward Charles Town.

"Well, what is your report?"

Peter wheeled to see General Lee looking at him impatiently. "Must we reorient our defenses — or, better still, evacuate this exposed position after all?"

Peter shook his head. "No, sir. The sightings were mistaken. There are no British troops here."

The general gave a brief nod and began striding back to where Moultrie stood issuing orders to some artillerymen.

"The new stock of gunpowder has arrived, General Lee," the South Carolinian said. "We are distributing it now."

"By all means resume your fire, Colonel Moultrie," Lee said. "The reports of British landings on the beach are erroneous."

Then the general raised the volume of his voice so all the Americans surrounding them could hear. "I have seen many bombardments and cannonades in my time, gentlemen, but none comparable to this in one day. Colonel, I see that you are doing very well here!"

Moultrie acknowledged the compliment with a short, respectful bow.

"You have no occasion for me, so I will go up to the town again," Lee continued. "Colonel Muhlenberg, when we reach shore, you may get your regiment loaded onto boats and conveyed to the advance guard. Let us ensure that General Clinton's forces never set foot on this island."

▲▲▲

By the time the Virginians were fully assembled on the northeast corner of Sullivan's Island, it was late afternoon. Peter could still hear British ships and Moultrie's batteries exchanging fire behind him. Ahead, he saw Colonel Thomson's men behind their own mile-long breastworks, pointing their rifles and their two cannons over the inlet.

"We have repulsed three attempts to land, but our ammunition is nearly spent," Thomson informed Peter. "We have but a single charge left for one of our guns and three for the other. Your reinforcement is most timely and most welcome, sir."

"The position will be held," Peter promised, directing his men into the positions being vacated by Thomson's exhausted Carolinians.

And so it was.

▲▲▲

The next day, they fully expected a new round of British assaults, but none came. The defenders of Charles Town had defeated the professional soldiers, sailors, and marines of the mighty British empire with few losses: twelve Americans killed and twenty-six wounded.

Peter was present in the fort, along with other officers and civilian leaders from the city, when General Lee addressed Colonel Moultrie and his men. "You have the congratulations and appreciations of your country, your comrades-in-arms, and your commander for your gallant defense of the fort."

Moultrie slapped one of the palmetto logs in the wall. "We have these to thank as much as anything else. They absorbed the British cannonballs like sponges."

Unbeknownst to anyone except Peter, another person had played a key role in ensuring the American victory: Har the Tower. It was from the Dwarf that Peter had first learned of spells that could make humans see things that weren't really there. It was also from Har that Peter had learned of the possibility of fairies helping the British win the war.

Still, as he walked back to his regiment, Peter was plagued with troubling questions. What kind of fairy was the little red-capped illusionist on the island? How many others backed the British cause? And what would they do next?

He recalled the words of the Prophet Jeremiah: *Call unto me, and I will answer thee, and show thee great and mighty things, which thou knowest not.*

Then the young American colonel knelt and prayed.

Chapter 16 — The Plan

FROM THE AIR, LONG ISLAND-ON-THE-HOLSTON looked like a narrow moccasin with an elongated heel. As Goran flew toward the island from the southeast, he could see the mountain on his left where he, Daniel, Nanyehi, and Tana had defeated the Stoneclad so long ago. To the right, on the opposite bank of the river, lay his destination: Fort Patrick Henry. In shape and location, it looked like a small, jagged rock being kicked by the moccasin of Long Island.

The image was an apt one. The previous summer, the Cherokees had attacked all across the frontier. They had kicked hard, but soft moccasin was no match for hard rock.

The Americans had responded with overwhelming and brutal force. Thousands of angry and determined militiamen had marched into Cherokee territory, destroying crops, livestock, and towns. Dragging Canoe and his followers had migrated south and west to establish new towns on Chickamauga Creek and other remote sites, but the other displaced Cherokees had become pitiful refugees.

Now their leaders had come here, to the newly built Fort Henry, to build a new peace with Virginia and North Carolina. Goran, too, had come here — back to Long Island, a place of cherished memories, of better days — in search of peace. But what he sought was peace of mind. *If American and Cherokee leaders can settle their bloody struggle through negotiation,* Goran thought, *perhaps American and British leaders could do the same.*

It had become his fondest hope. The American rebellion had brought great privation, suffering, and bloodshed to the colonies. It had also brought something dark and troubling to the policy of the Sylphs and other pro-British Folk. Their interventions in human affairs were becoming more numerous, more conspicuous. They were taking more risks. Goran was hardly the most traditional of rangers. He had taken risks, as well. But he had done so for the sake of friendship, to defend the weak, to right a wrong. Goran had no desire to wield power over humanity. For Folk like Guildmaster Bren and Atta Yellow Jacket, however, that desire was not only evident but, to their way of thinking, entirely justifiable.

What scared him the most was that their way of thinking was spreading.

Goran expected to see at least one familiar face at Fort Henry: Joseph Winston of Town Fork Creek. During the American retaliation, Winston had led the Surry County militia as a major. Now he had come to Long Island, along with three other men, to represent North Carolina in treaty negotiations. The Virginians were sending three representatives of their own, although Goran hadn't heard who they were. Officially, Goran had been sent by his guild to monitor Winston's movements and report back the results of the treaty negotiations. That he would do, although Goran found his motivations increasingly divergent from those of his fellow Sylphs.

As he finished singing a concealment spell and flew over the wall into Fort Henry, Goran saw a familiar face all right. But it wasn't Winston's — and it was looking right back at him, unaffected by Goran's magic charm. Nodding amiably, Isaac Shelby continued driving two cows down the dirt path toward a low-roofed cabin surrounded by cookfires. Goran guessed the militiamen in the fort would be having beef for supper.

The Sylph flew over the fort for several minutes, seeing no sign of the North Carolinian he sought, and decided to investigate the Cherokee encampments just outside. It was there that Goran saw two more familiar faces, again neither belonging to Joseph Winston.

The first was of Tana Song Snake. She was lounging on a stretch of grass between the fort and the Cherokees, fingering her blowpipe absent-mindedly. When she caught sight of Goran approaching, Tana jumped to her feet. Unlike Isaac Shelby, she didn't return Goran's smile.

"Are you alone," Tana asked warily, "or are you the advance scout of a war party?"

Puzzled by her antagonistic question, Goran shook his head. "I am alone, Tana. What makes you think I would be part of an attacking force?"

"Are your Folk not allies of the British?" she replied. "And are the British not allied with the Pukwudgies and the Chickamaugas? What else

191

am I to think?"

Goran felt hurt, frustrated, and angry, all at the same time. But it wouldn't do to target Tana. Instead, he sighed in resignation.

"I understand your question, now, but no—I scout for no attack on your friends," he said, sitting on the grass to rest his legs and also to put Tana at ease.

She looked at him dubiously for a few moments, then visibly relaxed and joined him.

"Is she here?" Goran asked hopefully.

Tana nodded. "Look over there," she said, pointing to several women standing in a circle. Nanyehi didn't return the fairies' gaze. But she inclined her head in a way that Goran interpreted as a signal that she knew they were looking at her.

"Nanyehi refused to let her uncle Attakullakulla travel without her," Tana explained. "He is an old man, as the humans measure time, and increasingly frail."

"And I take it you refused to let Nanyehi make such a journey without you," Goran said.

"True enough," she agreed. "Her people have suffered horribly at the hands of the Americans. But the threat I fear, and would protect her from, comes not from them, or from any other humans."

Once more, Goran felt puzzled. "What threat do you mean?"

Tana looked away for a moment, visibly upset. Then her expression abruptly changed from concern to curiosity. "I see we are not alone," she said.

Goran looked in the direction the Nunnehi scout was looking, to a spot on the high bank of the river. There, looking right back at Tana and Goran, was a face nestled in a clump of weeds. It was heart-shaped, tapering to a sharp chin. The eyes were large. They were turned up at each corner. And they were blue-green — a lustrous shade Goran had never seen before, and one strikingly different from the pale blue skin of the face and the dark blue of the hair that cascaded around it.

Goran realized he was holding his breath, as if subconsciously fearing that if he let the breath out, the incomparable face before him might have blown away with it.

It was Dela.

Isaac Shelby's description was enough to identify her. *But it was far from enough to do her justice*, Goran thought.

▲▲▲

After most of the people in Fort Henry and the surrounding Cherokee camps had retired for the evening, Goran met Isaac Shelby at the gate and accompanied him to the riverbank, where Nanyehi and Tana were already waiting for them in the soft moonlight. "It is wonderful to see you again, Isaac," said Nanyehi, holding out her hand.

"You, too," said Isaac, shaking her hand and casting a warm smile at Tana. "I've been worried about you. The militia had no choice but to fight back against the vicious attacks by Dragging Canoe and his followers, but I know many others got caught in the middle."

"I *did* oppose my cousin," Nanyehi said, her eyes narrowing. "So did my uncle and many others. Yet here we are, desperate and hungry, begging for scraps on our own sacred island."

Isaac looked taken aback. "My father and the other two commissioners from Virginia are here to make a fair treaty. And I'm here with cattle and other provisions for your people and mine. But Virginia didn't attack first. The Carolinians and Georgians didn't attack first. Cherokees did."

Nanyehi's mouth formed a smirk. "If I keep peeling away the onion, what will we find? What about the illegal settlements on our hunting grounds? What about the unjust treatment of the Cherokees who helped your people win your war against the French?"

Stepping cautiously between his two friends, Goran held up a hand. "Please, I hoped our meeting would advance peace, not tear us further apart. The past may be prologue, but we can script the next act for ourselves. We write our own fates."

Isaac and Nanyehi looked at Goran and then at each other. No words passed between them, but Goran could feel the tension slipping away.

"Your words are wise, ranger of the Sylph," said a melodious voice.

Goran turned to see the Water Maiden step from the river, moisture dripping from her slender frame. He gulped. Having waxed poetic a moment before, he found he couldn't manage even to squeak out a hello.

"Welcome, Dela," Isaac said. "These are the friends I told you about before: Nanyehi, Tana, and Goran."

The Water Maiden acknowledged each with smile. Both Nanyehi and Tana returned the gesture. Goran just gulped again.

"Dela and I have been becoming reacquainted over the past couple of weeks," Isaac said. "Tana, you were the one who first told me you thought you saw one of Dela's people at Long Island. The first couple of times I came looking, I found nothing."

"I was away ranging," Dela interjected.

"But when my father said he was coming here to make a treaty, I jumped at the chance to get a supply contract for the meeting," he continued. "I still hoped to find her. And I did."

Dela touched Isaac's arm affectionately and turned to the others.

"It has been a difficult time for my Folk," she explained. "The Pukwudgie ambush was devastating."

Nanyehi looked at the Water Maiden with sympathy. "You stand with others who have lost much in war. My people have. Isaac's have."

Goran finally found his voice again. "So, the Gwragedd Annwn are living here?"

Dela nodded and pointed to Long Island. "Our underground village is there. The entrances are underwater and protected by Shimmer walls and... other means. "

The mysterious pause left Goran curious to know more. But he didn't want to seem too inquisitive. It was Tana, not Goran, who posed the next question.

"How are the Gwragedd Annwn aligned?" she asked.

Dela seemed at a loss. "How are we...*aligned*?"

Tana looked searchingly at the Water Maiden. "War has come to America. The humans are negotiating a treaty as we speak, although who knows how long it will last. What I would know is, do your Folk side with the British or with the Americans?"

The Water Maiden shook her head. "My people are not involved. We lack the will and the means. I told the other Sylph that in no uncertain terms."

Then Dela stepped in front of Goran and gave him a withering look. "If that is why you sought this meeting, you are wasting my time and yours."

"The *other* Sylph?" Goran exclaimed, forgetting to be tongue-tied by the Water Maiden standing so close to him. "Who was he? How long ago was he here?"

Cocking her head to one side, Dela studied Goran for a long while. The others watched in uncomfortable silence.

"I do not claim to understand Sylph ways," said the Water Maiden. "You are only the second I have met. Perhaps there is more than one Sylph colony in America?"

Goran shook his head.

"A ranger named Bren came to Long Island a short while ago," she explained. "I met with him not far from where we now stand. He told me many Folk had decided to help suppress the American rebellion. He asked if the Gwragedd Annwn would join their alliance."

"And you declined," said Goran.

"I felt no need to consult my guild on the matter," Dela said. "I knew what the answer would be. But before I could form the words, another stranger appeared at Bren's side. My temper got the better of me. I would have run him through with my trident had Bren not stepped between us."

"What did he say that so outraged you?" Tana wondered.

"I have no idea what he would have said," Dela said as her giant blue-green eyes flashed with fury. "I did not give him the chance. It was he who led the ambush of my people."

Goran grimaced. "It was Atta Yellow Jacket."

The Water Maiden looked surprised. "You speak as if you know him."

"I do," Goran agreed. "I have tangled with him before, as has my friend Daniel Boone. As much as I disagree with Bren, I never dreamed he would stoop to traveling with the likes of Atta."

Now it was Tana who stepped closer to Goran. "Are you saying, then, that Bren does not speak for your Folk?"

Goran felt embarrassment wash over him. "Alas, I fear that Bren *does* speak for the Sylphs, or at least a large share of them. The Knob received orders from King Briafael to help suppress the rebellion."

"Are you not bound by those orders yourself?" Nanyehi asked.

It was a question Goran had been asking himself for a long time. *Would it not be the height of arrogance to question the judgment of my king, elders, and guildmasters? On the other hand, how could I take up arms against people I love in service of a cause I deem unjust?*

"I...I cannot say," he stammered helplessly.

As he looked around the group, he saw pity on Isaac's face. Dela's was impassive. Nanyehi and Tana were conducting a wordless conversation of gesture and expressions.

Finally, Tana spoke again, her voice like flint.

"Goran, if what I am about to say comes as no surprise to you, then I will question everything you have told us tonight. On the other hand, if it shocks you, and if you are the man I thought you to be, it may help you decide where your true loyalties lie."

The Sylph ranger met her eyes and saw something behind the flint. Something like fear.

"Bren visited the Nunnehi of Blood Mountain, too, speaking of alliance with the British," Tana said. "Like Dela, I knew that my Folk were unlikely to agree. But I chose to humor him, to let him make his case and state his plans so I would better understand them. Sometimes I wish I had not. What they have in mind is truly monstrous."

While Nanyehi's look of concern suggested that she already knew what Tana knew, Dela and Isaac seemed just as mystified as Goran. "What is it?" the Sylph asked.

"Their plan is precisely what I said: monstrous," Tana said. "The war has been far longer and costlier than the British expected. They thought the rebellion a product of a few misguided or ambitious men. They had not guessed the extent of disaffection. They deem the forces they have deployed to America insufficient for victory."

"So, they plan to send more troops?" Isaac asked.

"Perhaps," Tana said, "but that is not the plan I mean. Bren told me Folk rangers have been helping the British and their allies in battle. The sheer size of the country and the population to be conquered is a daunting challenge, however. And some Folk even say that, for some reason, Americans are more resistant to spellsong than other humans. Besides, no matter how effective their spells, there are not enough rangers to ensure victory."

Goran was aghast. "Do Folk plan to take the field themselves?" He thought of his brother, of Kaden's friend Jodoc, of the other Sylph warriors who might be ordered into battle, to fight and perhaps die just so the British could retain their iron grip over the colonies.

Tana shook her head dejectedly.

Sudden recognition lit the face of Dela. "The monsters!" she breathed in horror. "They plan to unleash monsters on the rebels!"

It was a preposterous, outrageous, impossible idea. To pit monsters against humans would be unthinkable.

And yet, even as Goran tried to tell himself that Dela's conclusion couldn't be true, he knew, somehow, that it was. It was the logical extension of the philosophy Bren had described in his lectures on the Knob. Folk domination of humanity wasn't simply about exploitation. Bren insisted it was in the long-term interest of humans themselves. The Americans could never truly be happy without submission. Ideally, it would be freely and enthusiastically given, but if fear was required to bind humans to their traditions, Folk should be unafraid to use it. Even if individual humans suffered grievous harm, humanity would ultimately be better off.

"You knew about this?" Isaac asked Nanyehi.

"Tana caught up with the delegation from Chota just yesterday and told me," Nanyehi said. "Ever since, my mind has been filled with disturbing images."

While Goran's mind was filled with disturbing images of his own, he couldn't help but watch Dela. The Water Maiden had dropped to her knees and rested her forehead on her hands as if praying in the human fashion.

Then Dela looked up at Goran in exasperation. "My Folk have already suffered much. If you Sylphs do so wicked a thing, this wild country will grow still more dangerous."

The accusation felt like an arrow to his heart. "Sylphs have venerated duty, honor, and justice for generations. I cannot believe most of my Folk know what Bren is planning." He thought of his father. Brae talked too big and too much. He was too eager for approval and too willing to accept what King Briafael and the Council said. But Brae was not a callous man. He was not cruel. Neither were Ceredan and the other guildmasters.

Perhaps Tana misunderstood what Bren was proposing, Goran thought. *Or perhaps it was only Bren and Atta who concocted the scheme. It could be little more than the fancy of two fanatics.*

He was determined to find out. Goran was a ranger. He was skilled at gathering and assessing information. He would not confront Bren until he was ready. And, as he looked at Dela's anguished face, now wet with something other than river water, he resolved to prove to her that the Sylphs were a noble Folk, that they were not all like Bren.

That *he* was not like Bren.

▲▲▲

The peace treaties took weeks to draft and approve. Dela left right after their meeting and did not return, but Goran was able to spend more time with Isaac and Nanyehi. They watched together as Colonel Evan Shelby, Major Joseph Winston, and the other commissioners proposed new boundaries between Cherokee territory and the American settlers — boundaries that legalized the Overmountain settlements.

The Cherokees protested. While admitting it had been a mistake to accept British aid to attack the backcountry, they argued that the white settlers had violated prior treaties.

"The Great Spirit has stocked your land with cows and ours with buffalo, yours with hogs and ours with bear, yours with sheep and ours with deer," said Old Tassel, whom the aging War Chief Oconostota had asked to speak on his behalf. "He has given you the advantage that your animals are tame while ours are wild and demand not only a larger space to range but art to hunt and kill them. They are, nevertheless, as much our property as other animals are yours and ought not to be taken from us without our consent, or for something of equal value."

The American commissioners found these words compelling and did adjust the boundaries they originally proposed, but they firmly rejected any wider demands. Goran could see, as could everyone else, that the Cherokees, displaced and hungry, were in no position to press their case.

Shortly after the treaties were signed, Goran watched his friend Isaac depart Fort Henry with Evan Shelby. The next day, he watched Nanyehi and Tana leave Long Island-on-the-Holston for the journey home. Goran would have no companions on the journey he must make. It would be weeks of solitude and hard travel. He would visit as many Folk villages and put on as many pretenses as it took to discover the breadth and details of Bren's conspiracy.

Old Tassel's talk of tame and wild livestock lingered in Goran's head. *Would Folk truly resort to the threat of monsters to tame their human livestock?*

Chapter 17 — The Fog

October 1777

"GENERAL MUHLENBERG, WE CAN BARELY see our hands in front of our faces."

Peter turned in his saddle and shot a reassuring glance at Colonel George Mathews, commander of the Ninth Virginia Regiment. He had known Mathews for years. They'd both been elected to the Virginia House of Burgesses. After Lord Dunmore disbanded the legislature, the two young men had served as fellow delegates to the Virginia Convention. Mathews had made a military name for himself during the short war against Shawnee Chief Cornstalk. Now Mathews — a short, stout man with a shock of unruly red hair — was a colonel in Peter's brigade. And Peter was a brigadier general in George Washington's army.

"We must all do the best we can under the circumstances, Colonel Mathews," Peter said. "General Washington has done his fellow Virginians the honor of giving us a critical role in the attack on Germantown. We will not fail him."

Mathews grunted his assent and urged his brown horse to a trot so he could catch up with his regiment. Peter decided to accompany Mathews to the vanguard. As his own white horse picked up the pace, Peter's blue uniform coat and white waistcoat did not fully protect him from the chill of the early morning air. The fog rolling over the road from the nearby Schuylkill River was thicker than Peter had ever seen it. And he had seen a Schuylkill fog more times than he could recall.

While Peter was a Virginian commanding Virginians that day, he knew very well the path his brigade was following in the faint light of dawn. Peter had often traveled Pennsylvania's Limekiln Road. Indeed, during his childhood in Trappe, he had traveled all the paths that General Washington had selected as attack routes against Germantown. His familiarity with the area was one of the reasons Washington so frequently solicited Peter's counsel. The other was that they had been good friends before the war. Washington trusted him. Peter was determined to merit such trust.

No such opportunity had yet presented itself on the battlefield. Since Peter left the Southern Department in early 1777 to become a brigadier general in Washington's army, things had gone poorly for the Americans. Taking advantage of his naval supremacy, British General William Howe transported his army from New York to the mouth of Maryland's Elk River. From there, Howe threatened Philadelphia from the south. Outmaneuvered, Washington tried to halt the British advance but was defeated at Brandywine Creek. The Continental Congress fled the capital. The British marched triumphantly into Philadelphia a couple of weeks later.

It was a devastating blow. But just as Washington had responded to the loss of New York the previous year by launching surprise attacks on Trenton and Princeton, he now decided to respond to the loss of Philadelphia by launching a surprise attack at Germantown. Only a portion of Howe's army was stationed there, about nine thousand men. Washington's eleven thousand regulars and militia would have a fighting chance. And their general had a plan.

Peter's brigade, serving under Major General Nathaniel Greene, had played only a limited role at Brandywine. But now they had a critical assignment. Greene's force was one of four American columns marching on Germantown from four different directions. They would confuse and rout the British. They would avenge, and perhaps even reverse, the loss of Philadelphia.

As General Peter Muhlenberg and Colonel George Mathews rode past the Virginia Continentals marching down Limekiln Road, Peter took pride in their disciplined ranks and confident faces. Unlike the Virginians he'd commanded in South Carolina the previous summer, the four Virginia regiments making up his current brigade were dressed in uniform blue coats and carried French-made muskets. For months, Peter had drilled them in close-order infantry tactics — to fire their muskets in volleys and to fight with bayonets. With new tools and skills, it was time to take the offensive.

"General, I see my lieutenant colonel by that fence," Mathews said. "I need to confer with him about the line of deployment."

"By all means," Peter replied, watching as Colonel Mathews rode through a gap in the column.

"I thought I would never get you alone."

The unexpected but welcome voice instantly made Peter feel light as a feather.

"Lack of privacy is one of the burdens of command I've come to accept," he said, turning to look down at the smiling face of Har the Tower. It had been almost two years since Peter had seen the Dwarf ranger. Har looked almost the same as he had the morning of Peter's farewell sermon — with two exceptions. One was that his yellow-brown beard extended a little longer down his chest. The other was that Har looked elated, not troubled.

"How did you find me here?" Peter asked, reaching his hand down to clasp Har's outstretched arm.

"With great difficulty," said Har as Peter pulled the Dwarf up and onto the saddle behind him. "I was halfway to Charles Town before I learned that you had been reassigned to General Washington's army — and that you were now a general yourself. Congratulations on the promotion."

Peter inclined his head in acknowledgment. "I hope to be worthy of it, although so far I have done little more than drill. Our army has had a rough time of it."

"In that case, I have a piece of good news — and you are as responsible for it as anyone," Har said excitedly. "The queen agreed to hear my plea to intervene. She and the elders of Grünerberg debated the issue for nearly a month before reaching a decision."

"And?" Peter wondered.

"The answer is yes!" Har exclaimed. "Queen Virginal has ordered me and the other Grünerberg rangers to provide what assistance we can to the Continental Army."

I will praise thee, O Lord, with my whole heart, Peter prayed silently. *I will shew forth all thy marvelous works.*

"That is excellent news, my friend," he told Har. "We may have need of you this day."

As they continued to trot alongside the marching column, Peter explained General Washington's plan. "It has a reasonable chance of success, although it will require a great deal of coordination when we attack Germantown. I am worried about this fog. It's so thick that I may have trouble seeing what's happening and reacting with enough dispatch."

"I can help," Har said. "I can be another set of eyes and ears for you. And, when we get close to the enemy, I may find a good use for this." The Dwarf patted the stringed scheitholt slung over his shoulder.

Just then, the two heard distant gunfire. Peter turned to Har, who nodded and slipped off the horse. "I will scout the British positions and return as soon as I can," said the Dwarf as he jogged away. Peter quickly lost sight of him in the billowing fog.

▲▲▲

"Give the order!" General Muhlenberg shouted. As his men fixed their bayonets and prepared to charge, Peter looked across the field at two indistinct lines of red surrounding a gristmill. The fog had, if anything, gotten thicker in the half hour since Har left. Still, he saw no alternative but to proceed.

The regimental drummers sounded the order to charge. Peter felt his heartbeat quicken as the Virginians advanced. The steady beat of the drums soon mixed with musketry, savage cries, and shrill shouts of pain. Drawing his sword and galloping forward, Peter almost trampled one of his own Virginians stumbling backward, clutching a wounded shoulder.

"Push on, men, push on to victory!" Peter shouted, dodging the wounded man and heading for the line of redcoats a dozen paces ahead. A British soldier aimed his bayonet at Peter's thigh. The American was able to turn it aside with a sweep of his sword. Then Peter heard a loud report as a redcoat on the other side of Peter's horse fired his musket. Fortunately, the ball missed Peter completely. As Peter engaged his first attacker with his sword, he saw Colonel Mathews appear on his right and use his own blade to slash the second attacker in the face while the man was trying to reload.

"We have them on the run here!" Mathews yelled. "Do you know how the other regiments are faring?"

"Can't tell," Peter admitted as the redcoat he was fighting suddenly wheeled and ran.

"Peter!"

Har materialized on Peter's right. Panting from exertion, the Dwarf looked up with an expression of dismay. "The fog...the fog," he repeated between labored breaths. "There is a reason it is so thick. It is not natural."

Peter's feeling of exuberance at his brigade's initial success evaporated, replaced by dread. "What do you mean, 'not natural'?"

Har stared back at him with a horrified expression. "There is a monster in the river," he said. "Its magic is producing the fog blowing across the field of battle."

Peter felt as though a sword had slashed his own face. "Did you recognize the beast?"

Har considered the question for a moment. "I have only seen drawings of it in guild books," he began, "but I believe it is a Fuath. A tall, thin monster covered in green scales."

"If we don't do something about the fog, our attack will become increasingly hard to manage," Peter insisted. "What about spellsong?"

"I already tried," said Har, looking dejected. "I thought I had deflected it downriver, but then the Fuath reversed course. I came to let you know, but now I will go try again."

As the Dwarf hurried away, Peter turned to rejoin the battle — and saw Colonel Mathews gaping at him.

"Who was that little man?" Mathews stammered. "And what was that nonsense about a monster in the river?"

Peter was amazed. But his impatience took precedence. "I'll have to explain later, Colonel. We must press our advantage."

▲▲▲

It was afternoon when Har found Peter again. Many of Peter's men had advanced past the mill and through Germantown itself, driving the redcoats before them with bayonets and musket fire. When he saw the Dwarf out of the corner of his eye, Peter turned his horse and dropped back from the front line, casting a look around to see if Colonel Mathews was nearby. But the colonel and his Ninth Virginia Regiment had pursued the retreating British still farther, beyond the village.

"I take it you couldn't chase it away," Peter said as Har stumbled toward him.

"It is worse than that, Peter — far, far worse. At first, my summoning spell seemed to work. Then I saw them — or, to be more precise, I heard them first and *then* I saw them."

"Saw who?" Peter asked.

"The Brownies," Har replied. "There were at least two of them, using spellsong to prod the Fuath forward. The monster attacked me, Peter, and then it attacked the American troops closest to the river."

Peter was aghast.

"The Americans fired a couple of volleys, then ran," Har added. "The Fuath ignored them and kept going."

"It's coming this way?" Peter gasped.

"It could arrive at any moment," Har confirmed, "and I have even more bad tidings. As I ran, I saw one of your Continental units mistake another for the enemy and fire at them. They fired back. Now both units are retreating. Your entire battle line is collapsing. The dense fog has proved to be a potent weapon."

"If those units are broken, the British may be able to turn and take our men from multiple directions! We would be surrounded!"

Even as he expressed that worry, Peter heard drummers signal retreat and saw his Virginians respond. Nathaniel Greene must have correctly assessed the situation and decided on the only reasonable course. Pleased to see the Virginians backing up in good order, maintaining their formations and firing occasional volleys, Peter was nevertheless worried about Colonel Mathews and his regiment. They had enjoyed the most success. But their great progress had now put them in great danger.

"Come on, Har," Peter said as he pulled the Dwarf up on his horse once more. "We must find Mathews and save those men."

As his horse galloped forward, Peter spied a thin green shape looming ahead in the smoke and fog. Initially he thought it was a small pine tree and veered to avoid it. Then it moved.

First he saw a long snout, its fangs bared, followed by flared nostrils and two deep-set eyes, blazing red. Then a scaly, eleven-foot-tall green body materialized from the fog, dripping water and draped in weeds. Two long arms reached out vicious-looking claws. And Peter saw a dark-green ridge running along its back, from head to massive tail.

"The Fuath!" Har warned. "The Brownies will not be far behind."

Peter considered sheathing his sword and drawing his pistol. But there was no time. The beast was almost upon him. Instead, Peter grasped his sword more firmly and spurred his horse to faster speed. Belatedly, he realized that Har had slipped off the mount and scrambled away. Then the Fuath was upon him, emitting a low, ominous hiss as it aimed a claw at Peter's head.

Ducking underneath the swinging arm, Peter slashed at the torso of the Fuath as he rode by. The sword struck but did not penetrate the scaly hide. Peter wheeled his horse and looked again at his foe. The Fuath was draped in a fresh curtain of fog, its outline barely visible despite Peter's proximity. Was the monster actively channeling its magic to guard itself? Or was producing the fog a reflex? Peter had no idea. He only knew the fog made it hard to target the beast.

Peter urged his horse into another charge. This time, as he passed to the left of the Fuath, he aimed his cut at its right leg. He felt his mount start with surprise as the Fuath's claw scraped its flank. Peter also felt his sword scrape along the monster's hip.

At a safe distance, he glanced down at his horse. Fortunately, the monster's claw had opened no wound. Peter gritted his teeth and began a third attack. This time, he headed right for the fog-shrouded monster, leaning forward and extending the point of his sword. He hoped the sight might put the Fuath to flight.

It didn't. Instead, the Fuath planted its two broad feet on the ground and spread its arms wide, with the evident intent of yanking Peter from his horse. Even as it tried to do so, however, Peter's point struck home. The force of the impact drove the sword up to its hilt into the breast of the monster. It also knocked Peter off of his mount — which proved to be his salvation as the claws of the Fuath embraced only empty air above the empty saddle.

Rearing back on its legs and hissing, the monster backed away from Peter, who was struggling to his feet. The Fuath clutched at the sword hilt with its claws but could not dislodge it. Then, reeling in pain and fury, it eyed Peter. The beast slunk forward, menacingly. Peter could see fresh fog billowing from its scaly hide. Just as Peter was about to turn and run, he saw through the mist a low red shape approaching the high green shape of the Fuath.

It was the dark red cap on the head of Har the Tower.

The Dwarf held his battleaxe with both hands. "Go back!" he shouted. "Go back to your watery domain!" And then Har began to sing. As usual,

Peter couldn't understand the words of Har's spellsong. Still, weird images flitted past his mind's eye. Swaying riverweeds and passing fish. Through an inky blackness, a water-filled cave.

For a moment, Peter felt drawn to the cave's tight, comfortable confines. Then he came back to his senses, and began running at the Fuath. He would not leave his friend to face it alone.

When Peter reached Har's side, the monster turned first its head and then its body to Peter's left, toward the Schuylkill River. After a few moments of hesitation, it began lumbering away.

"Do we follow?" Peter asked quickly. "Will the Brownies counteract your spell again?"

"We have seen the last of them this day," Har the Tower replied, lowering his axe and looking down the blood-stained edge of its bronze blade. "After I took off the leg of one, the other dragged his companion away."

Peter watched the Fuath disappear, leaving a trail of glistening mist in its wake.

"I will follow to make sure it reaches the river," Har said before running off.

Peter looked around him to take in the scene of the battle. His soldiers were still retreating in good order. He couldn't see any redcoats but knew they must be close by. Spying his horse only a few paces away, Peter quickly crossed the distance and remounted.

Only then did he feel the weight of the day's events crush him. Peter had fought the British for hours. Then he had fought something eerie and terrifying — something out of a nightmare, not a military manual. He had survived the encounter, however improbably. Yet still there was work to be done. There were men to be led. And his friend Mathews and the Ninth Regiment still needed to be extricated from the trap closing around them.

Peter galloped back and forth in front of his retreating troops, shouting encouragement. No one could tell him in what direction Mathews had gone. Looking into the smoke and fog, now finally beginning to dissipate in the afternoon sun, Peter saw signs of movement. The signs looked steady, not jerky. They looked like they might signify men marching in formation, not men fleeing in desperation. Was it Mathews finally leading his regiment in an orderly retreat of his own?

The sound of unfamiliar drumbeats and unfamiliar voices answered

Peter's unspoken question even before he caught sight of redcoats. "Here they come, men!" he yelled to his troops. "Fall back, fall back, but keep your muskets at the ready!"

▲▲▲

As the sun began to set, Peter's men were still formed up, bayonets bristling, guns firing volleys at the advancing British. It was their job to protect the rest of Washington's army as it withdrew. It was their job to keep another costly American defeat from turning into a far-costlier American rout.

One of the last officers still on the field of battle, Peter removed his hat and wiped his sweaty brow. Even that modest exertion required intense concentration to keep the exhausted rider on his equally exhausted horse. Replacing his hat, he rode along the path. He hadn't seen Mathews all afternoon. Peter feared the worst, that the men of Mathews' regiment had been either captured or killed. But at least the rest of the brigade had escaped a similar fate.

"Huzza for General Muhlenberg!" cried one of his officers, a large fellow named Hubley, standing behind a fence. The man's face was covered in soot. His arm was covered in blood where a musket ball had grazed his shoulder. Other Virginians were climbing over the same high fence. Peter saw that it blocked his way, as well. Sighing in resignation, he turned his horse and prepared to go around.

"Hold on, General, we'll take care of that," Hubley said. He and others began to pull on the rails and posts of the fence. Peter thought it might be faster just to ride around it, but then he realized the men's efforts weren't about saving him time. They were showing respect and affection for their general. He wouldn't rob them of the moment.

As Peter watched them dismantle the fence, his eyelids felt increasingly heavy. He slumped in his saddle. Surely it wouldn't hurt to rest his eyes. Perhaps after he recovered some of his strength…

The sound of a musket ball whistling past his ear jolted Peter awake from his accidental nap. He saw a British officer standing only a few feet away, his musket pointing right at Peter. Behind him were many redcoats.

"Pick off that officer on the white horse!" shouted the British officer to his approaching men. Then the officer lowered his smoking musket, removed a paper cartridge from his pouch, and bit off the end of it to reload his gun. Peter reached for the only weapon he still possessed: his pistol. Lacking the time and the energy to take careful aim, Peter pointed it in the officer's direction and pulled the trigger.

The ball struck the British officer in the head. He screamed and fell.

"Come on, General Muhlenberg!" shouted one of the Virginians. "You can make it now."

Peter saw that was true. Only the lowest rail of the fence remained before him. He spurred his horse into a gallop. It hurdled the barrier and carried Peter away to safety.

▲▲▲

That night, just as Peter lay down in his tent to get some much-needed sleep, he heard the familiar voice of Har the Tower. Beckoning him in, Peter learned that the Fuath had, indeed, gone back to the river and disappeared beneath its surface. There was also no more sign of the Brownies.

"I have never heard of such a thing," Har said, his normally jovial face pulled tight in an expression of deep concern. "I knew Folk were championing the British cause, but this goes beyond the usual forms of intervention. It is not just brutal; it is reckless. Monsters are hard to control, and their presence risks exposure."

"There must be some reason for their recklessness," Peter observed. "Perhaps the British aren't in as strong a position as we think, although the fall of New York and Philadelphia would appear to suggest otherwise."

"There are many unanswered questions, Peter. I will start finding you answers. But today's events suggest I need help. I will return to Grünerberg and ask Virginal to mobilize the other rangers."

Peter managed a weak smile. "You only just arrived," he said. "Must you leave so soon?"

Har clasped Peter's arm in a tight grip. "My service to you and your cause requires it, although I would much rather…"

Peter lifted his other hand to his lips. Har felt silent. There were footsteps approaching.

"General Muhlenberg, are you resting?" asked a sonorous voice from outside the tent. "I would have an urgent word."

"It's General Washington," Peter whispered as he rose to his feet.

"Of course, sir," Peter answered as he smoothed the wrinkles in his uniform and glanced over at Har, who had hastened to the other side of the tent. "I'll be with you in just a…"

But Washington must have interpreted Peter's initial answer as an invitation to enter. The flap parted before Peter was able to finish his sentence. Startled, Peter glanced back at Har. But the Dwarf was nowhere to be seen. There hadn't been time for Har to conceal himself magically. And the spellsong wouldn't have worked on Peter, anyway. He concluded that the Dwarf must have slipped under the tent.

General Washington was looking intently at Peter, who felt himself wither in response. The awkward silence lasted for some time.

"Peter, I trust you have sustained no wounds," Washington said kindly.

"No, sir, I did not, thank God," Peter said, his voice feeling dry as a bone.

"Alas, Providence was not so generous to many others," Washington said, his eyes falling to a spot on the ground. "Our preliminary count suggests far more than a hundred killed, including many officers. Hundreds more are wounded, some severely. And we lost an entire regiment captured — one of your own, in fact, Colonel Matthews and his Virginians."

Peter groaned. "I take full responsibility, General Washington. I shouldn't have let Mathews advance so far without covering his flanks."

"As the other generals tell the tale, the biggest responsibility for the failure of our attack was the persistent and impenetrable fog," Washington replied, "although to my mind when a plan fails for lack of proper coordination, that is an indictment of the commanding general, not the choices of his subordinates or the accidents of weather."

Peter said nothing. He admired Washington for refusing to blame others. Yet he still believed Washington's attack plan had been a sound one. If not for the intervention of the Brownies and the Fuath, it might have brought victory instead of another frustrating defeat.

"Of course, that assumes the persistent and impenetrable fog was truly an accident," George Washington said, once again fixing his intense stare on Peter. "Might your Dwarf friend have something to say about that?"

Chapter 18 — The Forge

IT HAD BEEN A MILD winter by Har's standards. Peter, the native Pennsylvanian, agreed. But a mild Pennsylvania winter was still a Pennsylvania winter. And the Continental Army was woefully unprepared for it — unprepared, undersupplied, and underfed. Malnourishment and disease had wrought as much destruction as any British attack. More than a thousand American soldiers had died during their first three months at Valley Forge.

Nine miles from Valley Forge was the small town of Trappe. There the Dwarf ranger stood, next to a maple tree, admiring how the moonlight painted a warm glow on the red eaves and shutters of the two-story house across the street. Since Har had caught back up with the Continental Army in February, he'd come to know well the route from Valley Forge to Trappe. Many times, Peter had insisted on leaving the American camp to visit the home of his father, Henry Muhlenberg. Har the Tower had insisted on accompanying him.

Peter's father was in poor health, but that wasn't the only reason for their nighttime visits. Peter's wife Hannah and two-year-old son Henry had come all the way from Virginia to stay with their in-laws in Trappe. Other members of the family had taken refuge in the Muhlenberg house, too. That gave Peter a chance to see them all.

During every visit, Har maintained a nervous vigil. The Loyalists of Pennsylvania were no fools. They knew of General Peter Muhlenberg. And they knew where his father lived. On more than one occasion, Har saw riders pass by the house, obviously straining to see inside. As a precaution, the Muhlenbergs had draped all the windows with blankets. So far, Peter's visits had escaped detection. Har was determined to keep it that way.

▲▲▲

"I understand the human is your friend, Har, but you must not let such ties distract you."

Queen Virginal had spoken those words the day Har left Grünerberg to return to General Washington's army. He and the queen sat together in her chamber, a structure of log and stone built within one of the largest caverns of the colony. Har had removed his red stocking cap in her presence, of course, and left his battleaxe by the door. But just sitting at table alone with his queen in her chamber would have been highly improper back in Germany.

Virginal had adjusted rapidly to the informality of Dwarfkind's American colony. The Grünerberg settlement was only three months old, from the perspective of the Dwarfs living there. Much of it had yet to be fully excavated and furnished, although craftsmen and mages had quickly constructed rude living quarters, storehouses, a monster pen, and Virginal's chamber. For the time being, the latter served not only as her personal residence and seat of office but also as the host site for guild meetings.

Har seized every opportunity he could to spend time in the queen's chamber — even after Virginal agreed, somewhat reluctantly, with his argument that the new colony could not afford to stand aloof from the American war. He asked for private meetings to discuss ranger deployments. He volunteered to give her briefings on humanlore. He stopped by to tell her tales of his latest rangings.

Despite rehearsing every rationalization before voicing it, Har felt utterly transparent. Virginal must have known he was looking for excuses to spend time with her. Perhaps she thought he was just trying to ingratiate himself with his queen. Or that he wanted to enjoy her spacious chamber and generous meals rather than staying in cramped quarters with the others. Or perhaps Virginal had read Har like a book. Perhaps his feelings for the witty and vivacious Dwarf queen had grown beyond his limited ability to mask them.

Virginal's ability to mask her own feelings were masterful, however. Har had no idea whether she was pitying him, ridiculing him or, dare he hope, beginning to reciprocate his affection. All he knew was that whenever he asked for an audience, she granted it.

"I helped Peter fight the Fuath because it was necessary to save the army," Har insisted in response to Virginal's scolding. "If I had not been there, we would not have learned about the Brownies' crime. Besides, Peter is one of Washington's most trusted officers. To render effective aid to the Americans, I must stay close to the commander-in-chief."

The queen cast Har a skeptical look as she drained her tankard of ale. "I do not begrudge you your friendship with Peter Muhlenberg. I recognize its value. But it must be a means to an end, not an end in itself."

While Virginal's reasoning sounded prudent, its implication made Har squirm uncomfortably. *What if I have to sacrifice Peter's safety to achieve victory? Could I do that?*

Virginal stood and walked around the table, clearly signaling to Har that his audience was over and it was time to leave. "All your queen asks is that you do your duty to the best of your ability."

Then, as he slipped on his cap and turned toward the door, Virginal added, "Still, Har the Tower, I find I must ask a personal favor: please return to me safe and sound."

Har tried not to let the spring in his step or the broad smile on his face betray his exhilaration. Naturally, he failed at that, too.

▲▲▲

They'd been in Trappe for hours. Har was growing worried. The longer they stayed, the greater the danger. Har glanced at Peter's big white horse, fully saddled and tied to a fence post. At just that moment, it whinnied and shook its head. Immediately on alert, Har looked up and down the street. He saw nothing. The Dwarf closed his eyes and listened intently. He heard nothing but the wind rustling the leaves of the maple tree.

Har opened his eyes. A light streaked across the street as the door to the Muhlenberg home opened. He could see Peter giving his wife Hannah a parting embrace. Then the light disappeared. Peter motioned to Har and walked silently to his horse. Pulling himself into the saddle, with Har behind him, Peter directed his mount down the street.

When they'd ridden a couple of miles toward Valley Forge, Har felt his clenched muscles relax. If Peter had been spotted in town, surely their pursuers would already have accosted them. Har opened his mouth to ask Peter how the visit had gone.

"We have you now, *General* Muhlenberg," said a sneering voice.

Har felt Peter spur the horse into a fast gallop. Sounds of other voices crying out and other horses galloping seem to come from every direction.

Then came a gunshot.

"Don't fire!" shouted one of the pursuers. "The captain said to take him alive!"

Har closed his eyes and imagined six mounted Loyalists heading toward the road from different directions. He imagined them catching intermittent glimpses of their quarry in the moonlight as General Muhlenberg raced along on his easily recognizable white horse. Har imagined a dark cloud covering the moon, plunging the scene into darkness. Then, in the spellsinger's powerful imagination, the moonlight reappeared, illuminating an empty road and leaving the pursuing Loyalists puzzled and angry.

▲▲▲

The Valley Forge encampment lay just over the Schuylkill River. As they approached it, Har marveled, not for the first time, how the Continental Army's living conditions made the new Dwarf colony at Grünerberg look luxurious by comparison.

Squads of Americans were crammed into tiny huts built by digging pits in the ground and then throwing up walls of logs and mud. Har had heard one of General Washington's officers, a Frenchman named the Marquis de Lafayette, describe the huts as "scarcely more cheerful than dungeons." During the day, sick Virginians lay suffering in those dungeons while able-bodied Virginians drilled, foraged, and manned the fortifications that guarded the camp from possible attack from Philadelphia. All too often, the able-bodied served on burial detail. At night, they tried to get at least some fitful sleep in the cramped, smoky confines of the huts.

Har never tried to sleep in Peter's hut. He preferred to get what rest he could far away from camp, in the boles of trees or other natural shelter. He also preferred to sleep during the day so he could range at night.

It was safer, for one thing. The darkness provided Har with an extra layer of protection from any prying eyes. Spellsong might protect him from detection, but Har had no way of knowing if another human in the area possessed the Sight. He couldn't be sure all Sight-gifted humans would be as trustworthy as Peter Muhlenberg.

Or George Washington.

When Peter first told Har that the commander-in-chief had seen the Dwarf, Har immediately blamed himself. But once Peter explained that Washington already knew of the existence of Folk, the Dwarf ranger felt surprise and relief. It was only the second time he'd met a human with the Sight.

Washington proved to be tight-lipped about his own experiences with Folk. During his visits to see Peter and Har, the general preferred to ask questions rather than answer them. Har told Washington all he knew about British-allied Folk and updated the general after each of Har's nighttime rangings. Har also assured Washington that the Fuath incident at Germantown was unlikely to be repeated, no matter how much some Folk might desire a restoration of British sovereignty. Monsters were the enemies of all, Har explained.

"The sun will be up in just a couple of hours," said Peter as they reached his hut in the rear of the Virginians' camp. "I'm going to try getting a little sleep. I don't suppose it would do any good to suggest you do the same."

Har smiled. "No, it would not. I will make a final circuit first. Rest can wait."

"You know, you probably saved my life again tonight, or at least my liberty," Peter said.

The Dwarf ranger waved off his friend's words. "If I truly wanted to keep you safe, I would stop your nighttime rides altogether."

"I don't answer to you," Peter grinned, "I answer to my superior officers."

"Do *they* know where you go at night?" Har asked, only half-joking.

Peter left the question unanswered, which served only to answer it.

Reinforcing his concealment with a softly voiced spellsong, Har began walking along the river in the general direction of Washington's headquarters, a three-story stone building on the opposite side of the camp. On previous night-time excursions, Har had brought his pole to the river to fish for shad. This seemed no fit night for relaxation, however. The ambush near Trappe was unsettling. To be sure, a few mounted Loyalists posed no threat to the Continental Army. Still, Har couldn't help feeling uneasy.

Just ahead, the Dwarf ranger saw the outline of the bridge connecting the Valley Forge camp with supply routes to the north and west. Sentries stood at both ends of the bridge. Just two months earlier, when Har first arrived, there might well have been no sentries posted. The camp had been highly disorganized. But another German speaker had arrived about the same time Har did: a human calling himself Baron von Steuben. An experienced soldier from Prussia, he'd insisted on changing the layout of the camp, improving sanitation, and drilling the men constantly. Slowly but surely, discipline and morale had begun to improve.

Although Har had no reason to believe his concealment spell wouldn't hold, he decided not to take any chances. Rather than pass by the sentry, he walked closer to the riverbank and ducked underneath the bridge.

"Make no sound, Dwarf," said a low voice. "My arrow is aimed at your head."

"And my point at your breast," said another voice, higher pitched.

Har froze in place, wishing he'd been holding his battleaxe rather than letting it dangle from the loop of his belt. Had the Brownies of Philadelphia sneaked into the American camp to gather intelligence? Worse still, had the Brownies come to unleash some new monstrous horror?

As Har opened his mouth to speak, he felt something sharp press against his chest.

"If you try to signal your accomplices across the river, it will be the last sound you make," warned the higher pitched voice.

Har raised his hands, hoping he looked conciliatory. "I have no accomplices across the river," he said, keeping his voice level. "I am here in the service of George Washington and one of his generals, Peter Muhlenberg."

The point still pressed against him.

"Who are your Folk?" asked the first voice, which Har now realized came from the shadows ahead.

"I am Har, Dwarf ranger of Grünerberg. Some call me Har the Tower."

From the shadows came the sound of movement. The first feature that came into view wasn't a foot, a hand, a weapon, or a face. It was a wingtip.

"I can see why," said the fairy who emerged from the shadows, clad in a forest green cloak, leather jerkin, and light green stockings. He was still holding his bow with arrow nocked. "I am Goran, Sylph ranger of the Knob. I know of your Folk, although I was unable to locate your village during my last trip to the valley of the Shenandoah."

Har allowed himself a mischievous smirk. "Then I did my job well, for

I was the one who chose the site for our colony."

Lowering his bow slightly, Goran ignored Har's jibe. "According to my latest information, you Dwarfs did not join the Great Alliance. Has that changed?"

"I do not recognize that phrase," Har said, "but if you ask whether my Folk are allied with the British, surely my presence here and my service to General Washington serve to answer your question."

Then Har realized the point was no longer pressed against him.

"Your presence is no answer, and your service is nothing more than a claim," said the other voice. Har turned slowly to his right and saw a three-bladed polearm still inches from his chest. "The Sylphs helped to form the Great Alliance, yet Goran stands apart from them. You may stand apart from your Folk, for all we know."

Har felt his caution give way to irritation. "*I* am the one living with the army here," he said, struggling to keep his voice calm. "*You* are the outsiders. You could be working with the scoundrels of Philadelphia, for all I know."

"Which scoundrels do you mean?" Goran demanded.

Glaring at him, unable to disguise his contempt, Har responded. "The Brownies. The villains who loose monsters to sow fear and destruction."

Into the faint moonlight stepped the Sylph's companion, a slender woman with pale blue skin and large, shining eyes the color of seawater. She was some kind of Water Nixie, Har supposed, and the fact that her long, dark blue hair and short, dark blue gown were sopping wet suggested she'd just come from the river.

"It has already begun, Goran," she said, obviously distraught. "If only it had not taken so long for me to convince my Folk. I could have brought a warning."

"We are here now, Dela, and in a better position to help thanks to what we learned in the meantime," Goran replied.

Har's eyes widened as he caught their meaning. "You *knew* the Brownies were going to employ monsters in battle?"

The Sylph shook his head. "Our news was not specific to the Brownies. The entire Great Alliance is committed to the strategy. Folk of town, forest, river, and mountain. All plan to deploy monsters. We have come to warn the Americans of the danger."

Har staggered back a couple of steps and leaned against the wall of the bridge. "It is incredible, unimaginable," he sputtered. "How can Folk justify such a crime? And how can they hope to limit the devastation?"

"We have only partial answers, and they are not meant for your ears alone," Dela said. "We must speak with General Washington immediately."

Har glanced first at the Nixie, then at the Sylph. "How do you know the general will take the word of creatures most humans believe to be imaginary?"

Goran's mouth formed a slight smile. "Washington and I have encountered each other before. I even saved his life. Now we hope to save him and his army from ruin."

▲▲▲

At Har's suggestion, the three fairies waited on the thatched roof of Peter's hut until dawn. It wouldn't do to try to approach General Washington directly. Peter should request the meeting and, if possible, participate to vouch for their credibility.

"That assumes this human friend of yours is himself inclined to trust our credibility," Goran pointed out.

"Peter will, once I have explained," Har said. "Remember, he has seen and fought monsters before. And I have found him to be remarkably insightful, for a human."

That made Dela smile, and for the first time Har noticed the astonishing beauty of her heart-shaped face. The Dwarf also noticed Goran staring at her with a worshipful expression. *Is that what I look like when I stand close to Virginal? No wonder Peter laughs at me whenever I mention her name.*

As the first light of dawn struck the camp, Har decided to risk waking Peter up from his all-too-brief nap. The Dwarf rose and strode to the edge of the roof, preparing to jump down.

He stopped short when he heard a shout from the direction of the river. Other shouts followed. He watched as a soldier from the brigade took off running. A few minutes later, he came sprinting back, his face flushed with excitement.

"There are wagons pulling into camp," he told other soldiers standing near Peter's hut. "Someone told me the wagons are full of corn, and that Indians are driving them."

The men cheered and started running toward the bridge — until their sergeant barked at them to halt.

Har, Goran, and Dela hurried to investigate. It was, indeed, a supply train. A few of the Indians were driving wagons, but most walked alongside. "Judging by their clothing, I would guess they come from a Northern tribe," Har told his companions.

"They are from the Iroquois Confederacy — the Oneida, to be precise," Dela said.

Har and Goran looked at each other in surprise, then at Dela in joint admiration.

"You can tell by the headdresses," she explained, pointing to one of the men. The Oneida was wearing a hat made of wood and doeskin and covered in turkey feathers. There were three eagle feathers, as well. Two stood straight up. The other pointed to one side.

As the next wagon came into view, Har's eyes went wide and he put a nervous hand on the head of his battleaxe. Two of the Oneida, a man and a woman, were walking beside the wagon. The woman wore a long poncho that extended half down her doeskin leggings. She was taller than most of the others and walked with a majestic gait. Her sharp eyes and aquiline nose made for a striking face underneath a prominent brow and black hair swept back by a beaded headband.

But what had really put Har on alert was the man beside her. If she was tall, he was gigantic, his shape provoking an instinctively defensive response from Har. But it soon became clear the man was human. He wore his gray hair in a single stripe cut high across his head, which had at first made him appear impossibly large.

Even so, the man stood six and a half human feet, at least. He was bare-chested, a sash of woven wood extending from his right shoulder to his left side and a buckskin cloak tossed over his left shoulder. The sash was covered with intricate designs of bead and feather. From his waist hung a leather skirt, fringed with porcupine quills, over cloth leggings. Like the other Oneida males, he wore a headdress crowned with eagle feathers.

If that human has spent his whole life towering over everyone else in his village, he and I may be kindred spirits, Har thought, and smiled.

The tall man looked straight at Har and smiled back. A second later, the woman looked directly at Har, too, and gave him a playful wink.

Isn't the Sight supposed to be uncommon? Just how many humans in this camp can see me?

▲▲▲

He got his answer that evening, after Peter succeeded in arranging a private meeting with the general. As Peter approached the soldier guarding the path to the modest stone house that was Washington's headquarters, Har and Dela walked behind him and Goran hovered above his head, all three magically concealed.

The guard, who'd been leaning on his musket, suddenly straightened. "You may not pass."

Peter smiled politely. "What is your name, private?"

The guard gulped, seeming to notice Peter's officer uniform for the first time. "Nathaniel Chapman, sir, of the Ninth Massachusetts," he stammered.

"Well, Private Chapman, I am General Muhlenberg — and I am expected," Peter replied.

The guard was saved any need to reply when the door to the headquarters suddenly opened, revealing a black slave dressed in white livery. Har recognized Billy Lee, Washington's valet. Har had learned over the past two months that wherever Washington went, Lee was never far from his side.

The slave stood impassively until Peter, Har, Dela, and Goran came through the door.

"That will do, Billy," said Washington, who was seated at the head of a cluster of desks pushed together to form a large table in the front parlor. "Now, make sure we remain undisturbed."

Billy Lee walked through the entrance and turned to pull the door closed behind him. As he did so, he caught Har's eye and gave the briefest of nods.

That makes five, Har thought.

Then he looked around the table. *Make that six.*

Much to his surprise, he saw that he, Peter, and the other two fairies would not be meeting with Washington alone. The two tall Oneida visitors he'd seen earlier in the day were standing together on one side of the table, smiling at the newcomers. On the other side stood a young American officer whose name Har did not know. The young man was impeccably dressed — his uniform clean and pressed, his hair carefully groomed. He was

219

looking intently at Har, Dela, and Goran, as well. But unlike the Oneidas, the American officer wasn't smiling. His appraising look and shrewd expression made Har think of a fox preparing to pounce on a rabbit.

Am I the rabbit?

Washington cleared his throat and began the introductions. "General Muhlenberg, I trust you recall my aide-de-camp, Lieutenant Colonel Alexander Hamilton."

"Indeed, I do, sir," Peter replied, extending his hand.

Hamilton shook it but kept his expression guarded. "General, it pleases me to see you again and to learn of your relationship with these...uh...visitors." He swept his eyes over the fairies, then looked back at Peter.

"General Muhlenberg," Washington continued, "may I present Chief Skenandoah and Polly Cooper, both of the Oneida Nation." Peter nodded to both, and they returned the gesture.

"Please allow me to introduce our other visitors: Goran, Dela, and Har," said Peter, motioning to each in turn. "Each serves as rangers for their respective peoples."

"Which peoples are those, if I may ask?" said Chief Skenandoah, still smiling.

Har spoke first. "I come from a Dwarf colony named Grünerberg, in Virginia. Peter and I have been friends for a long time, since his student days back in Germany."

Peter chuckled and shook his head. "I wish you wouldn't keep reminding me of those days, Har."

"As for me," said Dela, "my people are known back in Wales as the Gwragedd Annwn. We are a people of lake and river."

"And what about you of the golden plumage?" asked Polly Cooper, her attention focused on the winged fairy.

"I am a Sylph of the Knob," Goran replied. "My Folk are originally from Cornwall."

Hamilton cocked an eyebrow. "A 'Sylph,' you say? I know that word. I've read my Paracelsus."

Har saw Goran wince. "My Folk are very well acquainted with the human who went by that name," said the Sylph.

"I must confess I am not," said General Washington, a bit impatiently.

"Paracelsus was a Swiss doctor who wrote a philosophical work linking the four classical elements of air, water, earth, and fire to four creatures with magical properties," Hamilton explained. "The Sylphs, if I recall correctly, represented air. I believe Paracelsus would call you" — he pointed to Dela — "an 'Undine' and your other companion a 'Gnome.'"

Har bristled at the comparison. "I am *not* a Gnome, sir. I am a Dwarf."

Hamilton looked taken aback at Har's vehemence and began a clumsy response, but the Oneida woman, Polly Cooper, cut it short with a screech of high-pitched laughter.

"Well said, Master Dwarf!" she exclaimed. "We all hate to be mistaken for something we are not."

A reproachful look from Chief Skenandoah seemed to silence her.

"I meant no disrespect," Hamilton told Har. "I meant only to cite a reference. In truth, I never developed a taste for Paracelsus, although his source material interests me. Ovid's *Metamorphoses*, for example, was one of my favorite books as a child."

"Your childhood was quite different from mine," Peter said. "I would scarcely have attempted such a book."

"For some children, books are a refuge," said Hamilton wistfully. "I became fascinated with Ovid's tales of transformations — of Daphne, Callisto, Philomela, Daedalion…"

"Ladies and gentlemen, if I may," Washington interrupted, "I have gathered you here tonight in seclusion to hear and discuss matters of some urgency."

"Of course, sir," Hamilton said, then sat. Peter and the Oneidas did the same, pulling chairs up to the makeshift conference table.

Only Washington continued to stand, looking at the three fairies with barely disguised amusement. "How may we accommodate you?" he asked.

Har took his meaning immediately. He walked to the end of the table opposite Washington, taking a seat sideways with his feet dangling over the edge. Dela followed his lead. Goran fluttered his wings, rose, and found a perch on a high cabinet. Har saw Hamilton's jaw drop in amazement, but the other humans seemed not to find Goran's feat so remarkable.

For the next half hour, Har mostly listened as Goran and Dela told the humans what they knew. It clearly pained Goran to relate the key role played by a master of his own guild, a Sylph named Bren, in organizing the Great Alliance. It included nearly all the Folk who resided in the cities or towns of the colonies. Some rural Folk had joined the Great Alliance, as well, such as the Elves of Georgia, as had the Pukwudgies and most other Folk indigenous to America.

"That includes the Jogah, whose misty cave in the Lesser Wilderness I first visited many decades ago," Chief Skenandoah interjected sadly. "My former fairy friends now make war on my American brothers, alongside all of our Confederacy except the Oneida."

"The Jogah are a Folk I do not know," Goran said. "Will they be as willing as the others to use monsters as weapons?"

Skenandoah looked over at Polly Cooper, and it seemed to Har that something passed silently between them. "I lived with them for more than a year," the chief said. "The Jogah are capable of that and more."

It took Har a moment to recognize the import of what the Oneida chief had said. "Sir, if I may ask, how old are you?"

The face that turned to Har looked relieved, as if the question had helped Skenandoah let go of some painful memory. "I have lived some forty-seven years on this earth," he said. "But my fellow Oneida believe me to be nearly seventy-three, although they grant that my needles and branches look surprisingly green and supple for such an old pine tree."

Har and the others allowed themselves a good laugh. The young American officer, Hamilton, was the conspicuous exception. *Perhaps he does not understand the different flow of time on either side of the Shimmer.*

Washington leaned over the table, laced his fingers, and rested his chin. "My officers and I are only just beginning to comprehend the magnitude of the conspiracy against us."

It seemed to Har the general's eyes had begun to blaze with an indignation that, if the human had possessed even a hint of magic, might have burned a hole clear through the table.

"Our frustration is that, as hard as our stay here at Valley Forge has been these past months, in some ways Providence has favored us," Washington continued. "Our men have grown tougher and more disciplined. The flow of arms and ammunition from France has steadily grown, and our mission in Paris continues to show progress. Our Northern Army has secured a major victory at Saratoga, an event that does the highest honor to American arms — and to the contributions of your brave Oneida warriors who have fought alongside our army in New York."

Chief Skenandoah acknowledged the expression of gratitude with a nod.

Washington swallowed and sat up straight, his eyes still directed downward. "I had hoped to take the field with greater resolve in the coming weeks, perhaps even to threaten General Howe's hold on Philadelphia. But now, you say, we must face a new, greater threat. My question is, how can we hope to defend ourselves against it?"

Har had followed Washington's eyes to the center of the makeshift conference table. As he considered the general's question, the Dwarf fancied that he could see images of monstrous beasts slide one by one across its surface. Then he cleared his throat.

"You will be far from defenseless, General Washington," Har said, trying to sound more confident than he felt. "As terrifying and dangerous as monsters can be, they can be defeated. Peter and I defeated the Fuath at Germantown."

"But not before our army suffered a great loss," Peter pointed out. "More such 'victories' can only end in defeat."

Goran pushed himself off the cabinet and hovered above the table. "Magical creatures are formidable foes, but do not forget that you possess potent weapons of your own. Magic and iron do not mix well, so enchanted armor — be it of bronze, scale, fur, or hide — is somewhat vulnerable to your musket balls and blades."

"Many monsters are susceptible to spellsong," said Dela. "They can be distracted, disheartened, even immobilized in some cases."

"We also have reason to believe your foes are not fully committed to their course," Goran said. "I have it on good authority that the British commander in Philadelphia, General Howe, is aware of the plan and opposes it. He was furious when he learned what the Brownies did at Germantown."

Dela lifted a pale-blue hand and pointed at Goran. "Howe is not the only one with scruples. Here is a Sylph who is horrified by what his people are doing and has the courage to do what is right and proper."

Har watched the mixture of emotions play across Goran's face — outrage at what his fellow Sylphs were doing, appreciation for Dela's kind words, and embarrassment at becoming the center of attention.

"Other Folk surely feel the same way," Dela continued. "Part of your strategy should be to play on these divisions, to encourage resistance from within the Great Alliance itself."

Chief Skenandoah nodded his head. "The surest path to victory lies not on battlefields but in the hearts of your enemies."

Polly Cooper was the next to speak. "I agree dissent can be a potent weapon, but so is fear. Were your foes to believe that if they use extreme measures against you, extreme measures will be used against them, they might lose their nerve."

Her suggestion met with an awkward silence. Everyone seemed to know precisely what the Oneida woman meant. Goran and Dela looked shocked. Washington and Hamilton looked thoughtful. Skenandoah was looking at Polly Cooper with wide, questioning eyes. She only arched an eyebrow and focused on Washington, drawing her eyes to narrow slits.

The American commander met her gaze. "We fight for more than our homes and property," he said firmly. "We fight for a principle, to live in liberty rather than abject submission. I will not sully our noble cause by resorting to the vile tactics of a cruel and unrelenting enemy."

Polly Cooper sank back in her chair, dropped her chin to her chest, and closed her eyes. Skenandoah did the same. Hamilton fidgeted nervously.

Har could see the anxiety written on the young officer's face, and at least the hint of anxiety in Washington's eyes. He knew he couldn't let their concern go unanswered. Har rose to his feet on the table.

"Magical threats *do* require a magical response," he said. "Queen Virginal offers you the services of our colony's rangers. There are twelve of us, two from each of Dwarfkind's six great nations. At least one ranger must remain in or around Grünerberg at all times to ensure our own security. But, as the remainder finish their current missions, each has instructions to come to Valley Forge and place themselves at your disposal. I expect the first arrivals any day now."

"Words fall short of expressing the depth of our gratitude to you and your queen," Washington said solemnly.

Har acknowledged the sentiment. "You will not face this peril alone."

Dela had hung her head as Har spoke. Now she rose to stand next to the Dwarf.

"I cannot offer you a similar pledge, General Washington," she said with evident anguish. "The Gwragedd Annwn have intervened before in the wars of humans. We have sometimes suffered for it. I tried to convince my Folk to do more than send a warning. They refused."

Washington stood and gave her a short, gallant bow. "Your warning, and the critical information you have imparted tonight, will be service enough."

Dela's blue-green eyes blinked as she responded with an appreciative smile. Har couldn't help but glance up at Goran, whose face had reddened. Har couldn't tell if the exchange between Dela and Washington had made the Sylph excited, flustered, or envious.

For a few moments, all seemed lost in their respective thoughts. For his part, Har spent the time thinking about the best way to deploy his rangers. The Dwarfs of the Ruhr tended to be the mostly scholarly, well-suited to identifying monsters and developing strategies to thwart them. The Dwarfs of the Rhineland and the Alps were especially skilled in spellsong. The stealthy Lutki would likely excel as couriers and spies. And the Dwarfs of Rügen Isle would be the fiercest warriors in battle.

It was Polly Cooper who broke the silence.

"In the land of the Oneida, there is a high cliff overlooking a deep lake," she said. "It is as if your enemies have pushed you and the entire American cause to the edge of that cliff. You cannot retreat. If you step off the cliff, you may fall into the lake and drown in its icy depths."

Then she turned her face up to Goran, still hovering above the table.

"Or, with the help of your new allies, you may take wing and find victory. Only *you* can reveal your fate — by taking a leap of faith."

▲▲▲

It was the next morning that the news spread like wildfire across the encampment: France had joined the war! Britain's disastrous defeat at Saratoga, and even the prowess Washington's army had shown during its spirited loss at Germantown, had impressed the French. They now believed the American colonies could win.

Peter shared the elation of everyone else at Valley Forge. As Har, Dela, and Goran met with him in his hut, Peter alternated between speculating about Washington's next move and offering prayers of thanksgiving.

"The French alliance presents new opportunities," Goran agreed. "It threatens Britain's complete control of the seas and may even bring French troops to these shores. But, General Muhlenberg, make no mistake: it brings new perils, as well."

"What do you mean?" Peter asked, clearly puzzled.

"I mean that now your enemies will be hard-pressed and impatient," the Sylph replied. "They may feel they have nothing to lose. And, for those who wield magic as a weapon, desperation may make them more dangerous."

Chapter 19 — The Devils

GORAN LOOKED DOWN ON THE open field and saw bands of shadow flicker eerily across its surface. Flying close to the ground, the Sylph ranger next passed over a cornfield and marveled at the curtain of crescent shapes cast by the dwindling sunlight shining through gaps in the cornstalks.

Hovering for a moment above that cornfield in northern New Jersey, Goran felt a wave of homesickness. The two sights, the shadow bands and shadow crescents cast that morning by the impending total eclipse of the sun, had reminded Goran of magecraft — of Shimmer walls and enchantment forges and the walls of monster pens. Both sights had brought to mind cherished memories of home.

Not of life on the Knob, but of his childhood in Cornwall. For many generations, the only home the Sylphs had known was Brown Willy. Unless they were rangers, the Sylphs had come to know the English countryside beyond only through short, Shimmer-shielded excursions.

The memory the solar eclipse triggered in Goran's mind was, indeed, of one of those excursions. It was of a journey he'd taken during a previous solar eclipse. His mother Wenna had been one of a party of Sylphs traveling by magical transport some one hundred and fifty miles east, to Wiltshire. Their mission was to observe the brief eclipse from the vantage point of a place known to the humans as Stonehenge.

During his humanlore classes at school, Goran had learned how the site came to be. He'd learned how, shortly after the Arrival, Folk settling in England had discovered the circular earthen bank and witnessed humans trying to carry huge stones to it from faraway quarries. He'd learned how the Folk bewitched the giants of England to help the ancient humans transport and raise the stones to build Stonehenge — and how, for generations afterward, both Folk and human had journeyed to the site to consult the astronomical information embedded in the arrangement of its standing stones.

As the village's most talented greenweaver, Wenna would be going along with the party to study the local vegetation. Because of the enchantments deeply embedded in the stones of Stonehenge, the flora of the area had absorbed great amounts of magic. Such botanical finds were invaluable to greenweavers. Young Goran had begged and pleaded with Wenna to take him along. Finally, she'd relented.

Goran could still feel the stiff breeze he'd felt that day when, holding his mother's hand tightly, he'd experienced his first transport spell. While Wenna and the others worked, surrounded by protective walls of magecraft and spellsong, young Goran had wandered through Stonehenge, looking up in wonder at the massive standing stones.

Now, as he witnessed the solar eclipse of June 24, 1778 from among the high cornstalks of a New Jersey farm, Goran imagined the monsters of America, bewitched by spellsong, wreaking destruction and death among the Continental Army.

His mother had taught Goran that magecraft and spellsong should be used for the common good of Folk and human alike. Stonehenge symbolized what she meant. Now Wenna was gone, and the Sylphs had abandoned such wisdom. It was up to Goran to remind them of it.

▲▲▲

He flew to the farmhouse and landed softly on a hood overlooking one of the windows. Although it was just mid-morning, the summer heat was already stifling. The window shutters were thrown wide open so those congregated inside could breathe fresh air. Soldiers guarded the perimeter to make sure Washington could confer with his generals in privacy. Of course, the guards presented no obstruction to a winged fairy shrouded in spellsong.

"It has been less than a week since General Clinton began evacuating his army from Philadelphia, and still we have taken no decisive action," said a voice the Sylph quickly recognized as belonging to the Marquis de Lafayette. "It would be disgraceful and humiliating to allow the enemy to cross the Jerseys in tranquility."

The identity of the responding voice was unmistakable. "Your counsel tends always toward the offensive," said Washington. "You urged probing Philadelphia's defenses shortly after Clinton replaced Howe as commanding general, and I agreed. But at Barren Hill, you were compelled to pull back. We sustained few casualties, thanks to the bravery of your men and the skill of the Oneida skirmishers sent by Chief Skenandoah. Next time, Providence may be less generous. And General Dickinson of the New Jersey militia believes Clinton is deliberately moving slowly in the hope we will attack him."

Goran heard some murmuring among the officers but couldn't pick out any words. He decided to lay flat among the shingles of the hood, draping his wings over his body and hanging his head slightly over the edge so he could see into the room.

The first thing he saw was the back of George Washington's head. Beyond it were the assembled officers, most of whom Goran recognized: the young Lafayette, the seasoned Baron von Steuben, the brave but sometimes foolhardy Anthony Wayne, Peter's immediate superior Nathaniel Greene, and the portly Henry Knox, the artillery commander.

Goran could see another general, too — a sickly looking man who must be Charles Lee. Goran had heard Peter talk of him. After joining Washington's army in New York, Lee had been captured in December 1776. He had only just been released in a prisoner exchange. Although some at Valley Forge, including Peter, nursed an intense dislike for the man, Washington had welcomed Lee back, no doubt continuing to value his military experience.

It was Lee who spoke next. "General, you are right to privilege prudence over pugnacity. We court defeat in every engagement that depends on maneuver."

"I know what you would counsel, as well, General Lee," said Washington, sounding exasperated. "You would have us withdraw to the backcountry and defend our liberty with raids and ambushes."

"By all means," Lee agreed. "To propose a decisive action on clear ground is talking nonsense. If Clinton means to take his entire army to New York, I would sooner build a bridge of gold to hasten him to his destination."

Nathaniel Greene stepped forward with some difficulty, favoring one leg over the other. "People expect something from us and our strength demands it. I am by no means for rash measures but we must preserve our reputations. I think we can make a very serious impression without any great risk and, if it should amount to a general action, I think the chance is greatly in our favor."

Lee smirked condescendingly as Greene limped back in line.

"And what is your feeling on the subject, General Wayne?" asked Washington.

The gruff Pennsylvanian officer cast a sidelong glance at Lee, then replied. "Fight, sir!"

As several officers began speaking at once, Goran heard the sound of approaching feet. He sat up and saw Har the Tower leading three other Dwarf rangers toward the farmhouse. He waved his hand to get their attention. Har motioned his companions to wait next to a fence, then ran to the window. Although the Sylph could never have been able to peer over the sill of the window from the ground, Har stood much higher. He shot Goran a quick grin and looked in.

Charles Lee was restating his case for caution. "The advantages to be gained by victory are not to be put in competition with the evils that might result from defeat."

"I am grateful to you all for your frank and timely counsel," General Washington said, with a finality that signaled the end of the conference. "For now, our policy will be to continue to harass and delay the British march to the sea. We shall also reinforce our vanguard with an additional force of fifteen hundred men to act as occasion may serve. That will be all."

The door opened and the officers exited. Goran stepped off the hood and flew through the window, Har pulling himself over the sill to follow. Washington had taken a seat, chin in hand, lost in thought. Nearby, Alexander Hamilton sat at a desk, furiously scribbling with quill and ink.

"General Washington, I have news," Har said.

"Can it wait?" Washington asked. "I need to determine which of our regiments to send forward to reinforce the militia."

Hamilton cleared his throat. "Pardon me, sir, but Lafayette had the right of it — we must attack in force before the opportunity escapes us."

"Lee argued passionately for the contrary view," Washington pointed out.

Hamilton snorted. "That meeting would have done honor to a body of midwives — and to them only."

Goran had gotten to know Har fairly well over the past few weeks. He could see impatience on the Dwarf ranger's face. Whether it was directed only at Hamilton or at both humans, Goran couldn't tell.

"You have another pressing concern, General Washington," Har said. "As you directed, we have been scouting far to the north and south. The rangers I sent northward detected no magical activity. The same cannot be said of the south."

Washington stood up quickly. "What did they find?"

"Late yesterday afternoon, five Brownies were spotted coming out of a pine forest southeast of Trenton. Just two hours later, another ranger saw a group of five Brownies drinking from Manalapan Brook, not far from here. Either there are more Brownies ranging across New Jersey than I would have guessed, or it was the same party."

Goran gathered Har's meaning faster than the humans did. "If it were a party of flying Sylphs, the speed of their advance would not be surprising," the Sylph said. "But Brownies are earth-bound and not particularly swift of foot. Either they used magical transport, which suggests the presence of Brownie mages and warriors…"

"Or," Har broke in, "the Brownie rangers made use of some other form of transport."

Hamilton sucked in a ragged breath. "Monsters," he whispered, horrified.

Washington cast a reassuring look at his aide-de-camp. "Alexander, this is a time for dispatch, not panic. Prepare to write orders. We will send a larger formation of foot and horse to seize whatever opportunity may present itself against Clinton. Colonel Morgan's riflemen will accompany them."

"Dan Morgan!" Goran exclaimed. "I know of him. He is a cousin of Daniel Boone's."

"He has proved to be a skillful leader," Washington said. "His service during the Saratoga campaign was exemplary. In this case, however, I am thinking not just of our human foes. If we are attacked from the south by something inhuman, I would rather trust our fate to Morgan and his riflemen than to any other."

Goran looked at Har, who approved the plan with a brief nod.

"Brave men may still quail at the unfamiliar sight of monsters, General Washington," Goran said. "I will accompany Morgan's riflemen to strengthen their resolve."

"Yes — and so will you and your rangers, Har," said Washington.

Har looked at the general with dismay. "Our place is with the main army, sir. If the probes by your vanguard were to broaden into a full-scale battle, you might need our help."

Since he had arrived at Valley Forge two months earlier, Goran had on many occasions witnessed George Washington hold meetings, guide discussions, and counsel subordinates. It had soon become evident why he'd been placed in command. Washington read faces expertly. His words defused tensions and motivated action. If Goran hadn't known better, he'd have guessed Washington possessed the power of spellsong himself.

Washington regarded Har with an expression much like Goran's teacher Ceredan had used when Goran was being obstinate. It was an expression that compelled obedience without seeming dismissive or threatening. It was the mask of command. Washington wore it well.

"Your orders are given, and your pledge binds you to follow them," the general said.

Har blinked and swallowed. "Yes, sir."

"I should add that of all the brigades serving under my command, none is more capable and has more of my confidence than the brigade led by your friend Peter Muhlenberg," Washington said. "They, and he, can take care of themselves. Now I need you and your companions to help take care of our southern flank."

▲▲▲

Goran spent the next three days with the Dwarfs as they marched with Morgan's Rifles. Already favorably impressed with Har the Tower's strength, good humor, and proficiency with the axe, Goran soon came to appreciate what the other three brought to the expedition.

The ranger named Onar, cloaked in black and gold and armed with a long-shafted halberd, was quick-witted and highly knowledgeable about both humanlore and monsterlore. The female Dwarf, Nithi, was dressed in dull gray. She was a skilled archer — and absolutely fearless. The third, slighter than the others and clad in shabby clothes of black and tan, was Meto. The Lutki ranger was fast. He didn't so much run as glide across the ground. His weapons of choice were javelins tipped with jagged triangles of bronze and enchanted to fly faster and farther than any ordinary arm could hurl them.

Looking up at the crescent moon overhead, Goran estimated it was still three or four hours before dawn. Colonel Morgan's men camped by a mill, and were soon joined by local militia. About two-thirds of the men were getting what sleep they could, along the millpond or the nearby road, while the remainder stood guard, cleaned their rifles, or talked around campfires. Har had sent Meto to scout the southwestern approach to Morgan's position, while Onar ranged to the southeast.

Goran spent the night in the air, scouting eastward. Seeing no sign of Brownies or monsters, he flew first over the British forces camped near Monmouth Courthouse and then over the several thousand Americans approaching them under the command of Charles Lee.

As he rested on a fencepost and looked across the campfires of Morgan's Rifles, some three miles south of Monmouth, Goran soon saw the face he expected: Dan Morgan's. Unlike many human officers the Sylph had observed over the years, Morgan didn't believe in distancing himself from his men. The burly colonel was joking with the soldiers huddled around their campfires and slapping their backs.

All of a sudden, Morgan jolted straight up. A moment later, Goran heard the sound of hoof beats in the distance. *Morgan must have the same keen ears as his cousin.* Goran leapt into the air and flew over the dawdling riflemen to the spot where Morgan was waiting for the approaching rider.

"Orders from General Lee, sir," said the courier. As Morgan read it, puzzlement spread across his face.

"It says here Lee plans to attack the British rear, and my riflemen are to serve as his right flank," he told the courier. "But it also says the attack will be in the early morning. Did General Lee mean today, right now? The sun will likely be up before we can reach him. Or does he mean early *tomorrow* morning?"

"I don't know, sir," replied the courier.

"Well, get a move on and find out!" barked Morgan. As the rider turned his mount to comply, the colonel let loose with a stream of expletives and stomped back toward the campfires lining the millpond.

Goran flew back to his perch on the fencepost. Despite his fluency in English, he was still struggling to decipher some of Morgan's metaphors when Har walked up to stand beside him. "Onar got back a few minutes ago," the Dwarf said. "Nothing out of the ordinary to report."

"Based on what I just overheard, General Lee could be attacking soon," Goran said. "If the Brownies mean to assist the British, their attempt may come at any time."

There was movement in the trees. Goran slipped his bow over his shoulder. His Dwarf companion now had his battleaxe in one brawny hand and a smaller throwing axe in the other. As they watched, something streaked out of the trees and glided across the intervening meadow.

"Har the Tower!" cried Meto as the Lutki ranger came within earshot. "It is coming!"

Goran scanned the horizon behind the rapidly approaching ranger, but saw nothing.

"What is coming?" Har asked as Meto reached their side. "What did you see?"

The Lutki was bent over, panting. "I saw only glimpses overhead. It has a long, thin body and a forked tail."

"Overhead, did you say?" Goran was even more alarmed. "Then it *is* a flying monster."

"Run to our base across the pond and tell Onar to prepare for spellsong," Har ordered. "Then bring Nithi back here with you."

Goran rose into the air and hovered to get a wider view of the southwestern approach to the camp. At first, he saw nothing in the faint moonlight. Then came the scream.

It was a long, shrill, blood-curdling scream. Even to Goran, it was terrifying. It was as if some unseen specter had reached a ghostly arm down his throat and stopped his heart.

The Sylph spun and looked down at the camp. The Americans hadn't been immune to the sound, either. Dozens had rushed to the fence where Har was still standing — he had to scramble out of their way — and looked anxiously across the meadow. Other soldiers, still groggy after being awakened by the scream, were donning hats and picking up rifles.

Then Goran heard another sound wafting over the camp, a completely different one. It was a fiddle playing a soothing melody, accompanied by a baritone voice singing in Folktongue. Onar's spellsong was well-chosen and expertly performed:

As nightingales in days of yore
Would fill a lonely night with song,
Now hear on this far-distant shore
The mockingbirds in chorus strong,
Their moonlit concert, evening score,
To fill the senses, dreams prolong.

Goran could see the soldiers along the fence begin to sway with the music, some waving their hands as if conducting the fiddler. Among the rest of the troops, he saw some sitting on the ground, listening dreamily, while others settled back down to sleep.

"Goran!" shouted Har. "Let us advance and trap the beast!"

The Dwarf ranger was already running across the meadow, accompanied by Nithi and Meto. Like Goran, Nithi had already removed and strung her bow. The Lutki had two javelins thrust through a strap on his back and carried the third — his hunting weapon, for the javelin was in one hand and the rope attached to it was coiled in the other.

The Sylph flapped his wings to gain altitude and then soared across the meadow, high above the sprinting Dwarfs. When he reached the edge of the forest and could see around it for the first time, Goran caught his first sight of the monster as it banked around a tall oak tree, its leathery wings outstretched.

The word that came immediately to his mind was "elk." Goran had seen his first American elk during his visit to Daniel Boone in Kentucky. But what was flying through the dim moonlight resembled an elk only in its long head, the antlers on either side of it, and the short, dark-brown fur running the length of its ten-foot-long body. The monster's forelimbs were short, ending in wicked-looking claws. Its hind limbs, on the other hand, were stretched and spindly, ending in cloven hooves and adding another five feet to its length. Whipping behind the beast was the thin, forked tail the Lutki ranger had described.

A human might have looked at the monster and thought it an impossible amalgam of mammalian and reptilian features concocted for some traveling show. But, although Goran had never seen its like before, he knew the beast was very real — and very dangerous, when it caught sight of Goran. Opening its long snout, baring enormous fangs that would have been completely out of place on the grazing animal it resembled, the monster issued another ear-piercing shriek.

Although every instinct told Goran to fly as fast as he could in the opposite direction, he forced himself to nock an arrow and take careful aim at the space between two red-glowing eyes. He loosed the arrow and then rolled over like a barrel, dropping toward the ground as he looked up and saw the monster fly through the space Goran had occupied only seconds before.

It dipped its right wing below its left and executed a turn as Goran hovered and reloaded. The Sylph saw that his first arrow had grazed the monster's snout, leaving behind a streak that crackled as its magic-infused blood came in contact with the air.

"Bring it down!"

Goran glanced to the ground and saw Har the Tower shouting up at him. Instantly recognizing the tactic the Dwarf had in mind, the Sylph flew at the charging monster, then banked and swooped toward the grassy meadow. Another scream from just behind his right shoulder told Goran the monster was following close behind.

Pushing himself to the limits of his endurance, Goran flapped his wings to gain velocity, knowing the much longer wingspan of the monster would inevitably win the race if it lasted too long. The faces of the three Dwarfs hurtled toward him at breakneck speed. Then he was past them. Goran heard the monster shriek and its attackers grunt. The Sylph pulled up, landed on the ground, and spun around.

Har and Meto were grasping the Lutki's rope with both hands and pulling mightily at the monster, its wings flapping furiously as it bucked and tried to use its claws to dislodge the javelin embedded in its furry flank. Har's battleaxe lay on the ground, either shoved aside or discarded. Nithi had put two arrows into an exposed breast and was nocking another when one of the monster's hooves struck her in the head, knocking her to the ground.

Even as he saw the battle unfolding, Goran was back in the air and flying at the monster, his fingers holding the nock of his arrow at his chin. Choosing the same patch of exposed breast Nithi had targeted, Goran fired. The bronze tip produced a rain of reddish sparks as the shaft struck home and buried itself to the fletching.

"We're losing our grip!" cried Har, his voice straining along with his bulging muscles.

Goran doubted his comparatively lean frame would change the outcome of the tug of war, but he knew the monster would be easier to defeat near the ground than if it took to the air. So he landed next to Meto, grabbed the end of the rope, and pulled.

Whether the additional weight on the rope or the enchanted arrows embedded in its chest were responsible, the monster's efforts grew less effective. Slowly but surely, the three fairies were drawing it closer and closer to the ground.

"What now?" Goran asked. "If one of us lets go to finish the beast, it may yet escape us!"

The Sylph never got a verbal answer to his question. One moment, the monster's mouth was shrieking. A second later, the mouth — along with the rest of its head — was rolling along the ground. A mist of smoke and sparks surrounded its severed neck. And Nithi, blood oozing from a hoof print-sized wound on the side of her head, hefted Har's battleaxe in her hand, eyeing it appraisingly.

"Nice blade," she said. "A little too weighted to the head for my taste, though."

Goran looked at her and then at Har, who was kneeling in the grass, catching his breath. Har caught his eye, breathed out a sigh of relief, and then began to laugh. Nithi, Meto, and Goran soon joined him, letting their excitement and fear subside.

After a while, they recovered their missiles from the carcass and walked back to the fence along the mill road, where they were met by Onar. Har gave him a brief synopsis of the battle with the elk-headed beast. As for Morgan's men, they were back to where they'd started — some lying down, some lounging around campfires, a few on sentry duty.

"As far as I can tell, the spellsong was entirely successful," Onar told them. "If that is all the Brownies have to throw at us, their failure is complete."

Har shrugged and leaned against the fence. Nithi sat down beside him, as did Meto.

"I hope you are right, Onar, but I fear your concert may not be over," Goran said.

The huge antler batted aside his knife as if it were a child's plaything. The massive jaws opened wide and emitted a piercing, bone-chilling shriek as they came at his unguarded neck...

Goran jerked to a sitting position, covered in sweat, his heart racing. He could distinctly see the green of the grass. He realized the sun must be up — and that he must have fallen asleep.

Then he heard the now-familiar scream again. It hadn't all been a dream. Another antlered monster was nearby.

As Goran got to his feet, Nithi fit an arrow to her bow and Meto passed a javelin from one hand to the other, mumbling a prayer. Onar and Har were a few paces away, talking excitedly. Har caught Goran's eye and pointed in the same direction they had encountered the first monster. Goran put a hand to his brow to shade his eyes from the mid-morning sun. There were several large shapes emerging from behind the trees.

Goran counted five, six — then seven flying creatures. They were heading almost due north. In that direction lay Monmouth Courthouse. And, from that direction, Goran just realized, he could hear the faint sound of gunfire. General Lee must have launched his attack on the British. Because of garbled orders, Colonel Morgan's riflemen had not marched north to help.

How their absence might affect the battle near the courthouse, Goran couldn't guess. But whether by accident or what General Washington would call "Providence," Morgan's Rifles were in a position to help counter the monster threat before it reached the rest of the army.

Har hurried over. "Ready for another round?" he asked, his lips twisted into a playful smirk.

Goran saw the stringed instrument in Har's hands. "Spellsong duty?"

The Dwarf nodded. "Onar and I will play — you, too, Meto. We'll send as many riflemen against the beasts as we think we can control, while using concealment spells to keep the rest from seeing anything that will panic them."

Nithi and Goran exchanged glances. "We are fighting, I guess," she said.

Picking up his bow, Goran nodded to Har and rose into the air. As he sped above the dirt road, catching up to and then passing the female Dwarf running below him, the Sylph heard the other rangers begin playing a lively jig. Once again, Goran was impressed by Onar's perfectly selected combination of illusion and mood spells:

At dawn awake, the branches shake,
A gathering cloud above the lake,
Their voices sing a song of spring,
A colorful choir in feathered wing.
So swift the game, no path the same,
A victory feast needs careful aim.

One of Morgan's captains, a big man with streaks of gray in his swept-back hair, began to whistle loudly. Then the captain cracked a broad smile and yelled "Come on, boys!" a couple of times, trying to prod the riflemen forward.

Colonel Morgan looked startled at first, then returned the captain's broad smile. "Samuel Houston is right, boys — it's a beautiful morning for a partridge hunt!"

Soon, there were four score or more riflemen following Morgan and Houston along the road, whooping and hollering. The noise attracted the attention of the flying monsters — and the Brownie rangers riding on five of them. The Brownies were City Folk, about the same height as Dwarfs but not as hairy or stocky. They were clad in tunics, stockings, and caps of many colors, their legs locked around the beasts' necks, their arms filled with loaded crossbows. With a whistle, they had turned all seven of the monsters and sent them diving swiftly toward the throng below, screeching at the top of their magical-infused lungs.

"Have at them — and we'll eat well tonight!" Morgan ordered.

An instant later, there were so many rifle shots that it sounded like a squad of drummers playing along with the Dwarfs' jig. Houston and the other riflemen thought they were firing at flocks of gamebirds. Instead, they were defending themselves against a line of monstrous foes that, had their appearance not been magically altered, would have filled the humans with an unfathomable terror.

Several riflemen struck home with their first volley. The wounded monsters screamed in pain but did not fall awkwardly from the sky. Instead, they continued their dive. Some lashed out with their hind legs, bashing soldiers to the ground with terrific blows to the head and shoulders. The other flyers plowed horizontally into the Americans, knocking riflemen right and left with their massive antlers.

Even as Goran selected a target — a Brownie riding one of the monsters — the Sylph could hear Onar adding more verses:

The first attacks of lobsterbacks,
Are bayonet thrusts and stabs and hacks.
But stand our ground, our courage found,
And into our trap are the lobsters bound.

Goran didn't allow the sounds of desperate struggle below him become a distraction. Matching the monster's speed for a moment, Goran loosed his arrow. It took the Brownie ranger in the thigh, dislodging him from the monster's neck. Screaming in terror, the twisting Brownie fell to the ground and then screamed no more.

Goran saw two of the monsters on the ground, twisting their massively antlered heads from side to side in an attempt to skewer soldiers who were either battling with rifle stocks or trying to stumble away. Two other monsters were high in the air and banking for their next attack runs. All four had Brownie riders. The remaining three monsters were riderless, but still under the Brownies' spell.

With Har, Onar, and Meto focused on keeping Morgan's men fortified and fighting, Goran thought it unwise to try to contest the Brownies' control of the beasts, at least not until the odds were less against him. Instead, he reloaded and selected another of the airborne Brownies.

This time, however, his target saw Goran coming and lifted a crossbow. Both rangers fired simultaneously. Goran saw his shot go wide. He felt the Brownie's crossbow bolt scrape his hip. Reaching his right hand, not for another arrow, but for the hilt of his hunting knife, Goran headed straight for the rider. The Brownie's eyes snapped wide in surprise.

With a savage cry, Goran smashed into the Brownie, plunging the knife into his chest and yanking him from his seat. Again a screaming, twisting Brownie met his end on the unforgiving ground below.

Goran felt a sting and realized the crossbow bolt must have slashed his hip. The realization kept him from noticing the monster's swinging claw until it was only inches from his face. Quickly he drew in his wings and let himself drop, just escaping the blow. Then he hovered for a moment to take stock of the battle, his blood-soaked knife still in his hand.

Dozens of Morgan's riflemen were lying on the ground, dazed or wounded. But so were two of the monsters, each riddled with bullet holes and writhing in agony. Their Brownie riders had abandoned them and, even as Goran watched, leapt onto the necks of two fresh mounts. A few paces away, he saw Nithi fire another arrow. Goran shouted in triumph as the arrow passed through the bottom of a monster's jaw, through its yawning maw, and into its brain. Instantly lifeless, the beast dropped like a stone.

That left four monsters — three bearing Brownie riders — against Goran, Nithi, and the remaining riflemen who had run up the dirt road from the main body to contend with what they still thought were either flocks of gamebirds in the sky or masses of British redcoats charging them with bayonets. Although Goran thought reinforcements were essential, he recognized the same danger Har must have: if the Dwarfs tried to charm and deploy too many humans, they might overtax their magic and lose control. Most of Morgan's riflemen were still at their camp, preparing for the more traditional battle they expected to join with the British within the next few hours.

While Goran was considering what to do next, the Brownies made the decision for him. Rather than converging on him, their only adversary in the air, or making another pass at the soldiers below, the monsters turned away from him and headed for the millpond.

"They are going after the rest of the colonel's men!" warned Nithi as she started running.

Goran flew in the same direction — then blanched. *No, the riflemen would not be the target. At least not at first.*

Ignoring the blazing pain in his hip, Goran chased after the monsters. He saw Har and the other two spellsingers sitting on the road about halfway between the millpond and the two wounded monsters still writhing on the ground. It was the right place from which to cast spells. But it was the wrong place to be at this moment.

"Har, look out!" Goran shouted.

Just in time, Har and Onar saw the monsters and managed to roll out of the way to either side of the road. But Meto, still clutching the squeezebox he'd been playing, wasn't so lucky. He screamed, and Goran winced as the riderless monster impaled the Lutki with an antler, landing and snorting as it slung Meto across the field. The ranger landed with a thump and kept rolling.

A handaxe spun end over end through the air and lodged itself in the creature's flank. Har stood, now holding his heavy battleaxe, shouting in defiance at the monster. Then Nithi's arrow grazed its back, throwing off sparks as it delivered another painful but not mortal wound. Goran saw Onar try to spear one of the other monsters with his long poleaxe, but it pushed his blade away with one of its enormous claws.

Pulling his wings together tightly, Goran dove straight at the Brownie atop Onar's adversary, locking his right arm straight in front of him, the point of his knife aimed at a point in between the shoulder blades of the Brownie.

But Goran never reached his target. The antler of another monster smashed into his head, knocking him roughly to the ground.

The Sylph sat up and tried clear his head. He heard grunts, shrieks, and sounds of struggle. He caught glimpses of a leathery wing, a black-and-gold cloak, the back of Nithi's gray tunic.

"Goran, can you hear me?" cried a voice.

He felt strong arms jerk him effortlessly to his feet. It was Har the Tower. "Are you hurt?"

"I can stand," Goran insisted. Behind Har, he saw Nithi backing away from the riderless beast while Onar tried to yank his halberd free from a furry hind leg. Har picked up his battleaxe, turned around, and launched himself at the snarling elk head of Nithi's antagonist. With a single stroke he chopped off one of the antlers, then spun on one heel and kicked hard at the monster's snout. With a sickening crunch, its face seemed to cave in, its glowing red eyes converging at the point where Har's heavy boot had crushed its skull.

The monster dropped to the ground. The three mounted Brownies shouted their anger and fired their crossbows. Goran gasped as he saw one of the bolts strike Nithi in the shoulder, spinning her like a top, and another strike Onar in the chest, forcing him roughly to the ground.

Unarmed, exhausted, and suffering excruciating pain from the wounds to his head and hip, Goran nevertheless stood undaunted next to Har the Tower and faced their foes. If it was to be his last battle, Goran was determined to sell his life dearly.

But it wasn't just determination that flowed through the Sylph and lent strength to his aching limbs. At the end, as he faced unconquerable odds, Goran would not face them alone. Har the Tower stood with him. After years of lonely ranging and painful estrangement from his family, Goran had found a comrade-in-arms, a confidant, a friend.

Har shouted a taunt. Goran joined him. The three terrifying monsters flew swiftly at them, their heads down, their antlers forming an irresistible wall of spear points.

Then, suddenly, Goran heard a clap of thunder — and it was as if the three monsters had themselves struck a wall. One was deflected downward, crashing into the ground with a howl of pain, while the other two bounced back into the air, puzzled and frustrated.

The Brownies fired again. Their bolts hurtled at Har and Goran, then suddenly twisted left and tumbled to the ground as if tossed by a stiff breeze.

Har and Goran exchanged puzzled looks. Goran saw nothing between them and their attackers, yet something was protecting them. The obvious explanation was magecraft, but a quick scan of their surroundings revealed no Folk other than Nithi and Onar, each still on the ground and clutching at the crossbow bolts protruding from them, and Meto, still motionless a dozen paces away. Goran could see some humans watching intently from Colonel Morgan's camp but, without spellsong bolstering their courage, they lacked the capacity to intervene or even to interpret the strange events happening before their fearful eyes.

The Brownies were just as puzzled but obviously loath to give up their final victory. Their three beasts were all airborne again, and seconds later they launched another diving attack.

This time Goran not only heard thunder but saw a flash of lightning as the monsters slammed into an invisible obstruction. There was a loud crack as the neck of one of the monsters broke almost cleanly in two. Then Goran heard a whooshing sound followed by a grunt as something struck another monster in the flank, sending it reeling into the air.

That did it. As the monster with the broken neck fell to the ground, the Brownie on its back leapt nimbly to one of the two remaining mounts and took a seat behind his fellow. Without a word, they soared into the air and began flying south. It seemed they'd finally had enough.

Goran staggered and fell to his knees, the pain in his hip burning intensely. He saw Har rush forward to Nithi, who waved him off and got to her feet. Clearing her head with a shake, she grasped the bolt and yanked it clear of her shoulder without even so much as a grimace.

"Had worse," she spat.

Har hurried to Onar, who was still lying on the ground. "It took the wind out of me," said the scholarly Dwarf with a wheezy chuckle, "but I think you will find the enchanted breastplate my brother lent me has done its job."

Har pulled the bolt out and whistled at the hole it had punched into the bronze armor. "A few inches more and it would have pierced through to your heart, Onar," he said, holding out an arm to lift the other man to his feet.

By this time Nithi had reached the side of Meto. A moment later, she looked back and shook her head gravely. Goran felt his heart skip a beat.

"He is not our only casualty," said Har, and he pointed to the scene of the initial melee. Some of the riflemen initially felled by the monsters had regained their feet but several others still lay on the ground. Fortunately, all were moving to some extent. Perhaps Meto's wound would be the only fatal one.

There could have been many more if not for the timely intervention of their mysterious savior. *If it was magecraft, how was the mage shielded from the view even of other Folk?* Goran wondered. *And if not magecraft, what was it that saved them?*

▲▲▲

With all four surviving Folk rangers playing and singing, it took less than an hour to erase the memories of Dan Morgan and the hundreds of riflemen who had either battled the monsters or saw glimpses of the final battle. By then it was a blazing hot afternoon. They could hear the sounds of battle still coming from Monmouth Court House. Colonel Morgan, however, had received no order to leave his position, and a courier he sent to clarify matters came back with a tale of confusion and retreat.

The rangers spent the afternoon tending to Meto and the slain monsters, using spellsong to recruit riflemen for a burial detail. Then the exhausted but bemused Sylph watched as Morgan received word that there *had* been a great battle at the courthouse — the largest of the entire war. The string of expletives that followed added a few more words to Goran's English vocabulary.

Morgan gave orders for the riflemen and militiamen under his command to march. Taking a roundabout way to rejoin Washington's main army, they managed to capture some German auxiliaries straggling behind the main body of Clinton's army, which was already on the march again toward the Jersey coast.

After several hours, Morgan's men and the rangers arrived at General

Washington's camp. Peter Muhlenberg rushed forward to greet Har. Then the human smiled and slapped Goran on the back, also offering praise to Nithi and Onar as they walked up behind Har. Goran hadn't found just one new friend in Har the Tower, he realized. He'd found several more.

"Tell us of the battle," Har demanded. "Was the army victorious?"

"It's hard to say," Peter replied. "We didn't keep General Clinton from continuing his march, so he will no doubt evacuate his army to New York. But we fought them all day, and General Washington seems to be pleased at the new tactics, discipline, and morale our men exhibited. Those hard months at Valley Forge weren't wasted."

"How many men did you lose?" Goran asked.

"Reports continue to come in," Peter said, "but surely hundreds were killed or wounded. We think the British lost hundreds, too. I saw that some of those casualties were men fainting not from wounds but from the heat. It was scorching hot. Thank God for the women."

Goran was puzzled. "The women? I do not understand."

Peter rubbed his chin. "There have been reports from across the army of women bringing pitcher after pitcher of water to the soldiers. Two different artillerymen even told me they saw water-carriers take the place of fallen men and help to fire the cannons."

Nithi grunted in appreciation. Har and the others smiled.

"But here's the strangest thing about it: every man who testifies about seeing a water-carrier or female gunner describes the same woman wearing the same clothes!" Peter exclaimed. "That's impossible. Rumor and hearsay are at work in these tales of Molly Pitcher, to be sure."

Mentally, Goran added another mystery to his list. As he looked out over the camp, he saw thin, sickly Charles Lee arguing strenuously with another officer.

Peter saw him, too, and shrugged. "There's another potential casualty. Washington is furious at Lee for launching an uncoordinated initial attack and retreating in disorder early in the battle. Alexander Hamilton told me that if Lee doesn't stop complaining, he risks a court martial."

Just then, two of Morgan's men walked by with their Hessian prisoners. One spied Peter and turned to his fellows, speaking rapidly in German. Goran didn't understand the language but he could tell the Hessian was looking at Peter with recognition.

"*Teufel Piet! Teufel Piet!*" shouted the prisoner excitedly. Peter groaned, then nodded amiably to the man.

When they were out of earshot, Goran asked Peter what had just happened.

"The prisoner's name is Dietrich," Peter replied. "Years ago, I served briefly with him in a dragoon unit in Saxony. What an odd coincidence."

"What was that he was shouting?" Goran pressed.

Peter looked down at his boots, evidently embarrassed. "It was the nickname they gave me back then," he said. "It means 'Devil Pete.' They were making fun of me for claiming to have seen a magical creature — this one in fact." He pointed to a laughing Har the Tower.

No, Har and the Dwarfs are not devils, Goran thought, *but it would be a good description of the monsters we fought. They were Devils, all right.*

Chapter 20 — The Siege

June 1778

BIG TURTLE CUPPED HIS HANDS to drink from the river. It was cool and refreshing in the summer heat. But he didn't like the taste of this Deer River — the Scioto, as the local Wyandot tribe called it — as much as he liked the taste of the Miami River that flowed near his father's village of Chillicothe to the west.

He expected his adoptive father, Chief Blackfish, to return soon from hunting. It was rare for Blackfish not to take him along. Everyone knew Big Turtle's skills at tracking and shooting were unmatched. He'd once chased a fox into the woods with nothing but a knife and come back the next day with a lovely new pelt for his adoptive mother, Watmeme. He'd killed a buck from so long a distance that the other hunters could scarcely see it. And Big Turtle had even shot a bird on the wing, a feat no Shawnee had seen before.

On this day, though, Blackfish had instructed Big Turtle to stay in camp with the women and prepare for a trip to the salt springs. Salt was an essential preservative — and one of the reasons Blackfish's party had come. The Shawnee and Mingo communities living on the Scioto always boasted the largest stores of salt in the territory. Blackfish had left Big Turtle behind to get ready because, even though he was an excellent hunter, he was also skilled at the craft of salt-making — of boiling large tubs of spring water and collecting the salt it left behind.

Big Turtle's skill came from years of experience. It had helped his family survive on the frontier. Unfortunately, salt-making had also led to his capture. It was the reason he was now called Big Turtle, or Sheltowee in the Shawnee tongue, instead of his real name, Daniel Boone.

Four months earlier, Daniel had been hunting game for an expedition of Boonesborough salt-makers when he was captured by Shawnee warriors. They'd taken him before Chief Blackfish, one of the Shawnees who, years earlier, chased and almost caught Daniel before he took his wild jump off a Kentucky cliff. Back then, Blackfish had been subordinate to the great Chief Cornstalk. But now Cornstalk was dead — murdered by American soldiers while trying to negotiate a peace treaty. Outraged Shawnees were on the warpath again. Blackfish was one of their war chiefs.

As he stood on that cold February day before Blackfish, Daniel realized the danger his fellow salt-makers were in. They were greatly outnumbered by vengeful Shawnees. Thinking quickly, Daniel had convinced Blackfish not to massacre his men but instead to capture and turn them over to the British for a large bounty. And, when Daniel learned that Blackfish's true goal was to march on Boonesborough, he had convinced the chief it would be too hard to capture the fort and then transport the captives north into Shawnee country in the dead of winter.

"Why not wait until spring, or better yet summer?" Daniel had suggested. "If you do, I promise to get Boonesborough to surrender without a fight."

Blackfish had agreed. After a harrowing trip over the Ohio River to Chillicothe, Daniel and many of the other salt-makers had been adopted into Shawnee households according to tribal tradition. Blackfish himself had adopted two of the Kentuckians. One was a sixteen-year-old youth named Ben Kelly, who became the constant playmate of a Shawnee orphan living with Blackfish, a spirited youth named Crouching Panther.

The other adoptee was Daniel, now called Big Turtle. Blackfish had adopted Daniel even after finding out he might be responsible for the fatal wound that took the life of Blackfish's natural-born son — one of the Indians who'd kidnapped Jemima Boone and the Callaway sisters nearly two years earlier.

"I shot one of the kidnappers, and one of my friends hit another one," Daniel had admitted. "I didn't know the wounds took their lives, but many things happen in war that are best forgotten."

Blackfish had considered Daniel's forthright explanation for a long while. Then he'd slapped his newly adopted son on the shoulder and called him a "brave man."

Perhaps turning me into his Shawnee son is a way to make me pay the debt he thinks I owe him, Daniel thought. *But who will pay me back for the murder of my son James?*

The next few months had been difficult ones for the Kentuckians. Some had been marched north to a British prison. Daniel had accompanied them to Fort Detroit, where the British governor, Henry Hamilton, had offered five times the usual bounty to acquire the infamous Daniel Boone. But Blackfish wouldn't hear of it. He'd grown attached to Big Turtle. And he was still counting on his adopted son to surrender Boonesborough.

Daniel spent the ensuing months plotting escape. Several opportunities presented themselves, but he preferred to wait until he could take other Boonesborough men with him. He also thought it impossible to make the journey home unarmed. Unfortunately, the Shawnees had been careful to limit Daniel's access to rifles and provide him only enough ammunition during hunting parties to fire a single shot.

Moreover, some of his fellow captives hadn't caught on to Daniel's scheme. First, he had surrendered without a fight and agreed to surrender Boonesborough later. Then he'd been pleasant, even friendly, to Blackfish, Watmeme, and Governor Hamilton in Detroit. Had Daniel gone native? Did he share the Tory sympathies of some of his wife's family back in North Carolina? No Kentuckian accused Daniel to his face, but he could tell they nursed suspicions.

Nevertheless, Daniel stuck to his plan. Every time the Shawnees let him go hunting, he secretly shaved off small amounts of gunpowder and collected spent balls. He hid his growing ammunition stash in his shirt. On one occasion, he was also able to pocket an extra flint. And, whenever he got the chance, he reassured the Boonesborough men.

"We aren't licked yet," he told them. And meant it.

▲▲▲

He was sitting by the campfire with Ben Kelly and young Crouching Panther when the sounds of galloping hooves and running moccasins brought Daniel to his feet. Blackfish and his hunters were due back any minute, but Daniel heard too many coming to be the hunting party alone. Feeling naked without a rifle, he steeled himself for what might come.

When Blackfish came into sight, Daniel initially relaxed. He tensed up again when he saw the Mingo, Lenape, Wyandot, and Cherokee warriors riding behind the Shawnee chief.

"Crouching Panther, Big Turtle — bring these brave men water to drink," Blackfish called out. "They have come all the way from Fort Randolph."

Located at Point Pleasant, the convergence of the Kanawha and Ohio Rivers, Fort Randolph was the place where Cornstalk had been murdered. In a strange twist of fate, it was also the place where the colonial militia, including Daniel's friend Isaac Shelby, had fought Cornstalk in 1774.

As Daniel approached with water, he heard one of the warriors talking to Blackfish. "We came for scalps and left with little more than tired horses."

"Those Virginians were well-fortified and well-supplied," Blackfish responded. "The trespassers in the Kentucky country are neither. Join us and you will find what you seek in the ashes of Boonesborough."

The attack has finally come! Daniel thought, trying to keep his face friendly and his hands from shaking. *There is no more time. I must get home and warn them.*

"We are low on powder and some of our rifles are fouled and broken," the visiting warrior said.

Blackfish dipped his hands in the water basin and took a long drink. "If you join us, you will go into the Kentucky country fed and supplied," he promised. "A squad of whites from Detroit will be with us, along with provisions. As for your weapons, I have a skilled gunsmith here in Big Turtle."

Within minutes, Daniel had a stack of rifles to fix. Some needed only modest adjustments or proper cleaning. Others were irreparable. While the arrival of the strangers presented Daniel with ominous news, it also brought him the means of his escape. While cobbling together functional new guns from the parts of the old ones, he was able to spirit away a rifle barrel and lock.

▲▲▲

After several more days of making salt, Blackfish's enlarged party began the trip back to Chillicothe. One morning, Daniel was walking next to his adoptive mother and leading a horse carrying two large brass kettles loaded with salt.

"You know what is coming, Big Turtle," Watmeme said. "I know you worry about your squaw and children. Soon they will be among us. It will be for the best, you will see."

Daniel had come to care for his "mother" who, in truth, was scarcely older than he was. But Watmeme's words fell on deaf ears. As rough as life was at Boonesborough, life among the Shawnees was worse. Their food was meager, their homes cold and filled with fleas. Despite Blackfish's assurances, Daniel deemed it unlikely that the men, women, and children of Boonesborough would be conducted safely to Detroit. There were too many desperate Indians bent on revenge. And, from what Daniel had seen in Detroit, captivity there might turn out to be a death sentence, anyway.

"Ho, there, look at that!" cried Blackfish.

Daniel stepped out of the line and held his hand over his eyes. A flock of wild turkeys filled the sky. Reflexively, his fingers itched to touch the trigger of his favorite rifle. His rumbling stomach endorsed the reflex. But Blackfish had become increasingly wary of putting a gun in Daniel's hands.

"Stay here with the women, Big Turtle," Blackfish commanded and then kicked his horse into a gallop, followed by the other warriors. Soon the men split up and dismounted, choosing targets among the flying turkeys or tracing others to the tops of trees.

As Daniel watched the distant hunters preparing to shoot, he knew his moment had come. Drawing a hunting knife from its buckskin sheath, he slashed the thongs holding the salt kettles against the flank of the horse, then jumped on its back.

"Big Turtle, what are you doing?" Watmeme demanded.

"I'm going home to see my squaw and children!" Daniel shouted as he raced off.

"Come back! You will never make it!" she cried, even as the other women began shouting and a few of the turkey hunters turned their heads to see what the commotion was about.

But Daniel was determined to get back to his friends and family, to Rebecca. Not for the first time, Daniel found himself wishing Goran would make a miraculous appearance and sing one of his spells. But the Sylph was no doubt hundreds of miles away — and his people were allied to the British, just as the Shawnees were.

The fate of everyone I care about depends on me — and on me alone.

▲▲▲▲

Daniel's mount was a pack horse. At full gallop, it gave him a few hours head start. He knew it couldn't carry him all the way, though. Just after dawn, he dismounted, bundled his supplies over his shoulder, and sent the exhausted horse on its way.

As the sun was about to set on the second day, he reached the Ohio River. Daniel stopped to rest and eat some venison jerky from his pouch. Then he saw a big log stretching from the bank into the river. Rolling up his gun parts and other supplies in a blanket and placing them on the log, Daniel pushed off the bank and swam alongside, pushing relentlessly through the swift current until he reached the Kentucky side of the river. Then he carried his supplies into the brush, slumped to the ground, and fell fast asleep.

Daniel awakened the next morning refreshed but hungry. The few bites of jerky he allowed himself didn't help much. His feet were blistered and burning from the previous day's exertions. Walking gingerly into the nearby forest, Daniel used his knife to slice long strips of bark from an oak tree. He also cut down a sapling of sourwood. Returning to his makeshift camp, Daniel scraped off the soft side of the bark and used his knife handle to pound it into a paste, rubbing it on the soles of his suffering feet as he'd seen Indians do. Then Daniel set to work on the sapling, carving and scraping until he had fashioned it into the semblance of a rifle stock. Unwrapping his blanket, Daniel removed the barrel, flint, and lock, fitting and strapping them as best he could to the carved sapling.

His skills as a frontier gunsmith were tested the following day when he spied a buffalo getting a drink. Without hesitation, Daniel brought the stock to his shoulder and fired. That evening, he had roasted buffalo for dinner. He even used the cookfire to smoke the buffalo's tongue, which he stowed away in his pack. His eight-year-old son, Daniel Morgan Boone, would consider it a great prize — a keepsake from his father's latest adventure.

I'll see him soon, Daniel told himself. *I'll see them all soon.*

In the late afternoon of June 20, 1778, several settlers were working in the field next to Boonesborough when they heard a familiar voice calling from the river. It was Daniel, tired and still walking gingerly on his blistered feet.

"Bless your soul," said one of the men. But others eyed Daniel dubiously.

As soon as he got inside the fort, he broke into a run. Reaching the Boone cabin, Daniel burst through the door, opening his arms wide to embrace his wife and family.

The cabin was empty.

Daniel ran back outside. "Where is Rebecca?" he shouted.

"Not here," said a settler. "She packed up long ago and was off to her old man's in Carolina with your little ones."

Disappointed, but relieved they were out of danger, Daniel walked slowly back to the empty cabin and sat down wearily in his favorite chair. He'd covered a hundred and sixty miles in five days. He'd made it home. But there was no one to greet him.

Then Daniel Boone heard a rustle in the corner. Nerves still on edge, he reached for his knife. Suddenly, something furry landed on his chest. It was Rebecca's cat, left behind when the family abandoned Boonesborough. The cat made two circuits of Daniel's lap, purred, curled up, and went to sleep. The man soon followed suit.

▲▲▲

Over the next several weeks, Daniel made three important discoveries about the state of things in Boonesborough. Two were disquieting.

First, the fort was still woefully unprepared for an Indian attack.

Second, when Daniel exhorted the Boonesborough men to work on it, some refused. A few salt-makers had escaped before Daniel did. They'd told the other settlers about his surrender to Blackfish, as well as his friendliness toward the Shawnees and the British governor. Some became convinced Daniel was a coward, a traitor, or both.

Nevertheless, Daniel kept warning of the danger. Eventually, enough Boonesborough men listened. Slowly but surely, the rotten timbers in the stockade were replaced with fresh ones and the final two bastions were added. The settlers gathered provisions, made bullets and bandages, and starting digging a new well inside the fort, just in case.

Daniel's third discovery, far more congenial, was that not all his family had fled. His daughter Jemima, now Jemima Callaway, still lived in Boonesborough with her husband, Flanders Callaway. And Daniel's brother Squire Boone had relocated to Boonesborough with his family. At least there would be a few people in the fort whose affection and trust were unquestionable.

In total, about sixty men were capable of bearing arms in Boonesborough, including enslaved blacks. A dozen women and twenty children filled out the fort's complement. Daniel knew Blackfish would be attacking with hundreds of warriors, including militiamen from Canada. No matter how much they prepared, the Americans would be grossly outnumbered.

"If men can be sent to us in five or six weeks, it would be an infinite service, as we shall lay up provisions for a siege," Daniel wrote out laboriously in a July 18 letter to the authorities in Virginia. "We are all in fine spirits, and have good crops growing, and intend to fight hard in order to secure them."

By mid-August, Daniel was itching to do something more than just wait in the fort and hope for the best. During his time with the Shawnees, he'd learned a lot about the layout of their villages along the Miami and Scioto Rivers. It appeared to him that staging a quick raid into the Ohio country might provide Boonesborough critical intelligence, or even distract the Indians from attacking the fort. It also appeared to Daniel that leading a raid into Shawnee territory might put to rest rumors of his disloyalty.

That appearance had deceived him.

"It is madness!" exclaimed Richard Callaway, recently appointed colonel of the Kentucky militia and Jemima's father-in-law. "You propose to take half our manpower on some fool's errand north of the Ohio?"

"It won't be a fool's errand if we can find out where Blackfish is, and how many men he has," insisted twenty-three-year-old Simon Kenton. The previous year, he'd saved Daniel's life during a skirmish at Boonesborough, and the two men had become close friends.

William Hancock, one of the other salt-makers who had escaped, remained deeply suspicious of Daniel's motives. "You promised Blackfish you would give up the fort," he said accusingly. "If he attacks while your raiding party is away, I'd consider that promise kept."

Keeping his temper in check, Daniel nodded and allowed a grim smile to come to his lips. "There is risk to my plan. But there is also the promise of reward. I'm going. Anyone else who wants to go is welcome."

For frontiersmen stuck in place for months and waiting anxiously to be attacked, the prospect of action proved attractive. After several days' travel, Daniel and eighteen of the Boonesborough men, including Simon Kenton, crossed the Ohio and came to within a few miles of a Shawnee village on Paint Creek.

Daniel sent Kenton forward to scout the terrain. The young man's report came not by mouth but by rifle shot.

"Come on, boys!" Daniel cried as his men raced forward. As they came around a grove of trees, they saw Kenton moving toward two wounded Shawnees lying in a canebrake. They also saw a large force of Shawnees coming at them from the other side of the field.

"Duck!" Daniel yelled to Kenton — but even as he yelled, the younger man was already diving into the cane. A moment later, the sides were engaged in a furious melee. Daniel shot one warrior in the thigh, then reversed his rifle and clubbed another Shawnee in the side of the head, knocking him roughly to the ground. A bullet whizzed past Daniel's nose. And his peripheral vision caught sight of a tomahawk slicing the air.

Instantly ducking and bringing his rifle around behind him, Daniel heard a satisfying thud as the butt struck the tomahawk wielder in the stomach, knocking the wind out of him. A moment later, another rifle shot rang out. The Indian crumpled into the cane as Kenton rushed forward, the muzzle of his gun still smoking.

"Are you hit?" he asked quickly.

"No, just fine and dandy," Daniel replied. "Let's get back to the job."

By that time, however, the Shawnees had begun to flee, leaving behind the warrior Kenton had killed while carrying off the two Daniel had wounded. They also left behind three horses, some baggage, and a question Daniel needed to answer. He sent Kenton ahead. It didn't take long for the young scout to return, eyes wide.

"The village is completely deserted," he reported. "All the Indians, all the horses are gone."

That was the answer Daniel had required, and dreaded.

"That can only mean one thing," he told the others. "The Shawnees were on their way to Blackfish. He's headed to Boonesborough. We've got to get there first!"

▲▲▲

Daniel's men did get there first —barely. As they crossed back over the

Ohio, they discovered that Blackfish's war party, now numbering four hundred fifty men, had already forded the river. By bypassing the main trail and moving as fast as they could, Daniel's men reached Boonesborough after dark.

Daniel wasted no time. "They're almost here!" he shouted as his raiding party entered the fort. "The attack will come at any time!"

Blackfish came the next day. But he didn't come to attack, at least not at first. Instead, he sent an interpreter forward to demand Boone surrender as promised. He even told the fort's defenders that the British governor had sent a letter guaranteeing the settlers' safe passage to Detroit.

"Let's see that letter," Daniel shouted back, seizing the opportunity to stall the attack.

He could hear some shouting from the Indians but couldn't make out what they were saying. Then the interpreter turned again to the fort.

"Blackfish calls out to Big Turtle," the man said. "The chief wants to see his son."

"Agreed!" Daniel called back. He set down his rifle against the stockade wall and walked through a gap in the gate, hearing it close firmly behind him.

A few dozen paces ahead, he stopped and waited. Blackfish emerged from the woods, accompanied by a chief Daniel did not recognize. When they got to him, Blackfish stood with his arms crossed, face painted for battle, looking fiercely into Daniel's eyes. The man was his enemy and former captor, but Daniel couldn't help but feel respect and even a little affection for the proud and crafty chief.

"Howdy, my son," said Blackfish, holding out a hand.

"Howdy, Father," answered Daniel, shaking it.

The three sat down on a blanket. Daniel knew his every move would be watched closely by his critics in the fort. But, if there was a chance to head off the attack, or at least delay it long enough for reinforcements to arrive from Virginia, he was determined to take it.

"What made you run away from me?" Blackfish demanded.

"I wanted to see my wife and children."

"If you had asked me, I would have let you come," the chief replied.

"You greet your adopted son most pleasantly," said the other chief, "while I will never greet mine again in this world because of this Big Turtle."

Daniel looked at him quizzically.

"Chief Moluntha's son was part of a war party coming to meet us from Paint Creek," Blackfish explained.

"He never arrived," Moluntha wailed, "because you squatters shot him dead!"

Daniel saw his chance rapidly disappearing. "No, I have not been there..."

"It *was* you," Moluntha insisted, "because I tracked you here to this place."

Thinking the conversation was about to come to an abrupt end, Daniel glanced at the fort sixty paces away. He doubted he could run the distance before a Shawnee shot him. On the other hand, he figured Simon Kenton and other riflemen stood ready to defend him if he needed it.

But it turned out that Blackfish was as keen as Daniel to keep the talks going. Waving Moluntha off, he handed Daniel the letter of transit from Governor Hamilton. Then he handed Daniel something else: a wampum belt of multicolored beads fashioned from shells.

"Here is Fort Detroit," Blackfish said, pointing to one end of the belt, "and here is your settlement." He traced along the three rows of beads connecting the two ends, each a different color.

"The red line is the warpath we followed to come here," the chief explained. "The white line is the path your people and mine can take back to Detroit."

"And the black?" Daniel asked.

"That is the path of death for, if you do not surrender as you promised, we will take the fort and put to death everyone inside it."

▲▲▲

"I always figured you for a traitor," Richard Callaway said, "and this letter from Governor Hamilton proves it. He would only guarantee safe passage to a friend and ally."

Daniel glowered at the militia colonel. "What I did was a *policy*. I was playing them to save my life and the lives of others."

Callaway snorted dismissively and some of the other men still seemed unsure.

Daniel swallowed hard. What he said next wouldn't be easy.

"I'm no traitor, but I think you all deserve the plain truth," he said. "There's a powerful army before our walls. They're painted for battle and many of them wish us all dead. Still, Blackfish may mean what he says. He could be willing to make peace."

Callaway stood up and glared menacingly. "I will kill the first man who proposes surrender."

The other men were silent for a moment, taken aback by the colonel's bold threat. Then Squire Boone stood up and nodded to his brother.

"Daniel's only laying out the choices," he said. "As for me, I will never give up. I'll fight till I die."

No one else spoke. The decision was made.

"Well, well," Daniel said as the men walked away. "I suppose I'll die with the rest."

But the negotiations weren't yet at an end. Even Callaway agreed it might be wise to keep Blackfish negotiating as long as possible. Daniel went back out to talk, assuring Blackfish that the leaders of Boonesborough were considering his offer and inviting the Shawnees to eat their fill of the settlers' unpicked corn and roving livestock.

Late the next afternoon, the Shawnee interpreter demanded an answer. Daniel and some of the other men walked out the gate, making sure to keep within rifle range of the fort.

"What is your answer?" Blackfish asked.

Daniel looked his adoptive father straight in the eyes. "The people have determined to resist surrender as long as there is a man living."

Was that shock and disappointment in the eyes of Blackfish? Daniel thought. He began to wonder if perhaps he had misjudged the situation.

"Your people spurn the path of wisdom, but it is not yet closed," Blackfish said. "Let us meet again tomorrow — all of the chiefs of my host, and all the chiefs of yours."

Daniel turned to the other men, who nodded their assent. "Agreed."

It was Jemima who came up with their next tactic. She suggested they lay out a large feast for the Indians, arguing that it would make the chiefs believe Boonesborough was thickly populated and well provisioned. So, the next morning, the settlers prepared multiple trays of venison, buffalo tongue, roasted corn, and other food. The Indians devoured the meal excitedly, and

Daniel caught enough snatches of conversation to hope that Jemima's trick might have worked.

The negotiations resumed. This time, Daniel and eight other men strode out of the fort. Blackfish met them in a sycamore hollow, along with enough Indians to outnumber the Americans two to one. Daniel was certain there were others in the forest, aiming their guns into the hollow just as the Boonesborough men were.

Blackfish was more effusive than ever. "Big Turtle, my son, you can still keep your word and your people can still keep their lives. If you agree to leave Kentucky within six weeks, we will withdraw back over the Ohio."

The offer took Daniel by surprise. They wouldn't have to become prisoners at all! It might have been a trick, of course. But perhaps Blackfish was looking for a face-saving way to avoid a bloody battle.

Thump. Thump. Swish-swish. Thump.

It was a sound Daniel hadn't heard for many years. Someone was playing a water drum. No doubt there were many drummers in Blackfish's host. But the unique rhythm tickled the back of Daniel's mind. It seemed vaguely familiar.

Colonel Callaway, who had insisted on joining the delegation, stepped out to face Blackfish. "We will never leave our homes. We are willing to die here. Are you?"

Thump. Thump. Swish-swish. Thump.

Blackfish's face darkened. "*Your* homes?" he thundered. "These are *our* hunting grounds. By what right have your people taken possession of this country?"

Daniel moved to intercede. "By the right of treaty," he replied, keeping his voice level. "There have been several treaties signed granting access to Kentucky for settlement. I witnessed one myself three years ago, at Sycamore Shoals, a treaty with the Cherokees."

A look of surprise came to the face of the Shawnee chief. Turning to one of the Cherokees in the party, Blackfish asked, "Did your people sell this country to the whites?"

The man grunted his assent. "Well, if that is the case," Blackfish continued, somewhat hesitantly, "our claim is no better than yours, and we should live in peace."

Thump. Thump. Swish-swish. Thump.

Daniel could see the other Indians looking at Blackfish intently, some puzzled, some angry. As for the Shawnee chief himself, he suddenly shook his head, as if trying to shed water from his hair, and turned to Daniel.

"I propose, then, that we make the Ohio the boundary of settlement," Blackfish said. "You stay on your side; we stay on ours. Perhaps later, we can talk of trade and other matters."

Thump. Thump. Swish-swish. Thump.

"We are no fools!" Callaway shouted. "You mean only to torture and kill us one by one instead of all at once!"

The Shawnee chief's countenance darkened once more, and his eyes seemed to gleam with malice. "Of course the offer only stands if you swear allegiance to your British king."

"Let's not be hasty," Daniel said. "All the people of Boonesborough have ever wanted is to live our lives and farm our lands. I swear to you, Father, that we truly want only peace with our neighbors."

It was Daniel's use of the term "Father" that seemed to snap Blackfish out of his foul mood. He grinned and nodded. Daniel could also see that his words had calmed the men of Boonesborough. Blackfish was offering all they had wanted from the Shawnees. And, if the Indians insisted on the oath of allegiance to King George, it would be purely symbolic.

After some additional conversation, both sides seemed satisfied. Then Blackfish held up both hands. "Brothers, we have made a long and lasting treaty. And now, we will shake long hands."

The chief stepped in front of Daniel. The other Indians did the same, two standing in front of every one American and offering both arms. Haltingly, the Americans offered their own arms and the two lines of leaders grasped each other.

Thump! Thump! Swish-Thump! Thump! Thump! Swish-Thump!

The pounding of the wet drum had suddenly risen in pace and volume. And then something else came to Daniel's sharp ears, another familiar sound. Someone was singing. And the words were neither English nor Shawnee.

"Wait!" Daniel exclaimed, "there is a force at work here that…"

But it was too late. Colonel Callaway began pulling away from the two Indians holding him. He shouted in alarm.

A shot rang out from the trees, and Daniel saw a ball strike the ground, kicking up dirt. Then he heard several shots from the fort as the

Boonesborough men returned fire.

In an instant, Blackfish seemed filled with a blinding rage. He yanked so hard Daniel feared his arms might pop out of their sockets. Rather than losing his footing, however, Daniel rolled to the side, using his momentum to spin Blackfish away from him and onto the ground. As Daniel rose, he saw a Cherokee warrior running at him with a tomahawk. Daniel spun on his heels and began running back to the fort — but not quickly enough. He felt the top corner of the tomahawk blade bite into the back of his head and the bottom corner dig into his back.

Crying out, but willing himself to keep going, Daniel saw Colonel Callaway, Squire Boone, and the other men running alongside him. As they reached the gate, Daniel heard Squire groan in pain as a bullet struck him in the shoulder and knocked him down. Daniel turned to help, but Squire waved him away, struggled to his feet, and stumbled into the fort. As both Boone brothers sank to their knees, Daniel heard the men bar the gate.

▲▲▲

Daniel's wound proved not to be serious — the tomahawk hadn't quite matched the speed of the target running away from it — but Squire nearly passed out when Daniel dug the ball out of his shoulder. His brother was confined to bed during the beginning of the siege.

For a siege it had become. On the first day, Blackfish's men tried rushing the fort in waves but fell back under intense fire. After a second day of inconsequential fighting, the Indians tried new strategies. After nightfall, brave warriors charged the fort not with guns but with torches, trying to set it ablaze. Some of the flames might indeed have spread dangerously far had Squire not converted the barrels of broken rifles into devices for shooting streams of water. During the night fires, his improvised "squirt guns" proved their worth.

In the daytime, Indian snipers on high ground tried picking off the fort's defenders. Both sides were running short on ammunition, however, so the rifle fire grew sporadic. Still, some snipers found victims. Boonesborough lost two men, and Daniel was again wounded as a rifle ball nicked his shoulder.

Daniel got more worried when the Indians tried yet another approach.

One of Squire's boys was the first to hear it: a scraping sound coming from the river. The Indians and their Canadian allies had started a digging a tunnel toward the wall of the stockade.

"They're going to mine it!" Daniel warned. If Blackfish's men could dig all the way under the wall, they could load up the hole with gunpowder and set it off, caving in the tunnel and causing the walls above to buckle and crumble.

It was to be nature that frustrated the Indians' designs, however. Heavy rains collapsed the tunnel while also making it harder to set the fort afire.

Alas, Blackfish's men weren't the only enemies outside the fort. Throughout the siege, the defenders of Boonesborough heard the steady beat of the Shawnee wet drum and the strong voice accompanying it with an eerie, otherworldly song. Only Daniel knew it to be the work of Atta Yellow Jacket. Daniel guessed the scout was using magic to strengthen the Indians' resolve.

Perhaps the Pukwudgie's spellsong was also responsible for the continuing abuse Daniel received from Richard Callaway and other defenders. They blamed him for Blackfish's attack and accused him of treason and cowardice. The dissension grew so intense that, on the tenth night of the siege, Callaway called a meeting in his cabin.

"I am the colonel of the militia here," he said, "and I insist we place Captain Boone under house arrest until the Indians leave or reinforcements arrive. He can't be trusted. Late some night, he may sneak over and open the gate for them."

The other men's unfriendly faces made Daniel fear that Callaway's command would be obeyed. "Think of what you're doing, friends," he pleaded. "You need every good rifle you can get."

His brother Squire spoke next. "We wouldn't have a real fort to defend without my brother!"

But the men were angry and frightened, and Atta's wet drum continued to pound its magical poison into their heads.

"At the very least," Squire continued, "why not postpone the matter until after the battle? If you would put Daniel on trial, do it then, not now in the middle of the night."

"The matter cannot wait — and he cannot be trusted to have run of the fort!" Callaway replied, and the others agreed.

Daniel tensed as he considered his options. Should he put up a fight? Should he submit and then try to escape confinement later? Should he keep arguing?

Then, in one of the darkest moments of his life, he heard it — like a ray of sunlight breaking through storm clouds. He heard the sound of a flute playing a light, lively tune.

He heard his salvation. He heard Goran.

The fairy's counterspell appeared to work quickly. Colonel Callaway stopped bellowing, stood for a while pondering the matter, and then spoke to Squire in a less bellicose voice.

"Your idea sounds reasonable," Callaway allowed. "We can put Captain Boone on trial when the crisis has passed." The others agreed. Daniel breathed a sigh of relief.

A little while later, he walked slowly along the walls of Boonesborough, looking up at the stars.

"Good evening, Daniel," said the Sylph, stepping out from behind a bushel of corn.

"Howdy, Goran," Daniel replied.

"I have a great deal to tell you," Goran said, "but I sense that the full tale will have to wait."

"That it will, *friend*," said Daniel, watching Goran's face for the smile he expected the term to invoke. He wasn't disappointed.

"I have never stopped being your friend, Daniel. Thank you for recognizing that."

"And thank you for saving me back there," Daniel said. "Now, I hope you aren't done making music."

▲▲▲

The next night, the Indians attacked in greater numbers, and with greater ferocity, than ever before. It was as if Atta's spellsong had turned the Indian warriors into something more than human. Some rushed the fort, grasping the logs with both hands and feet and scrambling up like squirrels, while others kept up a steady rate of precise fire. At almost the same time, another group of torch-bearers approached a different side of the fort, their war whoops magnified by Atta's spell into bestial cries sending chills up Daniel's spine and causing his stomach to lurch as if he was going to vomit.

But for every magically enhanced attack, the defenders had a magically enhanced response. Goran sang and played his flute for hours — building the settlers' courage, strengthening their determination, sharpening their aim. Many more Indians died than on any previous night of the siege. And, while the torch-bearers finally succeeded in setting an entire bastion of the fort ablaze, another heavy rain soon came to put it out.

Goran later denied his spellsong was capable of controlling the weather. Daniel could never seem to put the notion out of his head, though.

As dawn broke the next morning, it soon became clear that Blackfish's host had gone. Scouts ventured from the fort and found his camp deserted. They also found the Indians' tunnel had extended some forty feet before collapsing, making it a nearer miss than the defenders had realized.

The Pukwudgie must have retreated along with the attackers as well, because Daniel and Goran scouted the woods and found no sign of him.

▲▲▲

The shadow of Atta Yellow Jacket was a long one, however. Even freed from the Pukwudgie's spell, Callaway and the others insisted on convening a court-martial. Daniel, longing to head back to North Carolina to see Rebecca and the rest of his family, tried to talk them out of it. He failed.

The court-martial convened at Logan's Station, one of the few other Kentucky settlements that had remained occupied during years of incessant Shawnee attacks. Much of the population of Logan's Station, as well as settlers from Boonesborough, showed up for the trial.

"I accuse Daniel Boone of committing four grievous offenses," Richard Callaway told the assembled crowd. "First, he caused his fellow salt-makers to be captured. Second, while he was captive, he schemed with our enemies, going so far as to bargain with the British commander to give up all the people at Boonesborough. Third, I accuse him of endangering the settlement by taking many men on a pointless raid north of the Ohio. The fourth charge is that he nearly ended the defense of Boonesborough before it began by taking all our officers to the Indian camp to make peace out of sight of the fort."

For every point Callaway made, one or more of the spectators shouted a rebuttal, often throwing in an insult of Callaway for good measure.

Increasingly infuriated, the colonel shook his fist at the crowd. "It comes down to this: Captain Boone was in favor of the British government! All his conduct proves it. He ought to be stripped of his commission in the militia of our county, at the very least."

During Callaway's tirade, and subsequent testimony by William Hancock and another escaped salt-maker, Daniel sat looking at the ground and pondering his fate. *After all I've been through, if it's brought me to this, I can't say it was worth it.*

But when his turn came to speak, Daniel stood defiantly and spoke plainly. He explained the choices he made and why he saw them as risks worth taking. Whether Daniel was persuasive, or Goran had somehow worked magic without making a sound, the militia officers judging the case rendered their verdict quickly. Not only was Daniel cleared of all charges, but the court also promoted him to major.

"You are vindicated, Daniel, completely vindicated!" Goran said as the two began their journey back to Boonesborough. "Are you not delighted with the result?"

Daniel shook his head. "The verdict won't settle it. I know these frontier people. They'll keep talking and rumoring. I'll never be free from someone's scorn."

Goran swooped and landed on Daniel's shoulder. "I will quote a man that you and I both know, George Washington: 'Actions, not words, are the true criterion of the attachment of one's friends.' Your actions have earned you many friends."

Smiling, Daniel looked over at Goran's gesture of familiarity. "The first time you landed on my shoulder, we were in Carolina. Now that's where I'll be headed after I meet up with Jemima at Boonesborough. We're going to see Rebecca and the family."

Goran nodded and shrugged. "Then I guess you will be stuck with me for a while longer, because I am headed back to North Carolina, too."

"Oh?" Daniel asked. "Did General Washington send you on a new assignment?"

The fairy shook his head. "Remember, I remain first and foremost a journeyman ranger. Duty requires that I return to the Knob to make my report."

"Won't that be sort of like Daniel walking into the lion's den?" the human pressed.

"Perhaps," Goran shrugged. "But since you keep walking back out of that den alive yourself, Daniel, should I not be willing to follow your lead?"

Daniel smiled.

"Only I do not walk into danger," the fairy added. "I fly."

Chapter 21 — The Patriot

"I BEG YOU NOT TO do this."

Her hazel eyes bloodshot, her cheeks streaked with tears, Ailee's expression was like a mallet to Goran's stomach. He loved his sister dearly. He'd missed her terribly during his years of ranging. But what Ailee was asking for was unthinkable. Goran would not lie. He would not withhold the truth. He would not be complicit.

"If you go to the guildhall and tell the masters what you just told me, they will dismiss you," Ailee insisted. "The life you know will be gone forever."

"It is already gone, sister, that is what I would have you understand," Goran said. "What I have seen, what I have done, there is no…"

"It seems I am always the last to know the family's business," said Brae as he strode into the room and beamed at Goran. "When did you get back? What news have you brought of the war? Have the rebels surrendered and bent their knees?"

Goran endured his father's energetic backslap without wincing and forced a weak smile to his lips. "Hello, Father, I hope you are well," he managed.

"We can do better than that," said Brae, grasping Goran's arms and guiding him to the dining table. "I want to hear all about your latest adventures."

As gently as he could, Goran extricated himself from his father's embrace. "Now is not a good time. I have…an appointment."

Brae cocked his head and pretended to be offended. "Now, how can any appointment be more important than sitting down with your own father? Come, you can catch up with your friends later."

Goran looked helplessly to Ailee, who shrugged and wiped away another tear. *It will hurt him grievously if I tell him,* Goran thought. *But he will find out eventually, one way or the other.*

"My appointment is at the guildhall," he told Brae, trying to keep his voice from breaking. "If I do not leave right now, I will be late."

His father shouted in triumph, his wings flapping so hard in his excitement that Brae soared off the floor and nearly banged his head on the ceiling.

"I knew it would happen!" he exclaimed, shaking back and forth gleefully as he hovered in midair. "Becoming a guildmaster, at your age? An amazing achievement. I told Ceredan. I told Bren. They did not believe me — but I told them all!"

Ailee slumped into a chair. Goran swallowed hard. "It is not like that, Father — not at all."

Brae stopped in mid-hoot and let himself drop to the floor with a thump. "Just a routine briefing, then?" he asked, still looking satisfied.

Goran shook his head. He pulled out a chair. "Please, sit down. Let me explain."

Now his father knew something was wrong. Deflated, Brae turned and sat down, his stubby wings extending to either side of the backrest.

"I have been called to a disciplinary hearing," Goran said. "When I got to the Knob this morning and went to make my report, Ceredan handed me the summons without a word and bade me go home until the appointed hour."

Brae looked quizzical. "You must have misunderstood, Goran," he suggested. "Perhaps you are to testify in someone else's case. I hear one of the apprentices went on a humanware run in Salem and bungled the spellsong so badly that..."

"No, Father, the hearing is directed at me — and I know why." Goran avoided Brae's eyes as long as he could. But when he could resist the impulse no longer, he found Brae staring back in shock. No words came to his father's lips. Goran heard the unspoken question, anyway.

"Guildmaster Bren filed the complaint," Goran continued. "I am accused of insubordination, disobeying a direct order, and violating my ranger's oath."

The eyes that had shone with pride now simmered. "What did you do, Goran?" Brae demanded, his voice soft but far from calm. "Bren is one of my oldest friends. Perhaps I can prevail upon him to withdraw the complaint. Little mistakes here and there should not..."

"Bren will not withdraw it, no matter what you may say," Goran said, his voice rising in volume at least as much as Brae's had fallen. "Furthermore, I do not wish the matter dropped. I want to have my say."

Ailee slammed her hands on the table in frustration. "That will accomplish nothing! Your reasons will not matter. Your arguments will sway no one. All you will do is condemn yourself by your own words!"

Dropping his hands to his sides and gazing up at the ceiling, Goran struggled to control himself. His sister was only trying to protect him. But, while she loved him dearly, Ailee didn't really know who he was, who he had become.

Perhaps young Goran, an ambitious apprentice with something to prove, would be willing to admit to an offense he hadn't truly committed in order to preserve his future in the guild. Perhaps young Goran would be hesitant to say what he truly thought for fear it would cause the other Sylphs to think less of him. Perhaps young Goran would have said or done *anything* rather than injure the already poor reputation of his doddering, boastful, but well-meaning father.

After all he had been through, however, that young Goran no longer existed. He was now the Goran who had spent years in the Blur, who'd ranged far and learned much, who'd made friends and enemies, who'd fought alongside the former against the latter, who'd shed Folk blood in defense of humans.

Goran was a grown man. He had both the freedom and the responsibility that came with that.

"I have to try, Ailee," he said, gently but firmly. "What Bren and the others are doing is wrong — deeply wrong. They must face the consequences. The others must be made to see the light."

His sister brought her head down to the table for a moment, then looked up at Goran. "You will only offend them further."

"He who dares not offend cannot be honest," he replied. "A human wrote that, one of the Americans whom Bren would terrify into submission. But I did not take that lesson from an American, or from anyone else in the Blur. I learned it at our mother's knee, just as you did."

Goran immediately regretted mentioning Wenna, but the damage had already been done. Ailee twisted in her chair and placed her head in her hands. Brae shot to his feet.

"Do not bring her into this!" he said. "My Wenna wanted only the best for our children. She would never have approved of you disobeying your orders or breaking your vows. Never!"

There was nothing more to be said, and no more time to say it. "I must go," Goran said. "I know you do not understand why I do what I must do. Someday, perhaps you will."

As he walked to the door, he felt Ailee's sobs and Brae's mumbled curses wallop him a few more times in the gut.

▲▲▲

The guildhall was bustling with activity. The corridors were full of apprentices walking to and from class. As Goran passed the library, he saw journeymen poring over monster guides and spellsong books. Many more rangers were in the common room, talking in small groups. Nearly every ranger looked at him as he went by. They knew where Goran was headed. They knew why.

When he reached the council chamber, he found twelve guildmasters seated behind the semicircular council table. Grandmaster Cono and Bren were in the middle two seats, the table before them covered in stacks of paper and parchment. Borva and Ceredan sat on opposite ends.

"Journeyman, take your position and be judged," said Cono in his ancient, wavering voice. "All who testify will speak truly and completely. All who listen will judge truly and fairly. Let the Maker guide our actions. Let justice be done. So we all vow."

"So we all vow," intoned the other guildmasters.

"So we all vow," repeated Goran.

"Bren, as the complainant, you will speak first."

The thin, immaculately dressed guildmaster stood, stroked his closely cropped whiskers, and swept his eyes over the other guildmasters. He didn't bother to look at the defendant.

"We Sylphs, and indeed all the Folk of America, face a grave threat," Bren began. "Our own King Briafael recognized it earlier than most. But now, even the greenest of apprentices and the greatest of fools cannot fail to see it."

Bren's eyes then flicked to Goran, whose face reddened. But it wasn't from embarrassment. Bren's jibe had made Goran so angry that he felt as though he were about to burst into flames. *Fury is not my friend here*, he reminded himself. *Bren is trying to provoke me.*

"The American rebellion is about more than trade or taxes or governance," the guildmaster continued. "It concerns the traditions and allegiances that bind any people, human or Folk, together. It concerns the prosperity and security of the realm. It concerns the very roots of order in the American colonies, in Britain itself, indeed of any nation anywhere in the Blur."

Most of the council members were nodding. Ceredan looked pensive. Borva merely snorted.

"Without deference to legitimate authority, without respect for the law, there can be no peace," Bren said. "The Americans have broken that peace. Their reckless disobedience endangers everyone. It threatens to plunge their once preeminently envied realm into ruin. We must do our part to restore order — not just for the benefit of the humans whom it is our responsibility to shepherd but also to protect our own community. How else can we ensure uninterrupted access to humanwares and the continued success of our larder and monster hunts?"

Then Bren pointed an accusing finger at Goran. "This journeyman has taken it upon himself to reject the orders of his guild and the commands of his king. I will present testimony that will prove he has conspired with our enemies and even fought in battle against our allies. I will show that he has become confused by improper friendships with humans and blinded by his own youthful arrogance. I will prove that Goran is unfit to serve our guild and Folk as a ranger."

After Bren took his seat, most of the guildmasters started talking animatedly to each other. Three were silent. Ceredan stared at Goran, his face expressionless. Grandmaster Cono leaned back in his chair, lost in thought. And burly Guildmaster Borva stared off into space, tapping his foot impatiently on the stone floor.

Goran swallowed hard. "Ladies and gentlemen, if I may speak."

The buzz in the chamber quickly died down. Cono looked shocked at his temerity.

"You will have the opportunity to present your defense," the grandmaster told him sternly, "but now is not that time. First Bren will present his testimony."

"With respect, sir, there is no need to waste the council's time," Goran said. "I freely concede the facts contained in the complaint."

Cono and several other guildmasters gasped. Borva whipped his head around and looked at Goran, seemingly interested for the first time.

"So, you admit your guilt?" Bren asked, triumph in his voice.

"I admit only to the events you describe, not to your interpretation of them," Goran said. "To your authority, I have been insubordinate, yes. But, in doing so, I have *not* violated my oath as a ranger. I have fulfilled that oath. And I do not believe King Briafael's commands, issued from across the sea and based on outdated information, can either justify *your* crimes or bind me to help you carry them out."

Bren rose smoothly to his feet. The guildmaster's thin smile suggested disdain even as his eyes revealed something more, a rage tightly controlled. "*My* crimes? Your arrogance will not save you. It is not I who stands accused in this chamber."

"That is an injustice I mean to rectify," Goran said.

The council members gasped once more. Borva guffawed appreciatively. Bren only smiled indulgently. It appeared he was no more inclined than Goran to snap at obvious bait.

"Our command from King Briafael was to assist the royal governors in maintaining their control over the American colonies," Goran pointed out. "While for most Folk, this command came just months ago, within the Blur the war has raged for more than three years. Britain's governors are long departed. There is no royal control to maintain, and no prospect of reasserting it. The Americans have formed their own governments and chosen their own magistrates."

"They are children building towers of sand," Bren said with a dismissive wave. "Humans in any age are susceptible to delusion. These Americans are more self-deluded than most."

"Delusion is hardly a uniquely human temptation," said Goran, directing his attention to the rest of the council. "But it is telling that Guildmaster Bren would distinguish Americans from other humans. He has spent much time among them, as have I. He has studied them, as have I. They have an irrepressible spirit, a drive to explore and build, and a love of freedom that cannot be denied."

While Goran was speaking, Bren stood and walked around the semi-circle to stand near the accused. He folded his arms.

"Whatever these humans may have accomplished so far has occurred within the traditions of Britain itself," Bren said. "Britain's wise, lenient, and magnanimous government has bestowed a great gift. Now the rebels spurn that gift."

"The best of what they inherited from Britain, they intend to keep," Goran insisted. "But they refuse to surrender their rights to overlords across the sea. And on this question, are we so different? We respect the authority of King Briafael, but his commands are necessarily few and limited. For all practical purposes, the Knob governs itself. If our king across the sea tried to dissolve our councils, disband our guilds, or dispossess our leaders, we would resist. The cause of America is in great measure the cause of all mankind — and indeed of all Folk, as well."

Hope welled within Goran. The guildmasters were closely following the debate. Ceredan, in particular, was listening intently and taking notes. Grandmaster Cono still looked shocked but also attentive. And Borva seemed positively delighted, sitting on the edge of his seat as if watching fencers duel.

"You have gained a venomous tongue from the human fanatics you call friends," Bren said, "but your poison carries its own antidote. Ladies and gentlemen, did you notice that this journeyman has called for resisting the lawful commands King Briafael? He has indicted himself yet again."

Bren leaned back, clearly pleased with himself. Goran happened to be looking at Ceredan during Bren's last remark. Did he see a flicker of doubt, even of suspicion, in his teacher's eyes?

"I spoke of the crimes of Guildmaster Bren," Goran began, "so now let me be more specific. He has formed a Great Alliance of Folk to assist the British army in their war."

"I proudly performed my duty, as you should have performed yours," Bren said.

"Does our duty compel us to use our spellsong magic to foment Indian raids on frontier settlements?" Goran demanded. "Does our duty compel us to countenance and even to encourage brutal torture and the undistinguished destruction of all ages, sexes, and conditions?"

Bren smirked. "Boy, you know nothing of war. It is always and everywhere an awful, bloody affair. Only the end of the war, and the restoration of British sovereignty, can truly protect the innocent."

"How does unleashing monsters to attack humans protect the innocent?"

Goran's question struck the chamber like a thunderbolt. Guildmasters were arguing, shouting — Borva louder than anyone — while Grandmaster Cono banged on the table in a vain attempt to restore order. Bren glared at Goran, who willed himself to respond with nothing more than an arched eyebrow.

Bren walked the length of the semicircle. When he reached Borva, Bren lingered. "Desperate times call for desperate measures. No one regrets more than I the expedient of using fear to bring the rebellion quickly to a close. But if we do not, it must inevitably bring horror, misery, and desolation."

Unable to constrain himself any longer, Borva leapt up and spread his wings to their full extent, balling his thick hands into fists and glowering at the far-smaller guildmaster standing before him. If Borva meant to intimidate Bren, however, it didn't work. Bren just leaned back on one leg and crossed his arms again.

"The petty wars of human kings hold little interest for me," said Borva bluntly. "I care not which governments rule which nations of the Blur. But we are rangers of the Sylph. Our most solemn duty is to fight and subdue the monsters that threaten our supply of humanwares and our own safety. If you have loosed monsters into the Blur to shape some fleeting political outcome, you are an even greater fool than I thought."

"Wielding the reins of leadership requires callouses," Bren replied. "It requires a willingness to make difficult choices. There *is* peril in employing monsters against the Americans, of course, but letting their rebellion succeed presents a far greater peril."

"Why?" Goran dropped all pretense of control and stalked angrily toward Bren. "How could a newly independent America be so much more dangerous?"

For the first time, Goran thought he saw Bren's confidence waver. But then the guildmaster redonned his mask.

"I turn the question back on you, journeyman," Bren said. "You have spent much time among these Americans. How often have you discovered one who possesses the Sight?"

Goran wasn't sure what Bren was getting at, but could think of no reason not to answer. "I have met or seen more than a dozen such individuals, and I have heard tales of several more from other Folk."

Bren nodded and turned back to the council. "From my experience, the true count is far greater than that. Across Sylph history, our elders recall encountering only a few Sighted humans, truly rare individuals such as Piran of Penhale and Arthur Pendragon. For some reason, though, the Sight is comparatively common in America — and is becoming more so with every generation."

At this, Grandmaster Cono stirred. "That is so," he said in his quivering voice. "The grandmasters have discussed the causes at some length, without resolution."

"There is a broader concern," Bren continued. "Folk rangers report that even Americans without the Sight are remarkably resistant to spellsong. A spell that would have deceived or immobilized fifty humans back in England seems to affect scarcely half that many Americans."

Although it pained Goran to admit it, Bren's words rang true. Goran had no direct basis of comparison, to be sure. While his education had begun back in England, he started his field training in the Blur only after they came to America. Nevertheless, based on what Ceredan had taught him, Goran had expected spellsong to be more potent than he'd found it in the field.

Initially, he'd attributed that to his own inadequacies or distractions. Now that he knew other rangers, including experienced guildmasters such as Bren, had encountered the same limitations, Goran realized there must be a different explanation. But he had no guess as to what it might be.

The hearing turned once more into a series of smaller conversations. Grandmaster Cono picked up his mug and banged on the table. "The council will come to order," he said several times, although his rhythmic pounding was more effective than his reedy voice in breaking through the bedlam and silencing the Sylphs.

"We are far afield from the matter at hand," Cono said. "We are here to judge a serious complaint filed by a guildmaster against a journeyman."

"With respect, Grandmaster, the threat to our way of life *is* relevant to the matter at hand," said Bren, resuming his seat. "By themselves, the British lack the force to suppress the rebellion. Their troops and supplies must travel thousands of miles across the open sea. Victory will require assistance — from American Loyalists, from Indian nations, and, yes, from us."

Bren paused dramatically, and raised both hands as if surrendering to some unseen robber.

"We are compelled to employ all the means at our disposal," he continued. "Spellsong is insufficient. Direct intervention by force of arms will be required. I, for one, would rather send monsters against the Americans than send our own warriors and mages. If magical blood be shed, I would have it shed by mindless beasts, not our own Folk."

Then he pointed at Goran. "This reckless boy has taken it upon himself to ignore his orders, spurn his king, and take up arms with our enemies. Folk blood has, in fact, already been shed in this war — and this journeyman's hands are drenched in it!"

There was no buzz in the council chamber now, no side conversations. All eyes were fixed on Goran. He felt his insides writhe and coil like a snake at bay. But he could think of no way to strike back at his foe, no biting question, no venomous retort.

"So far, we Sylphs have seen fit not to take the battlefield ourselves," Bren said. "But what if we do? Would this stripling truly line up against his own Folk? I say to you, my fellow guildmasters: it only lies within our power to demote or discharge him. The Council of Elders, however, must answer a more troubling question. Do this journeyman's actions not constitute treason? Have they not earned him the ultimate punishment?"

The terrible silence that followed Bren's closing statement stung Goran more painfully than anything else his accuser had said.

After a while, Grandmaster Cono cleared his throat. "Journeyman Goran, have you anything more to say in your defense?"

Goran scanned the faces of the council just as Bren had done a moment earlier. Most looked unfriendly. A few looked outraged. Ceredan refused to meet Goran's eyes, turning his head as if studying something in the corner. Borva was continuing to snort and mutter under his breath, casting disdainful looks at both Goran and Bren.

"I have already explained the reasoning behind my actions," Goran began. "The Americans are in the process of building a new and independent nation. I would have us live in peace with it. If the power of our spellsong has weakened for some reason during our sojourn in America, I would have us study the problem and come up with remedies that do not make enemies of our human neighbors or violate our oldest traditions and strongest beliefs."

He paused, but not for dramatic effect. Goran suddenly found it impossible to speak. There was no surreptitious magic at work. Instead, it was as if the gravity of the situation had dropped a massive stone on him, pinning him to the floor. It was as if his entire life of experiences and relationships had led him to this moment, only to abandon him to paralysis and solitude.

But then the moment passed.

Images came flooding into Goran's mind. He saw Dan Morgan's riflemen, dogged in defense of their homes and freedoms. He saw George Washington and his advisors meet repeated adversities with creativity and courage. He saw the cities, villages, and farms he had visited across America, populated by strivers, builders, and believers. He saw the sturdy Isaac Shelby, the faithful Peter Muhlenberg, the compassionate Nanyehi, and countless other humans he'd come to respect and admire. He saw his friend Daniel Boone laughing and making new friends. He saw his friend Har the Tower laughing and taunting his foes. He saw Dela, indistinct, hauntingly beautiful, seen as through a morning mist, as if painted in blue watercolors on a canvass woven of riverweeds.

Then the young ranger met Bren's eyes.

"You ask if I would take up arms against my own Folk," Goran said. "I know I am just a journeyman with a lot to learn, but it seems to me that some of my own Folk have taken up arms against *me* — and against every other Sylph who would place honor above power, lasting peace above incessant war, and love and friendship above hate and fear."

Bren's eyes flashed in anger. For a fleeting second Goran saw another ember of hope. But that moment passed, as well. He realized he was no longer speaking to his judges. He was speaking to his father, his brother, his sister, to all the Sylphs who would hear and repeat the tale — even, he thought, perhaps grandiosely, to broader audiences he could not yet imagine.

"Bren says I am a reckless boy, and I suppose many see me that way," Goran said. "But I am older than you think. You may have spent more years on this Earth, but I have spent more years in the Blur than even the oldest of you — even more than Bren, who fancies himself an expert in humanlore but knows not a single human being well enough to understand them. I have nothing more to say to the guildmaster. To argue with one who has renounced the use and authority of reason is like administering medicine to the dead."

He saw several of the guildmasters, not just Bren, flinch at his blatant disrespect for an elder, but Goran pressed on.

"You see the Americans' mysterious resistance to magic as a threat. I see it merely as a puzzle to be solved. You deem the new American nation a coming flood, but the rickety dams you construct can never contain it. I would counsel that we learn to float on it, to navigate it."

"You still do not understand!" Bren shouted. "You do not see what is at stake!"

"Perhaps you are right," Goran allowed. "But I see this plainly: if our cause requires that we unleash monsters to inflict terror, suffering, and death on others, our cause is already lost. And it deserves to be."

With that, Goran turned, flapped his wings, and flew swiftly from the council chamber, down the long hallway of the guildhall, and through the giant doors of ash and bronze.

If it would be the last time he saw the inside of the guildhall, Goran had no regrets. The words of the American pamphleteer Thomas Paine came to mind: "Whatever country I may hereafter be in, I shall always feel an honest pride at the part I have taken and acted, and a gratitude to Nature and Providence for putting it in my power to be of some use to mankind."

Or to be of some use to my own Folk, even if they may never come to see it.

▲▲▲

"You cannot be sure of their decision," said Ailee as Goran packed his clothes and other possessions. "Why not stay for dinner? I know Father would not admit it, but I believe he would welcome the chance to speak kinder words than you and he exchanged before the hearing. Kaden will want to see you as well."

Goran walked over and embraced her, stroking her long chestnut hair soothingly like he had done when she woke up shaking after a nightmare. After Wenna's death, there had been no mother to comfort Ailee. Their father had often been absent, too — either at the guildhall, on a ranging, or in the emotional absence of a grieving widower. Kaden loved his sister but had been more at home in the training field.

It had fallen to Goran to care for Ailee. He was doing so again.

"Father and Kaden may well feel differently when they learn of what I said at the hearing," Goran told her. "And, even if they do not, it will be prudent to distance themselves from me. Perhaps it will be better if they truly resent and condemn me, rather than having to pretend."

"No, Goran, surely it will not come to that!"

"It *will*, Little Curlew," he said. "I walk a narrow bridge over a raging river. Unless you cross it with me, you must stay firmly on the other side or else be swept away."

Chapter 22 — The Mad River

August 1780

IT HAD BEEN MORE THAN two years since he was held captive in Chillicothe, yet Daniel Boone found the sights and smells of the Shawnee village achingly familiar.

He trudged through the cornfield, remembering Watmeme and the other women digging in it with their hoes. He passed a hut constructed of timber and bark, remembering the time "Big Turtle" had come to cheer up the sickly little boy who lay inside — Lalawethika, a younger brother of Crouching Panther. Daniel saw the great Council House in the center of town, and recalled the many ceremonies he'd witnessed there. He saw pots of corn, squash, and snap beans suspended over cookfires, and remembered how many times he'd eaten the same stew. And he stood in the clearing where captives had been made to "run the gauntlet" — to pass between two rows of Shawnee men, women, and children beating at them with sticks and antlers.

There were no Shawnees in the clearing now. There was no men, women, or children anywhere in Chillicothe. The village had been evacuated — obviously in haste, because the cookpots were still bubbling. Their scouts must have discovered General George Rogers Clark and his army of a thousand Americans approaching the village during the night.

General Clark knew all about Daniel's prior captivity in Chillicothe. That was why he'd sent Daniel ahead to investigate, along with his friend Simon Kenton. When they found the village empty, Kenton had headed back to tell the general. That left Daniel alone in Chillicothe. Alone but for his memories.

Despite his months of captivity and the harrowing siege of Boonesborough, Daniel had left Kentucky in late 1778 with every intention of returning. It had taken a year to organize a new expedition — by far the largest Daniel had ever been a part of. His wife Rebecca, their young children, their married daughters Jemima and Suzy, and a host of other relatives formed the core of the group.

As dangerous as Kentucky was, many of the settlers had judged it safer than North Carolina would be, now that Georgia and South Carolina had fallen to the British. In late 1778, troops had sailed south from New York to capture Savannah. A year later, Generals Henry Clinton and Charles Cornwallis had besieged Charles Town. The city's five thousand American defenders had, shockingly, surrendered. The prospect of the war moving further into the backcountry had prompted many settlers to join Daniel's new expedition.

By September, the Boones and a hundred others left North Carolina. Even more settlers from Virginia joined them along the way. One of the newcomers, a militia captain named Abraham Lincoln, had become a new friend of Daniel's. Indeed, the two discovered they were related: Daniel's cousin Anne Boone was married to one of Abraham Lincoln's uncles back in Pennsylvania.

After they arrived in Kentucky, Daniel secured a land claim and formed a new settlement, Boone's Station, about six miles from Boonesborough. As before, life on the frontier was difficult. Daniel had built a larger cabin than before — and yet his home had never been crowded. Five of his young children still lived at home, along with his daughter Suzy, her husband, their two children, and six of Rebecca's cousins.

Soon the cabin would gain yet another arrival. Shortly before Daniel headed north with General Clark, Rebecca surprised him with the news that she was carrying their tenth child. What kind of place would the baby be born into? Daniel had resolved to make Kentucky as safe as possible. That meant trying to bring to an end to constant Shawnee raids over the Ohio River. That meant coming back to Chillicothe.

Daniel would not face Blackfish again, for his adoptive father had died in battle while Daniel was in North Carolina. The new chief was Black Hoof, another Shawnee who'd besieged Boonesborough two years earlier.

Where had Black Hoof taken his people? Daniel figured they'd gone a dozen miles north to another village, Piqua, on the banks of the Mad River. Daniel decided to make one last sweep of Chillicothe for stragglers.

"You have walked out of my fondest dream, human."

Even as Daniel turned and cocked his rifle, he knew it would be difficult to get off a clear shot. He knew Atta Yellow Jacket didn't need spellsong to be a stealthy, dangerous foe.

"Are you too afraid to face me?" Daniel asked, hoping to bait the fairy into the open.

"Do you truly think such trickery will succeed?" Atta replied.

Daniel thought at least he'd be able to find the Pukwudgie by following the sound of his voice. But it seemed to be coming from more than one direction. Not for the first time, Daniel noted that his resistance to magic wasn't absolute. Folk rangers couldn't conceal themselves entirely, or do much to alter his mood against his will. But their spells *could* dull his senses, at least briefly.

"Here's what I think: I think I'm good at stopping you," Daniel said. "You tried kidnapping my daughter to run us off in fear. You tried capturing Boonesborough to carry us off in chains. You failed both times. Whatever you're up to here, you'll fail again."

Atta laughed — a mirthless, contemptuous cackle. "For one who purports to excel in hunting, you seem unable to follow obvious tracks. Because of our raids, hundreds of whites are dead or have fled back over the mountains."

Still unable to find the fairy, Daniel gestured with a sweep of his hand. "Here's the outcome of your plan. The Shawnees have also been killed, wounded, or forced to flee."

"Our humans have sustained losses, yes, but they are acceptable in service to our greater cause."

"I doubt those who used to live in this deserted village would agree — not if they were free from your spell," Daniel said.

After a long pause, Atta spoke. "It is *not* so deserted," he said with a tone of finality.

Daniel called out several more times, to no avail. As he approached the Council House, he saw a flicker of movement at the right end of the long, thin structure. Daniel brought his loaded rifle to his shoulder. The Yellow Jacket was swift of foot and low to the ground. But Daniel had long experience hitting small, fast-moving targets. And magic or not, the Pukwudgie ranger wasn't bulletproof.

Although Daniel was focused on the right end of the Council House, his keen ears didn't miss the burst of footsteps, like a roll on a snare drum, coming suddenly from the left end. He whipped his head around and again saw movement.

It wasn't Atta. The fleeting image was dark, not copper-colored. And it appeared to slither along the ground like a snake. But Daniel was sure he'd seen two feet propelling the object as it withdrew quickly around the building.

What he saw next was even more inexplicable. From behind the building came a loud hiss followed by a blast of small orange shapes. While blazing like fire, they fell to the earth like drops of water. As he watched in fascination, a clump of dry grass began to smolder.

The sound of scampering feet put Daniel back on immediate alert — and not a second too soon, because around the right side of the Council House came its source. The face of the creature was round, with the broad mouth and sloping chin of a frog but with slanted, forward-facing reptilian eyes that glowed a sickly yellow hue. The creature ran forward, revealing a snake-like body stretching at least twelve feet in length from head to stubby tail. Four short, powerful legs propelled the beast at a rapid speed. Its shiny skin was black, mottled with smears of orange.

Even as his brain registered the fact that some kind of giant Salamander was charging him, Daniel aimed at a spot between its glowing eyes and fired. Then Daniel spun and ran as fast as he could in the opposite direction.

The rat-a-tat-tat of the Salamander's legs told Daniel that whatever wound he may have inflicted, it hadn't slowed the beast. Ducking left between two lines of huts, Daniel chanced a look over his shoulder and saw the monster only a dozen strides behind. Making another hard turn, this time to the right, Daniel hoped to elude the Salamander among the huts long enough to stop and reload.

He heard a hiss and remembered the sight of flaming droplets. Executing another abrupt change of direction, Daniel ran behind one hut and then ducked into another, coming to an immediate stop. If the eyes of this monstrous Salamander worked like the frogs and newts Daniel had played with as a boy, they'd be highly sensitive to movement but struggle to pick out stationary objects. Daniel could never hope to outrun it for long. Perhaps he could outwit it.

Daniel carefully moved his hand down to his pouch. Every few seconds, he stopped to listen. He heard no footsteps. But, as Daniel loaded his rifle, he heard a crackling sound and smelled burning timber. The Salamander's fiery spittle must have set a hut ablaze.

Ready with another shot, Daniel crept to the door and chanced a look outside. He saw no sign of the beast. He headed back to the center of the village, placing his steps carefully so his moccasins would make little noise.

Rat-a-tat-tat!

Daniel whirled and saw the Salamander charge into sight. It halted a few seconds later and stood motionless, its eyes glowing fiercely as it sought its prey. As slowly as he could, Daniel lifted his gun to and took careful aim at the creature's right eye. He squeezed the trigger. The monstrous eye exploded in a burst of flesh, white liquid, and orange-looking blood. The Salamander's hiss was long and strained, not short and clipped like before, as the beast bucked its head and then rolled along the ground.

At first, Daniel thought he'd dealt the monster a mortal wound. But then the Salamander recovered its wits, rose to its feet, and stared with its remaining eye. The round face and long body of the monster was surrounded by flame — flame from the grass burning where it had rolled, flame leaping high into the air from the huts now burning on either side of the Salamander, and tiny drops of flaming liquid spurting from its mouth.

Inching his hand toward his powder horn, Daniel hoped to reload without catching the Salamander's attention. But his motions weren't slow enough. The creature jerked suddenly and charged. Out of options, Daniel ran.

He looked ahead to the Council House and saw obstructions in his path: carts, piles of firewood, and cookpots. He dodged them as best he could while maintaining his rapid pace. But, as the monster's feet drummed closer and closer behind Daniel, the distraction led him to stumble on a tree root. Daniel careened into two of the cookpots, knocking them over and spreading their contents on the hard ground.

Hopping for a moment and then regaining his stride, he heard the Salamander hiss. Daniel looked over his shoulder. The monster had halted its charge at the overturned cookpots, sputtering and jerking its head in apparent frustration. The beast seemed almost to prance as its legs pumped up and down. An image came to mind: the time Daniel had seen a horse wander into the embers of an extinguished campfire and yank its feet up in pain.

He looked more closely. While the Salamander had continued to hiss fiery droplets, setting several more huts and surrounding grasses ablaze, there was nothing burning in front of it. Then it came to him: the water from the cookpots! The Salamander had stopped where the ground was wet. Even as Daniel made the connection, the monster turned to its left and ran, scampering around a hut and then back to the main trail after its human prey.

Daniel was running, too, but this time with a clearer purpose in mind. He passed the Council House and kept heading north and west out of the town. Hisses and drumroll steps told him the Salamander was following — and gaining.

A few moments later, Daniel saw the trees lining the bank of the Miami River. Rushing to the edge, he waded in, holding his rifle and powder horn above the water line.

When he reached the other side, Daniel turned and saw the Salamander standing at the riverbank. Daniel had guessed correctly. Somehow, the creature was either afraid of water or harmed by it. Even as he congratulated himself, however, Daniel looked to his right and saw the potential instrument of his doom.

A large tree had fallen into a narrow section of the Miami. Although it stretched only halfway across the river, there were other logs and rocks visible above the water. If the Salamander judged the distances correctly, it might cross without getting more than the bottom of its feet wet.

Perhaps it would have taken the monster a long time to see what Daniel saw. But misfortune intervened. The rushing water was batting against the branches of the fallen tree. As Daniel watched in horror, the tree suddenly lurched to one side, the upward-pointing branches quivering in the air. A moment later, the Salamander was racing to the base of the fallen tree — and Daniel was reloading his rifle, this time as fast as he could.

By the time the Salamander reached the end of the tree and seemed about to leap to the line of rocks forming the second part of the natural bridge, Daniel was ready. He took careful aim at the creature's head and fired. Even as he squeezed the trigger, however, Daniel's heart skipped a beat. The Salamander had dipped its head to the side, no doubt trying to use its single remaining eye to judge the distance before jumping. Daniel's shot passed harmlessly over the monster.

At the rifle's report, the Salamander's head whipped around, trying to use its left eye to see the source of the sound. The motion threw it off-balance. Its left legs slipped off the log and, with a splash, the monster fell. A great bank of steam rose from the river.

The Salamander hissed and spat, its stubby legs fighting to propel itself to the bank as the current kept forcing it downstream. Where its fiery spittle struck the water, it fizzled. The skin of the monster seemed to ripple and bubble. Through an ever-thickening cloud of steam, Daniel watched the bucking, rolling Salamander drift out of sight.

He sat down, relief and fatigue taking their turns with his shaking body. After a short while, Daniel stood and shouted toward the abandoned village. "You have failed again, Yellow Jacket! Where is your sting?"

There was an answer, but not one Daniel expected.

"Who are you shouting at?" asked Simon Kenton, emerging from the trees.

Before Daniel could answer, he heard the sound of many approaching feet. It was General Clark's army. After recrossing the river, Daniel joined Kenton and the two walked back to the village. Daniel saw that a large number of huts were burning.

"The Shawnees must have put their village to the torch," Kenton said, "but I thought the place was already deserted. Were you chasing the ones who did it?"

Daniel glanced over at his friend. "I chased the culprits all right — well, one of them, anyway. The other appears to have run off. But one of these days, justice will catch up with him."

▲▲▲

Clark's hungry army spent the rest of the day eating the food the Shawnees left behind and then setting fire to everything that wasn't already burning. Daniel watched with a mixture of emotions. He understood the military necessity. General Clark was determined not to let Chillicothe serve as a base for raiding parties. But much of the Shawnee population consisted of women, children, and old men. They had lost their summertime home, and were now probably crowded into Piqua, hoping they wouldn't lose that home, as well.

And, after all, the chiefs were under the sway of Atta, who cared little for their suffering.

When the army left Chillicothe the next day, heading after Black Hoof, Daniel wasn't with them. General Clark left him behind with a small garrison. Daniel was relieved. He'd looked into the eyes of the haggard and embittered men of Clark's army. He saw vengeance in them. He saw madness. And now they marched toward the Mad River. What they were about to do, Daniel had no stomach for.

He held Atta primarily responsible. And perhaps, if the Yellow Jacket was still inclined to indulge his personal grudge, Daniel could bait him into another encounter by remaining behind.

But over the next couple of days, Daniel saw no sign of the Pukwudgie. And when the army came back through Chillicothe on its way home, Simon Kenton's account of the fight at Piqua left Daniel thinking Atta had played a role in the confused and costly battle.

"There were hundreds of them — mostly Shawnees, I think, but I saw Mingo, Wyandot, and Lenape warriors, too," Kenton said. "Their village had a stockade around it. General Clark sent three hundred men along the Mad River to keep the Indians from retreating that way. I went with them. But try as we might, we couldn't find a way across. Lots of Indians got past us somehow. It's a real mystery how that happened."

Daniel wasn't at all mystified. "So the rest of the army attacked?"

"Well, at first the Indians fired from the village while their women and children ran off. Then the warriors ran off, too, into the forest, and kept shooting as the army ran across a field toward Piqua. Dozens of our men got hit before General Clark pulled back. Then the Indians ran back behind their stockade."

"So General Clark left without taking the place?"

"Not at all," Kenton replied. "They hadn't counted on us having cannons. After we blasted their stockade into kindling, they came out for a last hard fight, then ran off again into the woods. We stayed for a while, burning huts and crops, then we headed back here."

More fires. More destruction. And more deaths to come as winter approached. Maybe, amid all their suffering, the Shawnees would stop their raids. But Daniel rather doubted it. And judging by the grim faces of his fellow Americans, their thirst for vengeance hadn't been slaked by a "victory" that, the way Kenton described it, had cost them many more casualties than they'd inflicted on the Indians.

The madness was still in the eyes of the Americans, as it was likely still in the eyes of their enemies. *Which is exactly what Atta wants*, Daniel thought.

Chapter 23 — The Overmountain Men

September 1780

DELA WAS LATE.

Isaac Shelby had been sitting at their usual meeting spot for hours. But he hadn't minded the wait. The water lapping the shore of Long Island-on-the-Holston calmed his nerves. The moonlight glistening on the surface of the river stirred his imagination. And the soft mud of the riverbank made him think of the first time he'd seen the Water Maiden, when she was lying unconscious among his bellowing cows.

That had been more than six years ago. Since then, Isaac and Dela had met many times. And, every time, Isaac asked if her people had changed their minds about joining the war.

He'd related what he heard from traders and settlers. He'd passed along accounts from newspapers. He'd told her of the successful expedition led the previous year by his father, Colonel Evan Shelby, against Dragging Canoe's Chickamauga towns. And, in July, when he last stopped at Long Island to say goodbye before leading his county militia over the mountains and into the thick of the fighting, Isaac had talked of their mutual friends.

"I saw Daniel Boone in Kentucky a few weeks ago," Isaac had told her. "He's going north with General Clark on an expedition against the Shawnees."

"Is Goran with him?" Dela had asked hopefully.

"No, Daniel hasn't seen him for more than a year, not since Goran visited him to say he'd been exiled from the Sylph village. Daniel assumes Goran went back to General Washington's army to try to be of some service."

The implication hadn't been lost on the Water Maiden.

"You know my feelings on the matter, Isaac — you have long known them. As much as I want to help, I am bound to service. My Folk will not intervene."

Isaac had given her a reassuring look. "I'm not blaming you. But, with all those fairies aiding the British, I can't stop hoping your people will decide to help balance the scales."

▲▲▲

That conversation had been only a couple of months ago. *And to Dela, it probably seems like just the other day*, he mused. *But it feels like a lifetime ago to me.*

He was Colonel Isaac Shelby now. In the past two months, he'd seen more fighting than ever before in his twenty-nine years. He'd led the militia into three engagements in South Carolina. They'd helped capture Fort Anderson. They'd tangled with Major Patrick Ferguson's Loyalists at Cedar Springs. And Isaac's men had won a big victory at Musgrove Mill — killing, wounding, or capturing hundreds of Loyalists.

Now Isaac was about to lead his Sullivan County neighbors into war again. How could he not? Most of the Overmountain settlements lay in the western counties of North Carolina. When the British attacked the Carolina backcountry, of course Isaac and the others had come over the mountains to do their duty. In response, Major Ferguson had threatened the Overmountain men, promising to "lay waste their country with fire and sword."

Isaac Shelby wouldn't stand for it. Neither would his friend John Sevier, now a militia leader in neighboring Washington County. Neither would the other Overmountain men, nor Isaac's friends and relatives on the east side of the mountains.

His uncles Thomas and Moses Shelby, for example, were militia captains in Mecklenburg County. The main British army under General Cornwallis had crushed the main American army at Camden. Now Cornwallis was threatening Charlotte Town, the very community where Isaac's uncles lived. No profane threat from a British major would keep Isaac from fighting alongside his kin.

"Greetings, Isaac Shelby," said a voice from the water. But it wasn't the one he was expecting.

"Goran!" Isaac exclaimed as the Sylph stepped out of the river, followed by Dela. Both Isaac and the Water Maiden burst out laughing as they watched Goran spread his wings and shake his wet feathers.

"I kept you waiting," said Dela, planting her trident in the mud and squeezing water from her dark-blue hair. "I am sorry, but Goran made his surprise visit and I…"

Isaac brushed off her apology. "I'm glad to see both of you. And Goran, I have news of Daniel."

As Isaac talked of the Boones' new settlement in Kentucky and continued trouble with the Indians, he could see eagerness give way to concern on Goran's face. And, when Isaac then described his battles in the Carolina backcountry, the British advance, and his immediate plans to return, he saw Dela's face adopt a similarly concerned expression.

"We're off tomorrow to Sycamore Shoals to join up with John Sevier and the others," Isaac said. "It'll be a large force, I think, and it'll get even larger when we get over the mountains."

"Have you room for one more?" Goran asked.

Isaac stared at him. "Of course, Goran. So far, we've only had to face British regulars and Tory militiamen. If some of your kind show up or, worse yet, one of those monsters you've warned us about, I sure would welcome your help."

"I am going, too," Dela stated firmly.

This time, Isaac's stare was accompanied by an open mouth. "Have your people finally declared sides?"

Dela shook her head. "The reason we were late is that Goran was meeting with our Council of Elders. He pleaded with them to enter the Blur in force, at least to subdue any monsters released along the frontier. My Folk are not ready to do that. But they did agree to send me to assess the monster threat."

"I have already seen the threat firsthand — no, I have already *fought* it hand to hand," Goran said resentfully. "They should have taken my word."

"Our encounter with the Pukwudgies cost many lives, Goran," she replied. "Our elders' caution is not unreasonable."

Isaac looked from Goran to Dela and sighed. "I'll take as much help as I can get. And, Dela, a verse or two of that courage song might go a long way."

Dela smiled and bowed deeply. He saw Goran steal a sideways glance at the Water Maiden. While hardly an expert in matters of the heart, Isaac read all he needed to in the Sylph's worshipful face.

"Well, if you're coming, you better get your gear together," Isaac said.

"We leave at first light."

Goran and Dela looked at each other and laughed. "We have all the gear we require," the Sylph said, one hand pointing to the pouch at his belt and the other touching the bow strung over his shoulder. Dela thumped her trident on the ground.

▲▲▲

The last time Isaac had seen so many people gathered at Sycamore Shoals was that day in 1775 when the Cherokee signed their treaty with the Transylvania Company. His and John Sevier's militiamen totaled about five hundred. From the Virginia side of the border, Colonel William Campbell had brought four hundred. Along with backcountry men who'd crossed the mountains to take refuge — Colonel Charles McDowell's Burke County men plus companies from Rutherford and Rowan — the army already exceeded a thousand men. Isaac was delighted to find some Mecklenburg militiamen there as well, including his uncles Moses and Thomas.

As the men waited for any last-minute arrivals, they cleaned their guns, cast rifle balls out of locally mined lead, cooked and stored field rations, filled their canteens, and foddered their horses. Friends and relatives who hadn't seen each other in months exchanged hearty greetings and slaps on the back.

At sundown, Isaac stood beneath a sycamore and looked over the sprawling encampment. His friend John Sevier sat against the tree and made loud chewing sounds.

"Is that chaw?" asked Isaac. "I'm surprised at you."

"Of course not," Sevier replied. "You know I don't chew tobacco. Nasty habit. Just nibbling on some jerky. I skipped dinner tonight."

"Did you now?" said Isaac thoughtfully. He'd missed dinner, too, because he'd gone into the woods to talk to Goran and Dela. Isaac felt his stomach rumble.

"Yep," Sevier said. "Had something important to do."

As did I, Isaac thought. He'd spent the time working out a plan with Goran and Dela for nightly conferences during the march.

Sevier stood up. "I guess you've heard the talk that there may be Tory spies here," he said, waving his arm at the camp.

"Yep, it's a risk," Isaac agreed. "We'll have to keep an eye on the men as we go."

"The ones we don't know very well, you mean?" Sevier asked.

Isaac shrugged. "It's hard to see into someone's heart. Their loyalties could be divided. People they know, maybe even fathers or brothers or sons, could be Tories. We can't be too careful."

"I agree," said Sevier, now standing face to face with Isaac. "That's why I followed you into the woods tonight."

Aghast, Isaac stared at his long-time friend. Then his heart skipped a beat. "What did you…"

"Don't jump to conclusions," Sevier assured him. "I didn't think you were sneaking off to warn the Tories. But I couldn't be sure you weren't being tricked into an ambush or something. Remember the business with Jacob Dykes last year?"

Isaac nodded, his mind still racing.

"He and his Tory friends would have done me in if my late wife Sarah hadn't heard about the plot from Mrs. Dykes," Sevier said.

They both lowered their heads for a moment. Even though Sevier had already remarried, to a bonny girl named Kate Sherrill, Isaac knew the death of Sarah had dealt his friend a painful blow.

"So," Isaac said after a respectful silence, "you followed me into the woods…"

"…and saw you talking to the little people, yes," Sevier interrupted with a knowing smile.

There was no point in denying it. Isaac had heard Goran sing a concealment spell. If Sevier had been able to watch them in spite of that, he obviously possessed the Sight. And his easy manner suggested that Goran and Dela were not the first magical creatures Sevier had seen.

So Isaac told his friend everything. He spoke of the Water Maiden and Goran, of Daniel and Nanyehi, of the Great Alliance, of monsters.

"Goran and Dela are coming with us," Isaac said. "They're the best scouts we could have and, if their kind of Folk or worse attack us, we'll need the help."

Still smiling, Sevier sat back down against the sycamore tree. He put his hand in his pouch and pulled out another strip of jerky. "Care for dinner? I'm having seconds."

▲▲▲

The next morning, the militiamen assembled to hear a sermon from the Reverend Samuel Doak, a Presbyterian minister and former neighbor of Isaac's. "My countrymen," Doak began, "you are about to set out on an expedition full of hardships and dangers, but one in which the Almighty will attend you. The Mother Country has her hand upon you, these American colonies, and takes that for which our fathers planted their homes in the wilderness — our liberty."

Some of the men hollered and whistled until their militia captains calmed them down.

"Your brethren across the mountains are crying like Macedonia for your help," the minister continued. "God forbid that you should refuse to hear and answer their call — but the call of your brethren is not all. The enemy is marching here to destroy your homes. Brave men, you are not unacquainted with battle. Your hands have already been taught to war and your fingers to fight. You have wrested these beautiful valleys of the Holston and Watauga from the savage hand. Will you tarry now until the other enemy carries fire and sword to your very doors? No, it shall not be. Go forth, then, in the strength of your manhood to the aid of your brethren, the defense of your liberty, and the protection of your homes. And may the God of Justice be with you and give you victory!"

Shortly thereafter, most of the assembled militiamen headed south from Sycamore Shoals. Only the boys and old men stayed behind in case the settlements were attacked by Tory or Chickamauga raiders. By nightfall, the column had traveled twenty miles, to the base of Roan Mountain. It started to rain, so the men camped for the evening, stowing their supply of gunpowder under a rocky ledge to keep it dry.

Late that night, when Isaac went out to meet Goran and Dela, John Sevier came along. The fairies were full of questions, but Sevier refused to answer them.

"At least tell us which Folk you have encountered," Goran insisted.

"That's a tale for another day," Sevier said, laughing amiably. "If I kept my secret from my friend Isaac for all these years, why would I spill it to someone I just met?"

"But if the Folk you know are part of the Great Alliance..." Goran began.

"They're not," Sevier said. "Their mortal enemies are. You have nothing to fear from them."

Isaac was about to pose another question when suddenly, from the top of Roan Mountain, there came an eerie cry. It reminded Isaac of the howl of a wolf. He'd often chased red wolves off his farm and heard them crying out in the night. But their howls had been short and high-pitched. This cry was long, low, and made the hair stand up on the back of his neck.

The others appeared to be similarly affected, looking at each other in alarm.

But it was the only howl they heard that night.

▲▲▲

The next morning, they headed up the slope to Yellow Mountain Gap and arrived at a meadow covered in fresh snow. The men stopped for a rest while the commanders took a headcount. The last of Isaac's captains had just reported when John Sevier rode up with a disgusted look on his face.

"We were right to be suspicious," he told Isaac. "Two of my men are unaccounted for. Either they got homesick real quick or..."

"Or they slipped away to warn Major Ferguson," Isaac finished grimly.

After several more hours, the expedition reached the banks of Roaring Creek and made camp. Throughout the afternoon, Isaac had been on edge. It wasn't just the suspected Tory spies that worried him. Although there'd been no more wolf howls, he couldn't shake the feeling they were being stalked.

That night, when Isaac and John Sevier went out to meet the fairies, they brought their rifles. As Isaac began to tell Goran and Dela about the missing men, they heard the same bestial cry as the night before — but much louder. Then came another howl from another direction. Then another.

"Sounds like a whole pack," Sevier said, glancing over his shoulder at the ridgeline. Then he tightened his grip on his rifle. "If they're hunting us, they'll go hungry tonight."

"I do not think they are natural animals," Dela whispered. "That is terror magic I hear."

"Terror magic?" Isaac asked.

"Monsters may not consciously sing spells, but the magic in their bodies enhances their natural abilities," Goran explained. "Snake venom becomes more venomous. Tough hides get tougher. Sharp claws get sharper. In this case, an unsettling sound can become a deeply terrifying one."

As if on cue, a chorus of howls sent chills up Isaac's spine.

Sevier spat in contempt. "The enemy knows we're coming. They're trying to scare off as many of our men as they can."

"That is their plan," Goran agreed. "And while Dela and I can use spellsong to weaken the effect, we cannot counteract it fully. Direct action is required."

"The hunted must become the hunters," said Sevier, brightening at the prospect.

Dela noticed. "John Sevier, do not take this task lightly. Monsters are elusive and dangerous foes. We rangers train extensively before we face them, and we never do so without enchanted weapons."

Isaac was just as surprised as the fairies when Sevier responded with a dismissive chuckle. "I appreciate the advice, my fair Water Maiden, but what makes you think this is the first time I've hunted monsters?"

He'll tell his tale if I have to drag it out of him, Isaac resolved. *But now is not the time.*

▲▲▲

Isaac and Dela walked cautiously through the forest. The Water Maiden held her bronze-tipped trident with one hand and her net in the other. Embedded in the net at regular intervals were beads of glass and devices of bronze. *Those must be enchanted, too*, Isaac thought. His own weapons — his hunting rifle, a knife, and a hatchet thrust into his belt — seemed pitifully inadequate by comparison. But he would do his part.

Then a long howl pierced the night.

Isaac had never been prone to loneliness. Often by himself, with his cattle or on some errand, solitude came naturally to him. But that night on the mountain, Isaac felt deeply, desperately alone. And he knew that, for the men back at camp who lacked his resistance to magic, the loneliness would be far more intense.

Dela cast a sideways glance at Isaac and smiled. Then, softly, beautifully, she began to hum. He drank in the melody and felt it quench his thirst. He wrapped himself in it and felt its warmth smother the chill of night.

JOHN HOOD

Abruptly, Dela went silent. Isaac froze in place. Before them glowed two green eyes. Before them stood the howler.

It was shaped like a canine. But it was bigger than any dog or wolf Isaac had ever seen. As tall as a pony, covered in shaggy black fur, and partially shrouded by a cloud of greenish smoke, the monster bared long, wicked-looking teeth and issued a long, wicked-sounding snarl.

"Hellhound," whispered the Water Maiden. "Its weakest spot will be its belly."

Even as she whispered, Dela began creeping to the right of the beast, her eyes locked with its eyes in a contest of wills. She began to sing a new melody in her strange Folktongue — a fierce song of menace. While her right hand grasped her trident, her left hand rose to the necklace of dark mussel shells at her throat. As Dela sang, her fingers thumped the shells, their rattle punctuating each beat. The Hellhound growled ominously in response, its head and then its body turning to face Dela as she continued to circle it.

She's making a bigger target for me, Isaac realized. He lifted his rifle to his shoulder, aimed at a spot on the monster's right side just above its underbelly, and fired.

The Hellhound jerked and cried out, although this time its howl was short and high-pitched. It stumbled back a few steps, shook its shaggy body, and then glared at Isaac with its strange green eyes. Suddenly, Isaac saw green-tinted smoke all around him. It felt like his body was being squeezed by invisible hands. He wanted to reload, to run, to do *something*. Instead, he could only watch as the Hellhound crouched, its tail stiffened, its teeth bared.

As the monster sprang, Isaac saw Dela racing at it with her trident. The longer central prong caught the beast low on its left side, its bronze tip casting off red sparks as it penetrated the skin. The two side prongs bit into the creature, too — and then the trident was wrenched from Dela's arms so forcefully that she was thrown to the ground.

The Water Maiden's grunt of pain freed Isaac from his smoky fetters. Bellowing in rage, he cast aside his rifle, pulled the hatchet from his belt, and charged at the monster.

"Look out!" Dela cried — but Isaac had already seen the front paw swinging at his face. He ducked, continuing his momentum underneath the blow as he lowered his head and bowled into the Hellhound.

It was a massive thing, but Isaac was no scrawny boy. Both tumbled to the ground, dazed. Isaac remembered the hatchet still in his hand and swung it at the snarling jaws. The blade struck a glancing blow but drew no blood. The monster retaliated by snapping at Isaac's outstretched arm. It might have taken his arm off at the elbow had Isaac not thrown himself backward.

The Hellhound poised to pounce, then suddenly yelped in agony. Dela had recovered her trident and thrust the enchanted weapon more than a foot into the beast's underbelly — through its magically toughened hide, through unnaturally strong sinew and muscle, into its heart.

This time the Water Maiden kept her grip as the monster pulled away, which had the effect of tearing off a chunk of bloody flesh. It was sizzling as if on a frying pan. Isaac found the stench almost unbearable. He scrambled to his feet, readying himself for another charge, but the Hellhound lay lifeless.

"You were magnificent, Dela!" Isaac cried.

"Hold your praise," she said quickly. "Remember — they hunt in packs."

Isaac picked up his rifle and started to reload. Dela stepped to the carcass of the dead monster and wiped the prongs of her trident on its black fur.

From behind them came another chorus of howls, then the sound of many feet. Isaac and Dela turned simultaneously to see two sets of glowing green eyes emerge from the dark forest, followed a moment later by a third.

"Run!" Dela shouted.

Neither was well suited for a foot race. Dela was naturally fleeter in water than on land, and her tiny legs were unlikely to keep her ahead of the pack for long. Isaac's legs were far longer but he carried more weight than average on his stocky frame. As the two fled along a small creek, Isaac yelled to his companion.

"We have to find a place to make our stand! They're coming up on us!"

"We barely overcame one," Dela shouted back. "Against three, we stand little chance!"

Isaac drew the only practical conclusion. He stopped short and turned.

"Keep going!" he cried. Then he knelt, balanced his arm on his knee, took careful aim, and fired at the small tuft of dark-gray fur he saw between the forelegs of the closest monster.

Isaac hooted with satisfaction when he saw flesh and blood burst from the chest of the creature. It crashed to the ground and rolled back and forth, its mixture of growls and whimpers prompting the other two Hellhounds to halt their advance.

Without hesitation, Isaac reached for his pouch and powder horn, intent on selling his life as dearly as he could. Then he felt a small hand lightly touch his arm.

"No, Dela, keep going!" he insisted.

"I will not abandon you," she insisted more fervently. "I will never again abandon my family or friends to save myself."

Isaac felt determination swell within him. Then he heard the Water Maiden resume her fierce, menacing song. At the sound of it, and the accompanying rattle of her necklace, the wounded Hellhound tried but failed to rise. And, at the sound of the song, the other two growled and bared their teeth. Just as Isaac and Dela had done to the lone monster before, now the two Hellhounds separated to come at their prey from different angles.

"Keep it up," he said. "I'm almost ready."

With savage growls, the Hellhounds rushed at Dela and Isaac. She couched her trident under one arm and spread her net with the other. Isaac had just enough time to fire his rifle from his hip before the beast crashed into the muzzle, knocking the gun from his hand.

Isaac rolled to his right, reaching for the hatchet at his belt. It wasn't there! It must have fallen out. Drawing his hunting knife instead, Isaac rose and braced himself for impact.

It came an instant later, knocking him back to the ground.

Isaac looked up at the snarling face of the Hellhound, its green eyes seeming to reach out and thrust thick green smoke down his throat, choking him. Somehow, Isaac managed to get hold of its throat with his left hand. It was the only thing keeping its teeth from clamping onto his jugular. His right arm was pinned under hundreds of pounds of magical monster, the knife in his hand irrelevant.

Try as he might, Isaac could draw no more than a shallow breath. The beast's massive weight was pressing too hard on his chest. His left arm was quivering. His strength was rapidly failing. In seconds, it would be over.

Then he felt the Hellhound jerk. It yelped. It yelped again after another jerk. The crushing weight disappeared. Isaac lay on the ground heaving, filling his aching lungs.

"That's some fancy bow-and-arrow work, Goran," said the familiar voice of John Sevier.

Isaac sat up and saw his friend and the Sylph approaching rapidly from the other side of the creek. The monster was on its side, twitching and grunting, two arrows protruding from its side. Dela appeared, trident in hand. With a single smooth stroke, she jabbed through the underbelly into its vital organs, finishing the Hellhound with a shower of red sparks.

Turning to the side, Isaac saw the third monster seemingly dead, as well — its head wrapped in Dela's enchanted net, the ends still twisted around its throat.

Sevier walked over and helped Isaac to his feet. "Just three of them, eh?"

"Four," Isaac corrected him. "There's another one lying up the creek a ways."

"That's impressive work — for a beginner," Sevier said with a smirk. "But I'd say it was more like three and a half, since our archer friend here helped with the last one. So, I guess that would make it, uh, six and a half for our team."

"Six?" Isaac was impressed.

"Six *and a half*," Sevier insisted. "Fair is fair."

▲▲▲

When Isaac and the others got back to camp, they found all of the men awake, most of them anxious, and many in a blind panic. After half an hour of restful spellsong, things finally settled almost back to normal. Even Isaac got a few hours of solid sleep. He hadn't gotten that much in weeks.

Over the next three days, as the army continued its southward journey, Isaac, Sevier, and the fairies braced for a repeat of their battle with the Hellhounds. They met up each night and took turns on watch while the others slept. Each night, their vigilance proved unnecessary.

When the column reached Colonel McDowell's Burke County plantation, Quaker Meadows, Isaac was delighted to find hundreds of reinforcements waiting: men from Wilkes County, led by Colonel Benjamin Cleveland, and a smaller force of Surry County militia under Major Joseph Winston.

"I am quite familiar with Major Winston," Goran told the others during their late-night meeting. "He lives close to the Sylph village. He is a good man and a fine leader."

"They are all good men, and many have fought Tories or Indians before," said Isaac. "But Patrick Ferguson has experienced fighters with him, too

— lots of them."

"And our encounter with the Hellhounds suggests the presence of Folk," Dela pointed out. "Those monsters were surely being guided."

"So, some of your sort might still be following us?" asked John Sevier. The two fairies nodded.

"Dela and I think it is time to split up," Goran said. "I will range west of the column while she ranges east. We will look for signs of Folk or other enemies, and report back to you every couple of days."

Isaac agreed to the plan, although it had been comforting to have the fairies with them. Now he and the other Patriot militia would have to continue their journey on their own.

▲▲▲

Alas, the journey would have to wait. Heavy rains turned the ground into mud and threatened to ruin their gunpowder. For two days, the men waited out the storms in their camp on a rise called Bedford Hill. The last known whereabouts of Major Ferguson's Tories was Gilbert Town, a settlement to the southwest. If the Patriots didn't get there soon, and in enough force, Ferguson might well escape them. The men were growing increasingly frustrated and anxious. There were many arguments in camp, and more than a few fistfights.

The tensions weren't limited to the rank and file. The leaders of the expedition had bickered for days about who should be in charge of the expedition.

"If this infernal rain ever lets up, we'll have to move quickly — and I don't think the men will do that without firm leadership," said Benjamin Cleveland.

"And you think you're the one to supply it," Sevier said dryly.

"I *am* a senator and I have plenty of experience fighting Tories," Cleveland insisted.

"Many men here could stake a similar claim," Sevier pointed out. "I've served in the North Carolina House. Isaac served in Virginia."

Glancing around the campfire, Isaac quickly read the faces of the others. Each of the Carolinians seemed inclined to assert his own claim. The safest course, he recognized, was not to pick any of them.

"I suggest Colonel William Campbell be put in overall command," Isaac said.

The others looked at him in surprise — Sevier more so than the others. But it made sense. Campbell was a Virginian. Elevating him wouldn't favor one Carolinian over the others.

The officers soon agreed to the proposal. As they voted, Isaac could see Joseph Winston eyeing him closely. He nodded to the Surry County man, who returned the gesture. Then Isaac decided to make another suggestion.

"One of our scouts intercepted a letter Major Ferguson sent yesterday to recruit more Tories," he began. "He knows we're coming. He mentions us by name — Colonel Campbell, Colonel Cleveland, even me."

"I'm honored to be mentioned," Cleveland drawled.

"The point is," Isaac continued, "we may be outnumbered by the time we reach him. Some of the men are already grumbling. I think we better talk to them in the morning."

"That's a fine idea, Isaac — I'm looking forward to hearing your speech," said Sevier, effecting a mocking grin.

Isaac shook his head. "I am no speaker. Perhaps someone with more experience…"

"Experience isn't the critical factor," said Winston, stepping forward to face Isaac. "I've seen many a fine speech during my own time in the legislature. My cousin Patrick Henry is one of the finest orators in America. But our men don't need a political discourse or fancy sermon. They just need to know what we're up against, and how we're going to beat Ferguson."

Reluctantly, Isaac agreed.

The next morning, the captains assembled their militia companies in a clearing at the base of a slope. Isaac rode his horse to the front and cupped his hands over his mouth.

"You know why we've come all this way," he shouted, his voice echoing off the surrounding hills. "We still have a way to go. And, when we catch Ferguson, it will be a rough fight. If you would turn back, now is the time. As for the rest, we head south this morning."

Isaac could see some of the men talking nervously. *Was their courage wavering?*

Something pricked the back of Isaac's neck like a sewing needle. But the cause wasn't the sight of anxious militiamen. It was the faint sound of some kind of pipe in the distance.

Spellsong! he thought. *And Dela and Goran aren't here to counteract it.*

He imagined masses of disgruntled men turning around and heading home. He couldn't let it happen, not with their enemy so tantalizingly close.

"Hold on, listen to me!" Isaac shouted over the din. "Will you not fight to avenge the men they've killed? Will you not fight for liberty?"

The pipe still played a mournful tune, but some of the men had quieted down enough to listen to him. He had to make the next words count. Then he remembered the intercepted letter. Pulling it out of his pocket, Isaac waved it furiously.

"Patrick Ferguson calls you barbarians! Here's a letter asking for Tory reinforcements. He calls you robbers and murderers! He calls you a pack of wild mongrels!"

The militiamen were silent now. The faces of those in the front ranks had become rigid, like iron masks.

"Patrick Ferguson says you are coming to abuse and rape the mothers and daughters of the Tories!" Isaac continued. "He says you are cowards who have no will to fight! Is he right?"

"No!" yelled the Burke County men to the right. "To the Devil with him!" shouted the South Carolinians on the left. "He'll get his!" warned one of Isaac's own men.

Isaac decided to force the issue. "You have all been informed of the offer. You who desire to decline it will, when the word is given, march three steps to the rear and stand."

Then Isaac paused. He looked at Sevier, who jabbed his arm up in defiance. He looked at Joseph Winston, who merely cocked an eyebrow. Isaac saw Benjamin Cleveland roaring his approval and William Campbell urging the Virginians to stomp their feet.

"Those who desire to back out, march back!" Isaac commanded.

Not a single man moved.

Isaac realized he'd been holding his breath and let it out slowly. "I am heartily glad to see you to a man resolve to meet and fight your country's foes!" he yelled. "Your officers will shrink from no danger — we will be consistently with you."

The men cheered once more. And the march resumed.

▲▲▲

When they reached Gilbert Town, Ferguson was no longer there. That night, Isaac and Sevier were pleased to find Goran and Dela waiting for them atop a nearby hill.

"It must have been the Lutin," said Goran, after Isaac narrated the strange events of the previous day. "I caught sight of a red cap as I was flying over a stream this morning and soon discovered it belonged to a ranger from the Lutin colony of Charleston. She was probably the one controlling the Hellhounds. I was unable to catch her."

"I don't understand," Isaac said. "If neither of you was with us, why didn't the Lutin's spell work? I was worried hundreds of men were about to desert."

"Spellsong is strong, Isaac, but it is hardly omnipotent," Dela explained. "Perhaps if she had focused her magic on discouraging some of the leaders, it might have worked. But charming hundreds of human beings at a time is difficult."

"And Americans are more resistant than most, it seems," added Goran, "although, if other Lutins had joined her, the result might have been very different. If there are Lutins traveling in significant numbers with the British, that may be why the Americans surrendered Charleston so readily and why so many Americans ran away from Cornwallis last month at Camden."

Sevier shot Isaac a sly look. "I think your pretty words saved the day."

Dela surprised them both by nodding in agreement. "Words need not be infused with magic to exercise great power."

▲▲▲

When the column crossed the South Carolina border and reached the Cowpens, a popular grazing and meeting spot, Isaac and the others got two big pieces of news.

First, there were even more reinforcements — hundreds of militiamen from the Carolinas and a few from Georgia. That swelled their ranks to some eighteen hundred men. The second piece of news came from a spy who'd just left Ferguson's camp. The Tories had gone east, apparently trying to reach the British army camped in Charlotte Town.

"How far away are they?" Isaac asked.

"About thirty miles," the man said, "at a place called Kings Mountain."

The only sure way to catch Ferguson before he could retreat again toward Charlotte Town would to ride all night. That meant leaving behind the hundreds of men without good horses. Still, a slower march to battle might mean no battle at all.

Shortly before nightfall, the chosen Patriots mounted their horses and galloped east toward Kings Mountain. It soon began to rain, turning the ground to mud and making the cold night even more uncomfortable.

Colonel Campbell rode up next to Isaac. "Maybe we ought to stop until the rain lets up."

"No," Isaac snapped. "I should not stop even if I follow Ferguson right into Cornwallis's lines."

By early afternoon of the next day, the Patriots had crossed Kings Creek, passed two rocky knobs, and were looking up at the mountain that shared the creek's name. The militiamen dismounted, tied their horses to the ancient trunks of chestnut and hickory trees, and began forming up in companies. Many pulled scraps of white paper from their pockets and attached them to their hats. Isaac watched the men with a mixture of excitement and anxiety. The army had sacrificed numbers for speed to get to Ferguson in time. And it wouldn't be easy to charge uphill in the face of enemy muskets.

Isaac could hear the Tories stirring at the top. He could hear his own men shuffling into position. And then, distinctly and ominously, he heard something else.

Pipes. Many pipes. Playing in unison. Playing in harmony. Playing spellsong.

This was no lone Lutin ranger. There must have been a chorus nearby.

Isaac's Sullivan County men began to mutter and glance around nervously. Even Isaac began to feel the spell's effects. His skin felt like it was covered with crawling ants.

Then he heard Dela's courage song. He heard the rhythmic rattle of her mussel necklace and the piercing tone of Goran's flute. Would their magic be strong enough to counteract the Lutin spell?

Not without help, he realized.

"We've had a long chase!" Isaac called to the militiamen. "Our reward is waiting up there!"

One of the young men, thin and long-faced, looked over at Isaac and let out a whoop. "Let's go catch our rabbit!" he shouted. Others soon took up the same cry.

Isaac ran up next to the wiry man. "Crockett, isn't it?"

"Yep — John Crockett," said the man before whooping again and starting up the mountain.

Trotting alongside Crockett, Isaac cupped his hand over his mouth. "Never shoot until you see an enemy. And never see an enemy without bringing him down. We fight until we die or win!"

"Die or win!" barked Crockett and the others as they climbed.

A fusillade of shots from the top of Kings Mountain got their attention but didn't stop them. Amid shouts and gunfire, Isaac could still hear the piping of the Lutins and the competing spellsong of Dela and Goran. As he listened more closely, it sounded as if there were more voices than Dela's singing her song, and more sounds than just her battling necklace beating out the rhythm. But there was no time to sort that out. The Patriots had reached the top of the slope. Isaac could see red-coated Tories formed into lines stretching across the narrow plateau. Behind them were other Tories dressed like Isaac's own men, in regular clothes, except that sticking up from their hats were sprigs of pine rather than pieces of white paper.

Now the battle began in earnest.

Isaac's men fired their rifles, yelling and whooping. Isaac was pleased to see many shots find their targets, even though one of the guns went off so close to Isaac's head that the blast singed his hair and left his ear ringing. Then he heard someone at the top of the hill blow a tin whistle. The Tories let loose their own yell, their muskets bristling with seventeen-inch-long bayonets. They charged.

There wasn't nearly enough time to reload. "Back down!" Isaac ordered.

Rapidly, but not frantically, the Patriots scrambled back down the slope as the Tories pursued, their bayonets glinting in the afternoon sun, a few of their guns firing shots at the backs of the Patriots.

Once the charge lost momentum, the Tories climbed back to the plateau. "Now, boys, reload and give them another hell of a fire!" yelled Isaac.

The Patriots crept back up the slope and fired again, their precise rifle shots claiming more victims, and then the Tories charged again, prompting a second downhill retreat.

The third time Isaac and his men climbed Kings Mountain, there was no need to retreat. The Tories had been decimated, while Patriot casualties were few. Some Tories were backing away in good order. But others were fleeing toward the broader part of the plateau to the northeast, where Isaac could see a large mass of men shouting, firing, and fighting.

"Quarters! Quarters!" cried some of the Tories.

"If you want quarters, throw down your arms!" Isaac replied.

After a few more minutes of confusion and death, the Tories finally did so, and Isaac ordered them marched quickly away. Across the top of Kings Mountain, he saw similar scenes — Tories surrendering and being marched off, Tories resisting and dying, Tories on the ground and dying more slowly.

Presently a group of Patriots came by bearing a man wearing a red-and-white checked duster over an officer's uniform. Isaac knew it must have been Major Ferguson. He was the only British regular there. Isaac looked down at the face of the major — his lean, handsome features, his shock of red hair tied back. The eyes were open and lifeless. His clothes were riddled with bullet holes. Patrick Ferguson was surely dead. But Isaac couldn't resist a final taunt.

"Major, the fatal blow is struck."

▲▲▲

That night, as the Patriots hurried west from Kings Mountain with their prisoners, Isaac left his men and went looking for John Sevier. But his friend was nowhere in sight.

Then, out of the corner of his eye, Isaac saw Goran waving from above a clump of oak trees. Isaac followed the Sylph until they reached the banks of a bubbling creek. He saw Dela sitting in the water, splashing water over her body. Next to her, a horse was drinking. It was Sevier's.

Isaac looked up at Goran and opened his mouth, but the fairy simply pointed to a spot a few dozen paces up the creek.

There was Sevier on one knee, talking excitedly to two small figures. The two fairies didn't look like Goran or Dela. The closest resemblance was to Tana, the Nunnehi scout, although these fairies wore their long black hair differently. The male was dressed in a deerskin breechcloth. The female wore a mantle fastened at her left shoulder.

As Isaac approached, the two fairies shot him a wary look. The woman placed her hand on Sevier's arm and the man held up his hand as if in farewell. Then, without a word or backward glance, they disappeared into the forest.

Sevier stood and cocked his head. "By God, they have burnt off your hair!"

Isaac reached up and brushed some of the soot and ash from the left side of his head. "Not quite," he said, laughing. Then Isaac pointed to the forest. "I take it theirs were the voices I heard singing with Dela and Goran at the battle. Who are they?"

"They are river people, much like your Dela," Sevier replied.

"You had allies in your pocket all along, yet chose not to tell me?" Isaac asked, trying to sound more annoyed than he felt.

Sevier shook his head. "They're in no one's pocket. They're wild and free."

"They just happened to be wild and free at Kings Mountain?" Isaac was dubious.

"I reckon so," said his friend, shrugging his shoulders. "By the way, don't you think we should change that name?"

"What name?" Isaac asked.

"Kings Mountain," Sevier said. "We just showed that none of our mountains belongs to the king. Not anymore."

Chapter 24 — The Den

November 1780

GORAN HAD EXPECTED HIS SONG to fail.

He figured that, after he left the Knob under a cloud of suspicion, Sylph guildmasters would surely have recast the Shimmer wall guarding the entrance with a different admission song. But when Goran flew past the rhododendron bush and hummed the familiar melody, he felt the same familiar tingle of magic. He stepped through the Shimmer.

But am I stepping into a trap?

Even if it was, Goran was determined to try one more time to explain himself to his family. Brae and Kaden might refuse to listen. He couldn't believe the same of Ailee.

After the battle of Kings Mountain, the South Carolinians had broken up into companies and scattered. Isaac Shelby, John Sevier, and William Campbell had taken their militia back over the high mountains. And Benjamin Cleveland and Joseph Winston's men had returned to the Carolina backcountry.

Goran had considered accompanying Shelby and Sevier. He knew they still faced significant peril from Dragging Canoe's raiders. But he'd found himself drawn to Joseph Winston's regiment. It had, after all, been headed in the direction of the Knob.

When Goran's senses readjusted to Folk reality, he saw that the sun was already low. Because it hurtled through the heavens twenty times a day on the Knob, he knew he wouldn't have long to wait until sundown. Then he'd have half an hour of darkness to conceal his movements. That would give him enough time to look for Ailee at the greenweaver hut.

As he headed for it, Goran flew over the monster pens and saw two mages emerge. They didn't look up. Then Goran saw a trio of heavily armed warriors flying from the village. Cursing his bad luck, he descended rapidly to a stretch of scrub brush between the monster pens and the greenweaver fields. Hiding behind a laurel bush, Goran held his breath, hoping the warriors hadn't seen him silhouetted against the sky.

They hadn't, although it took him half an hour to be sure. Goran decided to wait until the sun was again low in the western sky before venturing out.

There were several Sylphs working in the fields. None resembled Ailee. Landing softly behind the greenweaver hut, Goran peered through a crack in the wall and saw the backs of two Sylphs working at a table. They were talking about different ways to enchant the seeds of butternut squash. Goran didn't understand much of what they were saying. But he was elated when he recognized one of the voices as Ailee's.

After a few minutes, the other Sylph rose, said something, and walked out of the hut. Now was Goran's chance.

"Ailee," he called, tapping on the back wall. "Ailee, it is Goran."

She didn't respond. Goran knocked harder, thinking Ailee hadn't heard him, but when she raised her hand and waved it a couple of times, he knew better. There were probably other greenweavers standing nearby. She didn't want to call out. Satisfied, Goran retreated from the hut and entered a small barn filled with ears of corn and baskets of peas.

It was two sun cycles later before Ailee appeared at the door, the moonlight casting her faint shadow into the barn. "Goran?" she whispered.

"I am here," he replied, rushing forward to embrace her. Ailee returned it for a moment, then gently pushed him away.

"You are in great danger," she insisted. "When you left after the hearing, the masters voted to eject you from the Rangers Guild. Then the Council of Elders declared you guilty of treason. Goran, if they catch you…"

"I am not afraid of them," he said. "You do not know what I have had to do these past two years. What perils I faced. What enemies I fought."

"No, and I do not want to know," Ailee said with a shudder. "What I imagine is bad enough."

"What I mean is that, while I know it was dangerous to come here, it is also dangerous for me in the Blur. Danger is something I have come to accept."

Ailee put her hands on her hips. "How could it all be worth it? Why have you put yourself and the rest of us through this?"

Goran's heart beat faster. "Ailee, I came back to make you understand. To accept what Bren and the others are doing would have betrayed everything I believe in — everything I thought we Sylphs believed in. Without belief, what are we?"

Ailee jabbed a finger at him. "You speak of big ideas and grand principles but you cannot see what is right in front of you."

"I see *you*," Goran assured her. "I see how hard this has been for you and Kaden. How much I have hurt Father. But what I have done, I did for *you*, for all Sylphs. If we suffer villains like Bren to remain among us, we shall become as bad as they. And, by trying to conquer the Americans, we will in the end become the conquered."

"You say you still serve the Knob, but most Sylphs agree with Bren," Ailee said. "Who are you to decide what our Folk should do, who our Folk should be?"

Feeling suddenly fatigued, Goran sat on a crate and looked up at his sister with pleading eyes. "Yes, I am just one man trying to do what is right. Bren would have the humans stay forever boys and girls under our 'enlightened' supervision instead of treating them as grown men and women. But does he not truly mean the same fate for our own Folk? We cannot remain children at play in a wider world that we do not truly understand."

Ailee sat down beside him and took his hand. "You still speak of grand principles, Goran, when I would rather you speak of how all this can end. But right now, I will accept the gift that you are here."

He covered her hand with his. They sat quietly for a long time. Then Goran swallowed hard and opened his mouth to speak.

She silenced him with a finger. "I know what you would ask of me, and I am willing to try. Father will *not* come — that I already know. But Kaden is another story. I believe he wants to hear your defense from your own lips. He has said as much many times."

Goran nodded gratefully as she rose. "You must be careful, Little Curlew. If Bren finds out that I am at the Knob…"

"He is not here," Ailee said. "The guildmaster left yesterday on some kind of special expedition. The village has been abuzz about it."

"What could be so special about another ranging?"

"It may be more than that," she said. "The talk is that Bren and a master from the Mages Guild went to the pens, then transported away. Given the rumors that spread after your hearing, many suspect they have released a monster into the Blur."

Well, at least that means Bren is not waiting here to trap me. But that thought didn't comfort Goran very much.

▲▲▲

For almost three days, he hid himself in the barn. Ailee visited regularly to bring food and keep him company, but Goran grew impatient. First, Ailee said that Kaden was away on a monster hunt. Then, after Kaden returned, Ailee reported that he'd refused to meet. Goran had resolved to leave immediately, but Ailee requested one more try.

The sun had set once more when Goran finally stood up, slipped his bow over his shoulder, and headed for the door. Then he heard his sister outside the barn. "Goran," she said in a low voice. "He has come."

Goran stepped back into the shadows. A moment later, Ailee appeared in the doorway with Kaden. His brother was in full warrior dress: scale armor of polished bronze attached to a leather jerkin, a red-and-gray tunic underneath stretching to the knees, scale-armor greaves and leather boots. Kaden carried no spear or shield, but under his arm was his bronze helm with wing devices extending from both sides.

"Are you off to war, then?" asked Goran, although he instantly realized it was perhaps the worst greeting he could have offered.

Kaden seemed to take no offense, however. He merely smiled indulgently. "Are you not *back* from war, Brother? It is not I who have taken up arms."

I came here to explain myself, not to provoke him.

"I cede your point," Goran said, bowing slightly. "I would only say I believe the war was thrust upon me. It was not something I wanted."

"You may say whatever you like, but the facts are what they are," Kaden said. "In our guild, we learn not to try to interpret them alone. We learn to trust the judgments of those around us, especially our commanders. We learn to follow orders. We learn to seek the midpoint of courage between the extreme of cowardice and the extreme of foolhardiness. I will give you this, Brother: you are certainly no coward."

"So I guess that makes me the fool," said Goran. Kaden merely inclined his head, but that was enough to confirm the intended slight.

"I *have* sometimes played the fool, I suppose, but I am hardly alone," Goran continued. "That men never turn into rogues without first turning into fools seems universally true. Those who chose to thrust the Sylphs into a conflict on behalf of the British king followed such a course."

"You call Guildmaster Bren and the others rogues?" Kaden shed all pretense of equanimity. "You, who have truly gone rogue and become a traitor?"

Goran felt his face flush with anger. "I am no traitor! I serve my Folk by defending their interests and honor against those who would sacrifice both. I serve the Sylphs by reminding them of what makes our Folk worth defending in the first place."

Kaden sneered — and at that moment Goran realized his return to the Knob had been for nothing.

"You have a talent for sophistry, Goran, but not for strategy," his brother said. "Even as you spoke your treason, Jodoc and the others surrounded the barn. You will come with us to the village, one way or the other. I hope it will be peacefully."

"Kaden, how could you?" Ailee had been standing next to her brother, watching the conversation with a pained expression. "I swore you to secrecy! Goran is your own brother!"

The warrior captain turned to face her. "I do not blame you for being taken in. I, too, have yearned to give our brother the benefit of the doubt, but his every word is a confession. And remember, I swore a sacred warrior's oath to protect the Knob from all enemies, external and internal. My oath allows no exceptions. I think even Goran can understand that."

I do understand, Goran thought. *I do not agree. But I understand.*

"I forbid you to touch him!" Ailee cried. "If you will not talk, let him return to the Blur."

"Let him return to fight alongside our enemies?" Kaden's voice was cold and metallic, like the armor he wore. "Out of the question. Come, Goran, you truly have no choice."

Goran looked at his brother sadly and shook his head. "We always have a choice, Kaden — a choice whether truly to live according to our principles, or simply to survive by abandoning them. With that freedom to choose comes the responsibility to accept the consequences. I accept mine. I will *not* submit. I will *not* be complicit to tyranny. If that robs me of my home forever, so be it. But remember this: I will never stop being your brother."

Kaden seemed startled by Goran's final words, then jerked his head to the left at Ailee's heartfelt but also exquisitely timed sob.

It was the distraction Goran had been waiting for. He sprang into the air, flapped his wings, and stretched both arms over his head, balling his fists as he sped toward the thatched roof of the barn. With a crunch of broken sticks and rushes, he burst through the roof — only to cry out in pain as a hard fist struck the side of his face.

The blow made the stars streaking though the night sky look even blurrier than they usually did through the Shimmer. But Goran didn't need to see to know which way to go. He continued to gain altitude, beating his wings furiously.

Then he felt a hand grab his ankle. Goran looked down and saw a triumphant look on the face of Jodoc as the warrior yanked his leg with a heavily muscled arm.

Jodoc smiled contemptuously. "Did you think we would fail to cover all avenues of escape, traitor? You have lived among humans and wingless Folk so long you have forgotten to think like a Sylph!"

Goran could hear the shouts of other warriors rising into the air. One of the shouters, he knew, was Kaden himself. Only he might be inclined not to treat their quarry harshly. The others, like Jodoc, would show no mercy to a traitor.

To escape, I must be just as tough.

He kicked Jodoc in the chin, the only part of Jodoc's face not protected at least partially by his helm. The warrior cursed but did not loosen his hold.

Then Goran tried a different maneuver, suddenly rolling in the air. Unprepared for the twisting motion, Jodoc lost his grip. Goran seized the chance to gain more altitude even as he saw two Sylphs hurtle past Jodoc and rapidly close the gap.

Fighting one armored warrior would be challenging. Fighting four would be pointless — and he couldn't be sure they would use only fists, although he doubted Kaden would draw a blade on him. There had to be another answer.

Then Goran heard it — a long, mournful cry. It was a cry of loneliness. It was a cry of desolation. It was the cry of the Catawampyrie.

The monster pens!

Goran withdrew his six limbs suddenly and formed a ball, dropping like a stone even as the two pursuing warriors grasped the empty air above him. Then he stretched out his wings and resolved his descent into a swoop, heading for the pens.

Like most Sylphs not in the Mages Guild, Goran had never entered the monster pens, nor even approached the structures. But he had flown high above them. He knew which pen held the two captive Catawampyrie. One was the beast he'd subdued with Daniel Boone's help so many years ago. Since that time, another monster hunt must have snagged another Catawampyrie.

It was against the law to fly close to the pens. *But what is another broken law to a traitor?*

Goran heard Kaden calling to him to halt. The others issued threats. That confirmed his suspicion: he had stumbled on the only tactic that offered him at least a chance.

He dove directly at the Catawampyrie pen, from which came another horrible roar. Goran could see the outline of the monstrous cat in the pale moonlight, its face pointed upward, its eyes glowing yellow-orange. It seemed smaller, leaner, more haggard than Goran remembered — but this observation was a fleeting thought, quickly chased out of his mind by his urgency.

"You cannot hide in the pens for long, Goran," called Kaden. "We may not enter under the law, but the monster tenders will catch you and mages will be summoned. You are only adding to your crimes."

Goran gave no answer. It was exactly what he hoped his brother would say. He flew as close as he dared to the Catawampyrie. With a scream of rage, it swiped its paw at him as he cleared the fence, but he stayed just out of range.

Then Goran abruptly banked to his right, staying low and following the perimeter of the fence. Bizarre and frightening sounds came to his ears. The screeches of avians. The snorts of porcines. The yowls of ursines. Hisses, bleats, roars, and even a few bellowing cries that sounded almost human. Goran shuddered with dread. But he knew the chorus of monstrous noises would evoke just as much dread among his pursuers. He was counting on it.

"Jodoc has gone to fetch the mages," Kaden warned, his voice more distant now that Goran had turned the corner. Goran contemplated the distance he would have to travel across open ground until he got to the Shimmer.

It was a long way. He knew they would see him sooner or later. If sooner, he wouldn't make it. But if later …

There was no point waiting. His pursuers would only grow in number, and mages had other ways of keeping Goran from escaping. He gathered in a breath, blew it out slowly, then flapped his wings as hard as he could, hoping the head start would save him.

It was only seconds before he heard one of the Sylphs cry, "He is making a run for it!"

Goran flew faster than he'd ever flown before. He thought of Ailee, crushed not only by Goran's exile but now also by Kaden's betrayal of her trust. He thought of Daniel, Nanyehi, and his other human friends who needed him. He thought of Bren's smug superiority, of Atta's manipulative cruelty, of Lutins and Brownies and other Folk driving vicious monsters into the ranks of American soldiers.

His anger burned inside him. Its intensity drove him to greater speed. But, somehow, he knew it would not be enough.

Then came to mind the affable face of Har the Tower, his companion-at-arms, who now felt more like a brother to him than Kaden did. He thought of the other Dwarf rangers he'd fought alongside. He thought of Tana Song Snake and their perilous battle with the Stoneclad. And, most of all, he thought of the delicate, heart-shaped face of Dela the Water Maiden, another companion-at-arms — and more.

It felt as though a sudden gust of wind propelled Goran at blinding speed across the remaining stretch of ground and hurled him at the Shimmer door. In an instant, he was through. He was flying through the cold air of the Blur.

But he was not yet safe. As soon as the mages arrived, they'd transport Kaden and the others into the Blur under Shimmer protection. The warriors might still catch Goran, especially if he stayed near the door or headed in a predictable direction — either north toward Washington's army in New York or south toward the Patriots resisting General Cornwallis.

So Goran flew due east. He stayed underneath the canopy of trees as much as possible, although it slowed his pace. After about ten miles without a hint of pursuit, he felt safe enough to stop for a short rest. When he resumed his flight, Goran decided to risk a peek above the tree line — and saw a familiar sight only a few miles ahead. It was the same cliff-topped mountain where he had first met Daniel, where he and Daniel had tracked the Catawampyrie.

The Catawampyrie!

It occurred to Goran that he had seen just one beast in the pen. There was supposed to be second one. It wasn't there. And Ailee had said Bren had gone on a special mission. Could it have been to release the Catawampyrie into the wild, or to use it against the Patriots who faced Cornwallis near Charlotte Town? The thought made Goran want to streak south immediately to warn them. But he resisted the impulse. His pursuers might be looking for him that way. The safer course would be to hide out until they gave up the search.

Remembering the cool drinks he'd taken from the creek he and Daniel had followed during their long-ago hunt, Goran decided to make the mountain his refuge for a time. Perhaps he could even catch a fish or something to supplement his meager stock of field rations.

As he rose into the cold air of the Carolina night, he realized he'd been at the Knob so long that some three months had passed in the Blur. It was February as humans reckoned time. How had the Patriot cause fared in his absence? He was eager to find out. But satisfying his curiosity would have to wait.

Goran found the creek and began to descend — only to pull up short when he heard voices below. Hovering, he looked down and saw a party of half a dozen men riding rapidly along a trail.

What are they doing out in the dead of night?

He banked to his right and then soared gracefully toward the ground, casting a concealment spell and hoping to get close enough to hear the humans' conversation.

"They took everything they could find — even the clothes off my back!" said one of the riders. "I am clad in some of the colonel's clothes, if you can believe it."

"How many are we looking for, Ambrose?" asked another man.

"Oh, I'd say six or seven broke into my house, Joshua, but I think there were more Tories outside," said the first speaker.

Goran flew over the riders and got on their left side, trying to see their faces more clearly. Then another voice spoke up, one the Sylph immediately recognized.

"You're far from their only victim, Captain Blackburn," said Joseph Winston, who was riding in front of the others. "Captain Stanly's Tory raiders have made quite a name for themselves, even as far as Salem. But it's a villain's name — and we'll make them regret it."

The other riders loudly agreed, some with the florid curses that Goran had come to expect from backcountry men.

A few minutes later, they rounded a curve and saw another party of men standing next to a chestnut grove. One of them exclaimed, "Colonel Winston! Thank God!"

So it is Colonel Winston now. His heroic service at Kings Mountain must have gotten someone's attention.

"Is that you, Jack Martin?" Winston asked as they rode up to the grove.

"Yes, Colonel," the man replied. "We've come on urgent business — Captain Stanly's band kidnapped a young girl from the settlement and brought her this way!"

"Kidnapped a girl?" Winston sounded outraged. "Which girl? Whose daughter?"

"Can't say," Martin responded, shrugging his shoulders. "We just heard that they were riding this way."

Colonel Winston was silent for a moment. "That may be little more than a rumor, Captain Martin. You remember all the strange rumors we heard on the march to Kings Mountain, don't you? They were just stories. But it doesn't matter — we're after Stanly, too, and we have eyewitness testimony to his other crimes."

Martin's men mounted up and joined Winston's party, which by now numbered fifteen. About a mile later, they reached a steep slope. Winston motioned a halt.

"It's on foot from here," he said. "There's a small cave ahead, above a creek. If that's where they're hiding, we should come up on them quietly."

Now Goran had something to go on. He gained altitude and headed up the side of the mountain, looking for the cave Winston mentioned and any sign of the Tories the Surry County men were chasing.

The latter wasn't long in coming. As Goran flew over a clearing, he saw two men crouching behind a fallen log, aiming their guns downhill. Glimpses of hats and jackets in the surrounding forest told Goran the riflemen behind the log weren't alone.

The Tories were about to attack Colonel Winston's militia — that much was obvious. They might even have committed the robberies or spread the rumor about the kidnapped girl just to bait Winston into the ambush.

But Goran could do something about it. Hovering above the clearing, he pulled out his flute and played a confusion spell. A few moments later, one of the crouching Tories fired his rifle. The other turned to the shooter, arguing and gesturing. Goran saw cocked hats moving through the trees and guessed the argument was about to get even more heated.

From down the steep slope, Goran could hear shouts. The rifle shot had alerted Winston. There would be no ambush. And Goran was going to make sure the Tories lost the coming skirmish.

Then the Catawampyrie roared.

There was no mistaking it. Goran had just heard the same sound during his escape from the Knob. So *this* was where Bren had brought the second monster. Goran instantly recognized that the Tory ambush was no human scheme. It had been orchestrated by the guildmaster. Somewhere nearby, the Catawampyrie was waiting to spring on the Patriots. And Bren was probably there, too.

"You will never reach the cave."

The short spear fletched in black and gold sank into Goran's left bicep, knocking him backward and into the top of a pine tree. As he fell through the branches, the speed of his descent slowed but the branches put cuts and scrapes across his face, arms, and wings.

Goran was able to halt his fall on the lowest branch of the tree. The spear had been torn away during the fall, leaving a bloody, painful wound. With his right hand, he felt into his pouch for a kerchief to bind up his injury. But then his hand went to his belt, and he drew his knife, for scrambling toward him was Atta Yellow Jacket, spear-thrower in hand, about to hurl another missile.

Goran jumped to the ground and rolled, hearing a thud as the spear struck the tree. Then he leapt up, holding his knife in a reverse grip, and hurled himself at the Pukwudgie ranger, who was struggling to draw his tomahawk in time.

Atta failed. Goran crashed into him, wincing as his left shoulder and curled wing struck the Yellow Jacket in the chest. Atta managed to catch Goran's knife hand before they hit the ground. The two rolled over and over, Goran trying to drive his blade into Atta's throat, the Pukwudgie struggling to push the knife away. The pain in Goran's left arm was excruciating, and sharpened every time his left side hit Atta or the rocky ground.

"You bleed, Sylph!" exulted the Yellow Jacket. "You weaken! You cannot last!"

Goran made no answer. Instead, finding himself on top for the moment, he did something Atta apparently didn't consider. He flapped his wings and rose into the air, with Atta still grasping his arm. From deep within the Pukwudgie's throat came a groan. He stared directly into Goran's face, his eyes burning with hatred, as the Sylph continued to lift the two upward. A moment later, the hand let go of Goran's wrist. Atta dropped rapidly through the air, slammed into the ground, and lay still.

His left arm useless and throbbing with pain, Goran couldn't indulge the temptation to shoot a couple of arrows into Atta's body. Besides, the Catawampyrie was still out there somewhere. Goran was in no condition to fight such a dangerous monster himself, and he rather doubted a Sylph hunting party would come if he called for help. But perhaps he could at least lead the beast away from Winston and the other humans. He had to try.

The cold air stung Goran's face as he raced up the tree canopy in the direction he'd originally heard the roar. Just past a rushing waterfall, he found what he sought — the cave. It wasn't deep. But it was large enough to hold its single occupant: the Catawampyrie. Its massive feline face, its elongated jaws, its tawny eyes blazing as if about to discharge bolts of lightning — all was as it was thirty Blur years ago, when he and Daniel had first faced it only a short distance away.

The monster saw Goran. It snarled, gnashing its long teeth as its eyes burned yellow-orange. Goran could see its stubby legs flexing as it prepared to spring at him. But the Catawampyrie made it only a few inches before it abruptly stopped and cried out. It was if as the monster had slammed into an invisible barrier stretching across the mouth of the cave.

Goran tensed, holding his knife in his hand, when he thought the beast was about to pounce. When it became clear that the Catawampyrie wouldn't or couldn't emerge from the cave, Goran took the opportunity to tie his kerchief around the wound on his arm.

He remained wary, however, which is why Goran wasn't surprised when Bren walked into view. Standing on a ledge above the cave, the guildmaster smiled indulgently.

"You are persistent, I must give you that," he said. "Your determination could have made you a guildmaster of unsurpassed renown — if you had possessed the judgment to go along with it."

Goran winced at the pain in his arm, not at Bren's feckless insult. "I have no interest in resuming our debate. I have come to bring an end to your crime. If you try to intervene, I will bring an end to you."

"Threats from you are like the squeaks of a field mouse," said the older ranger. "And I can see from the blood spilling on the ground that you have already been stung once this night. You will not survive another."

With that, Bren drew a long, thin sword from his belt, twirling its jeweled handle in his left hand and making the blade of polished bronze flash in the moonlight. Just below him, the Catawampyrie roared again from the cave, as if punctuating Bren's threat.

Armed only with his knife, and hampered by his wounded arm, Goran rated his odds low in a duel with Bren. But surrender was not an option. He knew how that would end, both for him and for the humans down the hillside. From the shouts, grunts, and occasional gunshots, he could tell Winston's men were still fighting the Tories. Even if the Patriots prevailed, they'd be exhausted. Fighting a Wampus Cat, or even just fleeing it down the steep slope, would likely be beyond them.

As he advanced to battle, a most unexpected memory came to his mind: an evening seated around a campfire with Har the Tower and Peter Muhlenberg. Peter had been telling the fairies about one of the sermons he'd delivered shortly before going to war. Peter had quoted a passage of scripture about a wicked man who "lies in wait secretly like a lion in his den" to "murder the innocent."

Not this night.

Bren sprung at Goran with the point of his sword aimed at Goran's throat. The young Sylph managed to parry it with a sweep of his knife, then kicked out with his left foot, hoping to knock the guildmaster off balance. But Bren was a practiced fencer and danced away from the kick, bringing his sword down in a chopping motion. It would have taken Goran's leg at the knee had he not used the momentum of his kick to spin away, crouching low as he did so.

"This is pointless," said the guildmaster, his eyes gleaming as he brought his blade up to his face, waved it with an ostentatious flourish, and then thrust it out again with the tip pointing at Goran. "You cannot defeat me."

Why is he talking instead of attacking?

Then Goran understood.

Bren was, indeed, a practiced fencer. As far as Goran knew, however, the man had never fought in battle. He may have directed others to kill, but he had never taken a life by his own hand. Goran had, alas, been forced to do both — many times. The experience had changed him, in ways that frankly terrified him. In this case, it also gave him a crucial advantage.

In his best imitation of the battle cry of the Overmountain men at Kings Mountain, Goran shouted savagely and launched himself at Bren. The sound made the Catawampyrie issue its own savage cry as if in response.

The guildmaster's mocking expression melted into shock as he involuntarily shrank from Goran's charge, his blade still thrust forward but wavering.

And then Goran was upon him, stabbing downward with his knife and snarling like the bestial Hellhounds he'd fought alongside John Sevier. The knife bit into the shoulder of Bren's sword arm. The older man shrieked in pain and dropped his blade. But, with his other hand, the guildmaster punched Goran's wounded arm — and now it was the younger Sylph who cried out.

Capitalizing on the distraction, Bren scrambled out from underneath Goran, holding his hand to his bleeding shoulder and spitting out curses as he backed away. Then, as Goran stood up and reset his knife in his hand, he saw the guildmaster's eyes widen and his mouth twist into a satisfied grin.

The warning came just in time. Goran leapt into the air and flapped his wings, shooting up from the ground just as Atta rushed through the space he'd just occupied, the Yellow Jacket's sharp tomahawk clutched in his hand. The Pukwudgie's momentum carried him to the mouth of the cave before he stopped and turned around.

"Now you will pay, traitor!" exclaimed Bren, still backing away and holding his wounded shoulder. Atta glared menacingly up at Goran — who then felt himself wobble in the air. It wasn't Atta's glare. Goran had simply lost too much blood. He could feel the strength ebbing from him. Soon he would be unable to keep himself aloft.

Then, behind him, Goran heard Joseph Winston's voice and the sound of the other militiamen climbing toward the cave. Perhaps they thought the kidnapped girl was inside. Perhaps they thought it the hiding place for the

Tories' stolen loot. They couldn't see Goran and his adversaries, of course, because of the concealment charm…

That's it! Goran's inner voice shouted. And then he sang.

It only took a moment for his counterspell to reveal the three fairies to the startled humans. Bren and Atta could, of course, restore their concealment. But it would require that they concentrate on the task for a few seconds.

If the Patriots had done nothing during those few seconds but gape at the scene, it would have availed Goran nothing. But Joseph Winston wasn't that kind of man. He saw a queer little man with wings hovering above the mouth of the cave. He saw another little man, dressed in Indian fashion, wielding a tomahawk. He saw a third little man, also winged but walking slowly backward along the rocky ground.

Most importantly of all, Joseph Winston saw the roaring face of a gargantuan cougar at the mouth of the cave. Without hesitation, Winston brought his rifle to his shoulder and fired.

The shot missed. It passed harmlessly past the left ear of the monster. But it had an unexpected effect.

Bren and Atta were both singing, their efforts focused on restoring their veil of invisibility ripped off by Goran's revelation spell. It occurred to neither Folk ranger that an iron ball had just passed through the magic barrier over the mouth of the cave. Iron disrupts magic. It would have been a simple thing to reactivate the enchanted rope that kept the barrier in place. But neither conspirator thought to do it.

Infuriated by the near-miss of the rifle ball, the Catawampyrie roared, bounded out of the cave, and pounced on the target closest to it. Atta managed a short, strangled cry before the jaws closed around his head. The cat yanked its victim into the air. Goran heard a sickening crack. Then the monster spat the Pukwudgie onto the ground.

His back broken, his breaths short and labored, Atta Yellow Jacket survived just long enough to watch with horror as one of the Catawampyrie's fangs punctured his throat. Then the monster began to drink.

Bren turned and retched, wailing in pain and anguish. "You…you barbarian!" he croaked at Goran, who'd landed in front of the guildmaster. "You are the lowest of the low. You would side with these mindless humans over your own kind."

Goran clinched his teeth and pointed at the feeding Catawampyrie.

"This is what you and Atta had in store for the humans. He has received his just reward. You are next."

As if in answer, Bren flapped his wings and rose rapidly into the air. Goran made to follow but realized he didn't have it in him.

"Until we meet again, journeyman," Bren called down to him, his shaky voice robbing the taunt of its menace.

Goran did not reply. He was nearly spent. There were still memory songs to sing and much distance to put between himself and the Wampus Cat before he could rest and heal. And, while his arm wound had robbed him of his physical strength, Goran knew he had sustained a deeper wound that would be prove much harder to heal, if it could be healed at all.

The Knob, and all those who dwelt upon it, were now lost to him for good.

Chapter 25 — The Governor

April 1781

HAR THE TOWER COULD SEE Peter Muhlenberg's army melting before their eyes, and there was little he could do about it.

Ever since General Washington sent Peter south in September to take command of American forces in Virginia, Peter had struggled to contain the growing British threat there. From their main base at Portsmouth, at the mouth of the James River, the British had raided far inland. In January, the notorious traitor Benedict Arnold had even led a brief but destructive attack on Virginia's capital itself, forcing the governor to flee Richmond for a time.

Three months later, Peter's situation had become impossible. His commanding officer, Baron von Steuben, ordered Peter to retreat up the James River — but also to put as much pressure as possible on Arnold and the British to slow their advance.

Peter was willing, Har knew, but many of Peter's troops were not. Mostly local militiamen recruited to short-term enlistments, they were leaving in droves. Hundreds had left already. In Peter's camp, hundreds more were stacking their muskets in piles and preparing to go home.

If Peter had faced only human foes, he might have held out longer, even with his ragtag army. But the British had enjoyed significant assistance from a squad of Pixie rangers from Norfolk. Har and two of his Dwarf rangers, Onar and Nithi, had accompanied Peter south from New York. But other Dwarfs were serving with Washington's army or at other key posts.

"I wish there was more we could do," Har said as he sat in Peter's makeshift headquarters, an old farmhouse. "But the Pixies are here in larger numbers. Their magic has turned the natural homesickness and fear of your militiamen into disaffection and panic."

"We'll just have to make do until Lafayette and Wayne arrive with reinforcements," Peter replied.

If it was to be a race between the two generals' Continentals trudging overland from New York and the British invaders sailing swiftly up the river, Har knew who the winners would be. But he also knew his friend would never give up hope.

"If we can just hold out a while longer, we can still defend Richmond," said Peter, bringing his hands together as if in prayer. "We can still keep Thomas Jefferson safe."

▲▲▲

The next morning, a scout entered Peter's headquarters to announce that the British ships had just offloaded thousands of troops at Westover, a plantation on the north bank of the James.

Peter got up from the breakfast table and quickly dismissed the scout. Then he walked to a chair and retrieved his coat. "I must confer with General von Steuben," he told Har, who'd dropped by for an early morning chat. "But I think I already know what his decision will be. We can't just let the British take Petersburg without a fight. The town is our main supply depot. And, when it falls, Richmond will be the next target."

Har could hear the resignation in Peter's voice. It scared him. "You will be heavily outnumbered, and morale is already low," Har said. "There must be some other way."

"Not if we want to slow the British down," said Peter, reaching for his cocked hat. "Don't worry. We won't do anything reckless. As long as our men keep their heads, we can make the British pay for every foot of ground they take."

"But that is precisely the risk you face — that the Pixies' spellsong will cause your men to break and run," Har insisted. "My rangers will try to hold it off, but we are only three and we count at least nine Pixies traveling with Benedict Arnold."

Peter strode to the door, opened it, and then turned his head. "Just do your best, Har. As King David once told Solomon, 'Be strong, and of good courage, and do it. Fear not, nor be dismayed.'"

Har admired Peter's unshakeable faith, now more than ever. *But do Peter's men share it?*

▲▲▲

Har stood with Nithi and Onar on top of a small house and looked northeast, over the waters of the placid Appomattox River. It flowed past Petersburg and the adjacent village of Blandford before joining the James about twelve miles downriver at Hopewell. That's where the British column would begin its march.

The first line of Peter's militiamen stretched through Blandford. The second line was further back, over a creek. Some Virginians were also on the far side of the Appomattox, guarding the north end of the bridge that would be the Americans' avenue of retreat.

It was a logical plan. It was the best the Americans could do with limited manpower. But it was doomed to failure, Har feared, unless he and his rangers could do something about the Pixies.

"I am tired of singing, anyway," muttered Nithi as she ran a stubby finger along the bronze point of an arrow. "No offense, Onar."

"None taken," said the scholarly ranger. "There is a time to sing and a time to fight."

Har shook his head amiably. "Now you are starting to sound like Peter."

The three Dwarfs jumped to the ledge of a window, then to the ground. Reinforcing their concealment spell, they headed down the Appomattox River. If they could intercept and silence the Pixies, the Patriots would still have a chance.

But the Pixies were no mean fighters. And there would be many of them.

Several hours later, the Dwarfs reached the point where three branches of the river came together. Onar suddenly raised his hand.

"I hear it!" he said excitedly. "I hear spellsong."

A moment later, Har began to hear it, too — first the shrill melody of a jig, played by tin whistle, then the accompaniment of fiddle, voice, and crowdy-crawn drum. As Onar had previously observed, the Pixies had made an ingenious choice by casting their mood spells not with sad dirges or ghostly tunes but with lively music that tempted the Patriots with hearth and home. Because it fit the natural mood of the impatient militiamen, it was harder for the Dwarfs to counteract.

"Disperse," he said, and his two companions immediately ran off in different directions as previously arranged.

Har slid his battleaxe out of the loop in his belt and placed it in his left hand, then filled his right with one of his smaller throwing axes. He looked down at the shirt of scale armor he wore and grimaced. He wasn't used to carrying so much weight. But unless he could keep multiple Pixies focused on him in a drawn-out melee, the Dwarfs would have no chance.

He lumbered off as fast as the extra pounds would allow, leaving the bank of the Appomattox and heading into the forest. He didn't bother with stealth. The jingling sound of his mail shirt made it impossible.

The first sign he'd been discovered was that the Pixie spellsong abruptly ended. The second sign was a rustling sound coming from a white-flowered shrub. The third sign was the spear that came hurtling from it.

Striking it aside with his battleaxe, Har lifted his right arm to throwing position. A second later, three male Pixies appeared. Two of them held spears, also in throwing position, while the third had drawn a wide, double-bladed shortsword. All three were garbed entirely in shades of green, from the dark moss green of their caps and cloaks to the fern green of their tunics and the yellow-green of their stockings.

"You are The Tower," said the swordsman, his green eyes twinkling mischievously under a mop of bright orange hair. "You are as big as the talk would have it. But all towers fall if struck in the right place."

"You will find my base sturdy and my walls thick," Har said.

The swordsman looked to either side of the Dwarf. "Where are your friends? You have not been alone during our contests of spellsong. Your companions must be hidden close by."

Har laughed heartily. "I need no companions to contend with you. One Dwarf is worth three Pixies any day of the week."

"And if the ratio is *six* to one?"

The new voice was female, and came from his left. Har turned warily and saw three more Pixies emerging into the glade — two spearmen and a slim female with long red hair brushed over one shoulder, a shortsword in hand. Har also heard, far off in the distance, the sound of stomping feet, many of them. The British column was continuing its march toward Petersburg.

"We can handle this pest, Lady Joan," said the Pixie swordsman.

"Perhaps," agreed Joan as a malicious smile creased her face, "but why should you have all the fun? I tire of marching with humans and casting spells on humans. I find the change of routine welcome."

Har's three initial antagonists looked exasperated. *Is there a spark I can fan into flame?*

"I am not in the habit of killing beautiful women," he said. "Perhaps you ought to go back to the British and let the men settle this."

Lady Joan merely leered at Har, although her verdant eyes looked fierce. "You are an oaf with far less guile than you imagine. And now you will die for your foolish choice of friends."

Well, divide and conquer did neither. Time to try something else.

"The Americans have right on their side," Har said, "while your Great Alliance sacrifices principle for the sake of power."

The other Pixies snorted in derision. But Joan regarded Har with a surprisingly serious expression.

"You truly do not understand, do you?" she said. "The Great Alliance is about safeguarding our future. Royal authority must be maintained. Without it, chaos will reign. Without it, the Americans will pose a growing threat. Even the Sylphs, our ancestral enemies, fight alongside us in this cause."

Not all of them.

"I understand only that you consort with tyrants and monsters," Har snapped.

"Your insults bore me." The Pixie appeared to relish her next words. "Soon the government of Virginia will fall, the Americans will lose their largest colony, and the rebellion will sputter to a halt."

Har bared his teeth. "Your overconfidence will be…"

The Pixies were done talking. The first two spears, thrown from Lady Joan's faraway companions, were easy to dodge. But the other two spearmen had crept closer. One of their missiles skated harmlessly along the right side of Har's bronze helm. The other spear struck him in the shoulder, knocking him off his feet.

Har landed on his back, then immediately rolled to his left when he saw a sword thrusting at his stomach. He only just escaped it. The broken haft of the Pixie spear lay at Har's feet while the spearhead was still embedded in his shoulder. His mail shirt, expertly enchanted by the craftsmen of Grünerberg, had done its job well. Har barely felt the point poking his skin.

The Pixie swordsman recovered quickly from the failed thrust and lifted his blade for a hack. It never landed. Har's throwing axe found the Pixie's throat. The two other nearby Pixies drew their own swords while Joan and her companions ran forward.

Har knew he would soon be overwhelmed. So he decided to rush his two closest antagonists. His battleaxe chopped the air. One of the Pixies spun away while the other aimed a slice at Har's legs. Despite the extra weight he was carrying, Har managed to jump above the swing, then landed on the Pixie's sword arm with a sickening crunch, eliciting a scream of pain. Har kicked his booted left leg into the man's face, silencing him, then brought his axe up to block another savage sword thrust.

By this time, four Pixies surrounded Har. The other Pixie rangers were probably coming, too. He could last only seconds now.

Then Har heard the spellsong, clear and strong:

To arms, to arms, the rebels come,
So lift your standards, beat your drum,
Behind their trees might pose some threat,
But run they will from bayonet.

Lady Joan looked puzzled. "Your Dwarf ranger summons British soldiers? What will that avail you? Nothing. You will soon be dead."

Then one of the Pixies gasped and looked down to find an arrowhead had erupted from his chest. He crumpled to the ground.

"They mean to pick us off!" Joan shouted as she ran to the wounded man. "Finish him quickly and scatter!"

The two Pixies still on their feet closed with Har. It was all the Dwarf could do to block their slashes and thrusts. He couldn't penetrate their curtain of bronze.

Nithi's next arrow found no fleshy target. But, after planting itself the ground, the arrow's fletching wobbled back and forth in a manner that seemed to unnerve the Pixies. Nithi's third arrow passed through the cloak of one of Har's antagonists, which distracted him long enough for Har to aim a heavy blow at the other swordsman. The Pixie parried it but the axe shattered his blade into multiple fragments.

Through it all, Onar's rich baritone voice continued to cast the summoning spell. The sound of running feet came closer. Then a dozen British redcoats came into the glade, their bayonets thrust before them.

"Bring them!" Joan ordered — and suddenly Har faced no opponents. The Pixies carried off their wounded comrades, leaving the dead Pixie with the handaxe still in his throat. Har heard Nithi call and lumbered off toward her while the redcoats continued to run through the glade, issuing challenges to no one in particular.

Nithi and Onar were crouching behind a fallen log.

"Your plan worked!" exclaimed the scholarly Dwarf.

"We have drawn first blood," said the gray-clad archer, a grim smile parting her lips.

Har shook his head. "The plan worked too quickly. We did not draw all the Pixies to us. We remain greatly outnumbered."

Onar looked thoughtful. "If there were still Pixie rangers with the British army, why did they not counteract my spell? Their spellsong would have easily overwhelmed my solo."

It took only moments for the answer to come. *Soon the government of Virginia will fall,* Lady Joan had said.

"The other Pixies were never here," Har concluded. "They are already headed to Richmond. They are going after Governor Jefferson!"

▲▲▲

When Thomas Jefferson originally moved Virginia's capital from stately Williamsburg to the more defensible location of Richmond, it was a small but bustling town on the James. As Har trotted into town just after sundown, however, he saw little other than burned houses and piles of debris — the result of Benedict Arnold's devastating January raid.

There were plenty of people around, though. Some were filling wagons and carts with food and household possessions. Others were scurrying from hollowed-out house to hollowed-out house, searching for family or friends.

Word of the British marching up the river had clearly preceded Har. While he was confident Nithi and Onar could keep the fight at Petersburg from becoming a rout, Peter's militia could only delay the British arrival. It no longer seemed possible to save the capital. The residents of Richmond were preparing to leave. Now, Har had to ensure Governor Jefferson joined them.

Under magical concealment, Har ran through the streets. When he reached the center of town, he spotted a single-story brick house on a hill. Deeming it a likely location for a provincial government, Har headed for it, deftly dodging an elegantly dressed woman and two slaves as they rushed in the opposite direction.

When he reached the brick house, Har could tell immediately that it had been abandoned in haste. The door was wide open and documents lay strewn on the ground. As he stooped to pick one up, he heard spellsong — a chorus of voices coming from his right. Har turned and noticed a small, two-story house that had survived Arnold's raid intact.

A governor's residence?

Har ran toward the house, a throwing axe in each hand. The Pixies were producing a melancholy tune, a ponderous procession of minor chords. Through the open window, Har saw three Pixies standing in the drawing room, swords drawn, singing in the flickering candlelight.

Without a second thought, Har leapt to the windowsill and charged into the room, hurling his axes. One Pixie crashed into the far wall, the axe buried deep in his chest. Another ducked under Har's other missile. Then the two Pixies closed in.

Har barely had time to draw his battleaxe and parry the first cut. The second Pixie's sword swept Har's right leg, cutting into his thigh and knocking the Dwarf to the floor. Trying desperately to block out the sharp lance of pain, Har reached out his left arm and grabbed the ankle of his antagonist, then yanked it with all his might. The Pixie toppled backward, his head striking the edge of a table with such force that the wood cracked.

While the Pixie fell senseless to the floor, Har struggled to rise from it. His battleaxe had fallen beyond his grasp. The remaining swordsman stepped in for the kill.

Then a shot rang out.

The sound startled the Pixie so much that it spoiled the swing of his sword. Rather than striking Har's lifted left arm, the blade flashed by it and sank into the solid planking of the floor — wrenching the hilt from the Pixie's hand.

Har managed to rise to his knees. Given his great stature, that was high enough to drive his fist into the chin of his astonished foe. The Pixie staggered back, looking first at Har and then at the human standing in the doorway with a smoking pistol in his trembling hand.

Without another word, the Pixie stumbled to the open window, jumped through it, and ran off. Har groaned and fell back, pressing his hand against the bloody cut on his thigh.

A moment later, he looked up into the face of his rescuer. It was a long face containing hazel eyes, an angular nose, and a pointed chin. Strands of loose reddish hair fell over his ears while the rest was swept back and tied. The tall human wore a dressing gown. He looked tired, the skin around his eyes reddened and puffy as if he had been weeping. But his thin lips formed a genial smile.

"I take it you have come for me," said Thomas Jefferson. He pointed to the two Pixies, one clearly dead and the other at least unconscious. "Were these the fairies who meant me harm, or is that you?"

▲▲▲

Much later, his wound cleaned and sutured with catgut, Har lay on Jefferson's bed and watched the governor pace the floor.

"If these Pixies were here to kill me, why didn't they just come up and do the deed?" Jefferson asked.

"They may have considered it wise to render you defenseless first," Har replied, wincing as he shifted position. "Or perhaps their plan was to put you under a spell and have you issue orders to weaken the defense of Richmond. They had no way of knowing you possess the Sight, that their spellsong would fail."

Jefferson shook his head. "It did not fail, not entirely. I was already grieving. Less than a fortnight ago, my youngest daughter, Lucy, passed from this world. Moreover, for a few more weeks, I am governor of an invaded land full of desperate people I lack the power to help. When I heard the song, I knew it was fairy work. But it still drove me deeper into sadness."

It took several moments for Har to grasp the import of Jefferson's words. "You say you will be governor for only a few more weeks?"

"That is so. My term ends in June. The General Assembly is convening here in a few days. They will elect a new governor. I will then retire to my home at Monticello."

"I suggest you hasten your plans," Har said. "The British are intent on capturing you. It will not matter whether you still hold the governorship. Making the author of the Declaration of Independence a British prisoner will deal a blow to the American cause."

"I have already sent my wife and family to Tuckahoe, a few miles up the James," Jefferson said. "As soon as the legislature convenes and we can get the affairs of state in proper order, I will join them — and together we will journey home."

"With respect, sir, there is nothing so important as getting you to safety," Har insisted.

The governor stopped his pacing and looked down his long nose at Har.

"You and I are not well acquainted, Master Dwarf, so it does not surprise me to hear you say that. But, although I am no soldier, I have obligations under the Constitution. The General Assembly is meeting here in Richmond. So here I must stay until our business is concluded."

With great effort, Har slipped to the end of the bed and stood up, holding the bedpost to steady himself. "Then I will remain with you, Governor, until your duties permit you to depart."

Jefferson nodded respectfully. "Your presence will be most welcome, Master Dwarf."

"Sir, everyone just calls me Har the Tower."

"Ah," said Jefferson with a wry smile, "and here I was content simply to name you Merry Wanderer of the Night, although we are hardly ill-met by moonlight."

These words left Har completely mystified. Jefferson quickly seemed to perceive that.

"While you heal, you are free to read from my library," the governor said. "Might I suggest my favorite William Shakespeare play? It is entitled *A Midsummer Night's Dream.*"

Chapter 26 — The Escape

May 1781

THE MARQUIS DE LAFAYETTE ARRIVED in Richmond at the end of April with nearly a thousand Continentals — just in the nick of time, according to talk around town.

Lafayette's timely arrival was why the British army hadn't advanced all the way to the capital. It was why the town wasn't completely abandoned, why Governor Jefferson was still in his executive residence, and why the Virginia General Assembly was about to convene in the brick house nearby.

Daniel Boone wasn't looking forward to that. Not in the least.

"I'm no politician, and I won't dress the part. If they don't want to see me in buckskins, I reckon they can refuse to seat me."

Goran, hovering above Daniel's left shoulder, held up his hands in surrender. "I did not mean to rile you, Daniel. But *you* are the one who asked me about the government meetings I witnessed in Philadelphia. I can only tell you what I saw: even the delegates from the Pennsylvania backcountry wore coats, breeches, and stockings."

"The settlers of Fayette County sent me here to Richmond to look after their interests," said Daniel as he walked toward the center of town. "I'm no speechmaker. Maybe the best I can do is remind them that the frontier people are Virginians, too."

He glanced up at the Sylph flying overhead, then returned his eyes to the largely deserted street. How many delegates would join him the first day of session? Daniel suspected many had not made the trip yet, or had turned back prematurely when they heard about the latest British invasion. The way Daniel heard it, the Virginia militia had surprised even their commanders by putting up a tough fight at Petersburg, then retreating in good order to the outskirts of Richmond.

A few minutes later, Daniel glimpsed the brick building that was serving as the government's meeting house, and headed for it. There didn't seem to be anyone else around. "I guess you can stay a bit longer," he told Goran.

"That would suit me fine," the Sylph replied. "Accompanying you on the journey from Boone's Station to Richmond was a good idea for many reasons. One was hearing more about your adventures in the Shawnee country. I still have a few questions."

Daniel stopped short. "They'll have to wait."

Goran followed his eyes and saw the tall, elegantly dressed man walking toward the brick house from the opposite direction.

"Another delegate?" Goran wondered.

Daniel was about to reply when a movement next to the approaching man caught his eye. A moment later, he looked up at Goran.

"Friend or foe?" he asked.

Goran had seen the same thing. "Friend, Daniel — a very good friend. And unless I am mistaken, we are about to meet another."

The tall man and the Dwarf had stopped in their tracks.

"Har the Tower!" Goran shouted as he swooped forward, landed, and stuck his arm out excitedly to clasp the arm of the other.

"Goran, you are a sight for sore eyes!" said the Dwarf.

As Daniel strode over to join them, Har was introducing Goran to his human companion. "This is Governor Thomas Jefferson."

"I am honored, sir," said Goran. "And I have the honor to present my long-time friend Daniel Boone. He is here to represent Fayette County in the House of Delegates."

The governor looked down at Daniel's hunting shirt and leggings, then smiled. "You are most welcome, Colonel Boone."

Perhaps as a younger man, Daniel would have been surprised by the whole scene — surprised that anyone but himself was acquainted with fairies, surprised at the ease with which fairies could interact with humans, and surprised that someone like Thomas Jefferson would know to call Daniel by his recently elevated rank.

Jefferson immediately dispelled the latter mystery. "My friend George Rogers Clark spoke of you. He passed along stories of your captivity in the Ohio Country and the siege of Boonesborough. General Clark also mentioned you had been elected lieutenant colonel of the Fayette County militia.

But I did not know you were coming here as a legislator."

"Neither did I until a few weeks ago," said Daniel dubiously. "I fear I may take to politics about as well as a fish would take to a forest."

They all laughed.

Jefferson inclined his head. "I speak as someone who would rather be home at Monticello, tending to my gardens and continuing my studies, Colonel Boone. You will fare no worse, and perhaps better than most, for your lack of experience in government."

The four repaired to a grassy spot on the hill and spent an hour in deep conversation.

"Lafayette has fortified the capital for now," the governor explained. "But, with the British enjoying full and free navigation of the river, Richmond remains vulnerable. And we have neither the boats nor the artillery to change that calculation."

Goran was the first to spot the arriving delegates: two men in coats, breeches, and cocked hats standing next to the brick house. "Perhaps Har and I should take our leave and make plans," he suggested.

"By all means," Jefferson said. "Let us reconvene this evening at my residence."

After Goran and Har left, Daniel and the governor stood up and walked toward the meeting house. "Did you ever imagine a time when you would sit on a hill and talk of an American Revolution with two fairies and an old deer hunter?" Daniel asked.

Jefferson shook his head amiably. "I did not. But, in truth, I have always liked the dreams of the future better than the history of the past. How will our dream end, I wonder?"

▲▲▲

During the first three days of the legislative session, little happened. But, on May 10, word arrived that General Charles Cornwallis and Britain's entire Southern army, save the garrisons at Charles Town and a few other posts, were converging on Petersburg to join forces with Benedict Arnold's force. Once combined, they would far outnumber Lafayette's defenders, including the Continentals now under the command of General Peter Muhlenberg.

The only choice was to flee. Daniel voted along with the handful of other delegates present to relocate the General Assembly to Charlottesville and reconvene in two weeks. Then he, Goran, and Har spent the next couple of days helping Jefferson pack up his official papers and other possessions for an urgent departure from Richmond.

"I will go with the governor to meet his family at Tuckahoe Plantation, and see them safely to Monticello," Har said.

"That leaves us the task of escorting the other delegates west to your new temporary capital," Goran told Daniel, who nodded grimly. It would hardly be the first time he'd found rapid flight the better part of valor. Only this time, Daniel's pursuers wouldn't be clad in buckskins and moccasins. They wore uniform coats and stiff boots.

▲▲▲

The trip was largely uneventful, although Daniel encountered several travelers who told stories of British advances, American retreats, and vengeful raids by Whig and Tory partisans. When they arrived in the small town of Charlottesville, its population suddenly swelled by the relocation of the capital, Goran went in search of Har and the governor while Daniel went in search of lodging.

"Most of the newcomers are staying at Jouett's place," said a young mechanic Daniel passed in the road.

"And where might that be?" Daniel pressed.

"Just look for the sign," said the youth as he hurried away.

But try as he might, Daniel could find no sign with the name "Jouett" on it. *Some tracker I am.*

Finally, he saw two well-dressed gentlemen enter a house labeled as "Swan Tavern." That seemed as good a place as any to start. Daniel followed them through the door and saw a young man wiping a table.

"I'm looking for a Mister Jouett," said Daniel hesitantly.

The youth straightened. "I reckon you've found two of them."

"Oh?" Daniel looked more closely. The youth was a strapping fellow, well over six feet in height and thickly built.

"I am John Jouett the Junior," said the young man, "but everyone calls me Jack. My Pa is John the Senior."

"Which of you do I ask about lodging? I'm Daniel Boone, a delegate."

"Pa can get you settled," Jack replied. "I'm just about to leave — got an errand over in Louisa County. Nice to meet you, Mister Boone. Maybe I'll see you again in a few days."

Daniel's room proved to be small but comfortable. Although he felt self-conscious mingling with the gentry of Virginia, Daniel's natural gregariousness soon took over. By May 24, when the legislature was set to reconvene, Daniel had made half-a-dozen new friends. It wasn't until four days later, however, that enough lawmakers made it to Charlottesville to form a quorum.

They reelected one of Daniel's new friends, a former member of the Continental Congress named Benjamin Harrison, to serve as Speaker of the House. "The people expect that effectual and decisive measures will be taken to rid them of an implacable enemy that is even now roaming at large in the very bowels of our country," Harrison told the other delegates.

They immediately began the work of receiving and issuing correspondence, forming committees, and passing resolutions. Daniel found the procedural niceties confusing but the import was clear enough: the legislature was acting to give Lafayette and the American army the militiamen, horses, and other supplies needed to defend Virginia. Daniel was glad of that. He also gladly voted for a resolution asking his cousin Dan Morgan to come out of retirement and command the newly raised militia.

The next day was Sunday. The legislature wouldn't be meeting, so Daniel was pleased to visit Monticello for the first time at Thomas Jefferson's invitation, along with Benjamin Harrison and several other legislators. As Har had agreed to accompany Goran on a brief ranging mission, the two fairies were delighted to hear Daniel would be at Monticello — just in case.

The governor's two-story house was not the largest Daniel had ever seen, but its eight rooms were ornately decorated and lavishly furnished. "It remains a work in progress," Jefferson said as the two men stood in the library. "Shortly the General Assembly will elect a new governor and then perhaps I will make some real headway. I will no longer need to spend hours a day drudging at my writing table."

Daniel looked out the window at dozens of black slaves working in the distant fields. He was no stranger to slavery, of course. There had even been a few slaves at Boonesborough. But he'd never seen so many enslaved people at one time. He couldn't help but think of the Bible stories he'd heard so often at his mother's knee. *Let my people go, that they may serve me.*

Jefferson followed his eyes and seemed to understand. "I once wrote that the abolition of domestic slavery should be the great object of desire in these colonies," he said. "But I fear that time has not yet come and the circumstances will not yet permit it."

To Daniel's ear, the governor sounded like he was trying to convince himself of something. "Sir, I don't know much about plantations and politics and such. But I've been stuck in enough thickets to know it's a lot easier to get into one than to get out."

▲▲▲

Daniel and the other guests spent the night at Jefferson's home — or, at least in Daniel's case, part of the night. He'd been cooped up too long. Rising from the bed, Daniel pulled on his clothes and tiptoed out of the house, trying not to disturb Jefferson's family or the other guests.

The moment he reached the grounds of Monticello, softly lit by a full moon, Daniel heard two men talking. Suddenly on alert, remembering what Har had told him about the previous attempt on Jefferson's life, he stalked toward the voices, which were coming from the gardens.

As he got closer, however, he recognized Jefferson's voice. Still wary, Daniel turned the corner and saw the governor speaking to a man Daniel immediately realized must be the gardener. There was a platter set on a brick wall. Incongruously to Daniel's eye, it contained a bottle of wine and two glasses.

"Colonel Boone, I trust we did not wake you," Jefferson said.

"No, Governor, I'm an early riser. I had a thought of doing some exploring..."

"...And perhaps a bit of hunting, no doubt," Jefferson interrupted. "Would that I could join you this morning. As to the species of exercise, I have always advised the gun. While it gives a moderate exercise to the body, it gives boldness, enterprise, and independence to the mind."

"It does," Daniel agreed. "To me, though, hunting is more than just exercise. It feeds and clothes my family."

"Indeed, I take your point," said the governor. "I would know more of..."

Jefferson stopped in mid-sentence as he, Daniel, and the gardener simultaneously heard hoof beats. *Why would a rider come to Monticello so early in the morning?*

"Get behind me, sir," Daniel ordered, wishing his rifle was in his hand rather than thrust through the saddlebags of his horse. The governor seemed about to protest but Daniel didn't give him the chance — he hurried to place himself between Jefferson and the approaching rider.

A few moments later, the rider came into view. Daniel immediately recognized the youthful face of Jack Jouett.

"Governor Jefferson!" shouted Jouett, his face flushed with excitement, "have you already heard?"

"Heard what, young man?"

"British dragoons! They're headed this way!" Jouett replied. "Banastre Tarleton has orders to capture you and the rest of the government. I saw 'em last night near the Louisa Courthouse."

"And you rode here during the night?" Jefferson seemed amazed. "Louisa is some forty miles away. How did you manage it?"

"Tarleton took the Notched Road, so I came by the Old Mountain Road. That way's longer but safer."

"Proceed on, then, and pass the word to the others to flee," the governor said. "Tell them I suggest taking the road over the Blue Ridge to Staunton. We will join them there."

"Yes, sir — but please hurry!" The young man still looked flushed and exhausted.

Jefferson patted Jouett on the arm. "No need to worry. We will act with appropriate haste. Anthony, if you please?"

The gardener seemed to know Jefferson's intention, though Daniel did not. The man went to the platter, filled one of the glasses, and brought it to the governor.

"This is a fine Madeira," said Jefferson as he extended the glass. "I have found good wine is a necessity of life. Draw strength from it and ride on, Master Jouett."

The young man was nonplussed for a moment, then took the glass and drained it. A smile spread across his face. Without another word, Jouett turned his horse and galloped off.

"Anthony, Colonel Boone, let us proceed inside and rouse the others,"

Jefferson said. "No doubt we have an exacting day ahead of us. I suggest we begin it with a hearty breakfast."

▲▲▲

While his guests finished their leisurely morning meal, Jefferson was actually busy making plans with Daniel and the two fairies, who arrived shortly after Jouett rode away. The governor sent his wife and daughters to a friend's plantation fourteen miles away. Goran volunteered to escort them, while Har insisted on patrolling Monticello until Jefferson got away.

"What can I do to help?" asked Daniel. "Want me to help you pack up?"

"I suspect you are more sorely needed in town, Colonel Boone," said Jefferson, bundling some books together. "Neither the government nor its sensitive documents can be allowed to fall into the hands of the enemy."

Daniel quickly took his leave and rode the two miles to Charlottesville, where he found residents and visitors alike in a panic. When he arrived at the modest house where the General Assembly had been meeting, he found several of his colleagues coming out in a hurry.

"We just moved the government to Staunton," explained one of the delegates as he hopped on a horse. Daniel was about to follow his lead when he saw through the open door several men stacking documents and placing them into baskets and bags.

He pitched in to help. *Here am I, Daniel Boone the Long Hunter, now a clerk.*

As he carried one of the baskets outside, a wagon drove up to the side of the house. "Colonel Boone, you're still here!" exclaimed the driver, who turned out to be none other than young Jack Jouett.

"Well, friend, I don't know if it's necessity or orneriness, but here I stand," Daniel replied. "Come to think of it, it's been a while since I was a wagoner in wartime."

Jouett helped Daniel and the others load bundle after bundle into the wagon. By the time they were finished, Charlottesville had significantly depopulated.

"Which of you knows the way to Staunton?" Daniel asked. Two of the men raised their hands, as did Jouett.

"Get this wagon there as fast as you can," Daniel said. "I'm going back to the Swan Tavern to make sure the others have headed out."

"I'm going with you, Colonel Boone," said Jouett. "I already helped a wounded general make his escape this morning. Others may need aid."

Daniel nodded and got on his horse. Jouett borrowed one of the wagoners' mounts and followed him. As they rode toward the tavern, Daniel saw flashes of green and red in the distance. Banastre Tarleton's column of British regulars and American Loyalists had reached Charlottesville.

"We can't go on to the tavern and lead them to the others," Jouett said, "and, if we suddenly gallop in the opposite direction, they'll chase us."

"We'll do neither," said Daniel, tugging meaningfully on the sleeve of his shirt. "I'm just a simple hunter, friend, and you're just a tavern keeper. They won't pay us much mind."

Daniel urged his horse to the left. Jouett followed. They ambled slowly along the dirt road and turned their heads only when a group of green-coated dragoons came close.

"Hold there, you two," ordered the sergeant. "Where is the General Assembly meeting?"

Daniel put on his best mask of indifference. "I'm not rightly sure, sir. I wasn't exactly invited."

The dragoons looked at Daniel's buckskins and laughed. "All the same," pressed the sergeant, "you'd know where they set up the government."

Daniel made a show of considering the sergeant's question. "I believe they were meeting over at the old Smith place, weren't they, Jack?"

Jouett caught on quickly. "Yep, I think that's right."

Daniel headed back into town, followed by the others. After a few minutes, he pointed to a house on the other side of the square from the actual meeting house. "That's the place," he announced.

Three dragoons galloped off. But the sergeant and several others remained.

"Well, we best be off, Jack, your mother will be worried if we aren't home for supper," Daniel drawled.

"Uh, sure, Pa, we best be off," the young man stammered.

They urged their horses away from the dragoons. After a few strides, Daniel cracked a smile. They were about to get away.

"Colonel, this is our road," said Jouett, pointing helpfully to the street they were about to cross.

"*Colonel*, eh?" bellowed the sergeant from behind them. "You two wait right there."

Daniel groaned.

▲▲▲

There were worse jails than the Charlottesville coalhouse. But it was still a jail.

During his days of confinement, Daniel had only two consolations. One was that among his fellow prisoners was Jack Jouett. Daniel enjoyed his company immensely, and was pleased to learn the young man intended to move to Kentucky.

"You're welcome at Boone's Station anytime, friend," said Daniel, "although my house was pretty crowded the last time I was there."

Jouett looked around at their cramped quarters and held up his hands. The gesture made Daniel guffaw. "Well, now, my house has a big edge over this one — I can go out hunting whenever I want."

Daniel's other consolation was that, based on what he overheard from the guards, Thomas Jefferson and most of the legislators had managed to escape. No doubt they were headed to safety in Staunton or some other western settlement.

Daniel kept up his spirits by leading the others in singing as many songs as they could recall. They sang church hymns, ribald camp songs, and everything in between. Daniel even hummed a few bars of one of Goran's spellsongs. Nobody else knew it, though, so they just clapped their hands and stomped their feet to it.

It was all the loud singing that saved him from whatever fate Banastre Tarleton might have had in store for him — or so Daniel found out later. One morning, after bringing the prisoners their breakfast, the guard left the door of the coalhouse wide open. Jouett walked to it and poked his head out hesitantly.

"I don't see any soldiers," he exclaimed. "They've all gone!"

Daniel went outside. He couldn't see any red-coated regulars or green-coated Loyalists in the vicinity, either. But, unlike Jouett, he *could* see the person hovering over the roof of the coalhouse, looking down at him with relief.

Shrugging, Daniel called out to the others. "Let's all get out of here, gentlemen. We've had a stroke of luck. I suppose you might say our adventure has had a fairy-tale ending."

Chapter 27 — The Mother

ALTHOUGH SO MANY OTHER THINGS had changed, the trail they followed was remarkably unaltered. Every twist and turn felt achingly familiar. The trail led in the same direction, to the same destination. Would following it produce anything other than the same result?

Nanyehi nursed no false hopes. She knew the suffering of her people would not soon be forgotten nor forgiven. But neither had it been foreordained.

If Dragging Canoe and the war faction, goaded by British agents and the fairies of the Great Alliance, hadn't ruthlessly attacked the white settlers, the American militia wouldn't have retaliated against Cherokee villages with such destructive force. And, if the American settlers had honored their governments' treaties, provided the food and other supplies they'd agreed to, and distinguished in good faith between friend and foe, they wouldn't have driven so many desperate Cherokees into the arms of Dragging Canoe.

There were no simple answers. There were only perilous choices among limited options. But Nanyehi remained convinced that the best trail to follow was that of peace. It was the trail that led north and east from her former home at Chota, across the Tennessee River, over peaks and valleys, across some one hundred forty miles of rough terrain. It led to Long Island-on-the-Holston. It led to the signing of another treaty.

"Was it really worth it?" asked Tana as the two women bypassed a syca-more tree that had fallen across the trail. "You did not need to travel all the way back to Chota."

Nanyehi smiled sadly. "My journey to Chota was not simply to meet up with you," she said. "I wanted to see my home again, even if it now sits deserted. I wanted to remember our lives, even if the memories taste bitter rather than sweet."

Chota lay deserted because it had been attacked, plundered, and depopulated by John Sevier and his militia. But the white settlers weren't the only ones responsible for the tragedy. So were Dragging Canoe and his Chickamauga. So were the British who'd used them as pawns.

And so am I.

When Sevier and the Overmountain men rode off to confront Patrick Ferguson and the Tories, the British agent had urged the Cherokees to attack. "Now is the time to get your land back," he'd told them. "All the men of the Watauga and Nolichucky will be gone and no one will be left to fight except old men and young boys. The king's soldiers will soon kill off all those untrained backwoodsmen who have crossed the mountains."

What the British agent advocated was cowardly and foolish. Nanyehi had said so — loudly and repeatedly. But whether it was an overwhelming desire for revenge, an overwhelming desire for British arms and supplies, fairy magic, or some combination, the war faction had prevailed.

Nanyehi couldn't just stand by and watch the women and children of the settlements be enslaved, tortured, or slaughtered. So, once again, she'd warned the Americans. One messenger had gone to Long Island to alert the American agent Joseph Martin, the husband of Nanyehi's daughter Betsy Ward. Another messenger had been waiting at John Sevier's home when the militia leader got back from Kings Mountain.

Sevier and his barely rested militiamen had defeated the attacking Cherokees at Boyd's Creek. Then, after the Virginians arrived to reinforce him, Sevier had proceeded to occupy Chota and other villages. They'd destroyed hundreds of Cherokee homes and consumed or burned all the provisions they could find.

When Sevier's militia returned home, Nanyehi and her family had accompanied them. There had been no other way to survive the winter.

Living with Betsy and her husband at Long Island, while enjoyable in some ways, had deprived Nanyehi of many comforts of home. One of them was the companionship of Tana, who'd spent months scouting for the Nunnehi in their war against the Elves of Georgia and didn't know at first about the destruction of Chota.

On the other hand, living at Long Island had given her the opportunity to spend time with another fairy friend: Dela the Water Maiden. Many a night, Nanyehi would sit next to the fairy on the bank of the Holston, looking out over the water as Dela told stories of the Gwragedd Annwn's life back in Wales, their emigration to America, their battles with the Pukwudgies, and the strange aquatic creatures that were the primary prey of their monster hunts.

"Tana, do your people hunt the Water Panther?" Nanyehi asked as the two women continued their journey to Long Island.

The Song Snake shook her head. "I have heard tales of it, but I have never seen one. Has Dela spoken of Water Panthers?"

"She has," replied Nanyehi. "Her people have encountered them several times, although Dela says they have succeeded only in driving them off, not in capturing them."

Tana looked thoughtful. "When I met Dela, I was impressed. Still, I wonder about her Folk. I fear they lack the courage to build a new life here."

"If you mean to say their neutrality in the American war amounts to cowardice, I disagree," Nanyehi said. "Their reasoning may be sound given their conditions."

"Knowing when and how best to fight for your people requires both wisdom and courage," granted the Song Snake. "But they strike me as too passive. They have come a long way to settle in a place teeming with potential enemies."

"Just as the whites have." Nanyehi tightened the sash that tied her blouse around her waist and pushed her tomahawk lower into its confines. "Ours is a huge country. There should be room enough for all, if only we would learn from each other rather than letting fear, resentment, and violence prevail."

"You speak a truth far too many ears seem not to hear," said Tana as the two women reached a small creek and stooped to take a drink.

Nanyehi wiped her mouth with her sleeve. "The next cycle of violence may start with the new 'peace' treaty. If the Americans demand we give up still more land, more of my people will join Dragging Canoe's cause. They will see no alternative."

"It is the way of things for the victors to dictate terms to the vanquished."

"That is just the point, Tana — they all see themselves as victors and vanquished," said Nanyehi. "There must be some way to break the cycle."

John Sevier, Evan Shelby, and Nanyehi's son-in-law Joseph Martin were among the seven commissioners authorized by General Nathaniel Greene, the commander of the Southern army, to negotiate a new treaty. As the participants gathered, Nanyehi saw the heavy-set figure of Isaac Shelby standing close to his father.

The Cherokee delegation was missing several familiar faces. Attakullakulla was dead. Aged Oconostota was now First Beloved Man. But the flight into the hills in response to John Sevier's invasion had rendered Oconostota too ill to make the journey to Long Island. Another cousin of Nanyehi, Old Tassel, now spoke for the people.

As Old Tassel stepped forward, an expression of grave concern on his weathered face, Nanyehi watched the other commissioners carefully. She knew General Greene had insisted the Americans treat fairly with her people. Would the commissioners resent the general's interference in their affairs? Or would they take it as a signal that their government wanted peace on the frontier?

"We come here to the Great Island with heavy hearts and open hands," Old Tassel began. "We were opposed to this war and tried to restrain the young chiefs, but they would not listen."

Then he looked directly at John Sevier.

"I know you are a man and a warrior. I have heard different talks by different people quite different from what I expected. I fear you must be angry and that it was caused by some evil persons."

From her fellow Cherokee, Nanyehi heard grumbling at the unflattering description of Dragging Canoe and his war faction, but Old Tassel's choice of words seemed to have the intended effect.

"My neighbors and I have never acted from hate or wished all Cherokees harm," John Sevier said. "But we defend ourselves when we are attacked — and we offer no apology for it."

"No apology is needed when a man acts as a man," Old Tassel replied. "You have risen up from a warrior to a Beloved Man. May your words be good and true."

It was Evan Shelby who spoke next.

"I will speak a truth that is not good. British agents have supplied your warriors and directed them against us. They have used you to wage war on behalf of King George. But his war does not fare well. His redcoats no longer roam the country at will. And, thanks to many here today, including my son Isaac and my friend John Sevier, they have no great army of Tories to rally to their cause, either."

Again Nanyehi heard grumbling among the Cherokee while the Americans beamed with pride.

"You bet on the wrong horse," insisted William Christian, one of Virginia's commissioners. "The British misled you. Now they cannot supply you with arms, or blankets, or food."

If the Americans' words were meant to pressure the Cherokee to capitulate, to sign yet another treaty giving up land, the words were ill-chosen. Old Tassel could see that, too.

"The men who wronged you, the men who have earned your anger, are not among us," he said. "But, if you close off all others, more will walk the warpath."

"They may not be among you today, but they are your brothers and sons, and those who feed and clothe them are your sisters and daughters," Evan Shelby pointed out.

Nanyehi could see the fate of the conference, perhaps even the fate of her people, teetering on the blade of a knife. Now was the time to do what she'd rehearsed repeatedly in her head during the journey from Chota to Long Island. Now was the time to act.

"I am Nanyehi. I would speak as Beloved Woman for my people."

All eyes turned to her as she strode forward. She saw shocked expressions on some faces, curiosity on others, and grudging admiration on a few more.

"You may not be accustomed to women speaking in council," Nanyehi told the Americans. "But, although our ways are different, there is much we have in common, your people and mine."

She saw her son-in-law glance nervously at the other commissioners. *Is he afraid the others will doubt his loyalty?*

"We know that women are often looked upon as nothing," Nanyehi continued, now letting her gaze take in the Cherokee men as well. "But we are your mothers. You are our sons. From our mouths, from our minds, from our hearts, our cry is the same: it is a cry for peace."

Nanyehi's voice broke. She found herself searching for the right words to speak next. Then she heard a familiar voice begin to sing a familiar song.

It was the lullaby Nanyehi had sung to her children when they were babies:

Cedar sways as night winds blow,
Brushing boughs a rhythm drum,
Mother Moon sings long and low,
Whispered words while heartbeat thrum.

The sweet tones of the lullaby — which only she, Isaac Shelby, and John Sevier could hear — brought back a flood of memories, memories of life in Chota that strengthened her resolve even as they brought tears to the corners of her eyes.

That had been Tana's intention, of course. The Song Snake knew Nanyehi wouldn't have wanted the Nunnehi scout to use spellsong on the Americans. *The agreement we strike here must be authentic, not some fairy trick.*

"The peace we make must continue beyond today," Nanyehi said, raising her arms along with the volume of her voice. "The peace must last forever. Let your women's sons be ours. Let our sons be yours. Hear our words. And let your women — your mothers, your sisters, your wives, your daughters — let them hear our words, as well. I have spoken."

There was silence as Nanyehi returned to her seat. Then William Christian cleared his throat.

"You spoke well for the mothers of your people, and to the mothers of ours," Christian said, clearly moved by Nanyehi's words. "And we have listened well."

She saw John Sevier nod his head enthusiastically. Behind Evan Shelby, Isaac had his head bowed as if in prayer.

"No man can hear it without being moved by it," Christian continued. "Such words and thoughts show the world that human nature is the same everywhere. Our women shall hear your words, and we know how they will feel and think of them."

Turning her head slightly, Nanyehi saw the other Cherokee women looking at each other wonderingly. Old Tassel caught her eye, arched his eyebrows, and inclined his head.

"We are all descendants of the same woman," Christian concluded. "We will not quarrel with you because you are our mothers. We will not meddle with your people if they will be still and quiet at home and let us live in peace."

That is a condition that may prove impossible to meet, Nanyehi thought. *But I would rather have a just peace on that condition than an unjust peace, or no peace at all.*

▲▲▲

"I had no idea, Tana — how did you manage to keep this secret from me during our entire journey from Chota?"

The fairy looked at Nanyehi with a mixture of amusement and embarrassment. "It was a matter of finding the right time. I knew you had a great many matters to ponder, so I…"

"So you did not think I would welcome the change of subject?" Nanyehi looked incredulously across the campfire at Tana.

"I can understand why she held back her news, Nanyehi." Dela's large, blue-green eyes were wider than usual, the reflected flames of the campfire making them appear to leap with excitement. "You are one of the most inquisitive people I have ever met. She guessed you would demand to know every detail, even if she was not ready to yield it."

"She expected correctly," Nanyehi replied, staring intensely at Tana.

"There is not much to tell," the Song Snake said. "Huli and I have talked of marriage for many years, ever since we were first sent out together to negotiate with the Yunwi Tsunsdi. But we of the Azalea Clan often walk lonely trails through the Land of Shadow. Huli and I were apart for months at a time. And, once war resumed with the Elves, marriage and family seemed no more than a forever dream."

"So, do your wedding plans signify your war is over?" Dela asked.

Tana nodded, fingering the blowpipe lying at her side.

"When the British arrived in Georgia, the Elves were emboldened," she said. "They sought both to help the British and to expand their own hunting grounds at our expense. They attacked our stronghold on Blood Mountain, using enchanted engines of war to batter down our magic shield. They are skilled warriors with sling, bow, and blade. But the warriors of our Rattlesnake Clan are also formidable, and the Elf mages were either too few or too weak to combat the powerful magecraft of our Tobacco Clan. We defeated their assault. And then we attacked their own stronghold, hidden in a forest near Augusta."

"Did you drive the Elves out?" Dela asked.

"No, such a feat was beyond our power to accomplish," Tana said. "But our war party took many lives that day. They were forced to sue for peace."

Nanyehi had already heard Tana's account of the Nunnehi victory, but its larger significance only now become clear to her. "The Elves did more than sue for peace — they pulled back from the American war, did they not?"

"That is our understanding, yes," Tana replied. "The British still receive aid from other Folk, from the Lutins and Pixies primarily, but losing the Elves was a blow."

Dela lowered her eyes for a moment, then fixed them again on Tana. "Will your Folk now intervene directly in the American war?"

"The Council is considering it, yes, given the continuing dangers posed by the Great Alliance," the Song Snake agreed. "Still, even if we do nothing more than keep the Elves tied down, we will be serving the American cause."

The three women sat by the fire, each lost in her own thoughts. It was Dela who broke the silence.

"Nanyehi, I was listening to the negotiations from the river when you made your speech."

"I assumed as much," Nanyehi said, drawing her swan-feather shawl higher to cover her shoulders.

"Your words made an impression on everyone," Dela began. "They certainly made an impression on me. And yet, I struggle to understand fully their meaning. Speaking as a mother, you call for peace. Yet you have also fought in battle for your people. Were you wrong to fight?"

This is no idle question, Nanyehi realized.

"It is an awful thing to go to war, Dela, and far too many resort to violence far too quickly," she said. "Still, there are circumstances when defending your homes and beliefs require it. It is better to win a peace by words than by arms. Unfortunately, there are times when only arms can win a *lasting* peace."

"But you oppose your cousin Dragging Canoe's war, even though the whites have taken Cherokee lands and killed Cherokee people," Dela pointed out.

Nanyehi stared into the fire and saw images in the dancing flames. She saw her bustling village of Chota, children playing in the streets, bountiful harvests, ceremonies in the Council House, and young men and women flirting over feasts of venison, partridge, corn, and bean. She saw the wise faces of kindly Attakullakulla and aged Oconostota. She saw the passionate face of Dragging Canoe as he argued against the elders. She saw brave young warriors go off to battle. She saw their agonized faces as they returned with grievous wounds, and the frozen faces of those who returned as empty shells. She saw the terrified faces of the women and children as they fled their homes.

She saw it all in the fire, just as she had so many times before. The weight of it was nearly unbearable. It nearly drove the breath from her lungs and the hope from her heart.

But only nearly.

"If I thought that Dragging Canoe's trail led to victory and a lasting peace, I would follow his footsteps," Nanyehi said. "There is great honor in defending your people and your way of life. That honor must be tempered with wisdom, however, just as the heavy blade of the tomahawk is tempered by forge and flame to an edge fine enough to cut rather than just to smash. If victory lies beyond your grasp — or if dishonorable means are needed to accomplish it — then honor and wisdom require that you seek another trail."

"And what of the American rebels?" Dela pressed.

"I believe they followed the trail of talk and argument as far as it could take them," Nanyehi said. "In the end, the Americans are a people who wish to govern themselves, just as your people and mine govern ourselves. Their king over the water refused. So war came."

"And now, with the Great Alliance unleashing monsters as weapons of war, the stakes are higher than before," Tana said. "The sooner the Americans force the British to make a just peace, the sooner we can regain control of the magical beasts that threaten us all."

The moon had long since passed from the night sky. Nanyehi gazed up at the stars, picking out the patterns and figures about which her elders had so often told campfire tales. She saw the Seven Brothers, for example, so angry at their mothers' constant scolding that they flew up and found new homes in the sky. And she saw two other bright stars, the Spirit Dogs that guarded each end of the starry Path of Souls — the route the recently deceased must pass as they leave this world for the next.

There would always be points of light traveling the night path, she knew. And some would always begin that journey by falling in battle — in unavoidable, honorable battle. But this night, the sky was lit too brilliantly. Too many souls had begun the journey before their appointed time.

She saw plainly what Dela was really asking her. And Nanyehi wondered if her answer would serve Dela and her people well. *Or will it just add more stars to the Path of Souls?*

Then the Water Maiden's final question left no doubt in Nanyehi's mind that the two women were wrestling with the same issue.

Dela pointed to a bright star directly overhead. "Back home in Wales, the humans called that star and its companions 'Arthur's Harp' and built legends around it," she said. "Among the Gwragedd Annwn, Arthur's Harp reminds us of the time our elders took a more active role in the affairs of Britain, in an attempt to save the humans from disruption and decay. It is a painful memory. And yet we still sing heroic songs of those days, as do the humans of Wales."

Then Dela turned to Nanyehi. "What songs will be sung of us?"

Chapter 28 — The Redoubts

October 1781

AS HE APPROACHED THE TENT of General George Washington, Peter Muhlenberg pulled out the spyglass he had borrowed from the commander-in-chief and looked across the field at a sea of colors. To the right, he saw thousands of Continental blue coats as well as dashes of brown, buff, and tan where companies of militiamen were huddled in small groups near tents and campfires. To the right, Peter saw thousands of white coats belonging to their allies, the French soldiers under the command of General Rochambeau.

Beyond the encampment, Peter saw the dark line of the ditch the French and Americans had dug some two thousand paces in a semicircle around the town. Hundreds of paces beyond the trench, Peter could see flashes of red — the coats of the British regulars — as well as the forest green coats of the British dragoons and the dark blue coats of their German auxiliaries.

Peter viewed that sea of colors at Yorktown, knowing the events of the next few days would likely paint it with another shade of red: not the bright scarlet of British coats but the dark red of blood.

▲▲▲

"We have never possessed the advantage at sea that we enjoy at this moment. Nor have we enjoyed greater advantage on land. The hand of Providence has been kind."

General Washington bent over the map of Yorktown, tracing his finger along the trench line. "Your artillery and ours have subjected General Cornwallis to such a bombardment as he and his army have never experienced."

Jean-Baptiste Donatien de Vimeur, Comte de Rochambeau, raised an eyebrow. "Good fortune is welcome, General Washington, but it neither planned our march nor fired our guns."

Several of the French and American generals in the room smiled and nodded, although Washington did neither. Peter, standing on the far side of the tent, now felt compelled to speak.

"Gentlemen," he began, "if I may quote the Book of Proverbs: 'A man's heart deviseth his way: but the Lord directeth his steps.' We have both divine guidance and human ingenuity to thank for our present position."

Peter was relieved to see the smiles grow broader on the faces of the assembled generals, even that of Washington himself. Maintaining the generals' morale was no less important than maintaining it among the common soldiers. They all knew travails still lay ahead. And, among the men in the room, only Peter and his commander-in-chief knew the full extent of the forces arrayed against them.

After the British forces had converged on Petersburg and forced the hasty evacuation of Richmond, it had taken weeks of campaigning by Continental regulars and Virginia militiamen to stymie the British advance. General Cornwallis had pulled back over the course of the summer, first to Williamsburg and then to Yorktown. There Cornwallis dug in, likely expecting a British fleet from New York to extricate his army.

All along, Har and his Dwarf rangers provided invaluable intelligence to Peter. When it concerned the movement of British troops, Peter passed it along to his immediate superiors and credited human scouts. However, when it involved the Pixies — who seemed to be gathering at Yorktown in ever-greater numbers — he sent the information directly to General Washington in New York, and by the best courier available: Goran the Sylph.

It was through Goran that Peter had learned in August of the French fleet sailing up from the Caribbean and the decision of Washington and Rochambeau to march their combined army secretly to Virginia. With the French fleet bottling up Chesapeake Bay, Washington and Rochambeau hoped to cut off all routes for reinforcement or retreat, forcing Cornwallis into a costly surrender.

But, as Washington's secret message to Peter conveyed, their plan required two unknowns to be resolved in America's favor. The first one *had* been resolved — the French fleet had defeated the British fleet on September 5 at the mouth of Chesapeake Bay. As long as the French continued to control the bay, Cornwallis was trapped at Yorktown.

The other unknown was how far the fairies of the Great Alliance would be willing to go to help Cornwallis. Pixie spellsong had clearly strengthened the morale of the British forces at Yorktown. On the American side, Har's squad of Dwarf rangers had expanded to eight during the siege, but they remained greatly outnumbered by the Pixies.

As for Goran, he'd left the camp days ago. Whether the Sylph was carrying a message or performing some other mission, Peter didn't know.

As they stood around a table in Washington's tent that night, the commander-in-chief looked across at Rochambeau. "It is now time to tighten the noose," Washington said. "It is time to dig the second trench."

The immaculately dressed Frenchman bent over and traced his own finger along the map. Washington gave a slight incline of his head. "I see that, General," Washington said. "If we move another three hundred paces closer to the town, we cannot extend the trench all the way to the river without doing something about those two redoubts."

Peter and the other generals stepped forward to see what Rochambeau was pointing to. On the south side of Yorktown, close to the river, there were two circular marks. Har the Tower had already scouted the two British fortifications and described their construction to Peter in some detail. The first line of defense was a row of sharpened logs. Next, attackers would have to climb a slope and make their way across a ditch of mud. Then came another slope, another line of sharpened logs, and a wooden parapet.

The redoubts were small but well-defended. Taking them would require taking them seriously.

Rochambeau straightened, looked back at Washington, and shrugged. "First we dig. Then we bombard their positions. After that, the redoubts shall be ours."

Sounds simple enough, Peter thought, *but something tells me it won't be.*

▲▲▲

The next morning, Har, Onar, and Nithi looked across the York River to Gloucester Point, a peninsula where some British troops were encamped — and the place to which British sailors were now laboriously rowing their flatboats. For days, French artillery had blasted anything floating on the

Yorktown side of the river. Taking their boats to Gloucester Point had been the only way for the British to save them.

"They are protecting their escape route, should it come to that," Onar observed, wiping his brow with the sleeve of his light-gray tunic.

Har considered the matter for a moment. "With so few boats, it would take many trips to carry their men across the river."

"By the time they flee, there may not be so many passengers left to carry," said Nithi.

They all laughed at her macabre jest.

"Have you heard from Goran?" Onar asked.

"No, and that worries me," Har replied. "Whether General Washington sent him on a mission or some other task, surely the intent was not for him to be absent for the final assault."

"Which will begin in a couple of days, I gather," Onar said.

Har nodded. "Some of Peter's troops will be among the assault force. I told him we would be on hand to help."

Nithi's eyes flashed with anticipation. "Good to see Pixies up close again," she said. "Moving targets make for better practice."

▲▲▲

For hours, the French and American guns pounded the British redoubts. Har spent the time finishing his own plan for the assault. Two Dwarf rangers would stay in reserve while the remaining six would accompany the attackers — Har, Onar, and Nithi with the Americans and the other three Dwarfs with the French column.

"The word around camp is that Colonel Alexander Hamilton will lead the American assault," Onar reported.

That will make it easier, Har thought. *Hamilton will see and hear whatever the Pixies may attempt.*

By mid-afternoon, the assault teams — four hundred French troops against the leftward redoubt and four hundred Americans against the rightward one — began to assemble along the newly dug outer trench. As Har, Onar, and Nithi approached the American position, they saw a French officer in a pristine white uniform talking animatedly to Lafayette. Har turned to Onar for a translation.

"The officer is questioning whether the Americans are truly capable of attacking with the speed and silence required," Onar said.

Lafayette shot the officer a withering look and responded in a level voice.

"'We are young soldiers and have only one way in these cases,'" Onar translated. "'That is to unload our guns and march right in with our bayonets.'"

Then Lafayette turned and walked away, leaving the French officer flustered and speechless. Soon those Americans with loaded muskets began to unload them. Most of the rest fixed their bayonets. A few did neither, for they held axes rather than muskets. These "pioneers" would go in front of the other soldiers to clear away any defenses not destroyed by bombardment. Har saw one of them, a young man in a tattered blue uniform coat, approach Hamilton.

"Colonel, my men want to know if they should go into the fort if the chance comes," he asked.

Hamilton turned and looked at the young man carefully. "Sergeant, what is your name?"

"Joseph Plumb Martin, sir," Martin answered.

"Sergeant Martin, once the signal is given — once you see three exploding shells fired in sequence — have your pioneers move quickly forward. After you clear the way, allow the fort to be charged by musket and bayonet."

"I understand, sir, but I fear it may be difficult to restrain the men," Martin said as he strode away.

The Americans were clearly impatient. Har suspected it would be hours before the attack began. Washington would want to use the full cover of night. Har and the other two Dwarfs edged up behind Colonel Hamilton, listening closely for Pixie spellsong. They heard nothing. Indeed, the field seemed impossibly quiet.

Suddenly, there was a flash of light. Then another. Then a third.

Has the signal been given so soon?

The American pioneers and soldiers seemed to think so. They climbed out of the trench and began to crawl forward. But Har had heard no artillery fire. And, as he trained his eyes toward the British redoubt, the three flashes of light were still clearly visible. No shell would be burning brightly so long after it exploded.

Then Har saw Hamilton whispering to the soldiers next to him. They ignored him and continued their advance. Obviously taken aback, Hamilton tugged at the sleeve of a soldier, but the man merely shrugged him off.

Har scrambled to Hamilton's side. The colonel turned around and tried ordering another group of soldiers to stop. They also ignored him. "Are they under some kind of spell?" Hamilton hissed. "I don't hear any fairy music."

"Nor do I," Har said, momentarily nonplussed. Then he heard footsteps behind him. Nithi and Onar appeared. The normally scholarly-looking Dwarf was bobbing in excitement.

"Look more closely, Har!" he insisted. "See how the lights are rounded, like globes? Can you not guess what they are?"

"Will-o'-the-wisp!" Har exclaimed.

"Indeed," Onar agreed, "although perhaps the more fitting name in this case would be Pixie Light."

"What are you two talking about?" Hamilton asked.

"A will-o'-the-wisp is a magical light used to lure humans," Har explained, "but it is a work of magecraft. No Pixie ranger could be generating it."

"Which means that…" Onar began.

But Har had already guessed the truth Onar would speak — and the sudden burst of wind that knocked his cap askew a second later served only to confirm his guess. Carried along the wind were whispered voices.

"There are mages ahead!" he warned. "And they may not be the only Pixies we face!"

As they looked once again at the will-o'-the-wisps enticing the American soldiers onward, the multicolored sparks of Shimmer were now clearly discernible behind the lighted globes. The wall's rippling contours distorted the image of the redoubt's sharpened logs, making them look like giant spears waving back and forth.

"Can you do nothing?" Hamilton asked.

"This magecraft is beyond our ability to counter," Onar said, shaking his head.

"But mages bleed as readily as any other mortal," snarled Nithi.

The three Dwarfs filled their hands with weapons and advanced. Hamilton drew his own sword and followed.

"I know not what we face," the colonel said, "but I am honored to face it with you."

Har glanced to his left and saw that the French soldiers were also creeping inexorably forward toward another set of lighted spheres. The Pixies were executing a coordinated plan. But what was its purpose?

The answer came as soon as they reached the Pixie lights and, without hesitation, pushed their way through the Shimmer. Many Americans had already done so — and were now sitting helplessly on the ground, their weapons discarded, their hands either clasped against their ears or shielding their eyes. Among them was Sergeant Martin, one arm across his face and the other held up as if trying to keep an unseen force from crushing him.

From the outside, the land encompassed by the Shimmer bubble would have looked only a few paces deep. But within it, the Pixies had conjured a large expanse. Har could see a dozen Pixie mages, three in each corner of the expanse, their arms lifted high and emanating the streams of Shimmer magic. Other Pixie rangers and mages were immobilizing the American soldiers with a combination of blinding light and terrifying spellsong.

And, behind them, Har could see nearly a hundred Pixie warriors standing five ranks deep, their bronze-tipped spears thrust forward, their armored breastplates, greaves, and helms tinted a dark green that contrasted sharply with the lighter green of their tunics and stockings.

The Pixies had come in overwhelming force. Their plan was to capture the attackers long before they could reach the British redoubts. And there was little Har and his friends could do to stop them.

The Dwarf looked up at Alexander Hamilton and watched a range of expressions pass over the young man's face: amazement, fear, frustration, rage. Then the human clenched his jaw and tightened his grip on his sword. The sight strengthened Har's own resolve. He raised his battleaxe above his head.

"If this be our end," Har cried, "let us make it a glorious one."

Nithi spat and drew an arrow. "Glory is a lonely man. Best marry him to Victory."

Har looked at her questioningly.

"They are *Pixies*," she insisted. "The odds are but even."

At that, Hamilton exploded in laughter. "Well said, my dear lady," he managed.

Nithi muttered "*dear lady*" under her breath disdainfully, then lifted her bow and fired in a single, graceful motion — not seeming to aim. Har knew

362

better. With a strangled cry, one of the Pixie mages sustaining the Shimmer fell, an arrow in his throat.

"Dwarfs!" shouted several Pixies at once.

Har moved his battleaxe to his left hand and yanked out a handaxe. Onar spun the halberd in his hands. Hamilton, who Har assumed had never fought Folk before, shifted nervously from foot to foot but otherwise seemed to keep his wits. Nithi reloaded her bow.

"Protect the mages!" shouted a female voice. "And take the Dwarfs and human alive. They may have valuable information."

Lady Joan strode forward, followed by some two dozen spearmen. Other Pixies ran to form screens in front of the mages. Even as the Pixies deployed, Har could hear more American soldiers walking through the Shimmer behind him and immediately crumpling to the ground in agony.

"You might as well surrender, *Tower*," Joan sneered. "Even if you were wearing your shirt of mail this time, you would soon be a pig on a spit."

"You hunt wild boar this night," Har replied. "We will stain our tusks red with Pixie blood."

Joan jerked her head. In rushed a line of green-clad spearmen, some leveling their points at the breasts of the Dwarfs and others pointing upward at Colonel Hamilton. Unlike their rangers, Pixie warriors preferred to fight at close quarters, thrusting rather than throwing their spears.

Har swatted the first two thrusts aside, producing a shower of reddish sparks, then felled a warrior with a throwing axe to the chest. Next to him, Onar's longer poleaxe was serving him well as he batted spears away. Hamilton's longer arms afforded him similar protection as he parried with his sword, its steel edge chipping the bronze blades and wooden shafts of the Pixie spears at every blow. Then Nithi stepped out from behind the cover of the larger human and sank another arrow into a Pixie chest.

But the weight of numbers had an inescapable logic. Even as Har blocked another thrust and forced a foe back with a sweep at the legs, he heard Onar groan. A spear had eluded the scholarly Dwarf's guard and pierced his side. An instant later, before Har could react, he heard Onar shriek as more spears punctured his falling body.

"Onar!" shouted Nithi, her usual gruffness replaced by shock and panic. She reemerged from behind Hamilton, fired another arrow, then drew a massive warhammer from her belt.

"Crush and burn!" she bellowed as she propelled herself into the melee.

Momentarily taken aback by her impetuosity, the Pixies wavered. Har saw Nithi smash into her first target, knocking the spear from his hands with her body and then bringing the hammer down on his head. With a sickening crunch, the Pixie's skull caved in. Red blood spurted from the wound, but it wasn't the only vivid color. Yellow-orange flames singed the dead warrior's scalp and leapt out to either side, causing the neighboring Pixies to cry out.

Nithi's warhammer had been expertly enchanted with fire magic. And, as Har watched in fascination, Nithi's eyes seemed to be aflame, too.

The next three Pixies met similar fates under the expertly wielded warhammer of the ferocious Dwarf. But Har's fascination soon turned to dismay. Warriors converged on Nithi from three sides. Har tried to fight his way to her, as did Hamilton, but both found themselves facing multiple spears.

The grunts and screams of Nithi and her enemies told the tale, even though Har could no longer see what was happening. More Pixies had met their end. But so had Nithi.

"Surrender, fool!" Lady Joan's imperious demand somehow rose above the clash of enchanted bronze and cold steel.

Despair made Har's stomach twist and churn. He saw Hamilton sweep away another thrust even as three more Pixies moved in for the kill. Har wasn't afraid to die, but he wasn't ready to. The vision of a broad, freckled face framed in braided auburn hair sprang to his mind. The face smiled. Har yearned to reveal himself to it — his secrets, his dreams, his love.

A love that would now never be expressed.

Then the pressure in Har's stomach and the ache in his heart were joined by a tingling sensation. *Have their spears found me at last?* Har wondered. But that couldn't be. He felt no pain, only pressure against his back and pinpricks along his skin.

"Dwarfs!" shouted several Pixies at once, just as they had when Har and the others had arrived a few minutes before.

Then the warriors surrounding Har stumbled back, as did those surrounding Hamilton. Har heard Lady Joan groan in frustration. And he heard the sound of booted feet marching up behind him. Many booted feet.

"Have you left us any foes to fight, Har the Tower?"

Queen Virginal appeared on Har's left, her eyes dancing. The rest of her face was covered by a bronze helm. Braids of auburn hair trailed down her armored back. Har looked past her to see a line of warriors clad in the royal blue and alpine white of Virginal's Dwarfs of the Tyrol, each holding a hooked sword in one hand and a stout buckler clasped in the other. Har turned and looked past Hamilton — whose face was frozen in surprise — to see a still-longer line of armored Dwarfs clad in a wide assortment of colors and brandishing a wide variety of weapons.

Glancing behind, Har saw Dwarf mages in long robes, cupping their hands in front of their long beards and focusing magic into balls of crackling energy. He saw a handful of unarmored Dwarf hunters, fitting arrows to their bows and leering audaciously at the Pixies.

And Har saw Goran, his own bow in hand, swooping down from the top of the Shimmer bubble.

"For honor and victory!" the Sylph shouted.

"For honor and victory!" Queen Virginal shouted.

"For honor and victory!" thundered the Dwarfs in answer.

A dozen arrows flew from a dozen bows. Most struck home. Har saw several Lutki warriors in black and tan rush forward, hurling their javelins to deadly effect. A few burly Dwarfs threw handaxes at the Pixies.

Then the battle began in earnest.

Har had no time to determine the precise size of Virginal's force but realized they were still significantly outnumbered. The momentum of the initial shock would have to carry the day. The Dwarfs crashed into the front rank of Pixies, slashing at legs with their swords, chopping down with their halberds and axes, smashing limbs with their warhammers.

Putting his full weight into a swing of his battleaxe, Har took the head clean off his first target, earning an admiring grunt from the queen. He returned the commendation as Virginal dodged a spear and slashed her hooked sword across the breast of her foe, opening a bloody wound through the Pixie's armor with a shower of sparks.

Remembering the colonel, Har stepped back for a moment and found Hamilton contending with two Pixies who'd drawn shortswords. This was no fencing match. It was a brutal fight to the death. The human used his superior size and strength to knock one of the Pixies to the ground, then finished him. Hamilton might have been finished by the second, however, had Har not charged in and taken the Pixie in the shoulder.

"Your reinforcements are timely, but we are still hard-pressed," gasped

Hamilton as he turned and began to look for his next target.

"Sir, you acquit yourself well, but your duty lies elsewhere," Har said quickly. "Your men — we must rally your men!"

He pointed at the Americans. With the Pixie rangers and mages distracted by the Dwarf attack, the soldiers were beginning to rise, groggy and perplexed. A few had recovered their senses enough to perceive the fairy battle, but that perception was producing a new round of confusion and fear.

Hamilton understood and rushed toward them, Har following close behind and trying to think of the right spellsong. *Onar would have known in an instant.* Suppressing his grief, Har focused on the task. First he began a song to counteract the Pixie terror spell. With only his one voice, he knew it would take a long time, but it had to be done. The Americans had to return to the Blur and carry out their assigned mission.

Then Har heard the dulcet tones of Goran's flute. Their duet was an incongruous one over the sounds of battle. But it soon worked its magic. Next, Har transitioned to memory spells to remove the encounter with the Pixies from the Americans' minds.

That would have to do, Har thought. "Goran, can you finish up here?"

"By all means, my friend," the Sylph replied — but Har was already running back to the melee.

Dozens of dead and dying Pixies lay on the ground. Unfortunately, there were many Dwarfs on the ground as well. He saw Virginal struggling to fend off two swordsmen and sprinted to her side, brushing one Pixie aside with his battleaxe and driving his fist into the jaw of the other, who fell senseless.

"You arrived just in time, Har the Tower," said the queen.

"I might say the same about you," Har said, lowering his axe when he realized they faced no foes at the moment.

"When your Sylph friend arrived at Grünerberg, he asked only for more rangers," Virginal explained. "But somehow I *knew* it was time for our army to take the field. Somehow, I *knew* that you…that Washington's army would come to harm if we did not."

Har said nothing. The words wouldn't come. So his body took over. His legs bent of their own accord. Kneeling before Virginal, Har removed his glove, clasped her hand, and drew it to his lips.

After a moment, the words came. "I am yours, my queen," he said simply.

"Your queen, eh?"

Lady Joan's derisive voice snapped Har out of his dream-like state. But, even as he tried to regain his feet, he saw the Pixie leader, a shortsword in each hand, leap at Virginal's back.

The Dwarf queen was hardly defenseless, however. She spun to her right, her royal-blue cloak whipping around and wrapping itself around Joan's sword arm. The motion threw the Pixie off-balance. Virginal sprang forward to seize the advantage, holding up her buckler with her left hand and bringing her hooked sword down with her right.

Joan parried the blow with one sword and aimed a vicious cut at Virginal's face with the other. It bounced off the buckler, the blade flaring green against the shield's crackling aura of red. Then the two antagonists, each recognizing the skill of the other, circled warily.

Har was watching their swordplay so closely he almost fell victim to a sword thrust himself. But the warrior running at him, blade in hand, fell screaming as an arrow from one of the Dwarf hunters took him in the groin. Har stepped forward and made the Pixie's screaming stop. Then he turned back to the duel.

"You have only brought more pigs to the butcher," Lady Joan hissed. "You cannot defeat us."

"You defeated yourself the moment you chose sides," Virginal replied. "You chose the dishonorable one."

"As one of royal rank, you should have been among the first to recognize the threat," Joan said, jabbing at Virginal's side to force her into a vulnerable position.

It didn't work.

"You look into the Blur and see only chaos," Virginal said. "I see change — inevitable, inexorable change. I see waves pounding the shore. You would order them to stop. I would wait and see what shapes they wrought."

Joan's eyes flashed. "Your inaction will…"

But Virginal had accomplished her design. The Pixie was angry and flustered, too intent on winning the argument. The queen abruptly lunged at her throat. Joan reflexively brought both swords up to block the thrust — but Virginal had already drawn herself into a ball, rolled along the ground, then shot up to drive the hooked point of her sword into Joan's thigh. As the Pixie leader cried out in anguish, Virginal brought the edge of her buckler down on Joan's exposed neck.

The duel was done.

Har felt a wave of exhilaration. He wanted nothing more than to rush to Virginal, reach out his arms to crush her to his chest, and cover her face with his long-repressed kisses.

"Lady Joan has fallen!" shouted a Pixie. Others took up the call. Despite their heavy casualties, there were still half a hundred Pixies standing. They outnumbered the two dozen Dwarfs still on their feet. Nevertheless, it was evident the fight had gone out of the Pixies.

"Gather to me!" exclaimed a Pixie in a pointed cap of yellow-green. The mage waved his hands above his head. Har saw a ball of magical energy appear between the mage's palms, then expand. Other mages rushed to his side and added their own magecraft to his. The sphere soon encompassed all the mages, then spread over the other Pixies converging on their position.

The Dwarf mages responded with their own magecraft. As the Shimmer seemed to liquefy and stream toward into the Pixie sphere, the Dwarf mages were creating their own, smaller bubble protect their own people. Then the Pixies began to disappear — their bodies turning into indistinct streaks as they passed through the magical tunnel.

Turning back to Queen Virginal, Har could see the delight and relief written on her face. Her eyes widened, as if issuing an invitation. He complied, first walking and then running toward her. A moment later, Virginal's eyes widened even more — but not in invitation. It was as if the flame of a candle had flickered in a strong breeze, then gone out.

Her eyes still stared directly into his. They saw nothing.

And all Har saw, all his eyes would allow him to see, was the bronze point of the spear protruding from Virginal's chest. He couldn't see the triumph in the face of the Pixie warrior who threw it. He couldn't see the remaining Pixies disappear. He couldn't see Goran land beside Virginal, weeping. He couldn't see the Dwarfs rush forward in anguish to the side of their queen.

Har saw only the wedge of bronze that had pierced his love's heart, and his own.

The Dwarf was inconsolable. As much as Goran wanted to stay and comfort him, the Sylph had to find the other will-o'-the-wisps, the one deployed against the French, and see if the second Dwarf detachment Virginal had brought to Yorktown had prevailed there.

They had, Goran discovered upon reentering the Blur. He found the French and American soldiers stretched out in front of their trenches, looking up expectantly at the darkened sky. Those who had been enticed through the Shimmer had recovered their wits but not, evidently, their memories. The Pixie diversion had failed.

Then Goran heard a French gun roar. A moment later, a shell exploded in the night sky. Then came two more. The signal was given.

The soldiers stood up and ran at the two redoubts. On the American side, Goran saw the pioneers hack and push at the first row of sharpened logs. Then the first wave of American soldiers reached the outer defenses and chose to worm their way around the stakes rather than waiting for them all to be felled. When the defenders popped up from the parapet to fire a volley, some Americans took shelter in the large holes created by their artillery barrage earlier in the day. Others fell into the holes after sustaining wounds from British musket balls and grenades.

Goran struggled to remember his priorities. He wanted to dive in and help, but he had heard no Pixie spellsong. So he banked and flew toward the other redoubt. Its defenses had survived the day's barrage largely intact. But, as he watched, the French pioneers — under heavy fire from the redoubt's defenders — created a large enough opening for the attack to commence.

"Vive le Roi!" shouted the French soldiers as they charged up the slope. Blue-coated Germans rose up in ranks and fired point-blank, to deadly effect. But it wasn't deadly enough. The French swarmed over the parapet. After a few minutes of melee, they lowered their bayonets and prepared to charge. The defenders threw up their hands and offered surrender in English, German, and a few words of broken French.

Glancing back to the river, Goran saw something similar occurring in the other redoubt. Some of the British defenders tried to escape back to Yorktown, but Hamilton had taken the precaution of sending a detachment around the fort to cut off any retreat. British soldiers were now surrendering in droves.

As the Americans cheered, Goran flew over the redoubt and counted three dozen dead and wounded attackers. He suspected the French had suffered heavier losses. But, other than Colonel Hamilton, the attackers had no inkling of how close the assault had come to disaster — and how many other lives, Folk lives, had been lost to forestall that disaster.

▲▲▲

"General Cornwallis must know his cause is lost," insisted the Marquis de Lafayette. "Now that our guns are closer to the town, his army cannot long survive."

Peter saw Washington and Rochambeau exchange meaningful looks. Lafayette's logic seemed sound enough. Indeed, the day after the redoubts fell, Cornwallis had ordered a frontal assault in an attempt to spike the French and American artillery. But the British had been quickly repulsed, and the guns they damaged were quickly repaired. The desperate assault showed that Cornwallis recognized his dire peril.

The other generals assembled in Washington's tent appeared to be of a similar mind to Lafayette. They were ebullient. The long war was not yet over. Still, if they could force Cornwallis to surrender, it would surely count as the greatest triumph they had yet achieved.

But no outcome was guaranteed in war. That much Peter had learned over five long years of service.

"There remains the question of the British navy," Washington said, exhibiting none of the elation written on the faces of the others. "We know Cornwallis has sent urgent messages to New York asking for succor. If the British were somehow to overcome Admiral de Grasse's French fleet at the mouth of the bay, Cornwallis might yet escape our noose."

"All the more reason to press our advantage and step up the bombardment," Lafayette exclaimed, although his face transformed from flushed with excitement to blushing with embarrassment as both Washington and Rochambeau fixed cold stares on the young officer.

Later, after the other officers left, Peter reentered with tent with Goran.

"What is your friend's condition?" Washington asked.

Goran grimaced. "Har's losses have been devastating. His queen is dead. Most of his friends are dead. He and the two Dwarfs left in reserve before the assault on the redoubts are the only rangers in camp — well, except for me."

"And, if battle with Cornwallis comes, or magical creatures of some kind intervene, can their assistance be assured?" Washington pressed.

"The other two are eager to help, General," said Goran. "As for Har, I believe that, if that time comes, he will rise to the occasion."

Peter cleared his throat. "General Washington, are you thinking of assaulting the town?"

"Siegecraft should accomplish our end without such a recourse, but as I am ever reminded, it is best to prepare for all eventualities where fairies are involved," said the commander-in-chief, effecting a faint smile.

It faded instantly when Billy Lee burst into the tent. "Pardon, sir," he said breathlessly, "but you'll want to see this for yourself."

"See what, Billy?" Washington replied testily.

"The river!" the slave responded. "Great waves come over the banks. And something's screeching and hissing!"

Peter, Goran, and Washington followed Billy Lee through the tent flap. Although the mid-morning sun clearly illuminated the grassy field that lay between the American lines and Yorktown, the sky above the river was unnaturally foggy. Every few seconds, Peter could see what looked like bolts of lightning within thick clouds. He could also see the water surging over the banks as Billy Lee had described.

But the most vivid sensation wasn't what Peter saw. It was what he heard. A howling of wind and a pounding of rain came from the river. All around him, in bright sunshine, soldiers and camp followers alike were yelling in consternation and pointing to the river. And through it all were two incongruous noises. One was the firing of a cannon — only it wasn't coming from York or the American lines. It came from somewhere far down the river.

The second incongruous noise was the screech Billy Lee had spoken of. Peter had heard magical beasts before. The Tatzelwurm he'd fought roared like a lion. The Fuath at the battle of Germantown hissed. The monstrous cry from the river was something else entirely. To describe it as a "screech" was to do it little justice. It was a cacophony — high-pitched shrieks, the blood-curdling scream of some giant bird of prey, and the guttural bellow of some great cat all mixed together, yet seeming to come from a single mouth.

"Cornwallis *did* have another trick up his sleeve," Washington said. "Goran, what can you tell me about the beast?"

There was no answer. Peter, Washington, and Billy Lee looked up simultaneously and saw no fairy hovering above them.

▲▲▲

The Sylph flew swiftly to the camp of the Dwarf rangers, his stomach churning, his limbs trembling with something other than exertion.

A Sea Serpent? In the York River?

The idea seemed preposterous, yet Goran knew it was the best explanation. Like the Fuath and some other aquatic monsters, the Sea Serpent had the ability to create stormy conditions as it raced along the surface — or, as in this case, while it was slithering along the river floor.

No doubt the Pixies were driving the creature. But to what end? If it were only meant to strike terror in the soldiers besieging Yorktown, the tactic might delay the inevitable for a short while. But, unless the soldiers came close to the river, the Sea Serpent could not do them any bodily harm, and the spellsong of Goran and the Dwarf rangers could eventually obscure the sight and sound of the beast.

Goran landed next to the campfire. Har was sitting alone, gazing into its fading embers.

"Can you not see and hear what we face?" the Sylph asked. "I know your heart grieves, but we must..."

The Dwarf held up his battleaxe. "I have not forgotten my duty, Goran. My two remaining rangers are already heading to the American lines to begin spellsong. I was just waiting here for you. Waiting and praying."

Feeling scolded, and feeling he deserved it, Goran bowed his head and offered his own prayer. Then he looked into the eyes of Har the Tower. What had once burned intensely in those eyes now but flickered. The once-youthful face now bore the haggard look of middle age. Har's normally wavy beard now looked matted and unkempt.

"We must discover their scheme," said the Dwarf — not in his characteristically light-hearted voice, but in a cold, flat tone.

Goran nodded. "What if I fly over the river and find the Folk prodding the Sea Serpent along while you investigate the source of the cannon shots?"

Har the Tower gave a brief nod of his head, rose, and trotted away. Goran returned to the sky, banked to his right, and headed for the center of the dark cloud overlooking the York.

▲▲▲

The cannon boomed again, much closer. Har stopped and tried to will his hands to stop shaking. She was gone. Onar, Nithi, and Meto were gone.

If I am not careful, I will join them. The thought made Har suck in a hasty breath. *Might that be what I truly desire?*

The Dwarf stood for several minutes, leaning against a tree and struggling for control. He looked down at his quivering arms, arms that had never once encircled her stout waist to draw her near. He looked further down, at the boots on his feet, boots that would never lay unlaced at the foot of her door. His world, once a place of uncounted wonders and uncountable possibilities, now seemed little more than an inventory of words not spoken, of moments not experienced, of roads not taken, of could-have-been's and never-would-be's.

Perhaps the next world offered another chance. Perhaps Virginal and the others Har had lost would be waiting for him there, waiting to guide him into a happier, easier existence.

Why not follow them on the Great Journey to what lies beyond?

Because there were still people counting on him in this world. The remaining Dwarfs of Grünerberg. His family back on the Brocken. Goran the Sylph and the other Folk he had befriended in America. And his human friends, Peter Muhlenberg most of all.

He would neither betray the faith of those in safety nor abandon the cause of those in peril. He would be the man that the likes of Onar, Nithi, Meto, and Goran could call a comrade-in-arms.

He would be the man who might have earned Virginal's love, if fate had allowed it.

Har's hands no longer shook. His knuckles whitened as he gripped his axe. Somewhere ahead were the kind of Folk who esteemed power over principle, who heartlessly sacrificed the freedom and well-being of others to achieve their ends, and who were willing to unleash terror against the innocent for some "greater good."

Boom!

Har crept forward, staying behind the scrub brush that extended across the field from the riverbank. Then he felt the tell-tale pressure against his body and pricks of his skin. He had crawled through a Shimmer wall.

The first thing he saw was the muzzle of the bronze cannon emitting a mixture of gray smoke and reddish sparks. Then he saw a set of hands pushing and withdrawing a sponge to clean the bore of the gun. Other sets of hands loaded powder and ball and rammed them into place. Then, after the unmistakable distortion of a Shimmer wall passed clear over the barrel of the cannon, Har saw a final set of hands push a long pole *through the Shimmer* to thrust a burning match to the touch hole of the cannon.

Boom!

Up close, the blast should have been deafening. But Har hardly noticed. His attention was fixed on the Shimmer wall now fully encompassing the bronze cannon again — and the team of four Sylph warriors who were hurriedly reloading it.

▲▲▲

As Goran approached the darkness hugging the river, a streak of blue lightning crackled along its surface. Banking to the left, Goran braced himself for the cold, wet cover of clouds — and what he would see beneath it.

Nothing in his imagination could have prepared him for what he saw, however. He saw an enormous mouth with two rows of teeth the width of tree trunks and a narrow forked tongue extending a foot beyond the jaws. Behind the gaping mouth, Goran saw an enormous reptilian snout and two enormous reptilian eyes, glowing blue with magic and bright with fury.

The Sea Serpent's face was leathery. The long, thick coils of the body were scaled and colored the same sea blue as the head, although the monster's ventral scales were aquamarine. A gold ridge ran from the top of its head down its dorsal scales. Two great fins emerged partly from the surface as the beast continued its leap from the water.

Continued its leap toward Goran.

In the nick of time, the Sylph spun and dropped suddenly toward the river, watching in horror as the giant jaws of the Sea Serpent snapped just above his feet.

The arc of the leaping monster took its head back to the surface of the river. Goran watched, horrified, as its body followed the arc through the cloudy sky and into the water. Was it sixty feet long? Eighty? Longer? He couldn't say for sure. He only knew it was far, far beyond his ability to combat.

A cannon fired from the southern bank of the river. Goran could hear the whistling sound as the projectile flew past and then landed with a splash upriver of the creature. There was a great whooshing, followed by a plume of water soaring high into the air, crackling with radiant energy. The head of the Sea Serpent broke the surface and emitted another cacophonous shriek. Then it used its massive fins to propel itself downriver.

That is how they are herding the creature! Goran thought. The cannon must be firing enchanted shot. That meant neither the gun nor its projectile would be made of iron. And it meant the crew would be Folk, not human.

But where are they herding it? And why?

"I was hoping you would come."

Goran instinctively drew his hunting knife at the sound of Bren's voice in his left ear. The guildmaster made no move. He merely hovered in midair, smiling triumphantly at Goran, the Sea Serpent's undulating body and flapping tail fin roiling the water below them.

"You will bear witness to the greatest feat of monstercraft in history — one that will snatch victory for the British from the jaws of seemingly assured defeat," Bren continued. "Perhaps you will finally learn what it means to be a ranger of the Sylph."

Yearning to close his hands around the neck of the despicable man, but also yearning to understand the scope of his plan, Goran was momentarily frozen in indecision.

Bren misinterpreted the reaction. "You are terrified, and I cannot blame you. Look down and behold the instrument of your destruction. See the face of real power, of a force that cannot be contained by hollow ideals or naïve fantasies. Watch the infernal devices of pathetic humans, their toys of wood and iron, reduced to nothingness by the magic only we can wield."

Toys of wood and iron?

"The French ships!" Goran exclaimed with alarm. "You mean to herd the beast into the fleet and smash the blockade!"

"Of course. And there is nothing you and your pitiful rabble can do to frustrate our design."

▲▲▲

Har's throw was imprecise. But it did enough. Instead of striking the broad back of the Sylph warrior closest to the Dwarf's position, the handaxe tore through her left wing. She cried out in pain, dropped the bag of gunpowder she was carrying, and sank to the ground.

Intent on assuring the second throw would be more accurate, Har rose and barreled toward the Sylphs, singing the traditional battle song of the Dwarfs of the Brocken as he drew back his arm and heaved his other handaxe. The Sylph holding the sponge was thinner. His chest was a smaller target than the first Sylph's back. But this time, Har the Tower's aim was true. The warrior pitched backward against the barrel of the cannon, then slumped lifeless to the earth.

"Curse you!" shouted the tallest of the remaining warriors. He stepped around the cannon, picking up a heavy shield with one hand and using the other to draw his sword. Its ornate guard encircled his hand, the rest of its long bronze blade glowing a dull red.

"Jodoc," snapped the swordsman, "take him from the left!"

The other Sylph now clutched a thick spear with a long-bladed tip. "I have him, Kaden," said Jodoc gleefully. "You have bumbled into your last battle, Dwarf."

Then the two Sylphs rose into the air. Har gritted his teeth, hefted his battleaxe, and crouched.

Jodoc's attack came first. The Sylph dove directly at Har, his spear point rapidly approaching the Dwarf's face. Knowing that Kaden was likely diving from the opposite direction, Har waited until the last possible moment — then swung his axe in an upward arc to bat away Jodoc's spear, making sure he struck with the flat of his axe blade rather than the edge so as not to get his weapon stuck. An instant later, Har dropped abruptly and rolled, allowing himself a satisfied smile as the two warriors collided in mid-air, grunting and swearing.

Har scrambled quickly to his feet and faced his antagonists, who were now eyeing him with greater caution. Off to the side, the Dwarf caught his first glimpse of a fifth Sylph — an older, slighter man, his long robes and upstretched hands marking him a mage. He must have been carefully waxing and waning the Shimmer wall between each shot, allowing the warriors to load the gun in safety and then placing the gun within the Blur to be fired. Har could tell from the beads of sweat on the mage's reddened face that the complex task had been taxing.

"You may play at war, Dwarf, but you are no warrior," said Kaden mockingly.

"I am only a ranger of Grünerberg," Har acknowledged. "Our Warriors Guild would not waste its time with such as you."

The provocation didn't work on Kaden, who Har had surmised was the leader of the cannon crew. But Jodoc readily took the bait.

"I will spear you like a fish!" he cried as he jumped into the air and swooped.

A moment later, Kaden hastened to add his sword to Jodoc's thrusting spear — but it was a beat too late to present Har with simultaneous threats from different directions. Instead, Har suddenly let go of the axe with his left hand, used his left forearm to deflect Jodoc's spear to the left, and somewhat awkwardly swung the heavy battleaxe with his right arm.

Awkward or not, the swing caught Jodoc on the side of the head. Even with the diminished force propelling it, the blade was sharp enough to cut deep into the Sylph warrior's skull. Jodoc did not groan. He did not scream. He simply perished.

"Jodoc!"

The rage and anguish in Kaden's yell made Har the Tower think of his own friends lost in battle at Yorktown. Friends, and perhaps more, who had chosen to fight by his side and paid the ultimate price.

Perhaps it was the debilitating memory, or Har's exhaustion, or merely the fact that Kaden's fury drew strength and vigor to his limbs. The Sylph's longsword came down hard on the haft of Har's hastily raised battleaxe, shattering it in two. Then Kaden was face to face with Har, leering as he pressed the metal boss of his shield against Har's chest and brought the tip of his sword up to Har's stomach, preparing to gut the Dwarf ranger.

▲▲▲

Goran hovered above the river, watching the Sea Serpent continue its course toward the bay. Straining his eyes, he saw the outline of small figures traveling just above the surface in the wake of the beast.

"More of your followers, I gather," said Goran, nodding his head in their direction.

"Loyal rangers of the Sylph, all of them," Bren agreed. "They and the warriors on the riverbank will drive our monster relentlessly to its objective. Their secondary mission is to frustrate any attempt by traitorous Folk to interfere. Of course, I need no assistance to deal with a single traitor."

"Truly?" asked Goran. "Do you not recall our last meeting at the den of the Tories?"

He wondered if he could keep Bren talking long enough to slip the bow over his shoulder.

The answer to his unspoken question was no. Bren had already drawn his thin rapier from his belt. Wordlessly, and thus surprisingly, the guildmaster flew right at Goran, who had time only to reverse his grip on his knife and then flap his wings to gain momentum, hoping to butt the incoming foe with his shoulder.

Artfully, Bren rolled to dodge the butt and slashed Goran's shoulder in a spurt of blood and crackling sparks.

Suppressing the impulse to cry out, Goran twisted in mid-air and kicked hard with his right boot, catching the guildmaster in the back. Bren grunted but managed to regain his balance, turning and bringing the handle of his sword from his side to his face in a dramatic flourish.

"Enough of this!" Bren launched himself into another attack run.

The blinding pain in his shoulder left Goran unsteady. He managed to knock the guildmaster's sword aside with his left arm, feeling the blade bite into his flesh once more. Goran tried stabbing downward with his knife, but Bren whirled and parried with his rapier — knocking the knife from Goran's hand. It tumbled into the water below.

The guildmaster's face contorted into a gloating smile. "Your final lesson ends here and now, journeyman!"

The next instant, Bren's face contorted again — but into an expression of shock, as a stocky figure crashed into him. Several feet below Goran, somehow managing to keep hold of his rapier, the shaken guildmaster halted his fall and stared, unbelieving, into the face of his new antagonist.

His long gray beard shaking, Guildmaster Borva held a shortsword in one pudgy fist as he belligerently shook the other. "How could you have sunk so low, Bren? To lure such a monster from the depths of the sea and endanger the lives of thousands? Does your oath truly mean nothing?"

"We swear allegiance to our Folk alone, you ponderous fool, not to other Folk and certainly not to humanity," Bren replied haughtily. "Now, move aside. Perhaps you cannot be bothered with our work any longer, but I intend to carry out my orders."

"Orders that you yourself orchestrated, by manipulating one old man at the Knob and another over the sea in Cornwall," Borva accused. "Grandmaster Cono no longer comprehends or even reads what you place before him. And Briafael has not received an honest report from the Knob in years."

"Once again, move aside," said Bren.

"I am no old man," insisted Borva. "I can taste your poison, and expel it." He punctuated the point by spitting in Bren's direction.

Goran was disappointed when the missile fell short.

"Taste this, then!" said Bren as he launched himself.

Borva was powerfully built and experienced. Still, it had been years ago, and many pounds ago, since he'd handled a blade in battle. He managed to parry Bren's first thrust, then tried to slash the chest of the smaller man. Bren easily blocked the move.

As the two guildmasters clashed swords over the York, Goran felt stabbing pain from his shoulder and stinging pain from his forearm. He felt his life's blood leaking from him. He felt himself start to fall.

But not before he saw Bren evade a downward hack from Borva, spin to the left, and then plunge his rapier, almost to the hilt, into the side of the larger man. And not before Goran saw Borva, bellowing in pain and fury, grab the neck of the prematurely triumphant Bren with a meaty hand and drive his shortsword, almost to the hilt, into the belly of his foe.

His wings flapping slower and slower, Goran continued to fall. But Bren and Borva — both impaled, and entangled together as each tried to strangle the other — fell faster. They passed from his sight. He only heard their bodies strike the water.

His wings gave out entirely when Goran was about a dozen feet above the surface. He managed to keep his legs together as he fell the rest of the way. The cold water of the river gripped him like a vice. His legs, arms, and wings felt pinned against his sides. Try as he might, Goran could barely move a muscle.

Down, down he sank, his lungs bursting for air, his skin encased in frigid cold, his eyes seeing only darkness.

The cold lasted an eternity.

"Goran, can you hear me?" asked a voice.

The darkness stretched into infinity.

"Come back, Goran — please come back to us," the voice pleaded.

A bright light stabbed his eyes. His lids opened a crack, letting in still more light.

Goran opened them wider and saw, leaning over him, a face drenched in sunlight. A heart-shaped face, framed by long strands of blue hair and a circle of shells around a graceful neck.

"Dela," he whispered.

Goran felt hands, several sets of hands, touching the shoulder and forearm that bore the wounds of Bren's rapier. The searing pain was now only a dull ache. Something tight and confining bound both wounds.

"We must press on, Dela," said another voice in Goran's left ear. "They have almost reached the river's mouth."

Goran saw the Water Maiden's lips form a thin line. Sitting up, he found himself on the north bank of the York, surrounded by more than a dozen blue-skinned rangers. All held long tridents in their hands. All had nets slung over their shoulders. And all but two were women.

Dela gave Goran a searching look. "Will you be all right here?"

"Do you pursue the Sea Serpent?" he asked in return.

The Water Maiden nodded. "It is about to attack the fleet of the French," she said.

"Then I cannot remain behind," Goran stated, rising unsteadily to his feet.

"Your wounds have only just been salved and bound, and you have lost a great deal of blood. You are in no condition…"

"I am coming along, even if I have to paddle like a dog behind you," he insisted.

The image made Dela smile. "I would like to see that. For now, just hold fast."

Without waiting for an answer, she dove gracefully into the river, as the rest of her companions had already done. Goran stumbled to the edge and flopped into the water. Then he felt Dela's hands clasp his and bring them around her waist.

As swiftly as Goran might shoot through the air, Dela and the Gwragedd Annwn shot through the river. In minutes, they'd caught up with the Sylph rangers who were flying just above the waterline, using spellsong and the noise of clashing swords and shields to help drive the Sea Serpent toward the French ships beyond the mouth of the river.

The Gwragedd Annwn were almost upon the Sylphs before the latter realized their danger. By chance, one of the Sylphs had abruptly changed direction to avoid a plume of water sent into the air by the Sea Serpent's massive tail fin. He saw the water fairies and sounded the alarm.

It was the last thing the Sylph did before a trident struck his neck and nearly cleaved it from his suddenly rigid body.

Goran expected an uneven battle between the Sylphs and the Gwragedd Annwn. There were twice as many of the former, and they had two other advantages: their winged mobility and their need only to delay the water fairies while the Sea Serpent wrought destruction among Admiral de Grasse's ships.

But four Sylph rangers died within seconds — because they counted too much on their first advantage. They stayed above the throwing range of the Gwragedd Annwn's tridents, firing arrows and taunting their water-bound foes. The Sylphs hadn't counted on the other missile weapon at the Gwragedd Annwn's disposal: their nets. Light, easy to throw, and expertly enchanted, the nets wrapped themselves around the wings of the Sylphs, who tumbled into the river to drown or be speared.

It soon became evident that the second advantage wasn't so advantageous, either. After the initial contest of bow, trident, and net, the Gwragedd Annwn simply swam under the hovering line of Sylph rangers and headed for the monster.

The Sylphs no longer drove it forward. And neither, Goran realized, had there been a magical cannonball shot from the riverbank for some time. But the Sea Serpent had seen the masts and sails of the French ships and needed no more prodding to seek their destruction.

Then Dela and the other water fairies began a song — a haunting melody accompanied by the rattle of shell necklaces and notes played on conch-shell horns. It sang of tides, of currents, of sunlight and moonlight dancing on the waves of the surface, and of succulent delicacies found only on the floors of oceans and the beds of rivers.

The Sea Serpent uttered its cacophonous screech and turned away from the French fleet. The Sylphs saw their scheme beginning to unravel. Drawing swords and knives, they dove at the Gwragedd Annwn, hoping to catch the water fairies by surprise.

Goran had struggled to flap his wings hard enough to rise above the water and join his strength to that of his allies, even though it meant fighting Sylph rangers he had once called friends. It was all for naught, however. He lacked the might to help.

Nor, it turned out, did the Gwragedd Annwn require it. Three times the Sylphs dove toward their enemies, cutting and slashing and stabbing. After each assault, fewer Sylphs rose back into the air. By Goran's count, four Gwragedd Annwn had sustained grievous or deadly wounds, but fully a dozen of the winged rangers had found a watery grave.

The remaining eight Sylphs had had enough. They soared far into the sky and flew out of sight.

Dela and her rangers still had a difficult task. They had to drive the monster back up the York River. Fortunately, the dark clouds the Sea Serpent had conjured above its head seemed to have obscured it from the thousands of French sailors who manned the blockading fleet. *They likely fear little more than a sudden squall*, Goran thought as he swam unsteadily to the riverbank. The Gwragedd Annwn needed no assistance from him. And Goran desperately wanted to rest.

He sat on the bank for the better part of an hour, watching the water fairies herd the slow-moving aquatic beast and thinking about all that had befallen him during the siege of Yorktown. He thought of the Pixie diversion, of the pitched battles at the British redoubts, of his final confrontation with Bren. The guildmaster had been wrong, of course, about so many things. Perhaps his most telling error was how much he undervalued the power of love and friendship. What else had brought Dela and her Folk to the right place at the right time to change the course of history? What else could explain…

Har the Tower!

Goran had forgotten about his other friend, the one who'd glumly but resolutely marched toward the source of the cannon shots while Goran flew to the river. Har could be facing multiple Sylphs. Alone.

"I know who you are," said Kaden as he pushed the point of his sword against Har. "I should have recognized you when I first saw your clumsy bulk stumble from the bushes. You are the Dwarf they call the Tower. You are one of those who turned my brother into a traitor."

The Dwarf ranger winced at the accusation. "I am Har of Grünerberg. I am honored to call Goran a friend."

The hard edge of Kaden's shield smashed into Har's temple.

"Honor? You speak to me of honor?" shouted the Sylph. "My brother is a traitorous fugitive. My father is a broken man. My sister is consumed with grief. Our family's honor is one of the many casualties of the rebellion you aid."

His ears ringing, his head throbbing with pain, his mind befuddled, Har could barely make out what Kaden was saying. He was in no condition to fashion a reply. The effort seemed pointless, anyway. He had only seconds to live.

"It is you who betrays everything our Folk has ever held dear."

Har recognized Goran's voice. But it sounded odd, strained. He opened his eyes and saw his friend standing a few paces from Kaden, his bow in hand, an arrow aimed straight for his brother's chest.

"I did not think I would see you again," said Kaden, turning to face the newcomer but maintaining his hold on Har. "And I never dreamed you could aim a weapon at your own brother."

Har saw Goran's arm trembling. Did Kaden's words sting him so badly? Or was it something else?

"I never dreamed I would see you endanger innocent lives, Kaden," said Goran, his voice still sounding labored. "We have reached an impasse."

"Really, have we? Your Dwarf friend lies in my power. It would take only a twitch of my arm to end his miserable life. And I can see your arms shaking. You look unsteady, unwilling. Would you really take the life of your own brother? I sincerely doubt it."

So did Har, if truth be told.

"You have no idea what I am willing to do, what I have already done," said Goran wearily.

"I can guess," Kaden replied. "He who has lost his way has no shortage of paths before him, all the wrong ones."

"I walk the true path of the Sylph, the honorable path," Goran said. "It is you who have so thoroughly lost your way, although I blame Bren and his noxious philosophy more than I blame those led astray by him."

Har felt Kaden's blade jab his skin. "Drop your weapon, Goran. My patience wears thin."

Goran's arm stopped shaking. "You threaten the life of one who has become more of a brother to me than you," he said, his voice recovering some of its usual intensity. "It is I whose patience is about to run out."

"You will not kill your own brother," Kaden insisted. "You know it. I know it. For all your brave words, you lack the courage."

There was silence. Har imagined what a human might have seen had he been peering through the Shimmer wall. The human would see three fairies seemingly as motionless as statues. An archer aiming an arrow at two other figures huddled on the ground. The human might gaze at that tableau for several minutes of Blur time and see only a few seconds worth of motion by the three statues. Still, that would be more than enough time to see the archer loose his arrow, or the swordsman drive his point home.

Goran loosed his arrow.

Kaden gaped. Har felt the pressure of the Sylph's shield disappear. The sword blade no longer poked his stomach. Har looked from the astonished face of Kaden to the agonized face of Goran, who sank to his knees.

And then Har felt it — the push of an invisible wind against his body. He saw sparks and streaks of light through the distorted air. Rising to his feet, Har turned and saw another face, that of the Sylph mage. It was no longer a living face. It wore a mask of death. A mask with one eye bare and the other filled with the fletching of an arrow.

Kaden drew in a ragged breath, then began to whimper. He sank to his knees, much as his brother had. But while Goran was weeping for a brother he had once admired, Kaden was weeping for reasons he could no longer understand. The Sylph warrior began to mumble, to mutter under his breath. He rolled over and over on the ground, speaking gibberish and sputtering and wailing.

Then Kaden began to scream. The screaming lasted until Har knocked the Sylph unconscious with a blow of his gloved fist. It was an act of mercy to a fairy who'd been entirely and permanently robbed of his sanity by the Blur — a fairy who possessed neither the natural resistance of a ranger nor the magical protection of the Shimmer.

▲▲▲

On the morning of October 17, 1781, General Peter Muhlenberg watched with satisfaction as the British and German defenders marched from Yorktown to the field where the American and French armies stood at attention. After a few bars of the song the British band played, Peter recognized the tune as "The World Turned Upside Down."

He saw a British officer — not, significantly, General Cornwallis — try to offer the sword of surrender to General Rochambeau, the French commander. After Rochambeau refused, the hapless British officer strode to George Washington, who also waved it away. If the British commander was going to refuse to offer the surrender himself, the American commander would refuse to accept it. Washington pointed to General Benjamin Lincoln, the American officer who'd been forced to surrender Charles Town more than a year earlier. Lincoln took the sword.

Peter wished his fairy friends had been there to see it. They had done so much to bring it about. Goran and the Dwarfs had defeated the Pixies. Dela and her people had kept the Sylphs from breaking the French blockade. And, when they drove the Sea Serpent back upriver, their work had even disrupted Cornwallis's final, desperate gambit — his attempt to evacuate his remaining troops across the York to Gloucester Point. The gambit might have worked if the Sea Serpent's stormy passing hadn't wrecked all the British flatboats.

But Goran and Har were not at Yorktown that morning. Their sacrifices had been too great, their physical and emotional wounds too grievous. The two rangers had left the American camp in the middle of the night.

"I will see them safely home, Peter, I swear it," the Water Maiden had assured him.

To what home did Dela mean? Peter wondered. Goran, still an exile, could not return to the Knob. And, without Queen Virginal reigning at Grünerberg, would Har ever truly feel at home there?

Surrounded by cheerful French and thankful Americans, exuberantly celebrating their hard-fought victory, Peter found his own thoughts turning bittersweet. He pictured returning to his home and family. Then Peter pictured the faces of two friends who had neither.

Peter pictured the future of his new nation, the American nation, born of toil and struggle but ready to stand on its own two feet and find its way in the wider world. And then he pictured that wider world still full of dangerous enemies — enemies both human and inhuman.

Then, still more clearly than the others, another image came to mind: a page from his father's favorite copy of the Bible. The page contained the tenth chapter of the gospel according to John. In his mind's eye, Peter saw the words leap from the page. The words transformed into notes. The verses became melody. And it sang to him:

I am the good shepherd, and know my sheep, and am known of mine.
As the Father knoweth me, even so know I the Father,
and I lay down my life for the sheep.
And other sheep I have, which are not of this fold:
Them also I must bring, and they shall hear my voice;
And there shall be one fold, and one shepherd.

Epilogue — The Meeting

April 1791

THE RIDER BENT HIS HEAD low and caressed the neck of his nervous horse. "Whoa, there, Prescott," he told the massive white charger, which was whinnying and stamping its feet. "Those people ahead of us are but the final guests we were expecting. Be still, now. Be still."

Prescott was one of the finest parade horses the Rider had ever owned. To his pleasant surprise, the animal had proved entirely oblivious to the roar of crowds, the fifing and drumming of bands, even the booming of cannon fire. But, for some reason, Prescott was unnerved by wheeled vehicles. On their recent trip south from Philadelphia, the party had been forced to place Prescott at the front of their procession, as far away as possible from the fine white carriage of the Rider, so Prescott wouldn't stomp and buck.

Now, having arrived the previous afternoon at his home in Virginia, the Rider had decided to take Prescott for an early morning constitutional along the banks of the Potomac River. Such rides were one of the many pleasures denied him during his lengthy stays in Philadelphia. Unfortunately, this morning's ride had been interrupted by the old wagon rambling and rumbling its way to the plantation house.

But the Rider knew his mount. His soothing words, together with the wagon's progress toward the house, soon served to calm the horse's agitation. With a subtle kick, he urged Prescott into a walk, then a trot.

As the two passed a small tree set apart from the nearby forest, the Rider's frustration with the wagon's interruption instantly disappeared. He stopped and stared wistfully at the tree's straight, purple-brown trunk and bright-green leaves. He hadn't consciously planned to pass by the tree. But he'd learned long ago not to take coincidences at face value.

How long had it been? Fifty-two years? Fifty-three? Thinking back to his childhood at Ferry Farm, his father's estate on the Rappahannock, always filled him with an uncharacteristic nostalgia.

It had all started on his sixth birthday. Thrilled by a surprising gift from his father, the boy had slipped out of the house to play with it. He had skipped through the meadow, spun like a top in the garden, and run circles around the trees that lined the dirt road, all the time reenacting the wondrous tales his older brother Lawrence had told him of heroes, monsters, and maidens in distress.

Unlike the younger boy, Lawrence had attended grammar school in England where, among other things, he studied epic poems and collected tales of Greek and Roman myth. Lawrence had loved nothing more than relating the mythological stories to his younger half-brother — who had, in turn, loved nothing more than hearing Lawrence tell them.

On his birthday jaunt, the little brother had taken to playing Zeus, father of the gods, swinging his mighty axe to smite monsters and conjure bolts of thunder. Wouldn't any newly six-year-old have done the same, if he'd received a shiny new hatchet as his birthday gift?

Only this little boy had caught a glimpse of a strange face seemingly embedded in the trunk of a tree. The face was long and narrow, with unnaturally large eyes and unnaturally pointed ears. It was the face of a fearsome tree monster, at least to the eyes of a six-year-old boy who might have been expected to flee in terror. But this six-year-old boy had been playing as an ageless storm god with a mighty double-bladed axe. Zeus would surely have swung his axe at the monster.

And so, of course, did the boy.

That was how George Washington came to chop down his father's prized cherry tree. And it was how he met his first fairy, a woodland Dryad named Hespera with whom George later developed a deep friendship.

On that fateful day in 1738, however, all young George knew was that he'd swung at a monster, missed, and destroyed the cherry tree. The boy had never once considered denying responsibility for the act. He'd gone right home and told his father everything.

Well, except for the part about the Dryad.

He hadn't told his father a lie, strictly speaking. He just hadn't told the complete truth. There was a big difference between the two — or so young George had assured himself.

▲▲▲

At the Rider's command, Prescott resumed trotting along the trail to the house, where the guests would likely be waking and dressing for breakfast. Mount Vernon was never more alluring than in the early morning. Over the past three years, George had been forced to imagine it far more than experience it. The duties of his office required him to reside elsewhere. For the past sixteen months, his duties had placed George, Martha, two of her two grandchildren, and some two dozen aides and slaves as residents of the Masters-Penn House in Philadelphia.

The Masters-Penn House was a fine, three-story brick mansion. It was a fitting seat for the president of the United States. But, for George, home would always be Mount Vernon.

A hundred paces ahead, he watched the old wagon roll past the bowling green, around the elliptical drive, and then to a stop in front of the house. Two tall figures climbed down from the seat, and were greeted by two slaves dressed in fine livery as other slaves stepped forward to drive the wagon to the coach house.

They were too far away for George to make out the features of the two new arrivals. But he was confident of their identities.

"Two more guests for breakfast, Your Excellency?"

Peter Muhlenberg stepped out from the woods to George's right, smiling pleasantly and carrying a fishing pole.

George returned his long-time friend's smile with the slightest of grins, exposing only a thin line of the uncomfortable dentures he wore. "How are they biting today, Congressman?"

Peter laughed and lifted the string in his hand, from which dangled a moderate-sized catfish. "Well enough, following the advice you gave me."

If only Peter followed my advice as faithfully on other matters, George thought.

Both Peter Muhlenberg and his brother Frederick Muhlenberg were members of Pennsylvania's delegation to Congress, which had just ended its inaugural 1789-1791 session. Frederick Muhlenberg was, in fact, the first Speaker of the House under America's new constitutional government. But, while Frederick proved to be a loyal supporter of George's administration, Peter had sometimes dissented from the president on matters of policy. They had not let their disagreements fray their ties of friendship, however.

The congressman walked alongside as the president rode Prescott to the house. George dismounted and handed the reins to a servant. Then he and Peter entered the central passage of the house.

"We will take our breakfast and greet our new guests in the New Room," George said. "But first, I recommend we don more appropriate dress for the occasion."

▲▲▲

When the breakfast bell rang a half-hour later, George was already walking through the elegantly appointed Front Parlor to enter spacious New Room, where his guests sat or stood along the green-papered walls, conversing in small groups and sipping from porcelain cups. It was the largest chamber at Mount Vernon, with a ceiling nearly seventeen feet high. In addition to the long serving table, the room was furnished with chairs and side tables arranged to accommodate a large gathering.

But Martha and I never dreamed we would host such a gathering as this.

Walking to the long table, George surveyed the platters of ham, herring, mutton, and corned beef the cooks had prepared for breakfast. He filled a small plate and poured a cup of tea. There would be no service today. The topic of conversation was fit for no ears other than those of his guests.

Having preceded George into the room, Peter Muhlenberg was drinking coffee and talking with two fellow members of Congress, John Sevier of North Carolina and George Mathews of Georgia. Sevier had played a significant role at Kings Mountain and in frontier conflicts during and after the war. As for Mathews, he'd served under Peter Muhlenberg as a colonel, been captured during the battle of Germantown, and spent the remainder of the war as a British prisoner. Mathews had served as governor of Georgia before his election to the House of Representatives in 1789.

George Washington nodded politely to the three congressmen and then turned to his right to find two of his other guests in a heated discussion. It was an all-too-familiar scene.

"To take a single step beyond the boundaries especially drawn around the powers of Congress is to take possession of a boundless field of power," said the secretary of state.

"Pray be practical," replied the secretary of the treasury. "The powers contained in a constitution must be construed liberally in advancement of the public good."

George walked briskly and with some difficulty placed himself between Thomas Jefferson and Alexander Hamilton. "Still debating the merits of the national bank bill, gentlemen?"

Jefferson nodded while Hamilton glowered. "I continue to maintain that the legislation sacrifices the interests of most of our countrymen to serve the interest of stock-jobbers, Your Excellency," said the Virginian.

"Now is not the time to continue this discussion," said the president. "We are gathered here for a rather different purpose, gentlemen."

Over his shoulder, a new voice chimed in. "A gathering of more than just gentlemen, for which I am thankful, sir."

Nancy Ward, known as Nanyehi among her people, strode forward with Isaac Shelby at her side. George had heard a great deal about the woman but had only met her for the first time the previous day, upon his arrival at Mount Vernon. He'd been deeply impressed.

"Your counsel will be most welcome, Most Beloved Woman of the Cherokee, as will that of everyone else here, as we confront the present threat," said the president, placing his cup and plate on a side table.

"And how would you describe that threat, Your Excellency, if I may ask?" pressed Shelby. "Was the Great Alliance not disbanded years ago?"

George considered both the question and the questioner. Isaac Shelby was another of his Mount Vernon guests who'd deeply impressed the president, although he'd made the man's acquaintance many years earlier. Well aware of Shelby's exploits during the latter years of the war, George had later come to appreciate his role in conciliating tensions between frontiersmen and newcomers in the west. And now that Congress, in one of its final acts of the session, had authorized the creation of Kentucky as an independent state, George was certain he was looking at the man likely to be elected the first governor of the new state. Shelby, a former state legislator in both Virginia and North Carolina, was already serving on the Kentucky district's Board of War and had come to Philadelphia to push for passage of the statehood bill.

"I think it best to defer explanations until our full company is present," George replied.

As if on cue, there was a tapping on the window at the far side of the room. George looked over at Billy Lee, who'd been sitting unobtrusively in a chair near the window. Billy made to stand but then grimaced, his hands rubbing the metal braces on his knees. His disabled legs were what had kept Billy from serving as the president's valet in Philadelphia, and why he now lived at Mount Vernon as the estate's cobbler.

Peter Muhlenberg took in the situation at a glance and walked quickly to the window, waving off Billy Lee's repeated attempts to rise. Opening the window, Muhlenberg offered a hand to help Dela the Water Maiden step down from the low sill.

Behind her came three other fairies: a copper-skinned woman clad in deerskin shirt and skirt, whom George had heard was named Tana Song Snake, as well as two familiar figures: Har the Tower and Goran.

George knew both fairies well. But neither looked as he remembered them. The hardy, happy-go-lucky Dwarf he had first met more than a dozen years ago now looked haggard and grim. As for Goran, the once thoughtful and passionate Sylph struck George as oddly distracted and withdrawn, not to mention weary and gaunt.

As Peter conducted the fairies to the circle of chairs in the center of the reception room, two seated figures stood, high and majestic, to offer greeting.

"It is agreeable to see you again, Dela of the Gwragedd Annwn and Goran of the Sylphs," said the Oneida chief Skenandoah, bending his lanky frame low enough to take the Water Maiden's tiny hand in his own.

"And to see you again, Master Dwarf," announced Polly Cooper, her striking face split by a broad smile.

Har acknowledged the greeting with a respectful nod but did not return the smile. "I trust you had a pleasant journey from New York."

"It *was* pleasant, Har the Tower," Skenandoah replied, clearly savoring the irony of a six-foot-six human calling a four-foot-high Dwarf by such a nickname. "But it was also a long journey, one I would have made more comfortably in my younger days. Now I am as an aged hemlock. The winds of many winters have whistled through my branches."

"And yet you stand tall and strong," said Dela.

Skenandoah smiled. "I take it you and your friends preceded us here."

"We arrived three days ago," said the Water Maiden. "Goran, Har, and I began our journey at Grünerberg, where we met two Dwarf mages and guided them to the transport station President Washington had arranged at an abandoned house in Philadelphia. There we met Secretary Hamilton, Secretary Jefferson, and the congressmen — and brought them all here."

Hamilton groaned as he and Jefferson took their seats. "It was one of the most unsettling experiences of my life," he said. "When the mages cast their spell, I felt as though my body were being drawn and quartered — although it offered me some comfort to know that my fellow travelers were feeling the same effect."

He cast a sly glance at Jefferson, who seemed to take the jest with good humor.

"I believe you chose the superior means of travel, Your Excellency, regardless of the number of days it took — and the number of ruts," Jefferson said.

"I made my choice not for comfort but for discretion," the president explained. "There are many prying eyes in the capital from whom I would conceal our purpose."

"So you made a big show of departing on a tour of the Southern states," Isaac Shelby observed, "while your real object was to gather us here for a conference."

"Indeed." George noted with satisfaction that almost all his guests had by now taken their seats. There remained but a single empty chair. "Although I should hasten to say that my stated design to acquaint myself more fully with the Carolinas and Georgia is a real and valuable one. That the first leg of my Southern tour also places me here, without raising suspicions, was a welcome combination."

There is a difference between telling a lie and withholding the whole truth, he mused, and thought again of the cherry tree.

Alexander Hamilton scowled as he looked across the room at the empty chair. "May we not just proceed, Your Excellency?" he asked. "God only knows when that one will return."

Sharing his young cabinet secretary's preference for punctuality, George was about to answer in the affirmative when he heard voices in the central passage, followed by approaching footsteps.

The question had become moot.

"Sorry to be late, friends. I lost track of time," said Daniel Boone as he entered the reception room. "General Washington, I don't know how well-stocked you are for vittles, but your cooks now have a couple more ducks on their hands."

Amidst hearty laughs from Sevier and Shelby, appreciative greetings from Nancy Ward and Jefferson, and a scornful look from Hamilton, Boone ambled across the room and sat in the empty chair between George Mathews and Peter Muhlenberg.

"I see the buckskins I was expecting, Colonel Boone, but not the coonskin cap," said Peter good-naturedly. "Having read my Filson, I feel sorely disappointed."

Boone snorted and made to spit, then thought better of it. "John Filson is a good storyteller, I grant you that. But I didn't speak half the words he put in my mouth. And I've never worn a coonskin cap in my life."

This time it was Jefferson who effected a sly grin. "As much as I cherish the books in my possession, and read the newspapers diligently as befits my current post, I often find that the written word embellishes more than it illuminates. I scarcely recognize the man described as the secretary of state by *The Gazette*."

"I might say the same for the bumbling secretary of the treasury as depicted in the pages of the *Daily Advertiser*," said Hamilton. But before Jefferson could object, Hamilton pivoted. "The subject does invite a question, Colonel Boone: now that you are made a national hero by such gifted storytellers, will you not seek a career in politics?"

The question elicited chuckles from others around the room, plus another loud snort from Boone.

"I've twice served in the Virginia legislature, sir, and in two weeks' time I journey to Fort Lee for what I suspect will be another election to that body," Boone said. "But if you mean to suggest a seat in Congress, I would as soon wrestle every bear the campfire stories say I did —in a single afternoon."

By this time the assorted chuckles had become a roomful of raucous laughter. Even Goran and Har joined in, an outcome George noted with satisfaction.

"The heroic actions and chivalrous adventures of Daniel Boone have, indeed, become legend," the president said. "But, ladies and gentlemen, we all know that such legends, concerning not only Colonel Boone but others in this room, are not simply fancies concocted to sell books. They are but confused and distorted accounts of real events shaped by magical beings."

JOHN HOOD

During the uncomfortable silence that followed, all human eyes turned to the fairies. Dela and Tana smiled appreciatively, while Har merely squirmed in his seat. Goran, who had been staring at the floor, now lifted his head and regarded Washington intensely.

"I would rather your people have human heroes to admire than fairies to fear," Goran said. "If your purpose in calling this meeting was to devise a means of revealing the full truth, I must strongly protest."

"As must I," said Har. "The deeds we performed, and the sacrifices we made, were to defend our highest principles and deepest loyalties. I will not have them devalued or dishonored."

The president shook his head. "You misunderstand me, sirs. I consider the legends surrounding Colonel Boone and others to be the tools of Providence. We must protect the secret of your existence — just as we must ensure the secrecy of that design for which I have gathered you."

Har and Goran exchanged surprised looks, as did others around the circle.

"I *was* wondering why you instructed us to take so many precautions," said Hamilton. "Writing letters with multiple dates and arranging for them to be delivered in Philadelphia on successive days, for example. Why was it so important to conceal our presence at Mount Vernon?"

George rose to his feet and clinched his jaw, again suffering discomfort as his dentures pressed against his gums. "Our young nation must contend with many powerful ones," he began. "Some nations would do us direct harm. Others would rather our experiment in self-government fail. The American people already know the human nations of which I speak. Must they also know of the fairy nations, and of the monsters that inhabit the fields, forests, hills, and waters of our land? I think not."

He paused for a moment, looked at the faces of his audience. The fairies seemed mollified, at least for the moment. The others seemed to be weighing his words carefully.

"Your Excellency," began Peter Muhlenberg, "you said that some wish our nation to fail. Do you speak even of our wartime allies, the French and Spanish? Why should they fear our success?"

"Because of what it may inspire — indeed, what it has already inspired," George replied. "The citizens of the United States of America have a right to applaud themselves for giving to mankind examples of an enlarged and

395

liberal policy, a policy worthy of imitation."

On the other side of the circle, Nancy Ward suddenly crossed her arms and looked up in exasperation.

"If you have something to say, madam, by all means please do so," George said.

"President Washington, among my people I am known for speaking my mind," she said. "I also have a reputation for peacemaking. These traits rarely conflict. Today, I must choose one over the other."

George felt a tinge of impatience. "Yes?" he asked.

"You say foreign nations fear that your liberal policy may inspire irrepressible demands from their people," Nancy Ward said. "Perhaps that is so. But within my nation, America has made its enemies by direct action. Where you see liberality and an 'experiment in self-government,' we see dishonesty, hypocrisy, and greed."

George watched silently as her words provoked protest and argument from the assembled leaders. Only Daniel Boone sat unperturbed, whittling a long hickory stick with his hunting knife.

The matter of relations with Indian nations was a delicate one, and George resolved not to let it disrupt the proceedings. *There is too much at stake to allow that to happen.* He held up his hand for silence. "It has always been my policy that the administration of Indian affairs should be directed entirely by the great principles of justice and humanity."

"And yet there has been too little of either," asserted Chief Skenandoah as he shifted uncomfortably in his too-small chair. "I, too, am known among my people as a believer in peace. Because of that, other chiefs of the Six Nations have called me a fool."

"American agents offer smooth words and tell us fair stories," Nancy Ward said. "All the while, we lose more and more land."

"Dragging Canoe and his Chickamaugas have continued to loot and kill," Sevier insisted. "I know you have always spoken for peace but, when your people ignore your words, what else can we do but..."

"This is an old argument between you and me, one we will not resolve this day," she interrupted. Then she turned back to George. "I recognize you have gathered us here for a different purpose — to share what we know of the fairies who still plot against your country. I have fought them myself, because they also plot against peace. There will be no resolution of other matters while those fairies, in their arrogance, continue to promote resentment and bloodshed. I merely asked that you not surrender to the same sort of arrogance."

Several bristled at her use of the word. Hamilton in particular seemed ready to leap out of his seat. But before George could fashion an appropriate response, another voice spoke up.

"While we are on the subject of setting examples, President Washington," began Goran the Sylph, rising slowly to his feet, "I feel compelled to point out that other nations surpass your United States in another key respect. They do not practice slavery."

George felt his stomach lurch as he glanced first at Billy Lee, still sitting quietly but attentively against the wall, and then at the others around the circle. *At this rate, our company will dissolve with nothing but ill effects.*

The expression on Hamilton's face had abruptly changed from outrage to triumph.

"Our fairy friend has identified a point of great contention, to be sure, but one that clearly flies in the face of our noble enterprise," he said. "Were not the disadvantages of slavery too obvious to stand in need of it, I might enumerate and describe the tedious train of calamities inseparable from it."

"None of us has need of a lecture on this subject from the secretary of the treasury," said Jefferson. "Nobody wishes more ardently than I to see an abolition of slavery. But abolishing the practice at a stroke would be exceedingly dangerous. To give liberty to, or rather, to abandon persons whose habits have been formed in slavery is like abandoning children."

Hamilton jumped to his feet. "By what right do you..."

George tried to master his own conflicting feelings while his mind raced. "I feel compelled to remind everyone of the task at hand: our policy regarding magical creatures."

Hamilton returned reluctantly to his seat. But the Sylph did not.

"With respect, sir, the question of slavery *has* a direct bearing on the task at hand," Goran said.

I know that better than most, George thought. His eyes flicked once again to Billy Lee, who'd spent an hour the previous evening telling George the latest tales of a mysterious figure called John the Conqueror — popular tales of a magical trickster who instilled hope in the hearts of slaves across Virginia.

For the moment, the president chose to keep those tales to himself. "What do you mean, Goran?" he asked.

"Folk nations seek to control and oppress you, and you properly resist," the Sylph replied. "But have you not resorted to the same practice against your own fellow human beings? Is that not more loathsome that what even the most tyrannical of Folk practice?"

There was a sudden commotion from the other side of the room. Chief Skenandoah was speaking rapidly in his native language to Polly Cooper, who'd walked into the middle of the circle, one hand pointing dismissively at the Oneida chief, her sharp eyes fixed on Goran.

"Stop trying to muzzle me, Skenandoah; you were never very good at it," the woman said, her eyes flashing with defiance. "If this is not the time to speak the truth, then it may never come."

The chief sat back in his chair, resignation on his face. Polly Cooper then addressed the Sylph. "Tell me, Goran, why is human slavery more loathsome than the oppression the fairies practice?"

"Because at least the Folk do not seek to enslave their own kind," he replied.

"And what of the monster pens?" she pressed.

Goran looked confused. "Monsters are not Folk. We capture and pen monsters to make our lands safe for humans and Folk alike. The monsters are nothing like the poor humans the Americans enslave to till their fields and run their households. The creatures in those pens are dangerous, mindless beasts."

"Are they now?"

Polly Cooper's question seemed to hang in mid-air. Unmistakable. But also unanswerable. Because, even as she voiced those three little words, the sound of her voice changed. The word "are" sounded impossibly deep. The word "they" seemed to crack like a whip. And the word "now" boomed like thunder.

As George and everyone else in the room watched with wonder, Polly Cooper's aquiline nose rippled and lengthened, turning gray as it did so. Her sharp eyes grew sharper, the brown irises turning yellow, with a hint of lightning behind them. The woman's long black-and-gray hair rippled and lengthened, as well, the gray becoming the predominant color, dappled with red. The head wasn't just changing shape and color. It was also rising higher and higher, until it was only inches from the ceiling.

Below it, the majestic body of what had been Polly Cooper filled much of the circle. Two massive yellow claws spread their talons on the floor. Red-orange metallic feathers covered the breast and underside, with darker feathers of brownish red covering two enormous wings and bright feathers of orange, striped in black and white, forming the tail.

From its gray beak head came a long, rumbling scream.

"A Tlanuwa!" cried Nancy Ward.

"A Thunderbird!" cried Dela.

She and the other fairies scrambled to their feet and surrounded the beast, weapons in hand.

The only other armed person in the room was Daniel Boone. He still held his hunting knife in his right hand and his whittling stick in the other. The old hunter gazed up at the head of the beast, its beak open, its yellow eyes, crackling with energy, looking back at him.

Then Boone uttered a single, hearty laugh, reversed the grip on his knife, and carved another long sliver of wood from his stick.

"You have nothing to fear from me, my friends," said the Thunderbird, its voice rumbling and echoing across the large room. "For the first time you see my true appearance. But I am still the same person you knew. I am Polly Cooper of the Oneida, although that was not always my name."

George found the constriction choking his own voice ease somewhat. "By what name were you known before?" he asked.

"I do not know," the Thunderbird answered. "I do not remember. I remember little of my life before I met Skenandoah in the village of the Jogah. And I have never met another creature capable of answering all my questions."

"She is what my people call a Thunderer," Skenandoah said. "I will do my best to explain." At his words, the four fairies lowered their weapons, warily.

"Many years ago, during my stay with the Jogah, I was given much freedom," the Oneida chief began. "I mingled with their warriors, shamans, and growers. I even went on outings with their hunters and scouts. But the one place I was forbidden to go was the monster pen. As the weeks passed, my curiosity grew beyond all bounds. Finally, I found I could no longer resist the temptation. During one fleeting period of night, I ran to the pen to see what was inside."

The claws of the Thunderbird rose and fell as the creature seemed to grow discomforted.

"The beasts I saw amazed and terrified me," Skenandoah continued. "But none was as tall as I. Now I understand that the Jogah had, by some kind of magic, reduced the size of the monsters so they could fit inside the pen. Back then, I knew only that, while some of the small creatures looked powerful and dangerous, others seemed shriveled and close to death. Polly was one of the latter. In fact, she was the most pitiful creature I ever saw. And, of all in the pen, she alone seemed to look back at me with something other than mindless fury or blank stares. I saw intelligence in those eyes. I saw a plea for help."

Skenandoah's words had painted a vivid picture in George's imagination. Then the president understood.

"You freed her," George guessed.

The Oneida chief nodded. "Yes. And when the Jogah discovered my crime, they banished me from their village. They also bewitched me, hoping to clear my memory. I played along so they would not be tempted to do something worse than banish me. Still, I remembered. And, before long, I was able to find her and nurse her back to health."

"I do not know how I came to be in the hands of the Jogah," the Thunderbird said. "And since my escape, most of the magical creatures I have met have deserved the name of monster. They do not answer when I speak. More often than not, they simply attack. They are the mindless, vicious brutes you fear."

"But not all?" observed Daniel Boone, who had perked up during Skenandoah's tale and now seemed intensely curious.

"No, I have met a few like me — monsters who talk, monsters with reason and purpose, a few who have even formed small communities of their own not unlike those of the Folk," she said. "For a time, I enjoyed the companionship of another of my kind, another Thunderbird. He taught me much of what I had forgotten, including how to use Thunder magic in attack and defense."

"Can you tell us more about this Thunder magic?" asked Dela.

With some difficulty, given the confined space, the Thunderbird turned and regarded the Water Maiden. "By sweeping our wings and concentrating our minds, we can shroud ourselves in invisible clouds and hurl gusts of wind at our foes."

"I have seen this," said Tana Song Snake, holding her blowgun in one hand as she gestured up at the face of the monster with the other. "I will admit that I have hunted Tlanuwa in the past, and seen them battle both monstrous and human enemies. I trust you are not offended by that."

"As you can see," continued the Thunderbird, appearing to ignore Tana's question, "some of my kind possess another ability. We can alter not just how others perceive us but our *actual* shapes, taking the form of humans for a time."

Suddenly Goran shouted out something in his fairy language that George could not understand. Har pounded his feet on the floor and exclaimed in what looked like agreement with Goran's declaration.

"Of course you are right, Sylph," the Thunderbird boomed. "It was *I* who intervened in your battle with the Brownies that day in 1778, just as I intervened to help the Americans during their battle at Monmouth."

George was thunderstruck. "You were at Monmouth? I do not seem to recall any reports of magical beasts or mystical gusts of wind there."

The Thunderbird's head began to shake, and from its beak came an eerie, rasping noise. It took George a moment to realize the beast was laughing.

"Your men saw me many times that day," she said. "They did not know me as a great bird. Nor did they know me as a woman of the Oneida. They knew only that I brought them succor and hope. So they devised their own name. They called me Molly Pitcher."

George felt almost giddy. *Of course* he'd heard the Molly Pitcher legends after the battle. He'd considered them fanciful exaggerations. As he looked around the room, he could see the anxiety draining from most of the others.

The conspicuous exception was Goran.

"I have many questions, most of which I concede you are in no more position to answer than the rest of us," the Sylph said. "But I must return to your original suggestion: what makes the monster pens of the Folk like the slave camps of the Americans? I confess I am horrified that intelligent creatures such as yourself may have been imprisoned in our monster pens. But unlike the slave owners, we were not aware we were committing an act of unjust cruelty. And we do not make the monsters in our pens suffer for our personal gain."

The Thunderbird known as Polly Cooper screamed once more, the shrill cry of a bird mixing ominously with the clap of thunder. George felt his body stiffen involuntarily.

"Have you not wondered, Sylph, why it is your *mages*, and not your more menial Folk, who tend the pens?" she demanded. "Can you not guess what they do there, and why it is so important that they insist you constantly replenish their stock? Can you not see, in your mind's eye, the figure of the shriveled creature Skenandoah found in the pen of the Jogah, and how — now freed from captivity — I can stand high and powerful before you?"

Goran gaped. So did the other fairy rangers.

George searched the faces of the other humans and discovered just as much puzzlement as he felt. "Goran, if you can draw meaning from her words, pray enlighten the rest of us."

The Sylph gulped, looked at the other fairies, then turned to George.

"She is saying that the monster pens have a purpose so brutal, and yet so essential, to the survival of the Folk that our mages have gone to tremendous lengths to hide the truth," Goran said. "She is saying the mages draw their elemental magic directly from the monsters we capture for them. That they store the monsters' magic and use it to sustain the Shimmer and other works of magecraft. And that, as the monsters are drained of magic, they lose their vitality — and maybe even their lives."

"That is the secret, awful purpose of our monster hunts," Har the Tower added hesitantly as he struggled with the implications. "Without fresh monsters for the pens, Folk magic would become impossible. Without them, our realms would cease to exist. And all Folk, save perhaps for rangers, would either go mad or perish in the Blur."

▲▲▲

For more than an hour, the company discussed the continuing Folk threat and agreed it would be prudent to meet regularly to share information. George thought the fairies were making an admirable effort to participate actively in the conversation, even though it was obvious Goran and the others had been shaken to their very cores by Polly Cooper's revelations.

Throughout the proceedings, both Hamilton and Jefferson took copious notes. During a lull in the conversation, the latter cleared his throat and turned to Goran.

"It is within my purview to gauge the sentiments of foreign governments," said the secretary of state. "But my understanding of fairy folk is rudimentary. Of the fairy nations who formed the Great Alliance, how many do we know for certain remain foes to our cause?"

"All of them, as far as I can tell," said the Sylph sadly. "They acknowledge the reality of American independence but continue to believe it profoundly disruptive and dangerous. President Washington is right: they will happily subvert your government if they can, and would welcome a restoration of British rule."

"Your people as well, I take it?" pressed Jefferson.

Goran stared at the floor for a moment, as did Har. Dela reached out a slender blue arm and touched Goran's arm in sympathy.

"My Folk no longer live within the boundaries of the United States," Goran said. "The Sylphs abandoned their village shortly after I conducted my brother, rendered insane by the Blur, back to the Knob. The Mages Guild has transported my Folk to a new home — somewhere in British Canada, I suspect."

George quickly read the meaning in Goran's words. "You aren't certain where they went because you weren't present to witness their departure."

"He did not even get a chance to offer a final farewell to his family," said Dela.

"Traitors are rarely welcome among those they betray," Goran said bitterly. "Your treacherous Benedict Arnold has lived in London and in Canada since the war, I understand, and never in happiness or comfort. Perhaps happiness and comfort will ever elude me as well."

After a respectful silence, Jefferson spoke again.

"Har, might I inquire as to the disposition of your host?" he asked. "Do they continue to inhabit their mountain in the Shenandoah Valley?"

The Dwarf nodded. "Grünerberg still rings with the tools of their craftsmen, the weapons of their hunters, and the words of their fallen queen. Remember that, to those behind the Shimmer, it has been but a few short months since Virginal's...sacrifice before the redoubts of Yorktown. A Council of Elders governs the colony in the interim, but it is assumed that a new Dwarfmoot has met back in Germany and a new monarch has been selected. The Dwarfs of Grünerberg await their new ruler."

Again the choice of words revealed much to George. "*Their* new ruler, you say, but not *our* new ruler. Are you not welcome to continue to dwell among your people?"

Now it was Har the Tower who received a sympathetic touch from the Water Maiden. "I am welcome — no, *we* are welcome to reside at Grünerberg as long as we wish," Har said, looking meaningfully at Goran. "But the place holds many memories. Some are hard to bear."

"You will always have a home among the Gwragedd Annwn at Long Island — *both* of you — if you so desire," Dela assured them.

"The same is true for the Nunnehi of Blood Mountain," said Tana.

Goran stood up and smiled appreciatively. "Both invitations are generous, invitations that I would be a fool to reject. Surely our paths will cross in the future. But to visit is not to settle. I no longer have a desire to make a permanent home."

Beside him, Har rose and placed his arm on the shoulder of the much-shorter fairy. "As for me, for now, my place is at the side of my friend — my brother."

During the conversation, Polly Cooper had assumed human form again. Nevertheless, her eyes retained the keen yellow irises of a Thunderbird. Now, as she regarded the two fairies standing before the circle, her eyes gleamed like polished gold.

"You have conducted yourselves with great honor, at great cost, and now the world you knew is no more," she told Har and Goran. "The world is far wider, and wilder, than you could have guessed. It contains more sights to see, more feats to perform, more honor to win. Will you not explore it, as I have?"

While Goran continued to hang his head, Har looked at Polly Cooper for a moment, a new light shining in his own eyes.

It was the Cherokee woman, Nancy Ward, who spoke next.

"Among my people, we follow a tradition that, as we grow and change over life's journey, our names should change to tell the tale," she said. "When I was a child, I was known by another name. After I met Tana, my mother began calling me Nanyehi, meaning 'she who walks with the Nunnehi' — who walks with fairies, you would say.

"During my first marriage, I gained the titles 'War Woman' and 'Most Beloved Woman.' After my second marriage, I was known among the whites as Nancy Ward. Through it all, I was not simply the same person bearing different names and titles. At each stage, I became someone new, someone whose earlier names were garments that no longer truly fit me."

Then she looked directly at Goran. "You who are no longer Goran of the Knob — you have become someone new. You are Sylph, yet not of the Sylphs. You are a fierce warrior, yet not war-like. You are a cherished friend, yet prefer to walk alone."

She stood and walked to the Sylph, removing something from a pouch. "I offer you this token of esteem — an emblem of my first husband that I have kept for nearly half a century."

She opened her hand. In it was a small feather of blue flecked with white. "It comes from the bird for which my first husband, Kingfisher, was named — a bird that, according to our traditions, has a special relationship to the Nunnehi."

At a loss for words, Goran accepted the gift. Removing his cap, the Sylph fumbled with it for a moment, overcome with emotion. Finally, he succeeded in affixing the token. Replacing his cap, Goran looked at Nancy Ward with gratitude, the single kingfisher feather standing straight above one ear.

She beamed. "I have no doubt that the adventures of Goran Lonefeather and Har the Tower have only just begun."

Made in the USA
Columbia, SC
24 May 2021